THE LAST PROPHECIES

by Jason M. Hardy

Facebook: Jason M. Hardy
Twitter: JasonMHardy

For Kat and Finn
and anyone else

Prologue

On June 18, fire fell on the altar of the Antigua cathedral of the Church of the Miraculous Creator. It began at the ceiling, sixty-five feet above the altar, and plunged in a narrow fall of spiky orange tongues and glowing sparks. It gave off no heat and left the altar undamaged. Believers congregated from miles around, because one hundred years earlier, Harriman Ellis had predicted the fire would come.

News of the fire spread quickly. All kinds of news, stories about anything imaginable related to the fire, ran across the world, but most of it was false. When they learned news of Antigua, people checked and double-checked what they heard, then checked again, and gradually people started to believe that significant portions of the stories floating around about the cathedral in Antigua were true.

High Adept Rowan Birch of the Hampton Cathedral first heard about the fire from one of his students. He disregarded it as idle chatter until his superior, Grand Adept Serl, confirmed it hours later.

Adept Lloyd Hsu learned of the fire from High Adept Birch, and he accepted it immediately. Adept Birch's word was enough for him.

Anderson Drauer, president of the United States of North America, learned about the fire almost as soon as it appeared because Anderson Drauer learned about most everything as soon as it occurred. His eyes were better than most. He didn't need to believe anything about it, because he knew.

Amelia Diaz had heard so many false reports of the fire that she automatically disbelieved the newest reports when they came in. By the time she was ready to accept the reports as true, she had other, far more difficult things to believe.

Adept Rafael Diego heard the news from Antiguans who ran at top speed to Guatemala City to spread the news. The next day he witnessed the fire firsthand, and regretted seeing it.

No one told Acolyte Terrin about the fire. If anyone had asked him the exact date the fire was supposed to occur, according to the prophecies of Harriman Ellis, he would have been able to give it to them (give or take three days). But no one asked.

Kale Faltergast did everything he could to not hear about Antigua, but information had a way of finding him. Just because he knew about it, though, didn't mean he couldn't ignore it.

Premier Adept Eliazer Dugwu knew things about the fire that he wouldn't tell anyone, because Premier Adept Dugwu understood the way things worked.

Courtney Whitaker heard about it, then forgot about it, since he didn't know where Antigua (or, for that matter, Guatemala City) was.

Nilda Yashie did not hear about too many current events, including the Antigua fire, during her incarceration. By the time she was free she had too many other things to think about. It always felt to her like a movie everyone else was talking about but she had never seen.

For a long time, very few people were certain what happened in Antigua and why. It took a long time, but eventually Lloyd Hsu understood the role Antigua played in everything else that happened, and understood why so much that happened traced its roots back to that place.

This is what happened.

Part One: Seeker

Chapter One

Everyone believed Acolyte Terrin exhaled dust. Watch when he speaks, they would say, and you could see the motes flying out of his mouth. He should get some fresh air, they said, for his health. But Terrin sat in the archives every day, never took a vacation, breathed in the archive air, and every day more dust settled deep inside him.

"I think he's hollow inside," Aron said. "The dust has been eroding his innards for a hundred years. There's nothing left."

Lloyd nodded his head absently as they descended the stairs to the archive, trying not to encourage Aron.

"The question is, did the dust erode his brain, too?" Aron continued. "I'd have to say no, because there wasn't much to erode in the first place. Can you imagine it—he's been an acolyte for seventy years. *Seventy years!* How dumb do you have to be to stay an acolyte for that long?"

"It's not about being smart or dumb," Lloyd said, almost to himself.

"That's what some people think. The ones that say you're born with it. That's spew. I wasn't born with anything. I couldn't read anyone's mind when I was a kid, and I tried, believe me. I didn't get it because I was born with it, I got it because I worked at it and was smart enough to learn. Terrin's problem has to be either that he's too dumb or too lazy. That's the only way to be an acolyte for that long. I just don't know why he's stayed. Most people, when they wash out, leave pretty quick. Guess he just accepted his mediocrity."

"Maybe he's happy where he is," Lloyd said.

Aron stopped abruptly, and Lloyd lightly bumped into him.

"Look around," Aron said, waving at the cramped stone staircase. "This is yellow limestone. It's supposed to be *yellow*. Does it look yellow to you? What you're seeing is not rock, my friend. It's decades of grime. And it only gets worse down below. Who in their right mind would be happy here?"

Lloyd only shrugged.

"No one," Aron said, then started moving down again. "I'm not saying I know why Terrin's here, but it ain't 'cause he's happy."

The staircase ended in a splintering door. Aron knocked twice, then shoved the door open.

Terrin's archives were dusty and crammed with papers, but, despite that, orderly. He reportedly knew exactly which papers were buried on which stacks. Organization was important to Terrin—but it seemed cleanliness was not.

Terrin's desk was just to the left of the door. He sat behind it, reading a book bound in crumbling leather and not looking up. He seldom looked up.

"Good morning, Acolyte Terrin," Aron said grandly. "Fortune has truly smiled upon us this day. The Creator has spoken to Grand Adept Serl, Grand Adept Serl has spoken to High Adept Birch, and High Adept Birch has spoken to us to tell us we are to speak to you. With the simple removal of two intermediaries, we see that the Creator Himself has ordered us to commune with you."

The mocking formality of Aron's speech had no effect on Terrin, who continued to study his book, as if waiting for Aron to say something that mattered.

"Have you heard about the fire in the Antigua cathedral?" Lloyd asked before Aron could say more.

"*Prophecies of Harriman*, 8:12," Terrin said, keeping his gaze fixed on his book, not moving any muscles besides the bare minimum required for speech. His voice sounded like rotted wood being torn apart.

"Yes … yes, I believe that's the one about Antigua," Lloyd said. "Adept Birch wanted to know if, now that this prophecy has been fulfilled, other prophecies might be coming to pass in the near future. The Church wants to know if there are any areas we should focus on."

"All of them," Terrin said.

Lloyd looked quickly toward Aron, who only shrugged, his mind apparently already elsewhere.

Lloyd turned back to Terrin. "All areas of the world? I think Adept Birch was hoping …"

"All of the prophecies," Terrin interrupted.

"Oh. Oh, of course. We know all of the prophecies will be fulfilled eventually, but in the near future, which ones are most likely …"

Terrin looked up, stopping Lloyd's sentence in its tracks. His eyes were rather ordinary—watery brown with large pouches underneath—but the direct gaze had force because it was seen so seldom. "All of them," Terrin said again.

Lloyd could not think of anything else to say. The cellar vault was silent for a few moments until Aron spoke.

"That's not really helpful. Is this what you want me to tell Adept Birch? He'll come down here himself and see if you can say anything that might give, you know, some sort of actual information."

Terrin looked briefly at Aron, then back at Lloyd. Then his eyes returned to his book. "Then let him come," he said, and the conversation was over.

"Seventy-six, seventy-seven, seventy-eight …" Aron said. "Seventy-nine, eighty. Eighty steps and counting. Double that and it's at least one hundred sixty stairs we've covered on the whole trip and we're not done yet. All so Terrin could tell us that all of the prophecies of Ellis would be fulfilled. Which is what our Sunday School teachers told us when we were blinkin' three years old. And I'm still counting, by the way. Just because I'm not counting out loud doesn't mean I'm not counting. We're at ninety-one."

Aron had been ranting the entire way up the stairs, bristling with energy that made his sandy hair even more spiky than usual. Around step forty-six, Lloyd had successfully tuned out his voice, making it blend into the background, like the pad of his footsteps or the distant sound of dripping water.

"And ninety-seven and we're done. One hundred ninety-four stairs we traversed today. All to tell Adept Birch nothing."

Lloyd didn't respond, mainly because he wasn't paying enough attention to Aron to know that he was expected to say something.

"I'm not going to let him blame me for the way this turned out. He told us to talk to Terrin. Fine. We talked to Terrin. It's not my fault—not our fault, I mean—that Terrin is senile and doesn't have anything useful to say. Birch didn't say we needed to get anything good, he just said he wanted us to talk to Terrin. And we did. I'd like to see Birch get more information himself. I would. I'd love to see Birch march down those ninety-seven steps and stare Terrin right in the face and get nothing. I'd love that."

They turned a corner. At the end of a long hallway was Adept Birch's office. Aron kept talking, but he didn't say anything more about Birch. He ranted plenty about Terrin, though. Unless Adept Birch was deaf, or more skilled at ignoring Aron than Lloyd was, he would have plenty of advance warning that their assignment had not gone well.

The door of Adept Birch's suite was like a portal to another world. Outside, the hallway was filled with harsh fluorescent light bouncing off chipped paint. The linoleum on the floor was twenty-five years old and completely worn through in several spots. The door was unlabeled except for the number "133" painted on the chicken-wire glass.

Once Aron and Lloyd walked through, though, they were bathed in a soft light from an indeterminate source (Adept Birch kept a light spell running whenever he was in the office). Satin-like wallpaper covered the room, and a rhododendron prospered in one corner. The reception area held a thin wooden desk and a few upright wooden chairs, all of them polished and smooth. Behind the desk sat Acolyte Devin, who had drawn reception duty for the week.

"May the light of the Creator shine upon you," Devin said with a smile when Aron and Lloyd walked in.

"May His powers bless your days," Lloyd said. "We have a report for the High Adept."

"He's expecting you. Go on back."

High Adept Birch had never really settled into his office. His desk, his shelves, and the floor held boxes that were propped open and half empty. What items he had unpacked were wedged between boxes. Anyone walking in would have thought he had just moved into the space, when in truth he had been in residence nearly a decade. His explanation for the office's condition was that he always had at least half a dozen more important things to do besides unpacking.

He was reading a thick textbook when Aron and Lloyd walked in. Unlike Terrin, he closed the book as soon as he saw them, stood up, and shook their hands warmly. His circular face beamed at them, and it was hard to believe the possessor of such a pleasant smile was deeply feared by most of the acolytes and adepts in the cathedral.

"Adept Nesbitt. Adept Hsu. Thank you for coming by so quickly. I am, as you know, quite eager to hear what Terrin had to say."

"I hope you won't be too disappointed in ..." Lloyd started, trying to cushion the blow.

Aron, though, wasn't having that. "Nothing. The old man told us nothing."

Birch raised an eyebrow. "He did not speak to you?"

"No, no, it's not that," Aron said. "But he might as well have. What he said wasn't worth anything."

"I'll be the judge of that," Birch replied. "Tell me what he said."

Aron prepared to blurt out something in anger, but this time Lloyd was too fast for him. "We asked him what prophecies we could expect to see fulfilled now that the fire in Antigua has appeared, and he said all of them. We could expect to see all of them fulfilled."

Lloyd's summary was far too neutral for Aron. "I tried to tell him what he was saying was worthless, but he just ignored us. I did the best ..."

Aron trailed off when he realized Adept Birch was no longer listening. The color had drained out of Birch's face, and his arms hung limply by his side.

"Adept? High Adept Birch? Are you all right?" Lloyd asked.

Birch remained perfectly still for a quarter of a minute, then stepped back. In truth, he practically fell backward into his chair, as if his knees had buckled.

He regained his composure quickly but did not stand. He placed one finger on his desk and tapped out a slow, steady rhythm. Aron and Lloyd hovered uncomfortably above him.

Finally, Adept Birch spoke.

"All of them," he said. "All of them. Well, well."

"This actually means something?" Aron asked.

Adept Birch's eyes, which had been unfocused, fixed on Aron. "He's never said it before," Birch said. "Do you know how many of Harriman Ellis's prophecies have been fulfilled?"

Aron looked at Lloyd, who carefully assembled an answer. "It's impossible to say, as some of the prophecies deal with areas where we may have trouble getting information ..."

"I'll refine the question," Adept Birch interrupted. "How many prophecies do we have concrete evidence—video, photographs, or otherwise—of their fulfillment?"

"I know of a few dozen."

"Fifty-one," Adept Birch said. "The Premier Adept has identified one hundred sixty-three prophecies in the Tarras transcript. Fifty-one of them have been fulfilled. Acolyte Terrin has all the evidence in the archives. At least fifteen times, I've sent adepts down to Terrin to ask him what to expect. Each time, the adepts have come back with a report of incremental progress, telling me that a few steps needed to happen before the floodgates open."

"And now the floodgates are open?"

"It would seem."

Birch walked around his desk two and a half times, occasionally shaking his head. Aron and Lloyd fidgeted and looked at each other.

Finally, Adept Birch stopped pacing and placed his palms on his desk. "You two will have to get to work immediately. We need to find a white field."

Chapter Two

"You don't have to keep trying to convince me," Amelia Diaz said. "I know what you believe." She leaned back in her chair, nonchalant in the face of aggression. Her dark eyes were impassive.

Slane threw up her hands angrily as she leaned forward, almost flinging herself to her feet. "It's not what I *believe*," she said. "It's what I know. It's what I saw. My word should be enough for you. It's been enough for you in the past. It's been enough for at least half a dozen netcasts, too."

"Netcasts—the bastion of reliability," Amelia muttered, which earned her a withering glare that was easy to see even in the dim light of sunshine filtered through lime-stained glass.

"I work hard at this. *Damn* hard. And if you're saying nothing I do can be trusted—that none of this is worthwhile—then you can go ..."

"Screw myself. Right," Amelia said, her impatience rising to meet Slane's. "I never said it wasn't worthwhile. I didn't even say I don't believe you. But don't expect me to jump at everything that comes in a netcast. Do you know how many times in the past five years some netcast or another has reported that Anderson Drauer is dead?"

"I don't see ..."

"Three. How about Eliazer Dugwu?"

"I ..."

"Twice. According to a video 'cast on at least three nets, how many people were beaten to death by police in the Mexican Independence Demonstrations of '33?"

"None," Slane said quietly, in a tone of resigned cooperation.

"And according to all reliable reports since that time, how many were actually killed?"

"Somewhere between two and three hundred."

"What did AlphaNet News declare as the top story of last year?"

"The creation of an ecclesiastical court in the CMC dedicated to purging adepts who were directly tampering with people's thoughts, forcing them into belief."

"What did Atmosphere News report about that story?"

"That there was no proof it had occurred, and that several leading psycho-kinetic researchers say it is only possible to force someone into religious belief for a brief period, and that any such long-term programs would be futile. Look, I've got it. No one said netcasts had a perfect track record. But this isn't a netcast I'm asking you to believe. It's me. I saw it. I saw the fire in Antigua. Don't believe any crap you see on the nets, I don't care, but believe *me*."

Amelia shrugged, bringing her shoulders almost up to the ragged ends of her black hair. "Okay, I believe you. It doesn't matter. I'm not the person you need to convince."

Slane picked idly at a loose piece of green vinyl upholstery on what happened to be the nicest chair in the small room. "Who is?"

"The chumchas. Go down to the cathedral and let them know what's going on. Tell them their people in Guatemala got one of their buildings back, so maybe if the clergy up here got off their asses, we could take something back in Queens. Or even put pressure on Manhattan."

"The NArds are getting clobbered in Guatemala. Isn't that enough for you?"

"I'm not in Guatemala."

Slane sighed. "All right, fine. Now, just as a formality, can you tell me what the ILF is planning next?"

"Of course not."

"Any comments on the firespout on Park Avenue yesterday?"

"Are you asking me to claim responsibility?"

"Did you do it?"

Amelia smiled faintly. "Me, myself? No."

"You know what I mean."

"Officially, we had nothing to do with the firespout, and we do not condone actions that could harm civilians."

"And unofficially?"

"Unofficially, we have no comment."

Slane shut off her recorder. "You're a lot of help."

Amelia shrugged. "Not my job to help you."

Slane's sharp, narrow face suddenly looked wilder when she smiled. "True enough. And it ain't my job to convince you what's true." She stood up. "I'll catch you later—sometime when we can be useful to each other."

Amelia watched her go, then walked into the back room of the shack. Like the front room, the walls were splitting wooden boards, the floor was a concrete slab, and the windows were dim grey squares. The front room held only a few pieces of battered furniture. The back room, by contrast, was packed with electronic equipment worth several times more than the house itself. Everything in the room was portable—it had taken Amelia about half an hour to set up shop here, and she could break it down in about half that time.

"Any news on the firespout?" she asked as she closed the plywood sheet that passed for a door.

"I've got the spectrographic analysis," said Waylon, a thin grey man who almost blended into his terminal. "The make-up of the spout is about the same as the air—no foreign chemicals added. So we're dealing with a pretty heavy-hitting pyro—at least class B, maybe class A."

Class A pyros—pyrotechnical psycho-kineticists—were rare. Almost all the ones Amelia knew were aligned, either in the army of the United States of North America or the clergy of the Church of the Miraculous Creator. The army wouldn't have set off the firespout and the clergy couldn't have—CMC clergy couldn't even get into Queens, let alone Manhattan. If the firespout was done by a pyro, it was a rogue, one not only powerful enough to set off the fire but clever enough to move around Manhattan undetected by USNA security.

"Did we get any video of the spout?" she asked.

"No, but we got a few stills. USNA nets got a hold of a few tourist snaps, all of them 3-D. Want a look?"

"Load them up."

Waylon punched up the stills. The flat display of the spectrograph results vanished while a three-dimensional street scene sprang forward.

"I've got three shots," Waylon said. "Two with the spout in full bloom, one with it fading. I like this one the best. Nicely framed and all."

The shot looked straight down Park Avenue. In the background, the battered granite of Penn Station was visible through the steel skeleton of the dilapidated, never-repaired SpeirAir Tower. The street was crowded in midday, which meant dozens of eyes were focused on the tower of fire in the middle of the street. Some people stood stiff and straight, others staggered back. Those closest to the fire fell from the heat. This wasn't just a light show, Amelia thought.

She pivoted the image. The spout rose up about thirty feet into the air and looked about three feet wide. It was placed perfectly for maximum visibility and minimum damage, hot enough for people to feel its effect but not close enough to seriously burn anyone. It hadn't done much to passing cars, either—a few singes here and there, but most of the automotive damage was caused by distracted drivers, not the spout itself.

The pyro who did this could have inflicted a lot more damage if he or she wanted. Setting it off inside a building, for starters—there would be a lot more people near the fire, and if the spout was hot enough the whole building might've gone up. Even setting it off on the sidewalk instead of the road would do more real damage.

But the pyro hadn't done that. He hadn't done real damage—he just wanted this to be seen. This was a simple message to the

USNA: Your guards may be good, but they're not perfect. If there was any other element to the message, it was a mystery to Amelia.

"Show me the next still," she said.

The next still had been taken only a few seconds later, from a worse angle. The cameraman had snapped a shot from the sixth floor of a building on the same block of the spout. The picture helped show just how tall the spout was but didn't show much else. Most of the people in the shot were tops of heads, not faces, and they only became more blurred when Amelia zoomed in on them. She told Waylon to bring up the third shot.

This one was the worst—street level, but taken hastily, out of focus. The spout could have just been an orange neon tube, for all the picture showed. It looked useless.

Still, she needed to give the picture at least a cursory examination before dismissing it. She looked at the shot from all angles, noting that each new angle showed her nothing.

Until she took a closer look at the lower right corner. There was a person on 36th Street who at first looked like he was ducking from the concrete the spout had thrown up. On a closer look, though, he seemed to be leaning toward the spout, getting a good look at it before moving away.

Amelia bent down to get a close look at the figure. Thanks to the snapper's ineptitude, this person was actually in slightly better focus than the spout. His clothes were indistinct—dark pants, dark shirt under a dark jacket, all combining into one in the blurry still. His face was partially hidden under a brown hat, but when she saw the round chin with the salt-and-pepper stubble, it was enough. She knew there were probably thousands of people in the metro area who had chins like that. But she still knew who it was.

"Stupid old man," she said, shaking her head. "Stupid old man."

Chapter Three

"It could be someone who lives in White Plains. It could be someone with a last name like Whitaker, Whiting, Whitney, or something like that. It could be someone who lives next to an actual white field, even though I don't know where we'd find one near here. For all I know, it could be a pilot."

Aron snorted. "When the prophecy said white fields, it meant white plains, and we're going to say that means white planes? No."

"I know, I know, but it's all I've got. Read it back to me again?"

"Don't you have it memorized yet?"

"Just read it," Lloyd said.

Aron read.

"Walking from a white field
Comes the fall.
The oppressor will meet
The one who is his end."

"It doesn't even say this person, 'the one,' comes from the field," Lloyd said petulantly.

"Where is the person first mentioned?" Aron said in the tone of a patronizing schoolmaster.

"First line," Lloyd said.

"Where is this 'one' mentioned?"

"Fourth line."

"In the prophecies, what is the typical relationship between the first line and the fourth line?"

"They speak about the same thing—each clarifies the other."

"So stop whining. Terrin says this prophecy means this 'one' will come from a white field, Adept Birch agrees, so here we are and what do we do next?"

"I don't know. Look up or call every Whitaker and Whitney and whatever in the area—I already checked, there's at least four hundred, and that's just the ones who have a listing, and most of them live in the USNA. And White Plains is in the USNA. Most of those candidates are out of our reach."

"So all that means …"

"That I have no idea what to do."

"Glad I asked, then."

Lloyd moved his hands back and forth across the chipped veneer of his black desk. To his left, Aron lay on his bed, feet near the wall, head hanging upside-down off the edge. One of the most trivial spells Aron had ever taught himself, in Lloyd's opinion, was the one that kept too much blood from flowing to his head when he stayed upside-down for long periods of time.

To facilitate concentration they had decorated their room like a Buddhist monastery today, austere with clean white lines, but parts of the décor occasionally flickered as their minds focused on the problem at hand.

"I don't think there's much we can do until we talk to Terrin again," Lloyd said.

"Which happens when?"

"Two days."

Aron shook his head. "Adept Birch isn't going to be too happy if we just sit around for a few days. We have to at least look like we're doing something."

"Maybe we could talk to some of the secular resistance—people in the Islip Liberation Front. See if they've got a Whiting or a Whitson. If they do, that could be who we're looking for. Someone who's already on the right side of things, kind of, you know?"

"Yeah. But you know anyone in the ILF?"

Lloyd smiled thinly—his narrow mouth never looked broad, no matter how cheerful he might feel. "No. But I think I know someone who knows someone who knows someone."

On a drizzly summer afternoon the next day Aron and Lloyd went to Central Islip, a good twenty-five miles west of the cathedral. Once they were off the ragged highway they went south on Carleton and turned left on a street with no name. The street—really no more than a patch of loosely connected pot holes—passed through a thick, overgrown clump of trees into a group of homes a world away from the Hamptons.

The shacks were scattered in overgrown grass tall enough to scrape on the dingy broken windows. The only creatures walking the streets were dogs.

"This is where the leaders of the revolution live?" Aron said as their cart jolted over the bumpy road. "If we join them in the struggle, will they show us how to free ourselves of the shackles of structurally sound housing so that we may all live in squalor as one? I think if they're going to be doing any leading, first thing they should do is lead themselves to a building that won't fall down in a strong wind."

"We're not meeting any leaders, just a contact. And I don't know if the contact actually lives here. This is just where they wanted to meet—a nice, isolated spot."

"Don't you think, if they really worked at it, they could find a pool house on the estate of a large mansion that's at least as isolated as this place?" Aron asked. He wore a wolfish grin. "The fact of the matter is, there's no cash in revolution, which is why these freedom fighters have problems galvanizing the masses. They don't set a great example to follow."

"You remember we're clergy, right? We're not exactly rich, but we want people to follow us."

"But we have nice churches."

Lloyd just smiled and shook his head. He looked for a place to pull off the road, but he didn't want to take the cart into the thick grass. There wasn't any other traffic, so he pulled over as far as he could and shut down the motive spell powering the engine. He was tired—he had wanted to take an electric cart out, since that required considerably less focus.

"I think this is it. We should probably take the engine cell with us."

Lloyd walked up to a screen door that hung by a single hinge while Aron reached under the cart's hood and pulled the cell out by its handle. He thought about knocking on the screen door, but was worried that a strong rap would bring it down. He knocked on the doorframe instead.

No one came to the door; no one called from the inside. Lloyd looked at Aron, shrugged, and gingerly pulled the door open.

He stepped through the doorway into an illusion and immediately shielded his mind. From the outside, the shack's interior had been too dark to see, but now he was standing in a simple, well-kept cabin. Lights, hidden behind tin sconces, provided an even glow across the room.

"Stay by the door," he told Aron. It was unnecessary—Aron felt the touch of the spell too, and was moving even more cautiously than Lloyd.

An old man sat in a rocking chair in a far corner. He rocked gently and kept his eyes on Lloyd. His eyes were grey—old, weary, but sharp. The rest of his face looked somewhat younger despite the smattering of grey stubble.

Lloyd sent careful feelers toward the old man. He was real, but that was all Lloyd could tell—the man had a mental shield like a brick wall.

The old man spoke in a tenor that sounded like it belonged to a man in his twenties. "You're CMC," he said.

"Yes."

"You're looking for Amelia."

"I don't know who I'm looking for," Lloyd said guardedly. "I wasn't given a name."

"Then I'll tell you. Amelia—that's who you're looking for. But why are two CMC adepts looking for an ILF operative like Amelia?"

Lloyd floundered. He had a cover story ready in case he ran into NArd security, who had been spotted a time or two in Islip, but he wasn't sure what to tell an unnamed old man who looked for all the world like a rogue PK.

Aron, though, was almost never at a loss for words. "We're looking for her because someone said we should talk to her. And since you're not that someone, and you're not her, and I'm pretty sure you're not us, I don't think you're involved in any of this."

The old man nodded gently. "All true. But you're here with me now, and you won't be going anywhere until I allow it. That is to say, I may not have been involved before you entered this room, but I have now managed to involve myself." He looked at Aron, and his eyes crinkled. "I understand you may want to see if you can force your way past me before I say anything more. That's fine. Go ahead. We'll talk after you're done."

Lloyd knew better than to take the man up on his challenge. He stood still and tried to look confident.

"Go ahead and talk," he said. For the moment, it wouldn't hurt to listen.

"Why do you want to find Amelia?" the old man said.

"We need information, and she might have it."

"That's not specific enough."

"That's all I can tell you right now," Lloyd said calmly before Aron could lash out.

The old man sat motionlessly. Lloyd wasn't sure if he was pondering something or if he had suddenly gone catatonic.

Finally, he spoke again. "All right. Then all you have to do is listen. I'm here to tell you that there are people, including me, who are watching out for her. If you try anything—if, for instance, you turn her into the NArds—we'll be on you instantly. You can go now."

Lloyd and Aron were hit by an invisible punch in the gut before they could put up any defenses. They were both hurled backward, Lloyd through the door, Aron through the window. The illusion dropped as they rolled out of the house. Lloyd ended up knocking the screen door off its last hinge, Aron scraped his arms and legs on the broken, glassless panes of the window frame.

Lloyd caught his breath for a few minutes and dusted himself off. He didn't see Aron, but an indentation in the overgrown grass showed where he was.

"Are you all right?" he called.

"Yeah," Aron said in a breathless voice. "Give me a sec."

Once Aron's breathing became less labored, he stood up and pushed his way through the tall grass to Lloyd.

"I hope that's not who we came here to meet," he said. "He wasn't helpful."

Lloyd grinned wanly.

"So, this Amelia," Aron continued. "Where are we supposed to find her, if she's not here?"

"Who says she's not here?"

"What do you mean, who says? We were just in there! We were thrown out! There's no Amelia in there, just a guy who doesn't like us much."

"That was an illusion. Mostly. If we walk back in, we'll see what's really inside. Maybe this Amelia's in there now."

"Right. Okay. You go first."

Lloyd stepped back to the doorway and tossed aside the fallen screen door. He took a deep breath and stepped through the door again.

There was no touch on his mind this time. The shack was benign—and a complete wreck. It held no furniture, just a few pieces of splintered wood lying here and there. The old man wasn't there, but neither was anyone who looked like they may be named Amelia. There wasn't anyone there at all.

Lloyd waved to Aron, and Aron strolled in.

"Looks like she got tired of waiting for us. Let's get out of here," Aron said.

"Wait. What's that door over there?"

Aron glanced at the narrow piece of warped wood hanging in a doorway. "Doesn't look like anything. And this whole place is so small, it could only be a closet or something."

"Might as well take a look."

Lloyd strolled over and pulled the door open. Disappointingly, it was indeed a closet—a closet as bare of human belongings as the shack. Some mouse droppings in the corner were the only signs of any life.

"This is a breakthrough find, all right," Aron said.

"Shh. Do you hear something?"

Aron didn't say anything, but the skeptical way he held his head spoke volumes. Lloyd, though, was convinced he heard a squeaking from behind the wall to his left. It sounded for ten seconds or so, then disappeared.

Aron looked like he was about to speak, but Lloyd held up his hand. The sound started up again, this time louder. Aron's eyes widened as he heard it, too.

With a sudden crack, a piece of the wall pulled away from the floor and swung upward, revealing a cramped staircase. The opening was dark, but traces of a faint light could be seen at the bottom of the steps. Lloyd tried to get a scan of what was ahead, but something was blocking him. Another PK or someone who had taken some first-class blockers. Usually, though, if someone tried to keep you from seeing something, that meant there was something to see.

"This is nonsense," Aron said in a tense whisper. "Don't these people know that if they come to a church, they get sanctuary? No threat to them at all! We should just have them come to the cathedral."

"You can tell that to whoever we find at the other end of this tunnel," Lloyd said, and he started cautiously down the steps.

The stairs descended about ten feet into a crude passage, where two-by-fours and sheets of plywood kept the dirt walls from collapsing. The smell of earth and damp wood was strong.

A small, battery powered lamp hung in the middle of the tunnel. Squinting ahead, Lloyd saw another staircase about fifty feet ahead.

"We're going there?" Aron guessed.

"We're going there," Lloyd confirmed, and walked ahead.

The tunnel was quiet except for the sound of mice running across the dirt. There was no indication if someone was waiting ahead or not.

The small screen in front of Amelia's right eye showed two men in the black, belted robes of CMC adepts walking cautiously through the tunnel leading to her. They'd taken long enough to find it, and they still weren't moving very fast.

It would be nice, she thought, to have a job where people could just walk into a normal office and find you. The cloak-and-dagger stuff had been fun for a year or two, but after that it was mostly inconvenient.

She flipped the surveillance camera image off her screen and took another look at the background file Waylon had put together. Either these chumchas were really what they claimed to be, or someone had thrown together a masterful fake background. The file said they both showed signs of the talent when they were young, and both of them were funneled into the priesthood before they were teenagers. Neither had family on the Island any more, and there wasn't much evidence of contact between the boys and their distant parents. There wasn't much beyond that—even Waylon couldn't penetrate CMC personnel files, so she had no idea what they had done inside the church. Outside the church, though, neither had made any waves.

She switched back to surveillance. They had finally made it to her end of the tunnel and up the stairs, and they were feeling the wall in front of them to find a door. She was tempted to stand up and open the door for them, but that would ruin the atmosphere.

The makeshift door swung up, and one of them—black hair, Asian features, so he must be Hsu—crawled into the dark room, followed by the second one. They probably tried to scan her the minute they saw her, but the blockers she'd taken an hour ago would keep them from getting much of a reading.

She pulled off her headband monitor while Hsu and Nesbitt blinked, adjusting their eyes to the darkness of the boarded-up shack. She waited until they were able to make out that another person was in the room with them, sitting in a thick leather chair. As soon as they started focusing on her, she turned on the lights.

The chumchas blinked again. Amelia smiled tightly, then made sure her mouth was a straight line again when they were able to re-focus.

"Did you enjoy that?" Nesbitt asked. She could see anger running up and down his short frame. Hsu, by contrast, stood very still.

Amelia shrugged. "Maybe. I'm doing you a favor, though, so you can just put up with it, can't you?"

Nesbitt glowered. Hsu spoke up before an argument broke out.

"Who was the man in the other shack?"

"What man?" Amelia had watched the entire encounter on surveillance, cursing out the old man the whole time. Hsu and Nesbitt, however, did not need to know that.

"Before we found the passageway here, there was a man in the other shack. An older man, with patchy stubble. He warned us about harming you. If you're Amelia."

"I am. But I don't know who this old man was. There's a lot of crazy men around here, and you just happened to run into one."

"Crazy men with the talent?"

Amelia cursed the old man again under her breath. "I don't know. I haven't inventoried every crazy man here. Is this what you came to ask me? Birch called in a favor to find out about some crazy man?"

Nesbitt started in anger, but Hsu managed to speak before him. "No, it's not. But this man threatened us. You understand why we would be curious about it. But if you say you don't know who the man was, you don't know who it was."

"I don't know who it was."

"Okay. Now. I'm Adept Lloyd Hsu, this is Adept Aron Nesbitt. As you know, High Adept Birch sent us to you."

Amelia repressed a smile, amused at Hsu's straining toward civility. Most of the people she met through the ILF didn't care for niceties.

"And here you are," she said. "What do you want?"

Hsu sat back a bit, and some of the tension moved out of his cheeks and jaw. "We're looking for someone."

Chapter Four

"To be honest—and this is based on a lot of experience—I think you can count on them going for exile. Under the law, they've got a few other options, but in a case like this, they're just going to want you out. There'll probably be some monitoring, maybe an implant—hey, hey, don't look so scared, I know it sounds bad, but it's nothing, really just a shot, in and out—I mean, that is, you go in and out of the doctor's office, not that the needle goes … well, you know, anyway, I think that's what they'll go for. And really, when you look at the alternatives, it's not so bad."

Nilda Yashie's forehead remained in her hands. She had no desire to look at the man on the other side of the glass. "It's not?" she said.

"No, really, it isn't. Now, I'm not trying to scare you here, but there's some people saying what you did, that is, what you're accused of doing, amounts to treason, and we know what the penalty for treason is, right? The good thing is, they're more concerned about getting Mira Corwin, not you, so there's not many people calling for your head, so to speak. I think they're willing to accept exile for you so they can focus on Corwin, and that gives us some bargaining room."

"Bargaining room? What are we bargaining for?"

"Well, let me tell this to you straight. The worse case scenario is they dump you on the Island with no money, no possessions, nothing, and they dump you at the border, and the border rats are there waiting for you. You don't want that—trust me, you don't want that. But if they want to wrap this up quickly, they might give us a little leeway—maybe they'll free up some of your assets, and let an agent find a place for you, so when they set you out, at least you'll have someplace to go, you know? We could get a good deal."

Nilda looked up at the horse-faced lawyer and his plaid bow tie. "How is that a good deal? I get exiled when I didn't do anything? And I'm supposed to accept that?"

The lawyer lifted his hands defensively. "We could talk for a while about who did or didn't do what, but that's not what my job is about right now. My job is making the best out of the situation that we've got, and this is it. I understand if you don't like thinking about exile right now—who would, really?—but you're not thinking about it right. You're thinking about exile for something you didn't do, which is bad, but when you think about the choice being either exile or death, you see that exile really isn't so. And that's all I'm going to be asking you to do for the next day. Just think about it. Think about it and we'll talk."

The lawyer stood up, still smiling. He picked up his hat, dropped it, picked it up again, and waved at the guard as he walked through the door.

There were plenty of books and 2-D films and archived news stories that made it clear that, even years ago when the Island and the City were part of the same country (same state, even), it wasn't easy to go from one to the other. The elevated trains stopped shy of the City's border, and the diesel trains didn't run anymore. The roads were perpetually clogged and slow, and the addition of checkpoints twenty-five years ago didn't help anything. Then the checkpoints became roadblocks, and before long no one knew how to leave the city for the Island because no one voluntarily did that anymore.

Two weeks ago, Nilda's lawyer had explained exile to her. Five minutes ago, the van carrying Nilda Yashie hit a road she had never been on. All the roads ahead of her would be roads she had never been on. For most of the journey out of the city, she had squinted through the porthole-like window in the side of the van, imprinting images of the New York City in her mind. Now, though, she didn't need to pay attention. She was seeing things for the first time now, and if it was the last time, too, that would be fine—the plain, blocky houses and battered stores were not worth remembering.

Then the van passed through the most closely guarded border on the continent without even pausing. Traffic wasn't a problem out here—very, very few people had clearance to cross the border. Those that did, passed quickly.

At least one PK, probably two, scanned the van as it crossed over, checking the number of people, reading the ID imprint buried inside the engine compartment. Everything cleared and the van rolled on.

She'd been told she'd be taken a half-hour away from the border. She didn't know where that would put her—she could only hope it would be past the worst of the borderlands. She had been thoroughly briefed on the procedure: the van would stop, the back door would swing open, and she would have thirty seconds to leave the van. After thirty seconds, a powerful electric charge would sweep through the van's interior. If she was inside she'd be killed. If she wanted, she could just sit in the van and choose electrocution.

She had heard that a lot of exiles chose that.

During the next half hour the sun sank. They timed it this way, Nilda thought bitterly to herself. NArds are suckers for cheap symbolism. She should know—she'd worked with them long enough.

Outside the van, a few fires in the east lit up the night, but she couldn't see any electric lights. Some houses near the road looked intact, others were rubble, but they had all been gutted years ago in the chaos following the Separation. She occasionally saw a few silhouettes running back and forth, but they kept their distance. They wouldn't come after her yet; they knew how the USNA protected their property. They'd likely stay back, wait for it to unload, then do whatever they wanted to her—unless, in the next half hour, the van brought her into civilization.

Her watch told her only five minutes had passed since she crossed the border. It seemed both longer and shorter—long enough that she felt she had been in the wastes forever, short enough that she believed that if she somehow got the van door open right now, she would be able to make it back to Queens and the USNA in a short sprint.

The van was traveling at least fifty miles per hour. She was already over two miles into the Island. She could sprint for maybe a few hundred yards, and the border rats would get her. If she could get the door open. Which she couldn't.

She sat down on the cold metal floor, closed her eyes, and counted seconds. In 1,380 seconds she would have a new life. How many seconds beyond that her life would last, she couldn't say.

The conversation centered on four lines:

"I can't give you any names."

"You can't tell us if you know of anybody named Whitaker, Whitfield, Whitton or Whitney in your organization?"

"I won't compromise any of our people."

"We won't compromise anyone. We want to *help* them. But we can't if we don't have their names."

And the cycle would start again. "I can't give you any names," Amelia said.

Blockers or no, mistrust radiated from Amelia like fumes from spilled gasoline. She'd talk with Lloyd and Aron as long as they wanted, but that didn't mean she was going to say a damn thing. It was getting dark outside, and the adepts weren't getting anywhere.

Aron was bouncing in his chair, torn between leaping for Amelia's throat or dashing out of the room in frustration. Lloyd hoped he looked calmer than Aron, but he didn't feel it.

"Maybe you can set up interviews for us. See if there's anyone who meets the description we gave you, and set up an interview. Then tell us where to go, we'll meet the person and go from there."

"If I'm not going to give you names, I'm certainly not going to turn anyone over to you in person."

"Maybe you can let us know how to contact people, and we'll see if they are willing to meet with us."

"I don't know how I could do that without giving you names. And I'm not giving you any names."

And so it went.

A good half-hour later, Lloyd blinked. The drizzle had stopped, and it was dark outside, darker even than it had been in the shack. When—if—he ever met Amelia again, he was sure she would ask to meet in a different location. Odds were, he would never set foot in that shack again. He was relieved.

"We have nothing," Aron said, just like Lloyd knew he would.

"We have her word."

"We have the promise of a terrorist that she'll look into a nonsensical request." Aron paused for effect. "We have nothing."

"I trust her."

"Oh, absolutely. If you can't trust evasive, icy felons, who can you trust? Is it because she was cute? Most felons you want to keep at arm's distance, but if they've got big, dark eyes and a perky little nose, hey, maybe they're all right."

Over the years, Lloyd had perfected a way to say Aron's name to get him to shut up, at least briefly. It was one syllable, short and clipped, the "o" dropped from the word. "ARN!"

Aron got the message. The topic was closed until one of them had something constructive to say, which most likely wouldn't happen until they met with Adept Birch.

Interlude: On Bureaucracy

Bureaucrats have gotten a bad rap. Slavish devotion to procedure is only a bad thing if the procedure itself is bad. But I worked very, very hard establishing the procedure, I've perfected it over the past fifty years, and slavish devotion to it is the most efficient way to get things done.

That doesn't mean people aren't important. People are crucial—specifically, people who understand the procedure. People who trust me enough to follow the procedure just because I made it are useful, but people who understand why the procedure is the way it is, that the procedure really is the best way to do things, are my most valuable asset.

The system has many purposes, one of the most significant being locating and recruiting the best PK talent in my nation—the best PK talent in to world. Do you think I could get out there and find each PK I needed myself? Sure, I did in the early days, but there were only a few of us. It took me only a month to find my first six, which meant I had doubled the number of known PKs in the world. Back then, that seemed like rapid progress. But we've gone from six to over six thousand, and I never could have tracked them down all by myself. They'd been found through the screening program, and the screening program works best through the procedure.

The trade-off, of course, is that those closest to the procedure lack imagination in their work, the ability to make adjustments or improvise. To be honest, though, improvisation is something I could often do without. There are certain people I trust to use their own judgment, and with them I can abide a degree of creativity. But with others, creativity leads to confusion more often than not. If they just do their job, the machine works smoothly. Generally speaking, people need to worry less about their own will and more about how well they serve the State.

I believe that part of people's difficulty with bureaucracy has come from dealing with systems with an uncertain goal. Too many systems were conglomerations of years of effort by many different leaders that resulted in chaos. People often complain that the chief purpose of many bureaucracies seemed to be preventing anyone from ever being served, and there is a certain truth to that. The systems were haphazard creations whose parts were confused and often contradictory.

That is why my government has been so successful—I was able to completely eliminate the organizations of the past and build my own from the ground up. The system does the work. The more I was able to expand the system, the more people I could draw into it, the better off I was, and the less work I had to do.

There is one other factor—the investment of my people. Once I had established that my systems would have a clear goal, I was able to find people invested in that goal. They're not part of the organization simply to pick up a salary, and they are too committed and intelligent to treat the people with whom they deal like they are annoyances. Those people are the reason we do what we do, and we need to treat them correctly so that our ultimate ends can be attained.

Note that I said "correctly," not "nicely." You do not find out the true capabilities of your people when they are comfortable. If your system is to be truly effective, you need occasionally to find opportunities to make your best people uncomfortable.

Chapter Five

"New exiles?"

"Two. Separate vans. One got dropped right at the border. Don't no know who he was, but the NArds must've wanted him bad dead. Drop at the border is next best thing to execution."

"How's he doing?"

"Surrounded. He make it through the rats, maybe we can help him, but best guess is he be dead in ten minutes. He lucky, maybe they make him a rat, too. But we can't no get to him soon enough."

Kale shook his head. There was a wall of screens in front of him, and most of it showed information in ways he didn't understand. The longer Spree was here, the more she customized everything to her preferences. It seemed to work—information flashed by faster than he could ever coax it—but now she had to tell him what he was looking at. There were a few images, direct surveillance that he could understand without a problem, but the other screens showed data, sometimes just words and numbers, other times colors floating and merging in ways that made sense only to Spree.

Spree was pointing at one screen that Kale figured was telling him information about the exile who had been dropped across the border. He couldn't make heads or tails of it, but that was okay. He'd rather not put a face to the poor sap. If Kale had been out there, he could shake the rats, get the exile somewhere safe. Then he'd see what this guy was made of. But he wasn't there, and there wasn't anyoany nearby who could deal with border rats. So that was it for the first exile. Kale didn't want to look at him too closely, or he'd humanize him, which would mean letting him die would make him feel like a callous son of a bitch.

"And the other?" he asked

"Is being dropped off a few miles in. Probably Yashie."

"Yashie?"

"Nilda Yashie. Friend of Corwin, they say."

"This is the woman who was supposed to have helped Mira?"

"This the one."

Kale tapped his fingertips together. "What's Mira going to do about it?"

Spree shrugged. "It's Mira. People get arrested, she tear up thinking how they martyrs, then she move on. She won't no think about Yashie unless somehow Yashie shows up at her doorstep begging to help the cause."

"All right, all right. Where's Yashie going to be dropped?"

"Just past Jericho. Got maybe five minutes."

"Anyone there to meet her?"

"Nope."

"Do we have any scooters?"

"Tied up or broken."

"As always. All right, I'll do what I can."

"Got that."

"Honduran ship come in?"

"Yeah—that's what all scooters is out doing, picking up shit and giving it out."

Kale had been carrying a tight knot in his abdomen for weeks—maybe for years—but Spree's news loosened it a bit. He wasn't a member of the Church of the Miraculous Creator, but on days like this, he was grateful for them. The only way a shipload of goods would ever come to the Island is if someone sent it out of charity. No merchants traded with the Island, since it had been years since it had any significant exports to offer. Without charity, they wouldn't get anything, and without the church, there wouldn't be much charity here.

"Okay, anything else?"

"Not for you old eyes."

Kale and Spree sat silently for a moment.

"How's Amelia?" Kale finally said.

"Amelia take care of herself."

"I know, I know. But how is she?"

Spree sighed and scratched the stubble behind her right ear. "Fine. You know she fine. She dealing with chumchas, and they're ain't no going to cause her any trouble. Don't no worry about her."

"I won't. Thanks, Spree."

Spree nodded as she stood and pulled on her cloak. It was long, sleeveless, and sheer, leaving her thin, dark shoulders uncovered.

"You should wear a hat," Kale said absently, trying to get the screens to show him something he understood. He managed to pull up some newsfeeds, and he started scanning through them while Spree got ready to leave.

"Don't no like nothing on the head," Spree said. "You seen the haircut?" The only hair she'd allowed to grow more than a few millimeters sat on her head like a yarmulke that was tilted a little to the left. "Be fine."

Kale didn't respond. He was deep into the feeds. Spree smiled and walked out.

As he watched the news, Kale wondered if the incoming boat might have some cable. The feed was choppy here and there, and if he patched into another network, that might erase some of the lag. Sure, the Island needed food, needed clothes, needed bricks and metal, but couldn't the boat also carry a few spools of cable?

The 2-D video feed finally started playing. It had taken fifteen seconds longer than Kale had wanted.

It's possible, he admitted, that there was more important work on the Island than cutting down his fifteen-second wait.

The temptation was to turn and look at the skyline. There were no trees, no buildings over ten feet tall, no lampposts or power lines to block the view. The skyline, with the USNA Pinnacle and its little brother, the Empire State Building, rose into a night sky so clear the stars seemed as bright as the distant windows. It would have been a nice view. But Nilda did not dare look at the sky, or do anything that would break her scan of her surroundings as she walked slowly forward.

Mines were one problem, but Nilda hoped previous exiles over the past decades had detonated the majority of them. Border rats, though, had only grown more numerous in recent years. Stealthier, too. Between the leaning shanties and the bare ground there were not many places to hide, but Nilda had no doubt the rats would manage.

Wind blew papers and plastic bags into her stockinged feet. Her prison shoes, completely inappropriate for walking long distances over rocky ground, lay in pieces far behind her. She kicked the trash off her feet, then stopped, listening for sound, thinking she heard someone else making noise. But when she was still, all sounds of movement stopped.

She moved again. The wind gusted, she shivered, then wiped drops of sweat off her forehead. The northern wind was cool, even though the night was still warm. The sweat all over her, though, was downright cold.

She lengthened her stride, hurrying toward nowhere, when she heard feet slapping on the packed dirt. Whirling, she saw nothing. But they had their eyes on her now. She had to move faster.

She was almost running, wondering how they'd appear. She could only think of how they looked in movies. In *Heretics*, the border rats were zombies, slow-moving but relentless. In *The Manfredd Candidacy*, they slithered, bellies to the ground, and sprang like panthers. In *Border Bounce*, they looked like club kids (being a comedy, though, the documentary value of the last film is questionable). Nilda pictured all of these images and more on her trail.

The first rat she saw looked like nothing from the movies. It was just a woman, sitting on a crate, leaning against a shanty. She looked like any person in the city, but dirtier and wearier. She did not leap to her feet as Nilda approached. She did not pounce.

But she didn't smile, either. Her eyes narrowed, her brow furrowed, and thousands of lines revealed themselves in her forehead.

"Keep moving," she said. "They're behind you."

Nilda whirled, still saw nothing, then started running. As she passed the woman, Nilda could think of only one question. "Which way should I go?"

The woman pointed north, to nothing—at least, nothing Nilda could see. "Away from them."

Nilda nodded her thanks and adjusted her course north. Why she should trust this woman over whoever else was out there, she didn't know. But it was what she was doing.

She kept jogging, her breathing and footfalls growing louder, but now she could hear them. Footsteps behind her. Not too fast, but steady. She put on a burst of speed, then had to slow as her side cramped. The noises behind her seemed neither closer nor farther away. Just steady.

She passed a few more buildings, most with traces of charring, none with visible inhabitants. The footsteps behind her slowly drew closer, and they approached even faster when she started walking again. She hadn't jogged for more than two miles since she left college, but tonight she must have covered at least three. She had to slow down.

She came to a row of four buildings, the longest continuous stretch of structures she'd seen since she left the van. She ran past two, then quickly dodged before the third, hoping to confuse her pursuers. Then she walked.

The footsteps came closer, following her. When they came out from behind the building, she finally saw them. They seemed low to the ground but did not run on all fours. They might just be short, or simply stooped. Probably malnourished.

Nilda tried to run, but pain in her side and legs hobbled her. Walking was difficult enough.

They gained. She looked over her shoulder with every step. She saw their faces. Their mouths did not gape, their eyes were neither empty nor filled with undying hatred. Their mouths were straight, the skin on their faces loose and jowly. Their eyes held no malice, just curiosity about the stranger in front of them and what they could get from her.

But they were people, Nilda told herself. Human. They can reason.

"What do you want?" she asked, burying any edges in her voice.

The group—there were four of them—stopped. "Everything you have," one of them, a tall man with a patchy beard, replied.

"They didn't let me take anything," she replied.

"You got clothes," the man said.

"Identification. Wallet," a shorter man to his left added.

"A necklace," said a woman missing her right eye.

"And after I give it to you?"

"We see then."

Nilda's throat tightened. "Promise me you'll leave me alone if I give you what I have."

The four of them snickered.

"There's four us," the bearded man said. "One you. We taking what we want. No terms."

"I can help you. We can work together. Finding food. I'll, I'll help build shelter. I can help."

"New exiles don't no help," the shorter man said.

"Usually die quick," the woman said.

"Eat more food than they bring in," the bearded man said. "Not no looking for your help." The four started forward.

Nilda ran, covering nearly a hundred yards before cramps seized her legs again. She slowed to a walk, almost fell as pain ran the length of her left leg. The four behind her hadn't run, but they didn't stumble, and the small gap she had opened started to close again.

She didn't know how long she managed to stay ahead of them. It might have been two miles, it might have been one, it might have been a quarter mile. Her feet bled, her muscles clamped in place, and four sets of hands grabbed her.

The necklace snapped off almost instantly. Her jacket went next, though they pulled it with an odd sensitivity, probably hoping to preserve it in as good shape as possible.

Nilda fell as they pulled, her hand landing on a rock. Not an especially large rock, but a rock. She grabbed it and swung.

Their reflexes were much better than hers, she only caught a glancing blow on the shorter man's thigh. He jumped back, rubbed it slightly, then moved toward her again with clutching hands. His expression never changed.

They had all jumped back, though. She had a gap of three feet. She scurried away, crawling. A few feet closer to somewhere else.

They closed again. Hands grabbed her pants. Ripping, this time, tearing pieces of fabric. One of them removed her socks, ripping fresh scabs off her heels. She clawed the ground, moving only inches at a time, not strong enough to pull away from the four.

Salvation came in the form of a flying rock. It struck the woman in the head, and she dropped silently. The three others looked up, opened their hands, and Nilda was free. She crawled fifteen feet before the newcomers arrived.

There were more rats, three of them. Dropping the woman behind Nilda had made the two groups equal. Nilda hoped the second group would set on the first as they converged.

Nilda stayed low. The six border rats closed in a mass of hands and weapons, grabbing at her jacket, grabbing at her necklace, grabbing at her. They landed blows on each other, they landed blows on her. The stick swung into her ribs, taking her breath away. Her arms gave way, and she ended up prone on the ground. The bearded man took a blow to the chin and fell, bouncing off her before coming to rest just to her right.

Someone stumbled backward—one of the only rats with shoes—and caught Nilda's head with his heel. She blinked in pain, and the world wavered.

She tried to focus but couldn't get her eyes to work right. No matter what she did, the rats looked like they were floating above her, even the bearded man who had fallen next to her. Ten feet in the air they looked, like she had fallen into a pit. She hadn't seen a pit.

She closed her eyes, rubbed her head where she had been kicked, then looked again. The six were still motionless in midair. And there was a seventh. She couldn't make out any of his features, as the night somehow seemed more intense around him.

"Can you roll?" he asked.

"Roll?"

"To your right."

"Yes, I think so." She rolled, and her shoulder hit a board lying next to her. She hadn't seen it before. She kept rolling until she lay on a smooth, hard surface that seemed infinitely more comfortable than the rough, hard surface she had been on before.

The six rats continued to float above her. Now that she could focus, she saw their muscles straining, their eyes trying to move, their mouths pushing to open, their limbs attempting to flail, but nothing worked. They hovered motionless.

Then they moved, floating slowly to the west. She wondered where they were going until she turned her head and saw she was moving, not them. The board felt like a large piece of plywood, but it flew. She had fallen out of the hands of the border rats and into the hands of a Long Island PK—a rogue, maybe, or a chumcha. When some of her pain ebbed, she would think about whether this was less trouble or more. For now, she enjoyed the fact that no one was kicking her or grabbing her, and that a blanket somehow found its way on top of her.

The seventh man, still enveloped in darkness, walked next to her, not saying anything, possibly not looking at her, but she couldn't really tell. She watched him, wondering who he was.

"I'm Kale," he said. "I'll get you somewhere safe. Sorry I couldn't provide better transportation—it doesn't do to take anything valuable into the borderlands."

"Why are you helping me?" she asked, not sure whether she had spoken in any more than a mumble.

"I owe you," he said. "Or at least, an acquaintance of mine owes you. I couldn't leave you to the rats."

"Acquaintance?"

"Not now. We'll talk when we're away from the borders."

Chapter Six

Aron had a game—developed long before he met Lloyd—called It Could Be Worse. The first dozen or so times he had tried to play it with Lloyd, Lloyd did not participate, since he thought it was stupid. But Aron kept at it, and Lloyd often got sucked into the game in spite of himself.

"It could have been worse if NArds broke in and arrested Amelia during the meeting, and took us in as accomplices," Aron said, starting the game without preamble.

"That would be worse," Lloyd agreed. "But they usually don't come out on the Island."

"They would to get a war criminal," Aron said.

"Maybe."

Below them the faithful flowed into and out of the Hampton Cathedral. The rumors about the miracle of Antigua were spreading, and more and more people were showing up at the cathedral to thank the Creator for that city's deliverance and to pray that New York—or at least Queens—would be next. Lloyd was monitoring the cathedral door, Aron was controlling lighting, tasks that the both of them could do without much effort.

Aron glanced at Stel Grant as she moved around the floor, wandering from person to person, stopping briefly to listen to anyone who wanted to talk with her, maybe casting a small spell, then moving on. Aron then turned back to Lloyd and raised an eyebrow to remind him it was his turn.

"It could be worse if we drew assistant archivist duty," Lloyd said. Aron reacted immediately, blanching as his brow furrowed.

"You're not supposed to go to the very bottom that quickly!" Aron scolded. "Geez, about the only worse place I can go from working with Terrin is if we were in hell for all eternity. Incremental steps is how the game is supposed to work."

"Right, right. My mistake."

Aron shook his head in mock despair. "You're really bad at this, you know."

"I'm doing my best, I swear."

"I know. That's what makes it so sad."

Below them, thoughts kept passing by, thoughts of gratitude, devotion, prayer, interspersed with curiosity, boredom, and doubt. No trace of hostility, though. No signs of disruption.

Stel looked up, made eye contact with Lloyd, and shrugged. He raised his hands helplessly. <<Duty,>> he sent to her. <<Gotta be done.>>

<<Is it wrong of me to want a mugger to come in?>> she sent back.

<<Wanting someone to sin so you'll have a few moments of your entertainment?>> he returned. <<Maybe. But I'd let it pass.>>

She waved briefly, then returned her thoughts to the flocking parishioners.

"Five minutes until the GA," Aron said, mainly to have something to say.

Lloyd dropped his head to the side, rested his hands between his cheek and shoulder, and closed his eyes. "I'm ready," he mumbled sleepily. Aron smiled.

Five more minutes of steady, mild-mannered parishioners passed. Stel helped the final stragglers find a seat, then took a position near the main doors, almost directly below Aron and Lloyd. They all faced the pulpit, assuming expressions of devout concentration.

Right on schedule, a choir of heavenly voices rose into song, lights throughout the cathedral dimmed except for a bright circle above the pulpit, and Grand Adept Serl descended, arms outstretched.

Lloyd remembered how impressive this whole ceremony seemed before he learned to do it himself. Every week, the ceremony began with the Grand Adept falling to the world from the heavens, as if returning from a direct consultation with God. In truth, he was returning from a quick climb up the stairs to a small meditative chamber atop the dome of the cathedral, but the effect was nonetheless awe-inspiring. Or at least, it had been, until Lloyd and Aron had snuck into the cathedral one night and duplicated the entire ceremony themselves, Lloyd providing the lighting while Aron descended, delivering a string of off-color jokes in a deep, resonant voice. Lloyd had laughed about it afterward, but he sometimes found himself missing the awe.

The crowd, though, had not seen Lloyd and Aron's demonstration, and they fell silent as the choir sung the Grand Adept to his perch. Grand Adept Malvoin Serl raised his hand in blessing, and pulses of light flew out over the congregation. A few muted gasps broke the reverent silence.

"The miracles of the Creator," the Grand Adept intoned. He was small, balding, and wizened, but his voice boomed across the cathedral and filled every corner. "They are what unite us. They are what call us here today. They are the continual manifestations of His power and grace. Amen."

"Amen," the crowd responded.

They had fifteen minutes of ceremony ahead, followed by a half hour or more of sermon, then a bit more ceremony. Lloyd's legs would be quite stiff by the time it was over. He wondered, not for the first time, what the harm would be in giving the adepts who were out of view a chair to sit in.

He divided his time between listening to the Grand Adept and scanning the parishioners' minds, which were far more interesting than the service. He found at least a half-dozen souls who should attend Penitence after the sermon, and one who made him wonder anew at the bounds of human imagination.

As he read signals from the front rows of the congregation, a small buzz wandered its way through their thoughts. He pulled back, cutting off all sendings from his mind, but the buzz remained.

<<Hear that?>> he sent to Aron.

<<What?>>

<<A buzzing.>>

<<Mental or physical?>>

<<Not certain, really.>>

Aron paused. <<I don't hear anything.>>

<<Okay.>> Convinced it was only in his head, Lloyd ignored the buzz. Which only made it grow louder.

He shook his head briefly, trying to keep his motions small since adepts in the cathedral were supposed to stay out of sight and not be noticed by the parishioners. The buzzing remained.

It seemed to be settled in the base of his skull. He wanted to rub it, but movement would cost him at least an hour in Penitence.

By the time the Grand Adept's sermon began, Lloyd couldn't hear a word he was saying. The buzz was louder and had been joined by pain, first mild, now approaching the level of a hatpin lodged in his spinal cord. Beads of sweat formed on his brow, as the act of standing still now required tremendous exertion.

<<You okay?>> Aron sent. <<You're leaking pain. Put a lid on it.>>

<<I'll try,>> Lloyd returned. <<Getting worse, though. You still don't hear it?>>

<<A buzzing? No.>>

Lloyd tried to focus on the nimbus of white surrounding the Grand Adept, looking for anything to think of besides the pain, but it didn't work. Waves of sharp agony ran up and down his spine, and his knees trembled. Grand Adept Serl misted out of focus, until all Lloyd could see was a white light. The light expanded, filling his whole vision, blanking the whole cathedral out in its bright shine. Below him, Lloyd heard the seemingly distant sound of the cathedral doors whispering open, and his vision flashed brighter, a blinding white filling his mind, a huge expanse of white covering all he could see for miles and miles and miles, everything, everywhere the purest white.

He screamed and fell to his knees. The Grand Adept paused, but only briefly. Aron, breaking protocol, dashed to Lloyd, but most of the congregation was unaware anything was happening. The scream had been psychic, silent to almost everyone in the cathedral.

Aron shook his shoulders. <<Lloyd!>> he sent, then whispered the same word. <<Lloyd, come back!>>

And he did. His vision returned, the light faded, the pain ran from his body like a stream down a mountain. The buzzing disappeared entirely.

He leapt to his feet, his head nearly bumping Aron's, hovering over him.

<<White field!>> he sent urgently. <<White field!>>

Aron responded wordlessly, with only confusion.

<<He just walked in. White field. The doors open, someone came in, and I was totally blinded by a white field. He's down there! Come on!>>

Aron and Lloyd ran down the stairs to the main floor. There, they slowed, knowing that a complete disruption of the service, no matter how well justified, would not be appreciated by the Grand Adept.

Lloyd approached Stel. <<Did you see the man who just came in?>> he sent.

<<Yes. He was clean.>>

<<Did you get anything else? Do you know who he is?>>

<<No,>> she sent.

<<Where is he? What did he look like?>>

<<I didn't really look at him,>> Stel sent. <<Ordinary, I guess. Brown hair. Medium build. Or a little thin. Kept his chin down and walked over to the pews.>>

<<Okay. Aron, watch the doors. Stel, help me find him.>>

Aron, never a good blocker, let loose a flare of resentment at being ordered around before tapping his emotions down. <<Got it,>> he returned.

Half the heads in the congregation watched Lloyd and Stel walk down the middle of the chapel aisle. Lloyd felt whisperings of respect and admiration, but these were sometimes buried under the apprehension and nervousness. Fifty-two Sundays each year they came here and were told that the miracles that had entered the world ever since the Six emerged were a true blessing from God, that they were more fortunate than any other people in history to have servants in the church who could put these wonderful gifts at their disposal, and the parishioners nodded in agreement and thought how great God was to have created the clergy and their miraculous powers. But when it came down to it, precious few of them felt comfortable having someone else look into their mind even if they believed the ability to do so was a boon from God.

Lloyd felt their resentment and wondered if they'd feel better if they knew the process made him about as uncomfortable as them. The private mind and the unconscious mind—especially the unconscious—were best left as they were, untouched and unknown to outsiders. When you were doing a broad scan like he was, it took focus to remember what you were supposed to be looking for and not let the odd notions and depraved thoughts you encountered distract you.

The vision Lloyd had seen helped keep him focused, though, and he scanned quickly, back and forth across the crowd. He skimmed over astonishment, embarrassment, revulsion, and even a streak of mental exhibitionism while looking for the white field.

He was with Stel at the front of the chapel, standing in the shadow of the Grand Adept. The litany was ending, and Grand Adept Serl was starting his sermon.

"One of the true tests we face as servants of the Creator is how we will act when our understanding is limited," the Grand Adept said. "When we have to fall back on something, to what do we

turn? Our own instincts? The logic of the world? Or do we use the
opportunity to deepen our obedience to the Creator?"

As the sermon continued, Lloyd turned to Stel and shrugged.

<<Nothing here, either,>> she sent.

<<Let's switch sides, walk back, and re-scan,>> he sent.
<<We need to find this.>>

As they turned, a new voice entered their minds. <<You will
prepare a report explaining this departure from protocol for me by
4:00,>> the Grand Adept sent sternly, while his speaking voice
continued the sermon without wavering. <<Please be certain High
Adept Birch receives a copy.>>

Normally the stern tone of the Grand Adept's voice would have
shaken Lloyd's knees, but he knew he had the best excuse for a
disruption he would ever have in his life.

"Perhaps the most difficult times we face is when the teachings
of God directly contradict the supposed wisdom of the world," the
Grand Adept continued. "How do we choose obedience when
everyone around us attempts to push us in a different direction?"

Lloyd scanned the south side of the chapel, finding it much the
same as the north. At the final row, doubts finally entered his mind.
Maybe he hadn't had a vision or been given a sign. Maybe he'd just
had a seizure.

Then he found it—not in the congregation, but in an apse, near
a statue of Harriman Ellis. The subject wasn't sending much, mainly
curiosity and confusion, but every thought carried a trace of the
white that had blinded Lloyd. This was the man.

Lloyd sent for Aron and Stel, and they quickly walked toward
him as he approached the man. Lloyd walked with the calmly
hurried pace acolytes were taught early in their studies, and it
worked—the man didn't notice their approach, or at least he didn't
care.

The dark corner of the cathedral hid the man's face, as only
traces of the central wizard light bled through. Lloyd was tempted

to shine a new light in this corner, but he didn't want to startle this person, as he was about to ask him for a tremendous favor.

The man—maybe not even a man, maybe still a boy, a few years younger than Lloyd—seemed engrossed by the statue of Ellis. Lloyd almost stopped in his tracks, thinking that artists may someday paint this moment, when the statue of the prophet looked down at the man who would deliver his fondest dream.

"Excuse me," Lloyd whispered, and the man started.

"I ... sorry, I ... was just looking. I'm sorry if I was doing something wrong." The man stepped back once, then twice when he saw the other two adepts behind Lloyd. He had floppy hair and an awkward gait.

"No, no, you weren't doing anything wrong," Lloyd said, trying to sound friendly while he kept his voice low. "We just wanted to talk to you."

The man's eyes darted between the three of them, moving faster and faster. "About ... what?"

"Just talk. Are you ... do you mind if I ask if you are a member of our church?"

"No. No, I'm not. I've ... been a few times but I've never joined. I don't know *how* you join. I've never, you know, looked into it. Sorry."

Lloyd carefully sent calm and trust while he spoke. "That's okay. We'd just like to talk. I see you like the statue—I could tell you a few things about the sculptor."

It backfired. The man fidgeted, moved backward, nearly pressing himself against the wall. "No, no, that's ... I was just leaving, anyway. I have to leave, I have somewhere to be."

"No, please, don't leave. Just ... wait." He reached out, hoping to get something from the man's mind, to learn something about him—his name at least. But all he could see was disorganized, flustered worry. He pushed harder.

Too much. The man must have felt the touch on his mind, then heard the edge of desperation in Lloyd's voice.

"No. I need to go." He peeled himself off the wall and strode toward the door.

Lloyd started to call after him, but a firm sending from the Grand Adept stopped him. <<Conduct your business outside.>> Lloyd sent acquiescence, then followed the man out. Aron and Stel were right behind him.

By the time he got to the cathedral doors, Lloyd was nearly running, and it turned into a sprint outside.

"Wait!"

"I can't talk!" the man yelled.

Lloyd watched, stunned, as the hope of the future ran away from him. But only for a moment. He was not trained to simply stand and watch.

There were ways Lloyd could run and run fast, catching up to the man and hopefully stopping him. He couldn't guarantee he'd catch him—running through Sunday traffic by the cathedral could be dicey—but he could make the attempt. But he'd probably end up making the man more scared, more angry. He'd have to find another way to approach him, and he had faith that if the Creator had already given him one sign of the man's presence, when the time came the Creator would give another.

There was, however, one more thing he could do. "He's gone," he said loudly. "And we didn't even get his name."

The man's thoughts may have been muddled, but when people hear any reference to their name, there's a reflex that happens in their head, information that floats to the surface of their thoughts. This time was no different.

At least, when I make my report to the Grand Adept, it will have that *piece of information,* Lloyd thought.

When Lloyd visited that night, High Adept Birch's office was quiet and soothing, as always. It calmed Lloyd a little bit, so he went from keyed up to somewhat jumpy.

"Courtney Whitaker," he said.

"Ummmm … no. I don't have him listed as a member. There are a few Whitakers here. Maybe they're relatives. Do you know his parents' names?"

"No."

Acolyte Devin sighed. "Well, there's a lot here. A few dozen. I could start calling, see if any of them know Courtney."

"Good."

"But what should I tell them?"

Lloyd drummed a finger on his leg. "I don't know. Something good. Like someone left a package for him."

"Someone left a package for him in our church?"

"I don't know, Brit, that's just off the top of my head. Think of something, okay? Adept Birch is waiting for me. Just give them a reason why it would be good for them to tell us if they know Courtney and where he is. I'm sure you'll think of something."

"Hmmmph. Give a guy one vision and all of the sudden he doesn't have time for lowly administrators." Devin held up a hand before Lloyd could protest. "I'm kidding, I'm kidding. Go in."

Lloyd entered the High Adept's office, not sure what his reception would be. He thought he gathered some good information, but he also knew he'd breached protocol in about half a dozen ways during the Grand Adept's sermon. He didn't know which issue High Adept Birch would address first. His confidence had continuously ebbed since the vision had faded, and he now felt sure that Adept Birch was about to deliver a long lecture and a serious reprimand. All the checks into this Courtney Whitaker would come to nothing, and Lloyd's standing as an adept would be forever tarnished.

Adept Birch erased his fears as soon as he sat down.

"You found him. Amazing, amazing work. Thanks be to the Creator."

"He is a God of miracles," Lloyd responded in rote form.

"You have put Acolyte Devin to work locating Mr. Whitaker?" It wasn't really a question—Adept Birch had full knowledge of what took place in his reception room.

Lloyd answered it anyway. "Yes."

"This means you will have to talk to that ILF contact again," Adept Birch said.

Lloyd wanted to say that Amelia Diaz had not been at all helpful before and he didn't expect her to be helpful now, but the High Adept had said what he wanted, so Lloyd just nodded and didn't say anything. He just felt good.

Interlude: From *The Way of Miracles*: "Limits of Power"

Very little of your training will focus on limits. The gifts of the Creator tell us to overcome boundaries, not be confined by what we believe we cannot do. Nevertheless, the world is given to common misperceptions of our abilities, and many who have joined our order have been tainted by these superstitions. In order to ensure that your training does not begin on improper footing, we wish to outline some limits of your abilities.

- **You cannot predict the future.** Society has a longstanding confusion between the gift of prophecy and mind-reading, which has only been compounded by charlatans claiming the ability to perform both functions. To be fair, we must admit that the fact that First Adept Ellis possessed both abilities has contributed to the confusion. He is the exception, though, not the rule, and the exact nature of his prophesying powers remains beyond our understanding.
  The so-called "mind-reading" ability we possess is more properly called "thought-reading." Though it makes us privy to an extraordinary amount of information, it does not show us the future. We may only read what our subjects are thinking, and most of them, quite naturally, are not sending prophecies of the future. Our gift is extraordinarily useful in illuminating the past and present, but the future remains as much an unknown to us as to the rest of the world.

- **You cannot know everything about a person simply by looking at him or her.** As mentioned above, we read thoughts, not entire minds. Thoughts cause shifts in electro-magnetic energy, which is what our gift can perceive. The mind, by contrast, is a number of patterns written into the brain, and our gift provides no methods to read that particular text. If we are to know something about a person, they must first think it, whether consciously or unconsciously. If they do not think it, it remains hidden to us.

- **You cannot read the thoughts of a large crowd all at once.** This conclusion should be clear to anyone who has ever attempted to listen to three or more people speaking at once. The multiple streams of words become gibberish. Part of your training will teach you how to move through a crowd, scanning individual minds briefly to obtain a feeling for the group as a whole, and also how to close your mind to sendings, putting a temporary stop to the voices that otherwise besiege us constantly. Neither of these abilities, though, allows you to read a large number of thoughts with a single mental swipe. Super-human mental focus is not part of the Talent.

- **You cannot teleport.** This may not be an absolute limit, and a small group of PKs has studied the topic practically since the day the Six escaped from the Area. The best solution they have devised to this point is demolecurizing the body, transmitting it to a chosen destination as a particle ray, then reassembling the body.
  The obstacles to such a procedure are daunting and are listed fully within this text. Here we simply point out that no one, including the greatest PK minds in existence, has solved this conundrum, meaning it is unlikely that anyone in the near future will accomplish the feat.

- **You cannot raise the dead.** There are certain powers the Creator has, to this point, reserved for himself, and that is one of them. The great difficulty rests in knowing just what it is that makes the difference between death and life in a human being. Many PKs have been able to send electric currents through dead brains, going so far as to make various muscles twitch and dance. But in the end, when the electricity is removed, the mind is still dead. We have not found a way to bring back what has left.

- **You cannot move mountains.** At least, not yet.

Chapter Seven

"I didn't help your friend. Everyone thinks I did, that's why I'm out here, that's why you're helping me, but I didn't. I don't *know* Mira Corwin. Why does everyone think I do?"

The woman, Nilda, still had not recovered from being exiled from her home and caught between half a dozen border rats. She'd spent twenty hours in bed, and what sleep she'd manage to get was restless. Once when Kale checked in on her he saw her lying with her eyes open, staring at the mottled off-white ceiling above her. Kale considered putting her to sleep himself, but that kind of unconsciousness seldom seemed to do anyone any good.

"I don't think you did anything," he said in level tones. "I believe what you say. I'm helping you because of what Mira did to you. She knew perfectly well you had nothing to do with her organization, but she let you twist in the wind anyway. I don't think that was fair, so I wanted to even the score a little."

The words sounded empty to Kale when he said them. The woman in front of him had lost everything in her life, and he knew he hadn't—and wouldn't—come anywhere near to replacing any of that. Fortunately, she seemed too tired to lash out at him.

"I was wondering if you were ready to eat yet," Kale said.

"I probably should …" Nilda said doubtfully, then paused. "No, not yet. Let me sleep a little first."

"Okay," Kale said. He thought again about putting her out himself, again decided not to, and left her alone.

I've been focused on her for too long, he thought as he wandered in search of Spree. He had more important work to do than cleaning up Mira's mess. He'd definitely have a few words with her the next time they happened to be in the same room, but until then he had other concerns to worry about.

"Spree! *Spree!* Where in hell ..."

Spree poked her head through a doorway, the back of her head brushing the frame and knocking free a few loose white paint chips. "Here. Place I always am. Where you would look first, you were thinking. What?"

Kale stomped down the hallway. "Was there cable on the boat?"

"A little."

"Can we get any of it?"

"A little."

"How much?"

"Enough to get us to FO2."

"That's *it?*"

"Better than most of the planet."

"I guess," Kale grumbled.

Kale walked into the tech room so that he could now talk to her face to face instead of yelling down the hall.

"Has Amelia set herself up in a good place?"

"Yeah. Nicer than the last one, less sneaking around. The diner."

"Is it wired?"

"Yeah."

"Load it up for me," Kale said.

Spree pointed to one of the screens on her grid. "Already there," she said. Amelia was on the left side of the screen, sitting in a corner booth in the mostly empty diner, away from any windows.

"She thinks she can trust this chumcha?" Kale asked.

"Guess so," said Spree, cocking her head. "Don't no know why he's meeting her again. Old bald heads in the church be up to something."

Kale stared dubiously at the screen. Despite the camera's poor angle, he could make out a distant roach scurrying across a leaf of lettuce lying on the floor. Or at least he thought he could.

"I hope she ate beforehand," he said.

Amelia watched the chumcha standing near the door to the
diner, staying away from the soap-painted windows and trying not
to appear nervous as he repeatedly scanned the room. She made eye
contact with him, he bobbed his head slightly, then tried to look
poised as he walked across the restaurant and slid across from
Amelia.

"Will the waitress be taking our order soon?" he said.

Amelia shrugged. "Maybe. There's a first time for everything."
Then she spoke again before Hsu could say anything else. "I'm not
interested in soaking up the atmosphere here any longer than I need
to. What do you want?"

"I have a name."

"Mmm-hmmm."

"I want to know if you know anything about this person. I'm
not sure what town he lives in, but I'm pretty sure he's within
walking distance of the cathedral. His name is Courtney Whitaker."

"Never heard of him." She may have spoken too quickly—it's
possible she had started her answer before the chumcha had even
finished the name.

Hsu's eyes narrowed. "Don't you want to take a minute to
maybe think about it?"

"No."

"Would you tell me if you had heard of him?"

Amelia remained silent.

"Haven't we done most of this before?" Hsu snapped. "Why did
you agree to meet with me if you're not going to say anything?"

"I met with you because people asked me to."

"Why did they tell you to meet with me?"

"I don't know—people repaying favors to other people. I don't
know the details."

Hsu stood. "Maybe I won't stay for lunch," he said, then
stomped away.

Amelia waited until he was gone to smile. Novices in this business were a godsend—they were always so willing to give up information, and not patient enough to get anything for it in return.

Chapter Eight

Kale treasured any time he spent with Amelia, but he wished he could find a way to change the first twenty minutes of every encounter they'd had in the past few years. They only met once or twice a year, and it seemed Amelia spent much of their time apart compiling a list of complaints against Kale, and as soon as she saw him the list shot right out of her brain through her mouth.

"A *firespout*? In *Manhattan*? What in *hell* were you trying to prove? And then you go off on your overprotective act, watching out for poor little Amelia, like I can't take care of myself. You don't have to worry about whether *I'm* safe, you'd do better keeping your ass out of New York! Watch out for your own damn self, don't watch out for me!"

He'd tried a number of techniques over the years. Silently nodding while looking ashamed, attempting to explain how his actions had been justified, trying to change the subject—nothing ever shortened the length of the lecture. There was a chance a total, abject, down-on-his-knees apology would ameliorate her temper somewhat, but that was one approach he was not yet ready to attempt.

"You want to help me, then *help* me. We'd have plenty of openings for you, plenty of ways to actually *contribute*, instead of freelancing yourself into trouble every other week. Sign up in the ILF and you could watch over me like a hawk instead of just popping up at the most annoying moments. You wouldn't even be interfering when you did—you'd be a part of the cause."

If only the fabric of time involved some sort of kinetic motion, Kale thought to himself. He could work with it then—speed it up, is what he'd do now—so that situations like this would be more bearable, and he could move right on to the more enjoyable and placid part of the encounter. But the fabric of time remained beyond his reach.

"All right? I'm not a little girl anymore. You can take less responsibility for me, more for yourself. Okay?"

Kale nodded gratefully, more because he knew the lecture was about over than because he agreed with anything she was saying.

"Okay," Amelia said. "Now. How are you?"

"Fine. And you?"

She flared slightly. "If you have to ask after what I've been telling you for the past …"

Kale held up his hands appeasingly. "All right, all right, I know how you are. I will be working to amend my future behavior."

"Mm hmm. Has anyone tied you to the spout?"

"Not that I know of."

"Did you want anyone to?"

Kale shrugged. "I don't know. I don't think it matters. I'm sure Andy could figure it out if he cared enough to give it a moment's thought."

Amelia blinked a few times before responding. "And if Andy—I mean, if Drauer figured it out you wouldn't be worried?"

Another shrug. "No. Why should I be? It's not like it'll make him any more mad at me than he already is."

"All right, all right." Amelia took a deep breath and pulled on the sleeves of her shiny black turtleneck. "You know, I didn't come by to yell at you. Or fight with you."

"Of course you didn't. It's just what tends to happen when you see me."

"I have a question."

"Go ahead."

"Those chumchas that came to see me, the ones you so gracefully intercepted before I had a chance to talk to them? One of them asked to meet me again. They keep asking about a certain person, and I was wondering if you might know what they're looking for. The first time they came by, they gave me a bunch of last names. Whitaker, Whitfield, Whitton, Whitney, I think they were."

"Okay," Kale said. A shadow flickered in a deep corner of his mind, and he ignored it.

"They wanted to know if we had anyone with a name like that on the rollflyover the extent we have any rolls. Naturally, I gave them nothing."

"Naturally."

"Then this one comes back and talks to me again, and he's asking the same basic question, but he's narrowed it down. He has a specific name, Courtney Whitaker, asked me if I knew anyone with that name, which I don't. So I asked him why he's so interested in it, and he just clams up. He's new to keeping secrets, he was pretty obvious about it, but he didn't give me anything. So I'm coming to you, the expert on all things chumcha. What are they looking for?"

Kale stood up. He was nowhere near the expert on the CMC that Harry or even Andy were, but neither of them were available. He paced the room, hoping the dark corner of his mind would just go away so he wouldn't have to deal with it. "They're looking for someone named Courtney Whitaker, I imagine."

"Right. But why the list of last names, then the specific name? They're digging for something. Any idea what?"

Kale stopped himself from saying yes. "I don't know. Maybe."

"Maybe? Well, do you or don't you? And stop pacing, you're making me dizzy."

Kale tried to restrain his steps, but his legs felt like he wanted to run. The dark corner of his mind, though, was even faster, spreading forward, flooding his entire skull with the information he knew was right but didn't want to admit. He tried to think of some way he could just tell Amelia that this was nothing to worry about, but he was too overwhelmed. All he could say now was what the dark corner was telling him.

"They think he's here. They think they know who he is."

Amelia sat stiffly in her chair, her hands gripping the seat firmly, responding to the odd urgency in Kale's tones. "Who is he?"

Kale spun, continuing his pacing, almost running back and forth across the room. "The one who's supposed to bring the whole bloody thing down."

The scooter—a larger model, with four wheels and a seat instead of just a platform to stand on—wheeled slowly under a crumbling overpass. Traffic was light enough to allow any other vehicles on the road to easily fly by the creeping scooter, as well as the two-wheeled counterpart behind it.

Twin droplets of water from the just-ended rain dropped off the end of the bridge as the scooter emerged. The condition of the road improved abruptly, becoming smoother with solidly painted lane dividers. The four-wheeled scooter crawled ahead, crossing a single line then a double one as it stayed straight as an arrow while the road dodged left then veered right.

A full car, with a roof and everything, flew up behind the scooter, horn blaring. The driver rolled down his window, yelled something unintelligible, and sped off.

The scooter was now in the wrong lane but it kept going straight. It didn't encounter any traffic before it bumped off the shoulder, rolled across a thin strip of grass and into a tangled hedge that forced the vehicle to stop.

The two-wheeler pulled up behind but stayed on the shoulder. Its driver folded his arms and leaned forward, resting them on the steering handle.

"Did you ever think that the Creator just doesn't like you much?" Aron said.

Lloyd grunted and willed his four-wheeler backward. "I hate this exercise."

"If the Creator kept trying to kill me, my enthusiasm would be pretty low too."

"How long before I get to give up?"

"You may quit once you reach the point where you don't even have the will to consider quitting anymore."

Lloyd rolled his eyes. "The First Adept and his damn paradoxes. Sometimes I think they're just a way to feign depth through easy contradiction."

Aron reeled backward, his hand flying to his forehead. "What's this? Muttering from the mouth of the faithful? I believe *I'm* supposed to say all the sacrilegious lines in our conversations."

"You don't keep riding into bushes."

"Because I have faith."

"Because you get to look where you're going."

"If you're going to get the plum assignments, you're going to have to ride into a few bushes. The Sayings of Nesbitt, chapter eight, verse fifteen. And if you keep rolling your eyes like that, one day you'll get stuck and have to look at your brain for all eternity."

Lloyd was back on the proper side of the road, Aron poised behind him. Water dripped from leaf to leaf on either side of the road.

"Blindfold down," Aron said.

"Can't I just close my eyes?" Lloyd asked for the fifth time.

"You'll cheat, and you know it. And stop whining to me—I'm just enforcing the rules here. High Adept Sternhaven said we need to do it this way, so we're gonna do it this way. Blindfold down."

Lloyd obediently covered his eyes and willed his scooter forward, keeping well under ten miles per hour.

A weak horn sounded behind him.

"Shut up, Aron," Lloyd said. Aron honked again.

Lloyd pushed out his mental image of the road and trees around him. He shut out the dripping water and the sound of birds just starting to emerge from whatever shelter they had found. He dropped his arms to his sides, leaving all operation of the scooter to his mind. He tried to forget about the sticky warmth of the air and the sweat on his brow. His mind lost all conscious thought, and he saw stars and lines darting against his closed eyelids. Then he shut those out, and everything was dark and he reached for the Creator. *Make me an instrument*, he thought.

He had no idea if the scooter turned. He focused solely on the interior of his mind, preventing all physical sensation from registering. He didn't know if Aron was still behind him, or if he was still on the road, or if Aron was a quarter mile back watching Lloyd slowly roll into the Sound. He could almost here the quiet rhythm of the waves, beating on his feet, then up his legs and finally covering all of him. The sea became both his breath and his heartbeat, and he didn't stop to wonder how he could still inhale as the water flooded over him.

He didn't think of Aron, or Courtney Whitaker, or anyone else. For all he knew there was no one else, the whole universe had dropped away, vanished as soon as he stopped thinking about it. The Creator had plucked him out of reality or mercifully erased the whole tangled mess that all the other people had made. The earth was just water again, the land was submerged, and soon the light would be taken away as well and everything would be as it was in the beginning and everything could start anew.

He bumped. A gentle bump, at slow speed, but his head pitched forward slightly and reality flooded back into it. He could hear Aron behind him. He could feel only air surrounding him—the world of water was gone.

"Dammit!" Lloyd exclaimed. He whipped off his blindfold and saw the curb he had just run into. "I can't get *anything*."

Aron didn't respond.

Lloyd whirled. "I don't know how much more snail's-pace wandering we can justify ..." Then he stopped, seeing Aron's wide eyes. "What?"

"You weren't steering?"

"No."

"You couldn't see through the blindfold?"

"Of course not. We went over all this before we left."

Aron inhaled. "The last time you went off the road was twenty minutes ago. You followed at least five twists in the road, never leaving your lane. You made a right, a left, and a right. You came to a stop sign at the same time as another scooter, and you waited until the intersection was clear, and you went. I was talking to you most of the time. At first I was kidding you, saying you must be cheating, but you didn't say anything. Then I was talking louder, I was yelling, trying to see if you could hear me, but you never flinched. I finally figured out what was going on and decided I should shut up for a change."

Lloyd looked around. "Where are we?" Two lines of split-level homes, identical in every respect but color, stretched down the street.

Aron shrugged. "North side, maybe half a mile inland. Other than that, I don't know." He nodded to a pale green house with a sun-bleached wooden door. "You were driving straight toward that door when you hit the curb."

Part Two: Chosen

Chapter Nine

Nearly thirty million people, about a tenth of whom lived within fifty miles of some USNA border or another, accepted Harriman Ellis as a prophet. In the old days, before wars and genocide swept from country to country and continent to continent, before Andy and Harry convinced a lot of PKs that they'd be better off following them then acting on their own, thirty million wouldn't make an especially large church. Nothing compared to the old Catholic Church. But the purges, the famines tied to devastated, blasted lands, and the other plagues tied to the wars made the world much, much smaller. And though it was scattered across many continents with its people divided, the church made its presence felt wherever its cathedrals stood.

Kale had learned long ago that, when so many people surrounding him believed in a particular thing, his own opinions on Harry's prophetic status weren't terribly important. He could believe or he could not believe, but as long as the majority of the people around him were convinced of the existence of prophecies waiting to be fulfilled, he had to acknowledge their relevance in their lives, and by extension in his own.

That didn't mean that he really thought they were going to come true. But people were going to act like they were, and they were going to do their damnedest to help them along in any way they could.

Even though he wasn't a believer, Kale had most of the prophecies memorized. Heaven knows he'd read them enough times, and he'd even heard a few of them come directly from the horse's mouth. Some of them he'd let slip away from his mind (minor verses that seemed to function more as parlor tricks proving Harry had a prophetic gift rather than actually increasing the level of goodness in the world), but how could he forget the one about the white field?

Walking from a white field
Comes the fall.
The oppressor will meet
The one who is his end.

Kale was not a chumcha, but he shared their opinion about the identity of the oppressor, as well as their eagerness to see him fall.

They'd been sitting idly on that prophecy for decades and now, out of the blue, they were moving on it. It had to be because of Antigua. For the first time, the CMC had taken back a significant plot of land, reversing their long backward march in the face of the USNA. They read the supposed miracle in the Guatemalan cathedral as the first step in a campaign that somehow would end in their ultimate victory.

Quite a reach, Kale thought, to go from a minor victory in Central America to the overthrow of the most powerful individual on the planet. But they believed it was their destiny.

This was going to suck in everyone. Amelia, whether she knew it or not, would be involved with whatever the chumchas were doing sooner or later. He'd have to keep a closer eye on her than usual (her recent lecture notwithstanding). Hell, he'd have to keep an eye on the whole operation to see how the chumchas were going to mess it up—or, on the off chance that the prophecy was legit and this really was The Big One, to see what kind of surreptitious assistance he could lend.

All that meant that this was a bad time to have a houseguest.

She had eaten. A little bread, some water, as if she were still a prisoner. She hadn't yet shown interest in the fruit he'd left for her, and Kale didn't think she'd built up much strength. She was going to have to start.

"I've arrived at kind of an awkward position," he announced to her without preamble when she opened the door to her room.

"You and me both," she said, managing a wan smile.

"First let me make it clear that you are free to stay here as long as you want. No place this close to the border is entirely safe, but my home is more secure than most. The difficulty is, I'm not sure how much Spree or myself will be around. I'll get some supplies—you know, food—that'll last you for a time, but I don't know how often I'll get back to restock, and I don't think you'll want to visit our local markets—the people there are not particularly kind to newcomers."

"So you're saying I'm stuck here with an ever-dwindling supply of food?"

"I'm afraid that's about the size of it, yes. While you're welcome to stay, like I said, you might want to head east, look for a more permanent residence, set up a new life."

"I wouldn't know where to begin."

Kale gestured vaguely toward what he thought was the east. "It's more sane out there, if you go far enough. Sort of civilized, even. You could talk to the CMC, they can help in a lot of ways."

Nilda visibly recoiled. "The chumchas? You want me to go to them for help?"

Kale blinked twice then remembered Nilda had spent her entire life in the USNA, where they were taught to see the CMC as little better than a primitive cult that used the talent to warp the minds of the members. Why the citizens thought CMC PKs would use this supposed mind control power but USNA PKs would not was a mystery to Kale, but that's the mindset he was dealing with.

"Well, like I said, you could stay here."

"Where are you going?"

"Nowhere specific. Lots of places. There's just lots of … things happening, things I need to keep track of. Things I can't keep track of here."

"Can't you watch from here?"

"Watch, yes. But there are things I may need to participate in."

"What things?"

"If they were things I wanted you to know about, I'd tell you."

"Take me with you."

Kale guffawed. "Impossible. Out of the question."

He sent a twist with his words, something he had learned decades ago. It didn't always work—the stronger the recipient's mind, the more likely they were to resist it—but it generally gave his words more weight, helping the listener perceive how serious he was and avoiding any further argument. He told himself it was just for emphasis, and nothing at all like mind control.

"All right," she said, "then let me go with Spree, wherever she is. I've seen her, with all her screens, she's got plenty to look at. Too much. She could use some help."

"She could," Kale admitted. "But why you?"

Nilda responded quickly. "Because I'm here. Because you and your people already got me in trouble, so I ought to see what's going on. Because I may know a few things that can help you. Because I have no idea what else I'm going to do."

What made this more difficult than it should have been were Nilda's emotions. She was being entirely honest and straightforward. She'd had all the guile worn out of her, at least for now, by exile. Now she was showing all her cards—no games, no deceit, just hoping that open honesty would carry the day for her. If it wasn't for that, Kale could have dismissed her without a thought. Because of it, though, he felt he owed her an explanation.

"Look, look, look here, no," Kale said, speaking quickly. "I've been working at this a long time, and you don't bring people in just because they've got nothing better to do. You're right that Spree is overworked, but, forgive me for saying this, that problem's not going to be solved by giving her an assistant that doesn't know anything. I'm sorry. I think the eastern half of the island is the best place for you."

It didn't take long for any trace of light to leave Nilda's eyes. She seemed to have little energy for anything, including this particular fight.

"All right. All right. You know the Island better than I do. I'll move east."

"Okay. Good." Kale suddenly felt embarrassed for pushing away a guest he had brought into his home. "You don't have to leave immediately, of course. When you're ready. You are my guest as long as you choose to remain so."

"Thank you," Nilda said, but her eyes stayed down.

"I don't think I can help you. I don't have the talent. I know, I've tried. So I really couldn't be anything to your church now, could I?"

Whitaker paused, took a breath, then talked some more. "Well, I could be an ordinary member, of course. But did you really come all the way out here just to recruit me? I don't know what to tell you, I don't know what you think I am. I think maybe you made a mistake coming here. Maybe you need to study harder in your classes. You have classes, right, to teach you how to use the thing? The what, talent? That's what I've heard. Well, if you study, you hopefully won't make this kind of mistake again."

Two miracles. The vision in the cathedral and the guidance of the Creator in finding this house and locating Courtney Whitaker. All to find a young man that Lloyd liked less and less with each passing moment.

Next to him, Aron bristled, as he had during practically every moment of the conversation. Were it not for a constant sending from Lloyd (<<Shut up shut up shut up shut up>>) he would have exploded long ago.

"I wish I could be more specific," Lloyd said, keeping all traces of exasperation out of his voice. "All I know is what I told you. I was directed to come here." Lloyd neglected to say he had been sent by the Creator, preferring to let Whitaker think he had just been sent by a higher-up at the cathedral. "I know people at the cathedral want to talk to you, they're very excited to meet you. If you would just come along with us …"

"Right, right, I understand, but aren't you guys in a lot of trouble most of the time?" Whitaker pushed a clump of dark brown hair back to the top of his head, but it immediately fell back in front of his right eye in a way that, for some reason, irritated Lloyd tremendously. "Not that I mean the two of you particularly, I don't know anything about you, and it's not like you're really highly placed, right? Just kind of like the errand boys of the clergy, right? But what I'm saying is, your church is always in trouble. Veering from disaster to disaster. It doesn't seem to be, you know, all that stable of an organization."

The bundle of sendings from Whitaker were truly unique. His thoughts were practically the exact duplicate of his words, framed in his mind a moment before his mouth moved. There was little trace of any ulterior motive, or secondary motivation for saying what he said. Whatever popped into his mind, he said. That was it. That at least gave Lloyd confidence in Whitaker's honesty, but he wondered how a person this simple was supposed to go up against the most powerful man in the western hemisphere.

"The church has plenty of difficulties. You're right. But truth and righteousness always have enemies, don't they?" Lloyd said.

"That's a little pompous isn't it? To assume you've got all that on your side? I mean, no offense."

Aron was bouncing up and down now, causing a rhythmic crinkle in the plastic cover of the couch they were sitting on. His right leg danced like a bare branch in a gale. But he still listened to Lloyd's steady admonition, and hopefully he was paying enough attention to Whitaker's mind to see he really didn't mean any offense.

"I'd simply invite you to come see for yourself. Judge for yourself. I'm sure High Adept Birch—he's our superior—has many wonderful things to tell you, and I know he wants to talk to you. If you'd just come with us."

Whitaker shifted in his worn green-and-yellow plaid chair. "Now? I don't think I can. I'm really busy, you know?" He gestured vaguely to the screen—a good sized one, 30 inches or so—perched on a white laminate desk.

Finally, Whitaker thought something besides the words he was saying. He clearly had little to no experience covering his thoughts, and Lloyd read them as easily as if Whitaker had painted them on a billboard. <<Lie enough hope they go away.>>

Lloyd had a sudden idea. "Do you have a camera you can use with that screen? We wouldn't have to go anywhere. We could just have the meeting here."

Whitaker recoiled from the screen as if it had just sprouted thorns. "No. No, that's okay, not right now. It's just not a good time." Lloyd could have read that as a lie even without the talent.

<<KNOCK HIM OUT, TIE HIM UP, DRAG HIM WITH US, AND LET'S GET THE HELL OUT OF HERE!>> The force of Aron's sending and all his pent-up frustration nearly melted Lloyd's brain.

"I'm sure you're quite busy," Lloyd said, though the items in the room—the screen, a collection of Tanya Fletcher films, a few printouts from gossip nets, and several crumpled items of clothing—provided no evidence to support that assertion. "If you can't come now, I'm sure we could arrange a time."

"Great," said Whitaker. He tapped the stained toe of a ripped red sneaker on the floor in a rhythm that almost exactly matched Aron's bouncing. "I'll call you. Just leave me your number, or the number of this Adept Birch, and I'll set something up."

<<He doesn't plan on calling.,>> Aron warned.

<<Thanks. Any other obvious observations you'd like to make? I can read as well as you, you know.>> Lloyd shot back, then regretted it as a wounded feeling, like that of a puppy being swatted with a newspaper, emerged from Aron before he tamped it down.

"No, I think it would be better if we set a time now," Lloyd said aloud.

"Well, you see, I don't think I know what my schedule is going to be for the next few days. When it's all a little clearer, then I'll give you a call and we can work something out. Okay?"

"No, really, why don't we just set a time …" Lloyd began, though he was despairing of getting anything accomplished in this encounter.

Once again, though, the Creator was prepared to assist him. This time, the assistance arrived in the person of Whitaker's mother, who appeared at the door to his room.

"Hello," she said in a smooth, polite tone. "I just thought I'd check in to see how things are progressing. It's so rare to see adepts in our neighborhood, let alone ones looking for my son. Is he telling you whatever you came here to find out?"

"He's being very helpful, ma'am."

Whitaker smiled briefly at the praise, then set his face back in the half-scowl he'd used to greet his mother. "It's fine, mom."

"All right. I'm sure you two … acolytes? Adepts? Yes, adepts. I'm sure you two adepts came a long way for this visit, so I hope my son is being accommodating."

Finally at his limit, Aron spoke. "Yes, ma'am. In fact, he's agreed to meet us at our cathedral tomorrow at noon. Our superior is anxious to meet him."

Whitaker's mother blinked. "Really? To meet Courtney? May I ask why?"

Lloyd just shrugged. "We're just the messengers," he said. "They don't always tell us those things."

"How curious. Well, if Courtney promised to be there, I'll make sure he's there."

"Thank you, Mrs. Whitaker. We appreciate your support." Aron ignored the fact that Whitaker's scowl had advanced well beyond the halfway point and was directed at him.

"You're quite welcome," Courtney's mother said. "You know, of course, that we're not members of your church—well, not practicing, anyway—but we can hardly live on the island without being aware of all the work you do, so I'm sure Courtney would be honored to talk with this superior of yours."

Aron grinned widely at both Whitaker and Lloyd. "It'll be a great conversation, I'm sure."

"Watch. Watch a while. See life out here, see what people do with their time, see what they normal is. Can't no see what's strange 'less you know what's normal, and Island normal ain't City normal. You stay—and you may not, way things are here—you'll help. Got lots of cameras, cameras all over, tapped into most of the damn Island, but cameras only worth something if they got eyes on them. We got to take in as much as we can. Even more now, with Kale jazzed 'bout something or other."

Nilda gently swayed her right leg, almost in a slow, gentle tap rhythm. "I'm not sure Kale really wanted me seeing all this stuff. Three days ago, I was USNA, part of the government even, and I've gathered that he's ... not. I want to help, but I don't think he trusts me."

Spree snorted and took a moment to make eye contact with Nilda. Most of the time her eyes were darting back and forth from screen to screen while her fingers darted here and there, interacting with this screen or that, switching between a seemingly infinite number of views.

"Kale don't no fully trust me, and I been here five years. But he don't no need to trust you. He just need to hear what you say, then he can scan and see if you lying. He like to pretend it's not that easy, but it is. Only people he worry about is people he can't read. And not no many people on that list."

"He's that powerful?" Nilda asked doubtfully. Rogue PKs, unaffiliated with either the CMC or USNA, were rare, and those that survived and remained independent as long as Kale generally succeeded because they weren't powerful enough to warrant the attention either organization would need to track them down.

"That powerful," Spree confirmed. "Now look, show you what we can see."

It only took fifteen minutes before Nilda's mind was reeling, and Spree was just getting warmed up. Images flashed by on the screen, some detailed, some fuzzy, some full color, some black and white, some mostly green. More than once, a color picture from the upper left seemed to dance down, skip right, and become a small monochrome image on the bottom line. At some points Nilda could see a person from the front, then the back, then each side as images flickered by in rapid succession. Sometimes she swore she saw the exact same location from twelve different angles. And Spree talked the whole time.

"Traffic cameras. Security. Cameras people put on their home net. Cameras we put up. Moving cameras, some on a remote, some programmed, some wandering, following an algorithm some egghead plugged into them. Cameras that swivel, cameras that zoom, and cameras that keep their ass in one place and can't no do much 'cept put out a single out-of-focus image. We look in homes, in businesses, on streets, in places that shouldn't no exist, and, when they careless, in churches. We get the right patch, we even get USNA images. We can patch into the docks and the border wall, stuff we need to see."

"What are you looking for?

"Whatever's there," Spree said. "The world and whatever the hell's happening in it."

"That's all?"

"That all."

Nilda was barely getting her mind around the geography of the Island and what places she could see when Spree started reviewing the commands. She could call up cameras with the right hand swipes, but sometimes it was quicker to type in the right code— provided you could memorize the hundreds of codes Spree seemed to have at her beck and call. 1-5-3-2-X-A brought up a series of cameras on Carleton in Islip, switching every few seconds, moving south. 1-5-3-2-X-B brought up the same cameras but in a reverse series, scanning north. Spree explained how these numbers came to be assigned to Carleton in a way that briefly made perfect sense until Nilda lost the information in the continuing deluge of words and images.

By the time Spree's vocal pace seemed to be easing, like a horse trotting after passing the finish line, Nilda was overwhelmed.

"I'd like to help, but it seems you have this station under control," she said, feeling guilty for attempting to beg off work she'd been requesting ninety minutes ago. "I know I'd be less effective sitting here than you would be, and I'd hate to take time away from you."

"Spew," Spree said cheerfully. She became more enthusiastic the more she talked about her station, a light behind her eyes turning the normal charcoal into heather grey. "I can't no be awake all day anyway. Could always use more eyes. 'Sides, if I decide I want to watch when you watching, we get more screens. I know how to do it. Be good to have 'nother eye here."

"Okay," Nilda said doubtfully. She stood for a while behind Spree, watching the images of the Island flash and change, hoping to catch glimpses of places farther east and decide if maybe she should go there after all.

Interlude: From *The Way of Miracles*, "The Paths of Life."

While we revere the Six as a group, acknowledging their role in starting the Age of Miracles and improving our understanding of the works of the Creator, we also must recognize the distinct flaws of members of that group. In fact, it may be said that each member of the Six represents a path or a temptation that faces those of us who have the gift of the talent. God has chosen us as vehicles to display His work, and such a calling can be a burden as well as a blessing. We must be ever watchful to ensure we are using our gift wisely, instead of falling into one of the many traps that lie in the path of the gifted. The Six can illustrate some of these pitfalls while also demonstrating how to avoid them.

Anderson Drauer: The Seduction of Power. With any power comes the opportunity to abuse it, to exploit power for personal gain. Few greater examples of this tendency exist than Anderson Drauer. From the earliest days of the Six, Drauer sought to use his power for his own advancement and gain. He built an organization dedicated to advancing his name and furthering his own personal glory, then ruthlessly seized control of a nation that had served as a beacon of freedom to the world and subverted it to his own ends, making it a vehicle for his own ego.

Nothing discredits Drauer more than his hostility to the Church of the Miraculous Creator, which he has battled with his full might. The fact that we have not succumbed to his onslaught is a testament to the power of truth, rather than an indication of any weakness in Drauer's desire to utterly destroy this body. He has been the enemy of the Church, an enemy of righteousness, and an enemy of God. That he has fought so after being given a greater measure of power than any person save one is perhaps the strongest possible statement about the corrupting nature of power.

Rachel Kallenbach: Despair. It is common for those newly discovered to possess the gift to feel overwhelmed, to believe that responsibilities are piling on top of them too rapidly. Typically this sensation passes and adepts move on to acceptance of their responsibilities, but some remain mired in doubt and low self-confidence. Rachel Kallenbach, who did not use her abilities at all for the last decades of her life and who made no discernable impact on the world, shows the final result of succumbing to such feelings.

By most accounts, Kallenbach was quite gifted—perhaps not to the level of Drauer or First Adept Ellis, but at least as strong as Diaz and Frau. She could have done as much good as them, but instead she sank under the supposed burden of her talent. What she never realized is that the gift is its own justification—one does not need to worry about living up to the gift, because the fact that the Creator has given it to you is evidence enough of your worthiness. The gift should be an inspiration to those who have it, something that pushes us to greater heights, rather than something overwhelming. Denying the gift and failing to use it to glorify God is tantamount to a denial of the Creator.

Armando Diaz: Delayed Penitence. It should be clear to all that people with the talent come from all walks of life and all backgrounds. Not everyone with the talent, however, is prepared to enter into the service of the Creator immediately upon the discovery of their gift. Some have habits and tendencies in their everyday life that Need to be excised over time before they can adequately dedicate themselves to God's work.

Sadly enough, some people use these tendencies as an excuse to delay their service, to wallow in their bad habits instead of eliminating them. Diaz should serve as a precautionary example to all such individuals. For too long, Diaz, who loved and trusted Drauer when they were young, followed in the more powerful man's footsteps, even when it should have been clear to him that

Drauer's only goal was to glorify himself. The position Drauer provided was too comfortable, too appealing, and Diaz buried his conscience in luxury.

Finally, though, Diaz listened to the call of the Creator and abandoned the service of Drauer. It was a noble move, but he waited too long. Once he started working against his former friend and master, Drauer was able to quickly root him out and assassinate him. He knew his old supporter's habits too well.

It is clear that, in his short time as an insurgent, Diaz accomplished some good in the USNA. How much more could he have done had he not delayed the day of his repentance?

Kale Faltergast: Lack of Direction. A common topic in the dormitories of young adepts is whether or not Faltergast was the equal, or even the better, of Drauer and Ellis in terms of power. If the stories about him are true, then he is at least their equal, but many of these accounts are surely exaggerated. Faltergast's life lends itself well to such stretching, as he seems to appear everywhere and nowhere, to be a part of everything without playing a strong role in anything.

With their strong powers, First Adept Ellis and Drauer each built tremendous organizations (though they are far from equal in terms of the quality of their impact on the world). Faltergast left nothing. His inability to focus his powers in any concrete direction is his legacy, a lasting example of the importance of pointing one's energy in a profitable direction so as to make a real difference with one's life.

Deegan Frau: Simple Persistence. While all of us should strive to follow the example of First Adept Ellis, the heights he attained are not available to most of us. We must remember, though, that we are capable of great good even if we possess weaker gifts.

In terms of the talent, Deegan Frau is generally recognized as the weakest of the Six, but in terms of spirit she is second only to First Adept Ellis. Her tireless devotion to helping women across the world, especially those in her increasingly strife-torn homeland, are an eternal testament to the values of perseverance and dedication. Her Frau Foundation continues without her, and the good of her efforts lives on.

Harriman Ellis: Perfecting Our Gifts. Summarizing the contributions of First Adept Ellis to the world is far beyond the scope of this section, or even of any single volume. Simply put, First Adept Ellis shows us why we have been given the gift, and how we should use it.

Chapter Ten

They had worked out a way of meeting because it seemed inappropriate not to. Personal history can't just be ignored, even if it was unpleasant.

They always met for lunch. They always sat outside, regardless of the weather, since, for the most part, external conditions had long since stopped causing them significant difficulties. They never thought about how they might attack each other, and they told themselves this was because of their dignity and manners. Along with each man's secret fear that the other might best him.

Today they were on Broadway. Kale preferred the park, because it was easier to find a more secluded spot, but Andy liked to take advantage of the opportunity to be among his people.

His face was the most famous in the USNA, probably in the world. Yet he sat at a green metal table with a frosted glass top on the busiest street in his nation and no one so much as gave him a second glance. While both Kale and Andy understood the power of being ignored at the appropriate time, Kale could usually be ignored without any effort on his part at all. Many people still knew Kale's name, but few knew his face anymore.

Kale had dressed up for the occasion, meaning the cuff of his blue striped shirt was only slightly frayed and well complimented by his black pants. The trousers, however, had white spots of wear on both knees and would only be good for a few more such meetings.

Andy, on the other hand, was his version of casual. A high-buttoned collar tracing a thin white circle around his neck, making him look like a priest from the old church that, long ago, Harry had used as the foundation of his own religion. Over it he wore a dark vest with gold veins swirling across the front. He still looked fifty years old, an age he had long ago decided presented the right combination of energy and gravity. Steel grey mixed smoothly with his black hair, which was short and combed back. His mouth was wide and gentle, his nose narrow and long. His eyes were, and had always been, unreadable.

There was no small talk between them, as neither was particularly eager to share details about people close to them with the other. Besides, Andy had something on his mind.

"That was a silly trick."

There was no reason to pretend he didn't know what Andy was talking about. "Probably."

"You got people to notice what you did, but you didn't really do yourself any good. Now I have to make at least a show of looking for you."

"Make more than a show if you want."

"Don't try to show off," Andy said, but kept his tone light. "We both know you'd evade anyone I sent after you for as long as you chose, making me waste manpower and resources. I'm not about to be sucked into that."

"Okay," Kale said diffidently. "Do whatever you need to. I hope your people will enjoy it."

"They always do."

A waitress came by for their order, made firm, friendly eye contact with them, then walked away as if they were two ordinary customers.

"So why did you do it?"

"Seemed like a good idea," Kale said. "I have to make sure you don't forget I'm around."

"Little chance of that," Andy said. "Next time, try a postcard."

"I don't trust the mail. Besides, I need a way to keep sharp."

"So you put a firespout in Park Avenue to say hi and keep yourself sharp." Andy shook his head. "I could make you a general. You could be using your gifts for more than practical jokes."

"Never really been a military man."

"I could put you in humanitarian aid. Distributing food across the country, across the world. All that stuff you and Harry were always so fond of."

"Haven't you made that offer before?"

"Yes. And for some reason, you prefer poverty and futility. Have you ever been inside the Plaza? Or any other hotel where the desk clerk doesn't sit behind bullet-proof glass?"

"Not recently," Kale said placidly. "And you probably won't believe that I'm not upset about that."

"There's so much life you could be living," Andy insisted. "The food alone ..."

"Yes, yes, nicer clothes, tastier food, faster cars, yes. I understand all that." Kale waved to the street, where taxis struggled to weave in and out of the slower luxury sedans. "It's tough to miss it. I'll ponder your offer."

"You've been pondering for more than fifty years."

"Haven't made my mind up yet."

Andy, who had obviously been keeping his eyes in check throughout the conversation, finally let them roll. "All right. So, would you like to have lunch in Austin next time?"

"Austin? Why?"

"I'm there most of the time, and I thought you might be wandering down there before too long."

"I don't think so. I didn't have any plans to visit Austin."

"Austin, no. But I thought maybe you'd make a pilgrimage to Guatemala, and Austin's not all that far from there."

"It's a thousand miles! And who said I'm going to Guatemala?"

"Fine. We can meet in Houston. It's right on the coast—just swing through the Gulf on your way back north."

"I'm not going to meet you in Houston, because I'm not going to Guatemala."

"Really?" Andy sounded genuinely surprised. "I thought you'd want to go down. Just to see."

"See what?"

"See Harry's church take it to me. After all these years."

Kale nodded. "It's not that I wouldn't like to see it. But that's a long way to travel just for a little vicarious enjoyment."

"True," Andy said. "And it's probably for the best. You'd probably arrive too late."

Kale raised an eyebrow. "Too late for what?"

"To see what you want to see."

"What's going to happen down there?"

Andy shrugged. "Not much. Everybody's expecting a response from me. So I have to respond."

"And you're confident about the success of whatever it is you're planning." It wasn't a question, so Andy respond except to smile.

That smile set off something in Kale. He leaned forward so far that the front of his shirt dipped into his food, but he didn't care. "Andy, what are you going to do to those people?"

"The same thing I always do. I'm going to secure my nation and make it stronger."

"Dammit, Andy …"

"I've been attacked," Andy said placidly. "Anything I do is self-defense. I don't see why you need to get all worked up about it."

"Because people are going to die, Andy! I know how you do things. How many lives is this going to cost?"

"However many it takes. If you'd ever bothered to take a position of leadership, you'd have a better understanding of how these things work."

Kale fumed for another moment, then took a breath and leaned back. "Damn but you're a smug bastard."

"Not smug. Just careful. If you ever saw the full picture …" Andy trailed off, his eyes unfocused, with a small smile on his face. Then he briefly shook his head and looked at Kale again. "Anyway, I have to say I'm a little disappointed that you weren't going to even go down there and see what was happening. I thought you, of all people, would take a little more enjoyment in any setback I face."

"Why me of all people? Don't you think Dugwu might enjoy it more?"

Andy's smile tightened. "I wouldn't expect him to go down there," he said.

Kale thought about asking for his reasoning for that, but he didn't want to discuss Dugwu with Andy. They'd gone down that road before, and each time Andy's contempt for the leader of the CMC became more noxious.

"Part of me wishes I could go down there," Kale said. "But there are other things I need to do."

"But they can't be more important than seeing me take one on the chin, can they?"

"Of course they can. Believe it or not, everything I do isn't about you."

"Maybe not everything, but still an awful damn lot. Look at Harry's church and their prophecies. Do you know how many of those bits of doggerel are about me in one way or another?"

"I know you've interpreted a lot of them that way."

"*Harry* interpreted a lot of them that way. If his annotated guide to them ever got out, his followers would be after me even worse than they already are."

Kale nearly dropped his fork. "You have the annotations?"

"Somewhere," Andy said with a vague wave. "I have a lot of things."

"How did you get them?"

"That would be telling."

Kale rolled his eyes. "That's the Andy I've always known. Always a step ahead of everyone else."

Andy took a sip of lemonade through a straw in an attempt to cover the smile making dents in the corners of his mouth. He swallowed, and said "You have no idea."

There wasn't much conversation for the rest of the lunch. They talked a little bit about Standish Fiske, the old king of New York and his short-lived reign, but the subject trailed off quickly. As usual, Andy had settled the bill before Kale could even reach for his wallet, and as usual they did not shake hands when they parted.

Whenever he'd thought about this prophecy—and he'd thought about it often, every adept did—Lloyd pictured how the person mentioned in the prophecy would react once they realized what their destiny was going to be. Would it be a solemn realization of responsibility? A sense of joy at the great task that was to be accomplished? Some fear at the largeness of the task?

Half the time he imagined the scene, Lloyd put himself of the role of the savior, the person destined to bring the church out of oppression. He knew he wasn't alone in that—he'd never met an adept who hadn't at least thought about the possibility a couple of times. What if it's me, they all asked. What if I'm the one?

He had imagined dozens of reactions this chosen one might have, but the one he'd never thought about was mocking disbelief. He could practically taste the amused superiority oozing from Whitaker's mind.

"I'm what? The who? What am I supposed to do?" Whitaker's hands twitched, folding and unfolding, as a nervous smile wandered around his mouth. "I'm sure you've got the wrong person."

Lloyd's mouth opened, closed, and opened again, fish-like. Not even a puff of air emerged.

High Adept Birch, however, was unfazed. "You're supposed to do good in the world, like all of us. You simply have a mission that is more clearly defined than most of ours."

"And that mission is ... ?" The condescension Whitaker radiated made Lloyd's teeth grind.

"To bring down Anderson Drauer."

"Anderson Drauer."

"Yes," Adept Birch said placidly.

"Is there another Anderson Drauer besides the President of the USNA?"

Adept Birch gently smiled. "None that I know of, no."

"So that's the one I'm supposed to bring down?"

"Yes."

"Ah. Well." Whitaker drummed his fingers on his knee. "I'd like to, really. I hear bad things about him." Sandy hair fell in front of his left eye. He flicked it away. "But I've got a lot going on right now besides, you know, overthrowing the most powerful man in the world, but I'm sure I can fit it in sometime in the future. So maybe we should be in touch again in a year or two, and I'll see what I can do for you then." He slowly stood as he delivered the last line.

Lloyd shot to his feet before Whitaker could move away from his chair. "This is a High Adept you're speaking to! We're talking about the prophecies of Harriman Ellis, not some yard work you need to talk your way out of!"

<<That will not win him over,>> High Adept Birch sent. <<We cannot drag him into his role. We can only show him the right path for his journey.>>

While Lloyd seethed, Birch attempted to keep Whitaker from sliding out of the office.

"I'm pleased you don't believe me," he said. "That is, I'm pleased you're not just taking my word for it. This is too large of a matter for you to charge in blindly, without a conviction of your own. At this point, I honestly wouldn't expect you to believe me, and I wouldn't ask it of you."

Whitaker hovered over his chair, arms crooked, knees bent, halfway to standing. "You wouldn't?"

"No," Adept Birch said with a warm chuckle. "This church has been the center of my life for over half a century, and if someone approached me with the same story I have told you, I wouldn't believe them, either."

"So ... if you wouldn't believe it about you, why do you believe it about me? You're more likely to be this chosen guy than I am, but you wouldn't believe you were the guy if someone told you that you were the guy, but someone tells you *I'm* the guy even though

I'm not qualified to be the guy and you immediately believe I'm the guy? Why?"

Lloyd was still trying to parse Whitaker's question while Adept Birch was answering it. "That is an excellent question. If you would indulge me for a time, I'd like to answer it to the best of my abilities. Would you come with me?"

"Sure. I guess." The superiority that had been accompanying Whitaker's words was not entirely gone, but it had decreased. And he was no longer on the verge of flight.

<<He seems much more willing to listen. Did you tweak him with a spell?>> Lloyd asked.

<<No. As I said, we cannot drag him where he needs to go.>>

Chapter Eleven

It had, Lloyd thought initially, been a disaster. Everything Terrin could do to drive Whitaker away, to convince him that this church was full of unbalanced people that he'd be better off without, he did. He had made them wait, standing silently, while he scribbled some illegible notes in his notebook. He spoke for several minutes in his dusty voice about the history of the prophecies and the importance of using them for a guide to planning the church's future. He made disparaging remarks about Whitaker's potential to do anything, let alone overthrow the most powerful man in the world—"Doesn't look like much. Short." "No trace of the talent. Not a bit. That should surprise them, at least." He repeatedly stated that the prophecies often seemed vague and open to interpretation, and he often did not truly understand how to interpret them until the action they described was already completed.

Then he had stood, his wizard light flickering as he did so. He looked up at Whitaker, trying to wipe dust from his eyes but only replacing it with the dust from his hands. He studied the young man carefully, staring until Whitaker started fidgeting, looking back and forth between Lloyd and High Adept Birch, his face twisted in supplication, hoping to leave and find some fresh air.

Then Terrin spoke again. "I will always remember the day you came down here. It will be recorded in my history, and it will be known. It will be known across the world." He turned to his desk, then abruptly looked back at Adept Birch. "The tremor of the sky is next." Then he sat back to his desk and continued on as if he had no visitors.

On the long climb from the archives, Whitaker repeatedly glanced back over his shoulder. Lloyd read him easily. His desire to leave was gone, replaced by a desire to be admired—a desire that, until this moment, Whitaker didn't know he had. Terrin's words, coming on the heels of his dry hostility, had done something to Whitaker. He realized he was going to be looked up to, and he liked it.

For the first time, Lloyd had to consider the possibility that Whitaker wasn't going to flee as soon as Adept Birch was done with him. He may still think all of the church people around him were crazy, but for now it seemed like a fun type of crazy to him, an insanity that he could go along with for a while and enjoy.

For most of the day, all Lloyd had wanted was to do his job right and bring Whitaker in. Now, though, when it looked like Whitaker was going to stay and take the first small steps along the long path Adept Birch had in mind for him, Lloyd had to quell the desire for Whitaker to leave. But the negative thoughts kept returning. *This is our savior? This is whom we'll be following? Couldn't we throw a dart in the adept's dormitory and hit a candidate more worthy than this one?*

Back at High Adept Birch's office, Whitaker was willing to sit without constantly glancing to the door. Adept Birch had obviously sensed the same things Lloyd had received, and he honed in on it as soon as he was behind his desk.

"Acolyte Terrin is only the first, you know. Everyone I introduce you to, everyone who understands what is happening the way Terrin does will have the same reaction. The people of this church can be *your* people, Courtney. You just have to let them."

"But I don't have … I can't *do* anything. And all of you can. I don't think …how could I be, like, a leader?" Petulance had crept back into Whitaker's voice. His hair flopped in front of his face and he let it stay for a moment.

Until a thought crossed his face. Lloyd watched its slow journey, moving from a twitched eyebrow to a quivering nose to a hesitant smile. It seemed to take forever for the nascent idea to become formed enough to be expressed.

"Unless ..." he finally said. "Unless you detected something? Saw something in my head? You know, like ..." Whitaker raised his hands in front of him and wiggled his fingers like a kid's-show magician preparing to reach into his top hat.

Lloyd's headache increased as he tried to keep his eyes from rolling. But Adept Birch only smiled.

"No. Nothing like that, I'm afraid. But you must remember that our talent is simply a gift from the Creator, and the Creator has many blessings to distribute among His children. If He did not give you the gift of the talent, that is because you do not need it for what you have to do. You have gifts enough of another sort to carry you."

"Gifts enough ..." Whitaker echoed hesitatingly. "Like what?"

Adept Birch gave Courtney the same smile Lloyd had seen after he'd taken his adept exam.

"Of a sort that we will discover," Adept Birch said. "That's part of your journey—the voyage you can undertake if you stay with us for a time and let us work together."

He had him. Whitaker didn't need to say a word for Lloyd (and, he imagined, Adept Birch) to see that he was on the hook now. That didn't mean he wouldn't wriggle off in the near future, but for now, he belonged to High Adept Birch.

Courtney sat in his chair, lightly drumming the armrests, clearly wondering what was going to happen next but unwilling to ask. Then something else popped into his mind.

"That thing the guy in the cellar said? Before we left? What was he talking about?"

"The tremor in the sky?" Adept Birch asked.

"Yeah."

"A prophecy. One of Harriman Ellis'. One in a series of prophecies that includes the words that led us to you. Acolyte Terrin is of the belief that all the remaining unfulfilled prophecies of our First Adept are on the verge of coming true, and he was letting me know the one he thinks is going to come up next."

"What's that one say?"

Adept Birch recited without hesitation.

"The sky shakes without cause
A single fall
The sign of precision
A lone collapse in the mass."

"What the hell does that crap mean?" Whitaker blurted.

Lloyd cringed. Referring to anything the First Adept said as "crap" was enough to cause CMC teachers to teach one of their special lessons to their acolytes—for example, raising the temperature of the blood in a single finger by twenty degrees. That usually was more than enough to instill respect for the First Adept.

But all the punishment Whitaker received was another warm smile from Adept Birch.

"The prophecies are not always crystal clear, and on their own, divorced from the context in which First Adept Ellis placed them, may seem like little more than gibberish."

Lloyd could not keep his mouth from dropping open. Adept Birch either didn't notice or just ignored it as he continued.

"Something is going to collapse. A single object in the middle of many similar objects. Beyond that, I cannot say. The object may be a tree, a mountain, a building, or even a person. Two things, though, are certain: first, it will happen, as with all the other prophecies of the First Adept. Second, we will notice when it does. The prophecies of First Adept Ellis were not meant to pass unnoticed."

"But you'll only notice it after it happens," Whitaker said.

"Yes."

"So what's the point? You're not going to do anything about what's going to happen, and you don't know why it's going to happen, and you don't know what kind of stuff comes after it, what it leads to—you know, the purpose of this collapse. Why did the First Adept tell you all this cra ... I mean, stuff?"

Lloyd noticed the slight change in tone, even though Adept Birch hadn't said anything. Had he planted something in Whitaker's mind, or was Whitaker just picking up on Adept Birch's tone? Either way, Whitaker had just asked a question Lloyd had been a little curious about himself, but he'd never asked it. He was anxious to hear Adept Birch's response.

"You're very observant," Adept Birch said. "When you apply your mind, it can be quite analytical." Lloyd wasn't sure Whitaker heard the rebuke in Adept Birch's words, but Lloyd, who had trained with Adept Birch for a long time, caught it easily.

"You have one false premise, however," Adept Birch continued, "and that is that we do not know the purpose of the collapse. The purpose of the prophecies, like so many other signs, is to indicate the proper direction. In the end, all the prophecies culminate in one single event."

"Which is …" Whitaker asked nervously, but Lloyd read him and saw that Whitaker had a good idea of what Adept Birch was going to say.

"Your work," Adept Birch said. "The more signs we see, the closer we are to your mission being accomplished."

"And this collapse is next?"

"So Acolyte Terrin tells me. And I have every reason in the world to trust his knowledge of such matters."

"And if this collapse happens … then I'm supposed to take over the world?"

Lloyd stifled a chuckle, and even Adept Birch smiled. "No, my son. The Creator is the only ruler of the world. You are simply supposed to make it easier for His work to be done."

Chapter Twelve

A screen showed a street, seen from barely above the ground. The image rolled slowly, bumping along as the camera's mount hit cracks, rocks, and sewer grates. These last were particularly dangerous—most of them were wide enough to swallow the camera and its mount whole. The camera, at the moment, didn't show much more than black asphalt and grey curb, with the occasional wet leaf thrown in.

Nilda leaned forward, squinting. "No wires at all?"

Spree shook her head. "Nope."

"How are you controlling it?"

"Radio signals."

The camera reached an intersection and turned right, clinging to the curb. It slid a little left to avoid the wheels of a parked car, then went back right.

"Radio? And I guess it's sending the images the same way?"

"Yeah."

The street the camera was traveling ended two blocks ahead. A dark building rose in front of the darker sky, two charcoal spires sticking into midnight blue. Yellow glowed softly around the gothic doors. That was the only light coming from the building.

"Won't they sense it before you see anything?" Nilda said.

"Hope not," Spree said. "They don't no always look."

"For cameras?"

"For radio signals," Spree said. "People don't no use them, so people don't no look for them. Big-time NArds, they sometimes remember. But these kids here, they training to be clergy. Not security. Can't no do it all. So the part they don't no do is radio, since ain't no one sells it no more, ain't no one uses it. They'll probably notice 'fore long, especially once we filming. But hopefully can get some footage 'fore then."

"'Some footage'?" Nilda asked. "How much?"

"A few seconds, probably. Not much, but more than if we use wired shit."

Nilda nodded. On screen, the motion had stopped. Spree took a deep breath.

"Best to move quickly now. Get to what we want to see, don't no waste time on the grass. Ready?"

Nilda shrugged. Everything was being recorded, so she didn't feel a pressing need to pay attention. But she said "Ready" anyway.

"'Kay." Spree pushed a small joystick forward and pressed a button. The camera darted toward the church.

The image bounced too roughly for Nilda to focus on anything. It was just a montage of greys, blues, and blacks.

Spree could only be steering on reflex and memory. She nudged her joystick right, moving toward the curb with a curb cut just ahead. Nilda watched the curb lurch closer, waiting for the camera to slam into it and stop, but instead it bounced up onto the sidewalk.

Something grey loomed ahead, and the camera darted right into it. The image settled into a close-up on smooth granite.

"Step one," Spree said.

The camera pulled back half a foot, turned right, and darted forward again. At the edge of the church it jumped to the left.

Spree was driving off-road now. The lens pushed aside black blades of grass as it trundled along.

"Did you get the right angle?" Nilda asked.

"Can only hope," Spree said. "Should put a compass or something on the thing, but the more junk I load on, the more obvious the thing is."

Still the screen showed nothing but a jittery image of grass with dark spaces between the blades.

"Is that the building ahead?" Nilda asked.

"Hope so."

Five more seconds passed, and once more the camera bumped to a halt. Stone filled the screen again.

Slowly the view rotated. The curtain wall of the building fell backward, and soon filled only the bottom half of the screen. The rest was taken up by clear night sky and a few stars poking through the glow from the Long Island lights.

The camera jerked left, then right.

"One window on that side," Spree noted. "Two on the other. Want the middle?"

Nilda glanced at notes on another screen. "Yeah. Middle."

The camera turned a little more and trundled forward. Nilda watched Spree's hands tremble a little on the stick.

"Nervous?" she asked.

Spree shrugged. "Hate to lose it now."

The camera stopped beneath the left edge of the window, and the window grew larger as the pole holding the camera telescoped up. Yellow light spilled out.

"Don't they have blinds down?" Nilda asked.

"They arrogant," Spree said. "It helps. They think God on their side, think He'll take care of them, thwart evildoers for them. Makes them forget details, like windows they think no one looks in."

The camera rotated level as it rose to the bottom edge of the window. Nilda saw some chumchas inside, and some others not wearing the church's robe. She couldn't see what they were doing, but it didn't seem like much—mostly sitting around.

The camera rotated right, panning to get the entire room. Spree stopped it every few degrees to get a still image. She managed to turn it all of fifteen degrees, getting a total of three still images, before the image exploded into white.

It was noiseless, but Nilda jerked backward anyway. The glow was blinding, like fiery magnesium.

Nilda's eyes stung as the light started to fade. Spree, though, had covered her eyes immediately, sensing the blow-up before it came. Now that the worst had passed, she could focus on the screen again.

The center of the glow took longer to fade than the exterior. Gradually, the last pieces of light flowed into letters on the screen, then surged briefly before the screen went irretrievably dark. The last flash was bright enough, though, that Nilda saw the red afterimage of the word the screen displayed each time she blinked.

The word was "infidel."

"Nice touch," Spree said. "They that good, though, they should have caught me sooner."

She picked up a phone and dialed rapidly. "Shut it down," she said after a brief pause, then hung up the phone.

Five miles away, Kale began dismantling a receiver. A few chumchas, unless they had slipped drastically in remembering how to trace radio signals, would be to this spot shortly. He had to be gone before they arrived.

The receiver went into a box, and ten feet of cable trailing from it wound around a spool. Kale grabbed the line tap that had let him patch into the net, climbed into his van and sped away.

He had broken down the remote receiving station in under a minute. The chumchas could trace the signal to the station, but they'd be lost once they got to the cable. That was the whole point of using a network of shielded cable—to keep people with the talent from messing with it.

Kale now had about ten seconds worth of footage waiting for him at the compound. Hopefully it would be enough to give him some clue what the chumchas were up to.

"I would not follow him to an ice-cream truck. I would not follow him in line at a movie theater. I would not follow him walking down the aisle of the cathedral. Am I making myself clear here?"

"Yes, Aron," Lloyd said.

They were in their dorm in the complex behind the cathedral. Tonight Lloyd had put a view of the Venetian canals outside their window, while Aron had piled a bunch of loose papers on their desk and put phantom fire on top, giving a warm glow to their room. To complete the effect, Aron had even managed to make some actual heat come the flame, though not, of course, as much as would come from a real fire.

"He knows nothing. *Nothing!* He keeps calling Deegan Frau 'Dylan.' Like she was a *man*. Or, I don't know, like he's never even *heard* of her. Probably hasn't heard of the Frau Foundation."

"You could make a fireplace for that," Lloyd suggested. "It'll make the room look homey, instead of like we were attacked by Vikings."

"Hasn't heard of the Frau Foundation," Aron said, not to be deterred. "They are now helping supply his food, and he knows nothing about them or their founder."

"Okay, okay, he's a little ignorant. You didn't know everything when you became an acolyte."

"*I knew who Deegan Frau was!*" Aron yelled.

Lloyd moved his hands to his ears, his common signal that he was placing a shield over his ears. Aron raised his arms appeasingly.

"All right, all right, I'll keep my voice down," Aron said.

"Just because you're jealous of Courtney doesn't mean you have to yell at me."

Aron immediately forgot his promise. "*Jealous?* Why would I be jealous?"

"Come on," Lloyd said. "You want to be the one to get Drauer. I know, we all do. I want it, too. But it's not us, it's him. So we're going to have to deal with it."

"You think I want to get Drauer? I don't. Believe me, I don't. That's a lot of pressure, you know, and I don't think the prophecies say anything about the guy who does it coming out alive. Which, come to think of it, could be a bright side of Whitaker being the guy that I hadn't thought of before."

"That's just mean," Lloyd said.

"Yeah, maybe it is. But I don't like him."

Lloyd wanted to argue some more on Courtney's behalf, but his heart wasn't in it.

"I know. I'm ... not especially fond of him either."

"Adept Birch has got a lot of convincing to do. A lot. I don't see anyone rallying around him. You, maybe. And the other guys that just follow Adept Birch without thinking."

Lloyd's eyes narrowed. He buried his face in a book as Aron tried to backpedal.

"No, no, no, not that that's what you do, not that you don't ... oh well, fine, I said the wrong thing, you know I didn't mean it, but you want to be mad at me, or at least you don't want to argue about Whitaker any more, so you'll use this to shut me out for a while. I get it. That's okay, that's what you do."

"You're not helping yourself any," Lloyd said.

"I'm not trying to. I said something to make you mad, you're going to be mad, that's the evening. I understand."

Lloyd shook his head. If Aron's mind moved as fast as his mouth—or if his lips would just slow down a little—that would be something.

The blessed silence lasted all of three minutes. Adept Brace flung there door open without preamble.

"There was a camera," he said. "Outside the Common."

Aron and Lloyd moved as soon as Brace's words sunk in, making his next comment—"High Adept Birch wants to see you"—unnecessary.

"Camera cost $2,500," Spree said. "For ten seconds of footage. That's $250 per second."

"Thanks," Kale said. "I probably couldn't have done the math myself."

Spree ignored him. "You should've just gone and peeked your eyes in the window. Done a few readings."

Kale shook his head. "No. They sometimes forget to look out for radio signals, but they never forget to guard against people like me. I wouldn't have gotten a thing."

"You don't no have no disguises? You sneak into the City every other day, right?"

"That's because only one person there knows my specific signal, and he usually leaves me alone. Malvoin Serl knows me a little too well, and he generally is on the lookout for me. I've got a few disguises, yeah, but I'm saving them."

"You'da used one tonight, wouldn't no be out $2,500," Spree said.

Kale shrugged. He felt implausibly optimistic about the footage the camera had shot, even though he hadn't seen a bit of it. Spree wasn't going to dampen his enthusiasm.

"We paid the money," he said simply. "Let's see what we got."

He glanced at Nilda, who sat silent near Spree. As always when Kale was present, she had fallen into a kind of awed silence, even though he had heard her chatting actively with Spree when he was coming down the hallway. He hoped she'd get over that soon.

He gave her a quick read. There was awe, gratitude, and, he was pleased to see, a kernel of resentment, as if he was forcing her to continue feeling grateful. That's good, he thought. That'll get her back on some independent footing eventually.

He dug a little deeper. She was curious to see the footage, mainly because she watched the mission as it happened. Her loyalty to Kale as the man who rescued her from the border rats far outweighed any vestiges of USNA allegiance. No matter how hard he looked, he couldn't find a trace of betrayal in her. So she could stay and watch.

Spree had the first steady image displayed on screen. It showed the left side of a large room. The walls were beige, with regularly spaced dark brown beams running to the ceiling. There was no ornamentation. The floor was blond wood, worn to grey in many spots. Several uncushioned wooden chairs, none of which matched another, were scattered across the floor.

The first still showed eight people. Five of them wore the black robes of CMC adepts; three did not. Those three, two men and a woman, all sat cross-legged on the floor. All three faces were calm, all three pairs of eyes focused on something besides the people near them. They were looking in three different directions, and Kale could not tell if they had their attention on any objects or if they were just staring vacantly into space.

All of the adepts stood. One, on the right side of the screen, was walking toward the edge of the frame. Three stood casually, hands on hips or stuck into the deep pockets of their robes. One stood more stiffly, his back turned to the camera. His left arm hung at his side, his right was horizontal. That arm may have been pointing at one of the lay people in the room, but the position of the camera and the body of the adept made it tough to see the exact angle of the arm.

"They doing something," Spree said.

"Remarkable observation," Kale responded.

"I mean they doing something beside standing and talking. Guy there almost rigid. Ain't no church party."

"Right. Okay, move on."

The picture blurred as the camera panned right, then it stopped and the room settled into focus again. Six people this time—one adept from the right edge of the previous picture, two more lay people, three other adepts.

"They're in groups of three," Kale said. "Two adepts, one lay."

"Yeah," Spree said, squinting at the screen. "Chumchas flanking the lay each time."

"What are they doing?" Nilda asked.

"Not much, at least not here," Kale said. "They're too relaxed, not focused on anything. They may be getting ready to do a spell, they may have just done one, but they're not doing one now."

Spree smiled but kept her eyes on the screen. "Don't no mean nothing," she said. "Seen you do spells while eating and sleeping."

"They're not me," Kale said. "Most adepts, when they're working on something, you can see it."

All three of them stared at the picture for a few more seconds. None of them announced a breakthrough observation about what was going on.

"Move it forward," Kale finally said

All three of them leaned forward when the next still picture came up. Spree's nose almost touched the screen. There were six more people, two more groups of three. No one in this image looked relaxed.

"That's the one that got us," Kale said, pointing to an adept on the right. Her face was twisted in a scowl as she pointed at the three of them through the soon-to-be-destroyed camera.

"Why the point?" Spree asked. "Never see you point."

"Matter of preference. Some people focus better when they make a gesture with the spell." He squinted. "But she's not the important one here. Look at the other group."

The three on the left side of the screen were arranged in the same pattern as all the other groups—two standing adepts flanking a sitting layperson. But in this group, the lay was about to fall out of his chair. His legs had shot out, his knees stiff, hips only slightly bent into the back of the chair. His arms were at his side, both hands at the waist, clutching the base of his shirt with white knuckles.

Kale pointed to the adept to the left of the screen. "This is the one getting him. Leaning forward, hands on his hips—he's practically throwing his brain at the guy."

"What is he doing to him?" Nilda asked.

"Can't say for sure. Probably a shock—ionizing the air around him, getting a current to run through the guy's body. Good torture technique, since you can control how much damage you do. You can just inflict pain without leaving any permanent damage if you want. And there's always the option of doing worse damage."

"Why torture a lay?"

"Good question."

"The other one's casting too."

Kale and Spree both looked at Nilda, who hadn't said anything about the images until then.

"What?" Spree said.

"I've seen it. You can't spend too much time in Manhattan without seeing that face, that expression," she said. "PKs are everywhere, squinting like that. Especially when they're just walking down the street."

Kale looked at the screen, then back at Nilda, shaking his hand. He should have seen it immediately. "They're blocking."

"How can you tell?" Spree asked.

"The face. Like she said. You see it all the time, especially with younger PKs and adepts. Everyone winds up squinting that way."

"Who's he blocking? Only ones with the talent there supposed to be his friends."

But Kale knew the answer. As soon as Nilda pointed out the expression, he knew what was going on.

"He's supposed to be blocking the other chumcha. The one shocking the lay."

"Shielding," Spree said flatly.

"Right. Blocking is tricky enough, shielding trickier still, and it's especially tough when you're shielding someone without the talent. Usually you don't need to use shielding too much—the NArds and chumchas are all PKs, so they can all block for themselves, and there's usually no one else between them. Not if they can help it. But sometimes you need someone around without the talent, and you need them safe. The church knows it comes up occasionally, so a few people are taught, usually once they've been casting for a number of years."

Spree waved to the screen. "These all young."

"Yeah. Five years casting or less, I'll wager. The CMC seems to think they're going to need some new shielders soon."

"Why?"

Kale wanted to say he didn't know. He didn't have the facts, he didn't have any concrete reason to say what was going on. But he knew. There was no reason why, but he knew.

"They've got someone," he said. "Someone without the talent. Someone they're going to want to shield because they think he's going to be targeted." He leaned back. The pictures didn't have anything else to show him. "They have their chosen one, and he doesn't have the talent. They're going to put him out there as soon as they can, and they need to be ready."

Spree nodded grimly, but Nilda looked confused. "Chosen one? Chosen for what?"

Kale exhaled. "We need someone closer. Someone who can give us more information." He didn't like what he was going to have to do, but he didn't have a wide range of options. And every read he'd done showed him she was trustworthy. "Someone they don't know."

Part Three: Witness

Chapter Thirteen

In the most desolate area of Long Island, a steel-and-glass tower blotted out a good portion of the sky. Years ago, Anderson Drauer had decided that the border, with the rats and constant outgoing traffic of exiles, provided the ideal training ground for young PKs. He built the Belmont Psycho-Kinetic Training Academy on the site of an abandoned racetrack (showing, many people insisted, how Drauer saw the PKs under his command), and a new city sprang up surrounding the training grounds. Research institutes, border security, and government recruiters all flocked to the area, and new buildings surrounded the Institute, though none as tall as the central spire. The buildings flowed east to the city's border until they bumped into the wall dividing the USNA from the CMC. The skyline, a smaller version of the collection of buildings on the island to the west, taunted the borderlands. Practically every room of every building there contained more wealth than every resident of the wastes (besides the church) possessed, combined.

Fifteen border rats were shuffling toward the wall of the city. It was a regular occurrence—the rats were drawn to the border, hoping some of the wealth it held would dribble out to them, until USNA security rode out and swept them back. They'd stay away for a week or so, then slowly drift back toward the city.

The morning sun gleamed off the buildings, nearly doubling the amount of light the dust and scattered grass on the ground received. It didn't make anything more inviting.

Five rats, already camped in the tower's reflected light, warily watched a new group of rats approaching them from the east. There wasn't enough garbage leaking out of the city to support even them, and this new crowd was going to make it leaner. Still, maybe they were carrying things with them. Maybe they could be robbed.

<<Don't try it.>>

The blast was forceful enough to come from a NArd. Impressed, the five stationary rats settled back into their patches of dirt. These newcomers weren't to be messed with.

<<That was well targeted,>> High Adept Kroll sent. <<Didn't get anywhere near the city.>>

<<Thank you,>> Lloyd sent back. He'd worried it had been too firm—the pressure of the mission, of living up to the expectations that had caused Adept Birch to recommend him for this job, made him tense. Too bad Aron hadn't been recommended as well—he'd help take some of the edge off.

"What're they going to do?" Courtney whispered. He scratched at the dirt on his arm—he'd been fidgeting with his disguise from the moment it had been put on.

"Nothing," Lloyd said in normal tones. "And don't worry about talking. Adept Kroll is keeping things quiet."

"Did he ... do something to the rats? To keep them calm?"

"No." An unreasonable desire to impress Courtney rose in Lloyd. "I did."

Courtney whistled. "Wow. That's ... I don't know how I'm supposed to lead any of you. When you can do that."

Lloyd didn't know either. "The Creator chose you, so He will provide a way."

"Yeah. That's what Birch said. Does this Creator ever tell you what He's going to do in advance, or does he just surprise you?"

"Usually it's a surprise."

"Great."

The towers of Belmont were close enough to see which windows had blinds down and curtains closed and which were open to the world. Since they faced the border, most of them were closed.

Adept Kroll led them like he knew where they were going. They had, by Lloyd's perception, made one slight course change since disembarking from their bus two miles back and walked in a straight line ever since. It looked like they'd end up north of the Belmont Academy, near a crook in the border wall that ran northwest before turning due north.

They had been seen. Lloyd didn't know when it had happened, but it surely had. All of the adepts in the group were well shielded, and they had Courtney covered as well. Hopefully the shields were camouflaged well enough to make the border guards pass over them without noticing the well of PK activity hovering over the heads of the shuffling border rats. If it worked, the guards would just leave them alone.

That was not his concern, though. Lloyd was there to watch the rats. And give Courtney someone to talk to.

"Where are we going? Are we going into the city? I'm pretty sure they don't let people just walk into the city."

"We're not going in," Lloyd said, resisting the urge to point out the giant wall in front of them. "They don't let anyone in."

"Okay. So we'll look and the prophecy will just ... fulfill itself?"

"Pretty much. That's what prophecies tend to do."

"All right," Courtney said, but, as usual, he sounded unconvinced.

They were now within five hundred feet of the wall, and Lloyd did everything he could to keep his eyes on the rats. He could almost feel the waves of PK energy coming from the wall. The NArds they couldn't see were far more dangerous than the rats they could. Maybe, around him, the air was catching fire, or electricity was darting out from the wall, or death was coming in any one of a thousand other forms that Lloyd's colleagues might or might not deflect. But Lloyd, watching the rats, would never see it coming, since it wasn't his job to look for it.

They stopped. The buildings towered above them. They were close enough to see people inside clearly, had any blinds or curtains been opened. There were several guard stations clearly visible along the top of the massive wall, but the occupants of those rooms were hidden behind tinted glass.

"So ... we're here now?" Courtney asked.

"We're here."

"And we just wait?"

"We just wait."

"Do they have guns? On the wall?"

"Yeah."

"Can they get us?"

"If you're asking if we're in range, yeah, we are. If you're asking if they can slip a bullet by us, no, they can't." They'd been testing their shielding abilities for weeks now, and only the best had come on this trip.

Behind Lloyd, High Adept Kroll started speaking. Lloyd had been waiting for this—the higher-ranking adepts had a clinical inability to let an opportunity to give a speech go by unused.

"History, as we all know, honors the doers. Those who break barriers, build something new, plow new ground." Adept Kroll's voice, unaugmented, rode on the wind rushing out of the city. "But remember that we wouldn't know anything about what these people did if there weren't people watching, witnesses who saw what they did and recorded it, or told others, so these deeds would be remembered. The names of the witnesses aren't always recalled as easily as the names of the doers, but they are no less important.

"You are all here to watch. To witness the fulfillment of one of the prophecies of the First Adept. You will be asked, time and time again, by people from many generations, what you saw here. They will depend on you for accuracy, for truth. If this day is remembered correctly, is because you do your jobs of watching and remembering.

"I brought you all with me because I knew you could do the job. You won't fail."

Lloyd noticed that Adept Kroll hadn't bothered to mention the small cameras that three of the adepts held, ready to record whatever happened for posterity, but he didn't mind the omission. The pictures could only tell the visual part of the story—it would be the adepts' job to fill in the rest.

While Adept Kroll spoke, a rat stood up. His body unfolded like an accordion being stretched, the creases in his long frame still visible. He ambled north, then south, then north, but the whole time his head stayed fixed on Lloyd and the people around him.

He didn't look threatening. His left arm poked through holes in a moth-eaten coat, and at its widest it looked about as narrow as a cane. If he tried to hit someone with that arm, Lloyd thought, it would most likely snap. Still, it was his assignment to watch the rats, so he watched this one.

And that was why he missed it when it started. Afterward, he watched the videos a thousand times, trying to correlate what he felt with what was happening behind him. In the end, the images of the tapes and his own memories became so intertwined that he eventually forgot what parts he saw for himself and what he watched after the fact.

One camera caught it right from the beginning. Its operator had already panned across the skyline a few times and was amusing herself by moving vertically up a few of the buildings that caught her eye. One of them, the Poulsen Tower, was jarring in its appearance, light stone in a mass of glass and steel. It was perhaps the third or fourth tallest building in the complex, and its windows seemed little more than slits when compared to those of its neighbors. The camera paid particular attention to the ziggurat top slashed through with triangles of darker stone.

The camera made a slight movement to the right, ready to move to another building, when the cloudless sky roiled. Concentric ripples of nothing spread over the top of the tower, expanding to exactly the width of the tower, then holding in place. Waves of PK energy poured from it, catching the attention of Lloyd and any other PK within five miles.

It was already starting when Lloyd turned. Cracks ran through the stone cladding, chips fell first, followed by larger pieces as the exterior fell to the street below. Windows broke but did not shatter, dissolving into a fine dust that glittered rain around the entire building.

Whatever the disturbance in the sky had done, it had pinpoint control. Much of the interior stood exposed but intact, except for papers blown out by the wind now passing through. USNA security footage, later discovered and released by hackers, showed people panicked inside, running for the stairs. Some even unthinkingly ran for the elevators, which somehow still functioned.

Outside, the three camera operators spread out, catching the building's breakup from as many angles as possible, moving back to the top spire to make sure the rippled disturbance was still in place.

Then there was a pause in the destruction, allowing time for the building's evacuation. According to the time stamps on the cameras, the delay lasted 73 minutes. The first half of that, in Lloyd's mind, seemed to pass in an instant. He kept forgetting to watch the border rats, but it didn't matter. Whenever he looked back at them, they were motionless, staring at the building that had lost its curtain wall.

Time started to drag. Lloyd found himself anxious for a definite sign that the occurrence was over so they could return to the cathedral and start their witnessing of the event, however they were going to do that. It seemed odd, but staring at the remains of the most impressive demonstration of PK power that Lloyd had ever seen started to bore him.

But then the wait was over, and the disturbance struck again. The ripples in the sky became narrower, moving faster. Waves of energy drilled into Lloyd's skull, and he felt his brain liquefying. Power moved downward, smothering the frame of the tower. One moment, the central frame of the structure was intact. The next, it was a tall collection of building-shaped dust. It held its shape for a brief instant, then collapsed.

NArd PKs lived up to their reputation by confining the dust to the footprint of the former building. It only billowed up. They couldn't save the building, but they kept the residents and workers of the Belmont area from inhaling the dust of tons of stone, steel, and glass.

On the other side of the wall, Lloyd and the other adepts stared in silence at the empty space in the city. When they regained their composure, a few of the adepts slowly clapped their hands together. Adept Kroll put a stop to that immediately.

"No time for that!" He barked. "Our job's just beginning. Move out!"

<<Hsu!>> he sent. <<What are the rats doing?>>

Lloyd, who'd forgotten to look at them during the final collapse, was grateful he'd glanced at them a moment before.

<<They were stunned, but they're over it,>> he sent. <<Mostly panicked now and moving west for a closer look, coming toward us. >>

<<Good,>> Kroll sent, then he broadened his reach and sent to everyone. <<We're heading right for the rats!>>

<<Something in the wall's opening,>> sent Adept Glorin, and Lloyd suddenly understood the haste in Kroll's sending.

<<I'm sending for the bus,>> Kroll told all the others, <<but we can't just sit here and wait for it. Let's go.>>

He set the pace at a near jog, glancing away from the rats to make sure Courtney was keeping up. He was ready for the next inevitable round of questions from Courtney, but nothing was forthcoming, and Lloyd saw an odd expression on Courtney's face. It took him a few moments to figure it out—for perhaps the first time since Lloyd met him, Courtney didn't look confused.

<<There's a truck coming out to the north ... no, not a truck ... boiling blood, it's like a small tank!>> Glorin couldn't keep an edge of panic from entering her thoughts.

<<The bus is coming,>> Kroll send with an edge of calming. <<We'll get to it before they get to us.>>

Lloyd ran, only to see that Courtney was already a step ahead of him, running right for the rats. He hadn't heard any of the messages—there was no way he could—but he was still following the instructions precisely. Maybe, Lloyd thought. Maybe he's here for a reason.

The rats were spurred by the pace of the adepts, and they started running too. As the adepts weren't making any threatening gestures, the rats kept themselves contained, though tense, in case the adepts broke a last-minute surprise on their heads.

Behind them, Belmont was in quiet chaos. Dust settled with a noise like wet falling snow, muffling the surrounding sirens. Lloyd imagined there were people yelling and screaming, but no sound carried past the wall.

The border rats drew closer, but behind them Lloyd saw the approaching bus, silver exterior glinting in the sunlight. The two adepts inside had it moving at a good clip, but nowhere near as fast as it would be going once the others climbed inside.

<<Bunch together!>> Kroll sent. <<Make the rats move aside>>

The adepts shifted into a tight phalanx, with Lloyd near the front of the wedge and Courtney to his right. Lloyd checked Courtney again, waiting for panic or uncertainty to show on his face, but the Savior-in-Training looked focused and firm as he watched the bus.

Border rats don't appreciate attempts at intimidation. They bunched together and picked up their pace. A few of them drew bits of sharpened scrap metal and waved them menacingly, though Lloyd thought the weapons were more likely to bend on impact than penetrate anyone's skin.

He took a second to look behind him. The USNA vehicle was moving briskly, but not, Lloyd was sure, at its top speed. They'd seen the building collapse, watched power materialize out of thin air and bring the whole thing down. USNA troops were not accustomed to dealing with any sort of defeat, or even minor setbacks. Feeling vulnerable was alien to them.

Dust rose behind the mini-tank, matching its grey-brown skin. The tank had three openings, two for NArds to look through and throw out whatever spells they wanted, the other a long barrel for hurling PK-powered shells. It was squat, blocky, and completely non-aerodynamic, because NArd PKs never let little things like wind resistance bother them. For now, nothing fired from any opening.

That was all the glancing Lloyd could spare, and he turned back to the rats. He could see their faces now, their determination (or maybe desperation) far more frightening than their primitive weapons. They weren't yielding.

<<Dammit!>> sent Kroll. <<All right, Estes, Krilow, level the right side of them. But make sure most of them stay on their feet. Everyone else, move right.>>

Another sending whispered past Lloyd's ear, but he only heard its passage, not its content. Probably some instructions for the bus.

The next order from Kroll came soon after. <<Flying entrance everyone. I've got Whitaker, the rest of you take care of yourselves. Cushions are already up.>>

The rats were seventy feet away when Estes and Krilow struck, hardening a column of air into a battering ram that leveled three rats. The other eight instinctively shied away from the fallen rats, and the adepts had their opening. They dashed by the rats, putting the refugees between them and the charging USNA mini-tank.

Now, as they passed, Lloyd could look behind him and keep an eye on both the rats and the tank. He hoped the rats would be a small obstacle for the onrushing tank. It wouldn't be much of a delay, but every second helped.

They didn't even get a second. The tank, keeping its speed, ran into and over the rats. One body flew into the air, limbs drooping, droplets of blood trailing as it was flung to lie in a final patch of dirt. The others fell like cut flowers, a quick and graceless drop to the ground. The tank didn't pause.

Kroll's sending had no words, just an urging for speed. Lloyd needed more than his legs could give him. He had the air behind him propel him forward, his feet skimming the ground occasionally to help maintain balance rather than move him. His shield got weaker, since running at this speed required focus—one slip of his feet, or a shift in the air pushing him, and he'd be skidding on his face at about twenty-five miles per hour. He wasn't sure how Kroll was able to push himself while also moving Courtney.

Behind them, the tank had to be hurtling at fifty miles per hour. It was closing fast, but the bus was just ahead, its open doors beckoning. The adepts shifted into a single-file line, Courtney at the head. Lloyd could no longer see his face, but he imagined panic had finally entered it—being pushed by hands of air had an unnerving effect on a first-timer.

What happened next was probably worse for Courtney. A piece of ground beneath him exploded, moving up like a springboard, and Courtney hurtled headfirst into the bus, arms wheeling.

The other adepts followed, firing into the bus like torpedos. Lloyd was in the rear now, keeping an eye on the approaching tank. He dropped his speed spell an instant before he used the ground to hurl him into the air.

His aim was good, and he entered the bus. An air cushion set up by one of the drivers bounced him off at an angle, flinging him into the middle of the bus. A second cushion caught him, and he landed a foot in front of the adept who had flown in just ahead of him.

The bus was moving again, turning and heading east. Most of the others were already seated, including Courtney, who sat on the floor, legs crossed, eyes closed, either scared out of his mind or phenomenally serene. The blockers kept Lloyd from reading him, though, and there wasn't time to talk. Lloyd ran to his position at the back of the bus.

He scanned the mini-tank for any traces of PK activity. He found a pocket of excited air near the tank, heating up past 200 degrees. It wasn't going to do anything yet—the NArds were keeping it ready in case they decided aggression was needed.

Lloyd didn't like looking down the barrel of a gun. He worked up a cold breeze and blew it through the pocket of heat, cooling it to only slightly warmer than the air. It blew apart easily—despite the adepts' bus-boarding display, the NArds still underestimated their strength.

The rest of the adepts were doing their part. The acceleration of the bus was smooth and rapid. With the broad, open space of the border wastes and no other vehicles around besides the one chasing them, they could work up plenty of speed. Clear plastic panels in the floor of the van revealed wheels with small paddles. The adepts focused on them, pushing them into a spin as fast as their minds allowed, generating power that flowed to the front of the bus, waiting to be used. Adept Gwin, in the front, steered and controlled how much of the adepts' power was allowed to flow into the kinetic engine. Right now, he was letting all of it come through. The body of the bus creaked with strain.

The USNA tank probably had the same set up, but it carried fewer PKs and probably had fewer paddlewheels. The NArds might, as they always claimed, be better wizards, but they couldn't overcome the disparity of numbers. The bus was pulling away.

They were going to try something. The tank knew the bus had PKs, it wouldn't be much of a mental leap to guess they were from the CMC, and CMCs fleeing from the scene of a collapsed skyscraper was not something the NArds would want to allow.

Lloyd took a little comfort that High Adept Kroll would be watching for the attack with him—he didn't have to defend the bus on his own. He hoped they would be enough.

The tank was falling further behind, but it wasn't happening fast enough. It was still in range. Lloyd wheeled his mind through any possible attack, every possible tactic the NArds might try. They'll know I'm watching the back, so they'll go high, then come down from above. Or they'll wait for me to look for a runaround attack, then throw something right in my face when my guard is down. Their attack might already be coming while he thought about it, snaking out the back of the tank, winding a torturous path that Lloyd could never follow.

Dust partially obscured air between the bus and the tank, but the line of sight remained clear enough for easy casting.

There was wind from the right, a tight stream whose signature was unmistakable. It wasn't natural.

It was also too obvious. It wasn't strong, it wasn't concealed. It was a distraction. Lloyd scanned everywhere except the direction of the wind, and he saw it. Nails, from the left, low to the ground, flying through a magnetic tunnel. Flying toward the bus' tires.

Lloyd attacked the tunnel first, altering the air around it to try to break it down and cancel the field the NArds had created. At the same time, he sent a warning to Adept Kroll.

<<Nails! Five o'clock.>>

<<Right. They're yours. NArds are trying to put a wall in front of us, I have to keep it down.>>

While Kroll sent that message, Lloyd's first effort was failing. The tunnel was well shielded, and the NArds rebuilt it as quickly as he could break it down. Lloyd abandoned that effort, tried to get a solid enough wall of air to stop the nails, but he couldn't push the molecules close enough together. The nails slid right through his efforts.

They were ten feet away, nine, eight, closing, then he saw the rock. He lifted it, hurled it through. The NArds were ready for all sorts of molecular attacks, but not a rock. It smashed into the nails, taking most of them out of the NArd's tunnel. They dropped harmlessly to the ground.

Lloyd's aim had been good, but not perfect. About a half dozen nails came through. He lost sight of them as they hit the bus, near, or possibly on, the tire. He waited to hear a rush of air, or an explosive blowout. He heard nothing. The tires, for the moment, survived.

The gust of wind hit the van at the same time, doing nothing more than rocking it a little side to side. Lloyd relaxed, let out a long exhale.

Which was exactly what the NArds were waiting for. They had a third attack ready.

It was fire, plain and simple. The air around the bus exploded, orange light devouring the world outside their windows. The temperature inside shot up, beads of sweat instantly appearing on most of the adepts' foreheads.

Lloyd knew better than to counter heat from a handful of NArds by himself. He couldn't distract ask any of the others by asking them for help—slowing down now could be fatal.

He didn't know where the answer came from, but he hoped it was from the same Creator that had prophesied the collapse of the tower. He sent a message Gwin.

<<Veer left as sharp as you can on three! One ... two ... three!>>

Ten seconds ago this wouldn't have worked. The NArds would've been reaching out, listening for sounds as quiet as heartbeats, and they would've seen right through Lloyd's little illusion. But now they were focused on speed and fire, so they weren't scanning carefully. They saw the bus continuing on its course, and they kept the flames on it, surrounding it. They even saw the paint on the roof and sides start the peel from the heat. But beyond that, the flames had no effect. The NArds thought the frame should be melting by now, but the bus kept cruising along at a steady speed, a hair faster than the tank. Then, after two minutes, the bus winked out of existence, and there was nothing but hot air.

Lloyd didn't know how long they'd be confused, but it should be enough. The bus was faster than the tank, and the NArds didn't know which way the bus had gone. They were clear.

The bus, becoming cooler each second, sped along under Lloyd's reflection spell, the bent rays of light throwing its image along its old course while it sped invisibly on its new. Figuring the constantly changing angles as the real bus and its image grew farther and farther apart put a strain on Lloyd's brain, but it was still better than the heat from the NArds' fire. He let it drop when he thought they had enough of a cushion, then slumped down in the bus' back seat.

"That was quick thinking," High Adept Kroll said, then scowled before Lloyd could accept the compliment. "But you should have seen that fire coming."

Lloyd only nodded. He glanced up at Courtney but saw only the back of his head—he was still staring firmly at the front of the bus. Lloyd thought about talking to him, but then figured Courtney's reaction wouldn't be much different between here and the cathedral. The conversation could wait.

Interlude: Death and Suffering

The real problem is not, and has never been, the evil that people do to each other. Well, let me correct myself—there are people who, in times of war and other such widespread strife, question how the Creator could let such things continue. In our church, scarcely a day goes by without someone—many people, really—wondering how long the Creator will make us suffer under the yoke of the USNA of Anderson Drauer. So, although it is perfectly clear that such suffering is caused by humanity's misuse of their own free agency and not by the actions of the Creator, there are still those whose faith is troubled by such actions. Often, though, this can be addressed through a discussion of free will and why the Creator insists that our choices have consequences.

It is other disasters, those without direct human cause, that cause deeper problems. God's reasons for allowing people to misuse free agency and harm others is, to the adequately educated, clear; God's reasons for allowing natural disasters inflict great harm on humanity are more opaque. The earth is not a freethinking organism; its actions can be changed without any threat to free agency whatsoever. It becomes quite easy, in these situations, to ask why the Creator allows such disasters to occur, and the best answer we can give is usually that we do not know. If we were infinite beings with infinite understanding, we may understand His purposes; but we are not, and we don't. We must use faith as a bridge to traverse our ignorance until we reach the day of enlightenment.

There is a third category of actions that create yet more difficulties. In natural disasters, the question is why the Creator did not stop them; most sophisticated theologians no longer bother with the notion that the Creator causes such things. But when we read the scriptures, both ancient and modern, we are occasionally confronted with actions where the Creator directly acted upon humanity, and many suffered from His actions. In some cases, such as the drowning of the Egyptians in the Red Sea, the loss of life causes little discomfort. This was the army that had enslaved God's people for over a century, and who were acting on the orders of the evil Pharaoh. Their loss was the inevitable consequence of their actions.

Other actions of God, though, may leave an unpleasant aftertaste. The constant slaughter, at the Creator's behest, as Israel enters Canaan; the death of children at the first Passover; or the slaughter of Job's children and servants with the implicit blessing of God; all these show a Creator that approves of, or even administers, death to the innocent. How could a loving, merciful Creator kill His children in such a fashion?

To understand the Creator's actions in such situations, we must adopt His mode of sight. We must see the larger currents in the world, the eventual outcomes of broad series of actions. It is not unlike a chess game, where the sacrifice of a single piece, even a highly valuable piece, can lead to victory. When the Creator acts, He does not do so randomly or ineffectively. His actions are carefully crafted to achieve His results, and, as He is a beneficent God, we know His actions must lead toward the greater good. Though it sounds heartless, in some cases a minimal loss of life is acceptable, even necessary, to direct the sweep of history as needed.

Though some people purport to find such arguments unconscionable, are they really far from things we are consistently taught as school children, things we believe and cherish to this day? Does anyone think the Revolutionary War, or the Civil War, were less noble in their causes because innocent people died in the conflicts? Would anyone argue that these wars were not truly necessary, that they did not lead to a greater good? If we are willing to sacrifice innocent life to build a better world, why can we not believe in a Creator who would do the same?

Chapter Fourteen

They didn't dare send news, let alone video images, of the collapse ahead of them. The airwaves were too insecure, and it wouldn't do to put anything in a place where the NArds, who were sure to be on high alert after the chase through the borderlands, could intercept it. The adepts and acolytes left behind at Hampton Cathedral weren't outside waiting to welcome the returning heroes—no one knew if there was going to be any USNA retaliation or what form it might take, so the cathedral was on high alert, with everyone at an assigned post.

Cathedral leadership also wanted to try to prevent the bus from being connected with the cathedral (though Lloyd didn't think the NArds would have any difficulty connecting the dots), so even after they had escaped the pursuing tank, the work of evasion was not done. Near Ronkonkoma, High Adept Kroll sent out a distortion burst, making the bus appear to waver and break apart like the picture on a faulty television. With that protecting illusion, all fifteen passengers dashed out and traveled back to the cathedral via fourteen different paths; most of them were on their own, but Courtney traveled with Lloyd.

While other adepts had been given routes that let them take public transportation or even a borrowed vehicle, Lloyd was on foot. He was pretty sure he wouldn't have to walk the entire twenty or so miles to the cathedral, though. He knew about a dozen ways to throw together a makeshift scooter that he could glide on to the cathedral. It would be harder, but still quite possible, to make one that could carry two people.

As they walked, most of Lloyd's attention was dedicated to scanning roadside litter for possible materials, which kept him from feeling like he had to say anything to Courtney, who still appeared to be lost in thought.

At this point on the Island, the desolation of the borderlands gave way to simple poverty. The shacks had rotting roofs, boards seemed more common than glass, and almost every painted surface was chipped. Still, most of the residents of the area had some sort of shelter to retire to at night, and most of them had a basic respect for the lives and belongings of their fellow residents. That alone made it safer than the borderlands.

The roadside here looked pretty well picked over. There was plenty of splintered wood and rusted pipes, but nothing that was useful—no wheels, not even any boards that he'd trust to hold the weight of a small child. He managed to find a few intact nails, though, and he picked them up in case they were needed.

"Did I do that?" Courtney's voice was even more hesitant that normal, and so quiet that Lloyd couldn't be sure he wasn't just talking to himself.

"Do what?"

"The building."

"Did you make it fall?"

"Yeah."

"No," Lloyd said. "We haven't seen any of the talent in you yet, and it would take an awful lot of ability to pull off what we saw."

"No, no, that's not what I meant," Courtney said. "I know I didn't *do* it. Believe me, I know. But did I *cause* it? The guy down in the basement, the acolyte guy, he said the prophecy about the building falling would be fulfilled. Because I'm here, I guess. So Birch and Kroll send us out to the border, and we watch, and the thing falls down. That sounds like I caused it, right? That it collapsed because I was there, right?"

Lloyd turned a few thoughts over on his tongue for a moment before he actually said anything. "Prophecies are going to happen by the very nature of what they are. We don't cause them, even when we seem to play a role in them. They are a sweep of events larger than free will, larger than humanity. They are the will of God in force."

Courtney stopped walking. "You sound like a textbook."

Lloyd stopped, too, and grinned awkwardly. "I do? Oh, yeah. I guess that's kind of what it says in *The Way of Miracles*. Not exactly, but close."

"*The Way of Miracles?*"

"It's a ... yeah, it's a textbook. Something they give to acolytes when they're training to be adepts."

"So what did you—well, what did the book say? What you just said—what did it mean?"

A speech, fully fleshed out and developed in an instant, appeared in Lloyd's mind, where he would explain to Courtney how ridiculous it was that someone being presented as the savior of the church, who would bring them out from under the heel of the most powerful nation on earth, couldn't even understand the church's basic text. The temptation to deliver it was very strong indeed.

But what good would it do? High Adept Birch wasn't going to be persuaded by anything Lloyd said. All his speech would do was annoy Courtney, and, when Courtney relayed it to Adept Birch (as he assuredly would), anger the High Adept. He swallowed his speech and decided to say something else.

"It says that no, you didn't cause the collapse of the building. It was going to happen regardless. High Adept Birch and High Adept Kroll just arranged a way for you to see it."

"Why?"

"Why what?"

"Why would they care if I saw it or not?"

"So you could see a prophecy come true."

Courtney almost asked another question, but then, perhaps for the first time since Lloyd had met him, the answer occurred to him first. "So I'd start to believe the stuff this Ellis guy said. And I'd start to believe the stuff he said about me."

"Right."

Courtney had smiled briefly at his understanding, but his mouth rapidly fell into a grimace. "Just because I watched a building fall down doesn't mean I believe I'm Birch's chosen person." He said it with an attempt at conviction for which his voice wasn't suited.

Lloyd almost laughed, but instead he concentrated on looking for wheels.

Kale tried to put a cold compress on his forehead, but that didn't get to the source of the pain. He was forced to build a cold compress on the inside of his skull, which was a tricky process, as making the brainpan too cold could cause real problems. This meant that a seemingly simple temperature alteration that no one else could see or feel took more concentration than many of the seemingly more complicated tasks he did on a routine basis.

The fact that he was working the spell with a splitting headache wasn't helping anything. He had felt the power in Belmont as soon as it appeared, and he monitored it the whole time. He was too close to it when the cloud shook the tower to the ground, and the power it had emitted had ground deep into his skull and stayed there.

"You didn't no recognize the mindprint?" Spree said. She said it for the third time, but she couldn't know when Kale was paying attention and when his mind was elsewhere.

"Print ... nnnoooo." Kale said, slurring his words.

"Someone new did this? Powerful PK, someone we haven't no heard of?" Spree was careful to put enough doubt in her tone to penetrate Kale's haze.

"No. Not nececececece ...necessarily."

Spree sat still, waiting for further explanation. Kale didn't offer anything. She looked at one wall of the small bedroom, then another one. Both were beige and blank.

She sighed, exaggerated and exasperated. "You didn't no recognize the print, but it's not no someone new. The hell?"

Kale remained stiff on his bed, eyes closed, but Spree saw him squint, working up his concentration for a multiple-word answer.

"Combined spell," he finally said. "Several working together. Planned in advance. Gives a unique mindprint."

"Any way to break it down? Trace any of the people involved?"

Kale raised a closed fist and swiveled it back and forth to indicate "no." It was far less painful than moving his head.

"But chumchas, they involved somehow. They probably responsible."

"Probably."

"But we can't no prove it."

Kale swiveled his fist again.

Spree rested her chin in her palms, waiting without showing much patience while Kale tried to speak.

"Otherthing. One. Other. Thing," Kale said with effort.

"What?"

"Creator."

Spree raised an eyebrow.

"The Creator?"

"Don't know His mindprint," Kale said. Then, since the pain that had carved into his head the moment the Poulsen Tower disintegrated showed no signs of easing, he let himself become unconscious, hoping Spree would find some information on her own before he woke up.

Chapter Fifteen

Reporters clustered near the front door of the cathedral, while the techs and camera crews congregated around the outdoor jackpoint the networks had installed there. It was currently filled beyond capacity. Most of the techs who made the trip knew it would be crowded so they brought splitters, hoping to get as many cables into the dual-plug jack as possible. Eight nets finally were able to plug in, while the rest were left either to make bargains to share the plugged-in cables or to attempt to relay their data through the air. A story like this, which wouldn't be making the USNA look very good, made aerial transmissions risky, with high odds that the data wouldn't make it to its source without interruption. The reporters would be best off waiting for time on the jackpoint, so they gathered around it as if it were their private altar.

The doors of the cathedral open. Two adepts walked out then stood flanking the doorway. Following them was an old man who walked with a perfectly straight back and had a full mane of grey hair on his head. He walked briskly to the top of the stairs and surveyed the reporters gathered beneath him.

High Adept Birch knew he could have knocked them all flat on their backs. That would shut them up. None of them had the talent, none of them could put up a shield, and only a few of them were on blockers. They were all accustomed to the CMC using its powers benevolently, to resisting the temptation to knock annoying reporters on their rear ends. *Others have resisted the temptation before me*, thought Adept Birch, *so I should try to follow their example.*

He wanted to shut them up with a nice, quick spell, but he did the next best thing—he shut them up by opening his mouth and talking. They were all there to listen to him, so it didn't take them long to fall into an appropriately reverent hush.

"Children of the Creator, welcome to Hampton Cathedral. My name is High Adept Rowan Birch, and I serve Grand Adept Malvoin

Serl as Director of Research and Information. The Grand Adept has asked that I speak with you today, and I have a brief statement to read before I will take some of your questions.

"Our prayers today are with our brothers and sisters in Queens as they recover from a terrible disaster. While we praise the Creator that the loss of life seems to be small for such a cataclysmic event, we still mourn with those who have lost loved ones this day.

"To some the events of this day may seem surprising and tragic. Those who pay heed to the word of the Creator, especially those prophecies given through his servant, First Adept Harriman Ellis, cannot be surprised by what has happened, and our sorrow for those who suffered in the disaster is combined with joy that the purposes of the Creator are moving forward.

"I would like to refer you to the Prophecies of Harriman Ellis, quatrain 231, which reads:

"The sky shakes without cause

A single fall

The sign of precision

A lone collapse in the mass.

"This is one of the prophecies of Harriman Ellis, and it presents a clear description of the day's events. The works of the Creator are proceeding, just as First Adept Ellis always said they would. Let this be a comfort to those who are faithful, those who have suffered so long under the oppression of a nation that does not recognize their faith. Let this also serve as a caution to those who fight the ways of the Creator. The time is late, but it is not yet too late. Cease your battles, join the ways of truth, and be united with us as we strive toward our final victory. Amen."

A few techs, but no reporters, echoed back the amen.

"I will now take some of your questions. Yes, the man in the red shirt."

"Thank you, Adept Birch. Are you saying the collapse of the Poulsen Tower was predicted by Harriman Ellis?"

Adept Birch thought it was already manifestly clear that he was indeed saying that, but dealing with the media required patience.

"Yes. He clearly described the event nearly forty years before it took place."

"So you believe the collapse of the tower was a good thing?" This from a woman with blond hair and a keen gaze.

"We believe the collapse was prophesied by the Creator as a sign to us. That does not mitigate the tragedy of the day—the fact that the Creator knew such a thing would happen does not necessarily mean it is good thing."

Every reporter had a hand in the air. The questions came as fast as Birch could point a finger at one of them.

"You say the collapse is a sign. A sign of what?"

"A sign that events are accelerating. First Adept Ellis prophesied a great many remarkable things, and as we mark the progress of his prophecies we see them leading to a single inevitable event—the fall of President Anderson Drauer and his oppressive administration."

"Weren't Harry Ellis and Anderson Drauer friends a long time ago, before they had a pretty severe break? Could this prophecy of Drauer's fall just be Ellis's way of working out a grudge?"

Inside, Birch bristled at the familiarity with First Adept Ellis's name. Outside, his face showed no change.

"All who knew First Adept Ellis describe him as kind, gentle, and completely guileless. He did not hold grudges—in fact, right up to the end of his life, he was asking President Drauer to join his church. He put his entire heart in the church he established and would never corrupt any part of it by using it for personal ends."

"Do you honestly believe Drauer can be brought down by your organization? You haven't had much success with that so far."

"I believe it because the First Adept prophesied it. And recent events, such as the collapse of the tower in Belmont and the miraculous fire in the cathedral of Antigua, show us there are cracks in President Drauer's vast structure. He is not, as is often believed, invulnerable, particularly when placed against the powers of the omnipotent Creator."

"But surely you've heard the latest stories coming out of Antigua. If they are true, the victory seems pretty short-lived."

"We have no confirmation of the stories. Until we do, we will continue to believe that the Antigua Cathedral remains in the church's hands."

"But confirmation's going to be tricky—if the stories are true, the last thing the USNA wants is any confirmation about what happened going around. Hearsay may be all you get."

Adept Birch smiled gently. "I believe that is a problem of news gathering, which puts it more in your bailiwick than mine."

A sturdy, balding man grabbed the line of questioning. "If the church believes the collapse of the tower to be the fulfilling of a prophecy leading up to the fall of tower, wouldn't it be fair to say the church has an interest in seeing this happen? Wouldn't the church want to lend a helping hand to those prophecies. You certainly have enough PK power in this cathedral to bring down a building, don't you?"

"The prophecies of First Adept Ellis do not need a helping hand," Birch said, working hard to prevent his smile from thinning. "While we have many talented adepts in our cathedral, they're generally kept quite busy, and tearing down buildings in the USNA is not often on their list of tasks." Birch was rewarded by a quiet chuckle from the press.

"If that's true, how would you respond to rumors that some adepts were seen near the tower when it collapsed?"

"The same way I respond to all rumors—I do not believe them until there is confirmation. In this case, though, I'm confident the rumors are untrue. I can state with certainty that our adepts have been going about their proscribed duties all day, with the exception of those who were asked to assist in preparations for this conference."

"Okay, so the tower collapsed as a sign that Drauer's on the way down. What's next? What should we be looking for?"

Good question, Birch said to himself. Good question.

Aloud, he said "The prophecies are there for all to read. Let those who have the will and the wisdom to understand them contemplate the words of the Creator. Thank you for your time."

All the reporters called his name simultaneously as he turned around, while techs plugged and unplugged cables from the datajack, sending footage back the their networks as quickly as they could. Birch would have to avoid the nets tonight or he'd face the embarrassment of seeing his own face on the screen. With the days that lay ahead, he had a thousand better things to do.

The tower had collapsed in fulfillment of prophecy, Lloyd had guarded the rear of the church's bus against an assault by USNA border security, and he'd ambled home in the company with the man Grand Adept Serl believed to be the chosen one. It had been the most extraordinary day of his life.

But at the end of it, he was sitting on his bunk with the plain white sheets and beige blanket, in a room with no decorative illusions. The window displayed its actual view—the back of a brick building with a brown metal door—and the walls were off-white cinder blocks. Lloyd was too tired to work up anything, and Aron was too cross. Lloyd hadn't yet figured out what Aron was put out about, and he wasn't planning on wasting too much effort to discovering it. He just wanted to rest.

But that wasn't going to happen.

"They're all hovering outside, you know."

"No they're not," Lloyd said without opening his eyes. "They're all in their rooms."

"They're not hovering *physically*, you dumbass. *Mentally*. Push your brain out a little, you'd feel it. They make a pass by our door every few minutes, each of them, seeing if we've changed our ward. The minute we make it anything more welcoming, they'll be running in."

"It's not changing until morning."

"Oh, come on. Don't tell me you don't want to bask a little."

Lloyd opened one eye. Aron was on top of a four-drawer file cabinet, sitting cross-legged. Aron preferred sitting anywhere in the room but in his chair. He'd been sitting with his legs dangling earlier, his heels swinging into the steel side every few minutes, making the cabinet emit a brief rumble of thunder. Lloyd had hoped that laying down and closing his eyes would get Aron to cut it out, but he knew he'd eventually have to tell Aron to be quiet before he changed his posture.

"Bask?" Lloyd asked.

"They want to know what you saw, what you did! You're famous—well, you're famous in our hall, anyway. You let them in here, they'll be hanging on your every word!"

"And that'd be fun?"

"That'd be great!"

Lloyd rolled onto his side. "I think I'll pass."

"*Flames*, you can be boring sometimes. I'd be milking it for all it was worth if I'd gone along."

"I know," Lloyd said, then shut his mouth before he finished saying the rest of his thought.

Too late. He was too tired, he'd thought it too strongly. Aron picked it up easily.

"'Maybe that's why they didn't ask me to go?' What the hell do you mean by that?"

"Nothing, Aron. Nothing. It's not what I think."

"Boiling blood it isn't. It's *exactly* what you thought."

"It's not what I *believe*, okay? Just one of those thoughts that pops up occasionally, but I knew it wasn't true. That's why I didn't say it. Okay?"

Aron uncrossed his legs and let them dangle next to the side of the cabinet. His right heel banged off the metal.

Lloyd knew he had about two choices at this point. One was to spellplug his ears and get some peace and quiet. The problem with that plan was that Aron would notice the spell and undoubtedly try to find some other way to harass him. There was no telling how much of the night that might take up.

The other option would be to let Aron have it out with him. That would be very unpleasant for a few minutes, but then it would be over and Lloyd could sleep.

"It's just that ..." Lloyd started, then stopped, trying to pick the right words. "It's just that maybe you like fame and things like that too much. Maybe your reasons for doing things sometimes get messed up, and you forget your focus. You could've done as good a job as I did, as anyone else did, I'm sure. But the problem's your focus—what you're doing it for."

He'd said enough. Aron slammed both feet into the cabinet then slid to the floor.

"Well of course I don't have *your* motives," Aron sneered, his voice buzzing like an electric plant. "I'm not totally selfless, totally focused on the Creator, like *you* are. I sometimes think about what *I* like, what *I* want, instead of giving every last boiling thought to the church. I still have a *self*, I haven't turned myself into a damned *cog* for the church yet."

To Lloyd's ears, Aron's tirade sounded small and tinny compared to the shattered rumble of the collapsing Poulsen Tower, the slow boom that still filled his ears.

"And I'll tell you another thing," Aron said after he had paused briefly and not gotten any response from Lloyd. "This church is in trouble if the only people who can offer service are the automatons. Some of us think a little different sometimes, okay. But aren't we adepts? Doesn't that mean that we have something to offer? Maybe we could do better if we allowed for creativity in the upper ranks, instead of just pushing a bunch of bootlicks forward."

Lloyd opened his eyes. "The fire in Antigua. The collapse of the tower. Both fulfilling prophecies. And you think the church can't go anywhere without *your* help?"

This stung Aron in the best possible way—it stung him into silence. Lloyd, still seeing the tower collapse over and over in his mind, fell asleep.

Chapter Sixteen

Two versions of the story went out, the USNA version and the version for the rest of the world. The USNA version mentioned that the tower collapsed, said there was no explanation for the disaster, and added that "USNA authorities, under the direct supervision of President Anderson Drauer, are investigating the incident." Every single USNA article contained that sentence, and none of them had any mention of casualties or the lack thereof.

The stories outside the USNA held as little hard information as the USNA stories, but they filled the vacuum with rampant speculation. Most of the guessing games had to do with the number of deaths from the collapse, but a few nets took some stabs at the reason for the collapse. AlphaNet estimated there were "anywhere from eight to 400 deaths" in the collapse, but most of their reports leaned toward the latter figure, allowing the articles to point to an alleged massive USNA cover-up. While not denying there was a USNA cover-up, both Atmosphere News and FreeNet claim any number higher than twenty deaths was not substantiated by any shred of evidence, and that the real number was likely closer to ten. The reports from these outlets, while careful to excoriate the USNA for not reporting any information on the deaths, offer grudging admiration for the efficiency of the evacuation operation.

As the coverage moved into its second day, speculation about possible causes of the collapse increased. Even one USNA net, ColumbiaCast, included this phrase in one report: "Investigation by President Drauer's task force is focusing on structural flaws in the tower." The idea that a skyscraper could collapse into a self-contained pile of dust and debris was met with widespread mockery on the nets outside the USNA—which meant, of course, that no one in the USNA, including their media, ever saw these rebuttals.

No one doubted the collapse had been the work of PKs, but the question of which PKs were responsible generated plenty of debate.

FreeNet, never a great friend of the CMC, claimed it was obviously the work of the church and expected severe retaliation by the USNA any day. Atmosphere News argued that the CMC had never made such a direct assault against the USNA in its history and was not about to start now. The culprits, their reporters said, was most likely rogue PKs formerly in the employ of the USNA. FreeNet responded by pointing out that former USNA PKs are quite rare and do not tend to live long once they've quit the service of their former nation. Such people are unlikely to call attention to themselves through actions as dramatic as bringing down the Poulsen Tower.

Those were the two most believable scenarios. All the rest were covered by AlphaNet: foreign agents, rust, supernatural phenomena, the direct hand of God, and anything else they could get someone to attach their name to.

Kale read all those articles, watched all the coverage, and still couldn't figure out just what had happened. Either the church had just attacked the USNA and Andy hadn't yet retaliated, or for some reason Andy's people took down their own building. Neither explanation made sense to him.

He walked away from his screen. It wasn't telling him what he wanted to know, and he was hungry. He made a trip to the kitchen, found it sadly empty, then stalked off to find Spree.

She was with her screens, where she always was.

"There's nothing to eat," he said.

"Yeah, yeah, yeah," Spree said, not looking at him. "Sent Amelia out, remember?"

"But there's really *nothing*. Not even a few scraps. What happened while I was out? You all went on a binge?"

Spree lifted her black tank top to the bottom of her ribs. "*Look* like I binge?"

"I don't care how thin you are, I care that I have nothing to *eat*. Do you know when the last time was that I ate?"

"'Bout an hour and a half 'fore the tower went down."

"Forty hours ago. I'm hungry."

"Not like you been burning much, lying on your back for a day. Don't no need much food for that."

"No double negatives!" Kale snapped.

"Look, food's coming. Maybe good you catch up on what you've missed. Time go by faster, keep you from complaining."

Kale stared at the open refrigerator a few more seconds. The black linoleum under his feet was cold from the air that had been pouring down on it for the past three minutes. Then he resigned himself to the fact that new food was not just going to appear in front of him and closed the door.

He followed Spree down the hall, shuffling his feet, feeling old. The clamping vise of the headache that had paralyzed him for nearly two days was gone, but its echo remained, pulsing in his temples.

At his age, he needed nearly constant maintenance of his body, at least when he was awake. Not being conscious for an entire day interrupted his regimen, and his body struck at him with a vengeance. But he'd be back to normal again once he got his maintenance spells running—after, of course, he had eaten something.

Spree walked into the tech room, and the peeling paint and worn floors of the rest of the house gave way to a dust-free room with sturdy, though unmatched, furniture.

"Been watching the nets most of the time you been out," Spree said. "USNA feeds keep blinking out—they shutting down pirate cables pretty quick now. Using the third backup now."

"Got anyone out tapping new cable?"

"Not yet. Ezziah—rat I know—is tied up for a little."

"Other jobs?"

"Knife fight."

"Oh."

"He survives, he be looking for a new jackpoint tomorrow. Got one more backup left, hopefully that'll last 'til Ezziah find something."

"All right. What have you seen?"

"Most nets just passing on NArd crap, stuff they heard from a spokesperson who don't no know nothing. Two whole layers of people who don't no know shit there, so nothing real gets through. But there's a guy, one guy, Edison Cain that knows something."

"Columbia guy?"

"Yeah. His face is all over now, on this show and that, and he's got this air, and … ah, watch yourself. Got some vid."

Kale lowered himself onto a charcoal grey chair that rumpled comfortably as he sat. Now that he was down, he wasn't sure he would be able to stand again until he ate.

He tried to listen to Cain talking while his gut grumbled. The clip Spree was showing him was from *Top of the News*, with Cain being interviewed by the always-calm and well-groomed Estella Bates. They sat in front of a backdrop photo of the Manhattan skyline, far from Belmont.

"What was the key to the success of the emergency response in this situation?" Bates asked.

"Preparation. These people are handpicked for their efficiency and have been thoroughly trained in the best simulations the Illusion Corps could devise. They are built for success, so their results are not surprising."

Spree lowered her voice to mimic Bates' timbre. "How is it that NArds manage to be so wonderful at everything they do?"

"Shh!" Kale said, staring at the vid, studying Cain's face intently every time it came on the screen.

"It could be said, then, that this was a perfect rescue operation?" Bates asked onscreen.

"I don't think there's any operation of this nature, on this scale, that could be called 'perfect.'" Cain replied. "There are too many people involved in too complex of a situation. But they did a remarkable job, despite the regrettable losses."

"By which I assume you mean the tower?" Bates said, speaking before Cain had fallen silent.

"Right." Cain cleared his throat. "Right. The loss of the tower is quite unfortunate."

"That's just one loss," Kale said, still staring at the vid. "He said 'losses' before."

"And you saw his face?" Spree asked.

"Yeah. Dropped some color. He must've known he'd made a little slip as soon as he said it and then started looking for ways to cover himself."

"Good thing kiss-ass interviewer there to help him out."

"Yeah. Do you know when he's on next?"

"His show comes on in an hour. The one where he and Spale bitch at each other."

"That should work. Assuming they're still talking about the collapse."

"Still the lead story on most nets," Spree said.

"Okay. Once Cain's on, it's recon time." He looked restlessly at the doorway to the room. "Could I get something to eat *before* I have to go read a NArd?"

"You're here early."

Courtney startled. He had apparently been interrupted in the middle of contemplating one of the chapel's marble pillars. He looked at Lloyd but didn't say anything.

"There are more interesting parts of the cathedral than that," Lloyd said. "I could show you …"

"That's okay," Courtney said. "I mean, thanks, but I've actually been looking around for a while. I'm kind of familiar with the place now."

"How long have you been here?"

Courtney turned. His eyes, which looked sleepy on the best of days, were puffy and red. His skin was loose and sallow. "Since we got back. Once High Adept Kroll said he was done with me. I came here and …" he waved a hand in a vague circle "… looked around. Thought I should know more about the place. The church."

Lloyd nodded, thinking this was the first time he'd heard Courtney refer to a church official by his full title. "You could talk to any of us. Instead of, you know, just wandering around the cathedral all night."

"Yeah. I guess."

Lloyd waited for further explanation from Courtney, but nothing was forthcoming.

"Is there anything I can tell you about? Any questions from looking around all night?"

Courtney shrugged, a very familiar gesture.

I'm pressing too hard, Lloyd thought. *Whatever he wants at the moment, Courtney isn't looking for a teacher.*

He changed tactics. "Are you hungry?"

Courtney blinked several times, then shifted from one foot to another a few times, pondering the question. "Yeah," he finally said. "I think I am."

"Let's get something to eat."

"Where? The dining hall?"

"Sure," Lloyd replied, but saw Courtney hesitate. "Unless you didn't want to go there."

"They all ... *you* all ... know me now. Who I'm supposed to be. You all act funny when I walk into a room." He thought for a minute. "Maybe I mean 'they all.' You don't seem to act like they do."

Lloyd just nodded. Then he gestured briefly to his right. "We can go somewhere else," he said. "Come on, I'll show you."

He led Courtney down the stairway behind the altar into the cathedral basement. The polished marble and detailed ornamentation of the chapel gave way to thick, blocky stone. Lloyd always thought the basement looked like a place that the original builders intended to make impressive someday, but they'd never gotten around to it.

He took a hallway to the left, walking into a dim corridor. He added some light as they walked along—he didn't want Courtney to feel nervous or uncomfortable.

They followed a few twists and turns, eventually walking past the stairway that led down to Acolyte Terrin's lair. Across the hall, a few feet farther down, was a narrow door that most people assumed was a janitorial closet. It was locked, though anyone who had been an adept for more than a week could easily shift the knob's tumblers around and open the door. Lloyd had it unlocked and the door swinging open before he was within five feet of the door, then felt bad for hoping Courtney was impressed with his simple trick.

"What's this?" Courtney asked as they walked in and Lloyd raised some lights.

"Study room," Lloyd replied. "Acolyte Terrin doesn't like to have anyone besides him in the archives for any more than five minutes, so if we have something we actually have to sit and look at, he sends us up here with it."

"Oh. Okay." Courtney, looking even more dazed than he had in the cathedral, took in the four wall-mounted carrels and the padded armchairs. He idly ran his fingers across the smooth black upholstery.

"You wouldn't believe what we had to do to get these in here," Lloyd said, smiling. "Once you've been in training long enough, you can get comfortable in any chair, even the straight metal ones they had in here. But we hadn't learned that when we were new, and Adept Birch had us in here every other day. Once, on our day off, Aron went to every furniture store he could, found these things and levitated them all the way back to the cathedral. Adept Birch saw him, of course—how could you miss someone trying to sneak into the dorms in front of four floating chairs?—and decided that if we cared about it that much, we could have the chairs we wanted."

Courtney had sat while Lloyd told his story, and now he was smiling. "You weren't supposed to get new chairs?" he asked.

"No. The High Adepts always say they've set things up the way they want, and it's not for the lower adepts to disturb their order." Lloyd grinned and shook his head. "But it's tough to study with a numb ass."

Courtney almost laughed. Then he settled into his chair and looked more comfortable than he had since he'd first come to Hampton Cathedral.

"Yeah, I guess they're not bad," Courtney said. "But why are we here?"

"After the triumph with the chairs, Aron was on a roll. We were comfortable, but we were still spending eight to ten straight hours in here without food. Aron threw out half a dozen bad ideas to get something to eat in here before he finally realized that we're sitting right under the kitchen. So—observe."

Lloyd walked to one corner of the room, looked up, and cast a spell to ball up some air and slam it into a wooden panel above him. Three solid knocks echoed through the room.

The panel lifted three inches, then slid to the side. "How many?" a voice called from above.

"Two," Lloyd replied.

"Three minutes," the first voice said, and the panel slid back into place.

Lloyd sat next to Courtney and leaned back, his hands behind his head. "There you go," he said.

Courtney's eyes still sagged, but he managed another small smile. "Terrin let you eat while you were looking at his stuff?"

Lloyd laughed. "Terrin would have Grand Adept Serl turn us inside out if he knew. This we kept secret.'

"Wow. Wasn't that tough?"

"Yeah, I suppose," Lloyd said, trying to remember even though it had only been a couple years ago. "We knew some good silence spells, though, so we could keep the sawing and other noise covered."

"Yeah, yeah, I'm sure you were, you know, careful, but you weren't just hiding something from some other adepts, right? This was Birch, and Serl, and all the others. And couldn't they notice a silence spell as easily as they could hear the work you were doing?"

Lloyd briefly wondered when Courtney had learned that much about the talent, but he was right. Now that he thought about it, their silence spell might have been *more* noticeable than the noise alone would have been. He'd been proud of their study room for a long time, and considered the silence spell he devised his most successful (and possibly only) act of covert rebellion. The leadership at Hampton, though, probably had not been fooled—they just thought that what Lloyd and Aron were doing was not important enough for them to bother with.

The panel raised and slid aside again, and a tray floated through. Lloyd reached out with his mind and slid the tray onto a cushion of air. "Got it," he called, and felt the kitchen staffer above withdraw her control. He took the tray the rest of the way down to the desk in front of Courtney.

Courtney grabbed a muffin before the tray had settled and pulled the paper off with one hand while the other stuffed it into his mouth.

"It's nice here," Courtney said as crumbs dropped from his mouth. "I like it."

"Thanks," Lloyd said, but he found himself thinking it was just an ordinary room.

Chapter Seventeen

Acolyte Brit Devin felt confident that one day he would draw an assignment that wasn't some sort of clerical duty. The people in the kitchen always told him he was lucky and claimed they'd pay hundreds of dollars just for a few days of the clerical work Brit typically performed. He'd calculated the odds of his streak once during a slow day in High Adept Birch's reception room. It wasn't hard, and he'd had plenty of time. He concluded that there was a one in thirty-six chance of drawing the same duty twice in a two-week period. He'd had reception duty at least once a week, and sometimes twice, every week for three months.

He asked High Adept Birch about that once, being as respectful as possible.

"The assignments are given randomly with no input from the High Adepts," Birch had said, then offered a hint of a smile. "However, if the Creator, who knows my needs for organized assistance, sees fit to ensure that the process provides an able acolyte with unusual frequency, who are we to question His designs?"

Brit took that to mean that schedules and filing were to be a regular part of his life until he became an adept, and that was the way things had worked out, no matter how much he longed for some good, solid manual labor.

At least today would be a little different than the normal filing. Today, he was conducting an orientation.

"Hello, I'm Acolyte Brit Devin. I understand you'll be doing some housekeeping for us?"

"Yes. I can't tell you how much I appreciate …"

Brit waved her off. "I'm the wrong person to thank. But I'm happy on your behalf."

The woman smiled hesitantly, her dark eyes squinting into straight slits as she did.

Brit looked over her file quickly, more for show than because he was actually concerned about her abilities. His job was to distract and relax her, get her to open up her mind a little for some basic probing. High Adept Birch had told him more than once that the purpose of orientation was to make sure the church remained secure—skills could be taught, so the first priority was on employees the church could trust.

"Okay, Ms. Yashie, where were you ... wow—you just came out of the USNA?"

"Yes."

"Why did you ... I mean, do you mind if I ask ..."

Yashie fidgeted uncomfortably in her chair. "I'd ... rather not talk about it. It was ... unpleasant."

"Oh, of course, I understand. That's fine. I'm sorry I brought it up." His body language was uncomfortable and apologetic, but his mind snapped forward, pushing ahead while he squirmed in his chair. Their teachers had taught them this trick early on—make people feel a little uncomfortable, then apologize. The subject almost always relaxes a bit and lets their guard down after the apology, and you may be able to get to some information they're trying to keep under wraps.

His scan didn't tell him anything he didn't already know—he'd recognized her name as soon as he'd seen it one the hiring form. This was the woman who had been exiled because she'd been accused of being involved with Mira Corwin. In truth, she didn't have anything to do with Mira—even a relative neophyte like Brit could read that easily, and he was sure the NArds had seen it too. But they prosecuted and convicted her anyway, and Brit was hoping to find out why. But when her thoughts touched on the events leading to her exile, she was as confused about the reasons for it as he was.

He didn't see any guile or repressed hatred for the CMC. In fact, her mistreatment by the USNA seemed to impress her favorably toward the church. So far, so good.

"What did you do in Manhattan? Before you left?"

"I worked with the government."

Brit had known that, too. It was in all the news reports. But he wanted to read her when she talked about the job, and he got a clear impression when she said "government"—resentment and anger. She hardly seemed like a USNA mole.

But the NArds had done this before, taking someone mad at one part of the government and recruiting them into intelligence. They knew that, for enough money, many people were willing to isolate their anger, to be mad only at their old department instead of at the USNA government as a whole.

"What kind of work did you do?"

"Pushing papers. In human services, paperwork connected to the soup kitchens. Arranging food donations, that sort of thing."

"Soup kitchens? In the USNA?" Brit said in mock surprise. "I thought they'd done away with poverty."

Yashie smiled wearily. "That's something President Drauer said years ago, so officially everyone has to stick to it and keep repeating the claim even though I never met anyone who thought it was remotely true."

She had liked her job, he saw, but she'd never bought into the propaganda. It was just a job to her, a source of income, which he guessed was why she hadn't risen very high in the bureaucracy. And why, when the time came, they were able to send her away.

They spoke for fifteen more minutes, with Yashie twice expressing surprise that the conversation remained so informal. Before the interview, Brit thought he might need to talk for as long as a half hour, but that clearly was not necessary. She had no loyalty to the USNA whatsoever. That didn't mean she was looking for the church to strike some blow against the USNA on her behalf—rather, once on the island, she did the same thing she had done in Manhattan. She found the sturdiest, most reliable organization around and went to see what she could do for them.

She wouldn't ever do anything for the church other than housekeeping. Brit did not detect a single trace of the talent in her, and she did not have the drive or enthusiasm for the church to advance in the ranks of the laity. But for what they needed, she'd be perfect.

"Well, Ms. Yashie, I appreciate you coming in. Welcome to the church."

She smiled, the most genuine smile Brit had seen on her. "Thank you. It's nice to have some semblance of order in my life again."

Brit nodded, his mind already moving to his next job of the day.

Nilda didn't know how to send, but apparently she didn't need to. Kale was watching her closely, and as soon as she went to the trouble to put a thought into words, he read it and responded.

<<I can't believe he couldn't sense you watching me,>> she thought.

Words entered her mind as if they were her own thoughts. <<If I can't maneuver around an acolyte, I'm in a lot of trouble.>>

She looked around nervously. She was only a quarter-mile from the cathedral, and there was a good chance a lot of the people she passed were CMC employees. None of them wore the robes of an adept, but she was pretty sure the church had some plainclothes adepts—she thought she'd heard that somewhere.

<<They don't,>> Kale said in her mind. <<They're happy to take credit for their own actions, so they don't feel the need to sneak around. Harry always favored the direct approach to almost any problem.>>

<<Harry?>>

<<Harriman Ellis. The guy who founded the church.>>

A lot of confused thoughts swirled in Nilda's head, but she couldn't make any of them coherent. She only formed a single word. <<Oh.>>

<<I knew him,>> Kale said. Clearly, he was getting more out of her mind than her most conscious thoughts.

<<You're reading more than you said you would!>> she snapped.

She felt an almost physical sensation in her head as Kale withdrew some of his presence from her mind. <<Sorry,>> he sent. <<Force of habit.>>

<<So what now?>>

<<Go home. I'll meet you there. You did pretty well—I really didn't shield you very much at all—but there's a couple things you need to do better before I send you in on your own.>>

Nilda walked to a quiet intersection. Healthy trees grew in every direction, the street next to her only had one or two visible potholes, and the stop signs at the intersection were intact and graffiti-free. She almost could have been back in the USNA.

She looked down one street, then another, then the first again.

<<I can't remember where I live.>>

<<Another mile and a half west,>> Kale sent. <<Then a little north.>>

<<Can I get some transportation? A scooter or something?>>

<<Sure. If you save enough from your paycheck.>>

<<Thanks,>> she thought, and hoped the sourness she tried to give the word transmitted to Kale.

<<Yeah, it did,>> he sent.

The buildings within a mile of the Hampton Cathedral were mostly occupied and in good repair. Just about a mile out, no matter which way you traveled, the neighborhood suddenly declined, well-maintained buildings giving way to boarded windows, gated doors, and scorched buildings that had burned years ago but had been neither repaired nor demolished.

For the next mile, maybe half of the buildings were inhabited, and half of those should have been abandoned due to the threat of imminent collapse. Beyond that, the neighborhood deteriorated further, improving only in clusters around stores that managed to keep a regular supply of goods in stock or small enclaves where the increasingly rare upper class kept council with each other.

Nilda's new home was not in such a cluster. Vacancies in such neighborhoods had long waiting lists and were far more expensive than what Nilda could afford with her new salary (she suspected Kale might have the resources to pay for a better place, but he did not volunteer them).

At the end of her long walk west on Montauk (during which she saw two cars and eight scooters) she turned right on Wisteria. The first house she passed had a collapsed roof and at least three different species of animals, not counting insects, living inside. The second had been given over to squatters.

A little farther down the road was a brick ranch house. From half a block away, Nilda could imagine what it looked like years ago, when it held only one family. Her door was where the living room window probably had been—the battered clinkers that had been used to fill in the gaps when the door was installed stood out against the finished red brick that made up most of the wall. The door just beyond hers probably had been a garage long ago. Carmen, who lived in that unit, had told Nilda that heat didn't make it to her part of the building very well.

Nilda unlocked her four deadbolts (Kale had insisted on that number) and walked into her new home. She had a bed, a chair, and a table, all courtesy of Kale and Spree. Judging by their quality, Nilda guessed they had been found somewhere. Her kitchen was a hotplate sitting on a shelf mounted on two metal brackets with chipped white paint. She hoped she wouldn't have to eat here very often.

Despite its haphazard appearance, the room met Kale's standards—the table was level and sturdy, and it sat next to a Coax1 datajack. Kale, of course, would have preferred an FO jack, or at least a Coax3, but he deemed a Coax1 to be sufficient— mainly since there wasn't much else to choose from.

Beneath the bed's mattress—the only possible hiding place in the closet-less, cupboard-less room—was her greatest treasure, the only item that seemed anything like what she had possessed in her old life. The computer was about a half-inch thick and only thirteen inches diagonal, but it could show her a million things that were not this apartment. And it was a quick and easy way to contact Spree, who was about forty miles west of her. She'd known Spree for about a week, but the strangely coiffed woman was the only friend she had (Kale was too remote and commanding to be classified as a friend), and that made the attachment feel much deeper.

She plugged in her computer, entered her codes as instructed, and waited as the machine danced through an intricate path to make a connection with Kale's base of operations. In all likelihood, the signal was darting around the world, passing through at least three points in the Far East in order to end up a few dozen miles down the Island.

The thin screen showed a circle with a line running from center to edge, rotating around the circumference once every two seconds or so. With little else to do, she counted the rotations before the connection clicked. It went around forty-two times before a dark image popped up. Nilda squinted at it until she could make out the six red spikes Spree had been wearing on top of her head the past couple of days.

"Spree?"

"One sec," Spree said without glancing toward the camera above one of her screens. She was doing her scans, glancing from monitor to monitor, taking in as much of the Island as one human could.

While Nilda waited, she dialed up a newsnet in a second window. At home, she would have happily tuned into the soothing headlines of *Newsday*, which always managed to make her feel that, no matter what was happening in the world, the USNA was on top of things and continuing on a steady course. The nets outside the USNA were considerably less comforting, though, and always made her feel like everything was out of control and there was little she could do about it. But they talked about things happening in Manhattan whenever they could get some word out, and that, at least, was something.

"K." Spree was looking at her now. "Livin' the posh life in Hampton yet?"

"Kind of," Nilda said. "It's not that bad out here. As long as you're near the cathedral."

"Nail that. You'll be there most time?"

"Yes. Most of the time I'm awake I should be in the area."

"K then. Start tomorrow?"

"Yeah, bright and early."

Spree was already looking away, scanning her screens again. Nilda probably could have continued the conversation, but she couldn't think of anything to say.

In her other window, FreeNet was talking about Antigua. Apparently they'd lost a reporter down there, like every other non-USNA net in the world. Most of the commentators said it seemed pretty clear that Antigua and its cathedral were back in the hands of the USNA, but, in the absence of hard evidence, a few talking heads insisted the CMC might still be in control.

Nilda had a guess about what had happened down there, and she didn't like to think about it. It turned her stomach. She was a little surprised no one had turned up any evidence of anything by now, but she knew how good the USNA was at keeping up appearances. And burying evidence.

She didn't have any inside knowledge of Antigua, just an ability to extrapolate from the facts she knew. When the miracle happened, when the fire fell in the cathedral, there was supposedly a packed house watching it fall, witnessing the executions that followed. They, along with numerous CMC adepts, were responsible for seizing the cathedral from the USNA. And now, with all the rumors swirling around, with all the questions about what had happened, no reporter could find a single witness to talk to. At least, no reporter could find a witness and survive long enough to report what they had said.

Keeping the witnesses silent for that long would take a lot of effort, Nilda knew, probably more effort than the USNA wanted to expend. There were easier, more effective ways to make sure the witnesses didn't tell what happened.

"Spree?" Nilda finally said, looking away from her 'cast.

"Say?"

"This guy—the guy who's supposed to be chosen? Is he legit?"

"Not no know," she said. "Never no met him."

"Do they have someone who'll take down Drauer?"

For the first time in the conversation, Spree focused all of her attention on Nilda, without her eyes flicking to one side or the other a single time.

"Not no one man take down Drauer," Spree said. "If one man could get him, would've done it. They don't no have the guy."

"Then why are we looking for him? What am I doing here?"

Spree gently rubbed her hand over the spikes on her head. "No one person'll take down Drauer. But if that one person's got followers—if it's one person with help ..." She shrugged. "Maybe make a difference. Don't no know."

"You're going to follow their guy? Be one of his people?"

"We don't no follow they chosen boy. That's chumchas' job. We help maybe—but we not no know what they're doing and they won't no tell us. Iffin we find out, we help. Be enough? Probably no not. Help a little, maybe do something good? Might. Maybe. Might."

That didn't sound convincing. But really, it wasn't all that different from her life in the USNA—had there ever been much of a chance there that she might maybe might do something tangibly good? She sat in her office, she took papers from one person and passed them on to the next, and wondered what effect she had on anything that mattered. Her surroundings were different now, but in this new phase of existence the possibility of making a real impact seemed as remote as it had in the old.

Chapter Eighteen

For the first ninety minutes of the discussion, Lloyd was overwhelmed by the fact that he was involved in it at all. After that, infatuation ended and frustration set in.

He was in a conference room he had never been in before, a room he didn't even know existed until High Adept Birch had led him to it. A winding stairway at the back of the cathedral rose to the organ loft, then a second, narrower stairway continued upward. It made a 180 degree turn midway and took Lloyd and Adept Birch to a spot Lloyd guessed was above the altar. There was a small hallway with a heavily lacquered wooden door, which Lloyd knew led to the Grand Adept's ready room, the chamber from which he descended at the start of each service. Lloyd always thought the hallway ended just a few feet beyond this door, so he was surprised when Adept Birch walked to the end of the hallway, turned right, and passed through the wall.

It was a simple illusion, the sort of thing most adepts could do it even before they received any formal training. If he'd wanted to, Lloyd could have sensed it easily. The one previous time he'd been in this hallway, though, he'd been too nervous to concentrate and had no real reason to suspect there was anything being kept from his view.

The illusory wall hid a second short hallway that ended in double wooden doors. Polished brass knobs gleamed softly.

Adept Birch had led him down the hall to a beautiful room where each wall was covered with oil paintings and silver wall sconces. At least one of the paintings, Lloyd believed, was a Kallenbach. There were rumored to be no more than twenty-three surviving Kallenbach paintings, all but three of them inside the USNA. This one, though, would make that total twenty-four.

It was, in Lloyd's eyes, an inspirational piece. Six people— there was no doubt who they were—stood at the top of a hill overlooking a railroad track at night. They looked off in six different directions and wore six different expressions. It was the morning after their escape, when they prepared to separate to avoid pursuit. In a week, Anderson Drauer would announce their presence to the world, starting their ascent from prisoners to the most famous, most loved, most feared, and most detested people in the world.

On the far right was Drauer, as dark-haired then as he was now. Only a few minor wrinkles here and there separated the face in the painting from the visage seen daily by millions. Brows furrowed, jaw clenched, he looked ready to burst forward and run off the edge of the painting. He was a ball of barely contained energy, eager to rush into a future that he seemed to have completely planned from that first day.

His opposite, on the left side, was Kale Faltergast. Eyes unfocused, posture slack, Faltergast looked like he might stay in the same spot for the rest of his life, unable to decide which way to go.

Next to him was Deegan Frau, arms folded, glaring across the painting at Drauer. Her suspicions of him, of course, turned out to be very well founded—unfortunately, she hadn't been able to convince any of the other Six of the hazard until it was far too late.

Her glare was intercepted by Armando Diaz, watching Drauer's back then as he had during their confinement and as he would for the next fifteen years. The break between the two, and the eventual assassination of Diaz, was far in the future. In the painting, his eyes knew only fierce loyalty.

The only unclear face in the entire painting was Kallenbach's. In her mind, she was starting to sink into the background from the first moment, trying to disappear from the spotlight for which she had no taste. The moonlight that lit up the faces of the other five somehow missed hers, and she was a slight shadow in the background.

In the middle stood Harriman Ellis. His long face, already prophetic even though it lacked the crags that marked it later in his life, looked straight ahead. While Drauer's eyes blazed, Ellis's glowed. His mouth wasn't as firm as Drauer's, his eyes betrayed a hint of worry. His purpose was as certain as Drauer's, but his future wasn't. While Drauer's plans centered on the advancement of himself, Ellis pondered the elevation of mankind. Lloyd could almost read him as he stood on the hilltop, tasting freedom for the first time, planning what he could do with powers that had never been seen in the world before. At that moment, the idea of the Church of the Miraculous Creator was coalescing in his mind—sent to him, some say, by the mind of the Creator himself. And that thought caused his eyes to glow.

Grand Adept Malvoin Serl sat directly in front of that painting, so First Adept Ellis gazed directly over his head. Lloyd's hands trembled as he sat.

Another High Adept, Elise Sternhaven, sat across from Adept Birch, to the Grand Adept's right. Lloyd knew her quite well—she directed acolytes preparing to be adepts, as well as adepts in their first year of training. Lloyd had been under her supervision for three years before being assigned to Adept Birch. He'd known very little about Adept Birch when his new assignment had come through, but he was grateful for the change—life under Adept Sternhaven's whip was demanding, to say the least.

Four other adepts joined them in the room—Stel Grant, Archie Gwin, Jefferson Balkin, and Bernadette Callow. Lloyd knew Stel and Archie fairly well, Jefferson and Bernadette very little. Aron had not been invited to the meeting, and as a result his sullen brood had only deepened.

High Adept Birch began the meeting with a prayer then immediately launched into business. He was more manic than Lloyd had ever seen him, a strong contrast to Grand Adept Serl's stillness.

"The prophecies will be fulfilled. They *are* being fulfilled. The only question is how ready we will be to respond to them when they happen. Courtney Whitaker will be instrumental in bringing down Anderson Drauer—but how will the church respond when he falls?"

"With prolonged shouts of joy, I would guess," Adept Gwin said dryly. A look from Adept Birch quickly let him know that attempts at humor were not welcome.

"The USNA will not fall just because Drauer is removed from power," Adept Birch continued. "There will be a void, there will be confusion, and we'll need to be ready to jump into it."

"With all due respect, I don't think that's our concern," Adept Sternhaven said. "Premier Adept Dugwu will be mobilizing the church's overall response. If he has directions for us, he will make them known."

"There is no 'if,'" the Grand Adept said, his voice rolling through the room like he was in the middle of a sermon. "There is a plan in place. There has always been a plan."

"Of course," Adept Birch said, rushing to show respect for the Premier Adept. "But there might need to be an adjustment now that we finally know the identity of the chosen one—and that he has shown up here, rather than any other place in the world."

Despite the shields everyone was employing, Lloyd could almost read the word that popped into most of the heads around the table—"So?" No one, though, actually said it.

Adept Birch answered the unspoken question. "We have to decide what to do with him. He has to be ready for what happens after Drauer's gone. He'll be one of the most powerful people in the nation. Is he ready for that?"

The answer was so obvious that everyone assumed the question was rhetorical.

"He isn't ready now, and he won't be ready for that when the time comes, either" Adept Birch continued. "Not with the way the prophecies are progressing. There's a lot we can do to build the character he'll need to lead us into whatever comes after Drauer, but that's a long process. We need a stopgap."

Adept Sternhaven's eyes flashed with a dark light that made Lloyd recoil. "If I had the right team, we could take care of it. We could make sure he said and did the right thing, every time, every place, from now until the end of time."

"No!" Adept Birch barked. "No possession! That won't shape him into the person we'll need him to be." He paused. "And it's unreliable beyond a few moments, anyway. Maintaining control is too difficult, even for a highly skilled group."

Adept Sternhaven frowned, pulling the skin on her cheeks so taut it seemed on the verge of tearing apart. She drummed her fingers on the polished table, and the thick wood absorbed most of the sound. "We need another way to control him."

"'Control' is not the word I'd choose," Adept Birch said. "I prefer 'guide.'"

"I am disappointed," the Grand Adept said, and all conversation stopped. Everyone looked at Malvoin Serl and waited patiently.

"Everything will be provided," Grand Adept Serl said. "We did not know how to find this chosen one, and then the way was made clear. Now, we do not know how this boy will become a leader— but as we move forward, the way will be made clear."

"Yes, Grand Adept," Adept Birch said. "But I do not think it's unwarranted for us to take action where it might be needed. To help the Creator where we can."

Everyone in the room waited.

The Grand Adept slowly smiled. It did not make him look either happy or amused.

"High Adept Birch," Grand Adept Serl said. "Have you ever given any thought to how it is that Hampton Cathedral still exists? That it remains in our hands? We live in the shadow of the largest city in the USNA. A considerable military force, which greatly outnumbers our clergy, is pointed at us daily. Yet they have not conquered us. They have not even tried. Have you pondered why that is?"

"Of course."

"And what answers have you come up with?"

"That while the conquest of the Island would be a winnable battle for Drauer, it would be costly. There is not enough benefit to removing us from our place—not enough to justify the cost."

"Not enough to justify the cost? His greatest enemy sits at his doorstep, and he allows it! Even after the collapse of the tower, which he cannot help but blame on us, he does nothing! In Central America he has taken town after town, regardless of the cost, even if they offered him nothing more than a few acres of dust and scorpions! So why does he withhold his wrath from us?"

No one replied to the question.

"Because the Creator wills it," Grand Adept Serl said, leaning forward over the table. "We are people of faith, and we are people who must be aware that every day we live on this Island is a miracle. When we have that proof before us, we should not be so worried about trying to force the Creator's hand in one direction or another. He will take care of us."

Grand Adept Serl leaned back, and Lloyd thought he saw a pained expression pass his face. Perhaps, with all that had been going on, the Grand Adept had neglected his daily physical treatments.

"The Grand Adept has spoken wisely, as usual," Adept Birch said in a humble voice. "Forgive me for my doubt. Perhaps, though, we may discuss the best uses of the chosen one's time while he is with us. I believe there are a few holes in his religious education."

Grand Adept Serl nodded. "The Creator will mold him as He sees fit, but that does not mean we cannot show the boy a few things that we know to be good. Things the acolytes learn."

"Courtney needs guidance—a *lot* of guidance," Lloyd said abruptly, then wondered if he was supposed to wait to be called on. "I think, though, that he might benefit from something other than the customary training and teaching that acolytes receive."

High Adept Sternhaven's eyes narrowed. "How do you mean?"

Lloyd carefully picked his way through a minefield of words. "There are certain techniques that High Adept Sternhaven employs that are very … effective at promoting learning in the acolytes. Courtney, however, does not have the talent and does not have the same motivation that most acolytes have. I'm afraid that some of High Adept Sternhaven's usual methods might not do much for Courtney." He swallowed. "I'm not criticizing the way she does her job. I'm just saying Courtney might need something different."

He looked around the room. The expression on High Adept Sternhaven's face told him that this might have been a meeting where he was not supposed to talk.

But High Adept Birch wore a much milder expression, and he spoke first.

"I forget how much time you've spent with Whit—with Courtney," he said. "And you're the one who found him for us in the first place. What do you think he needs?"

"Confidence," Lloyd replied. "He still has trouble believing he's this person we say he is. And even when he thinks there might be something to this whole prophecy business, he doesn't understand why *he*, of all people, should be singled out for this job."

"Okay," Adept Birch said, while Adept Sternhaven's lips and cheeks puckered inward. "Then one thing we need to teach him is what makes a good leader, and through that effort show him his own good qualities. Any traits you believe we could develop?"

Lloyd thought about Courtney's good traits. He thought about what might make Courtney a good leader. And he couldn't come up with a good response.

Adept Sternhaven noticed the silence. "What, exactly, is he supposed to be confident about, then?" she sneered.

Then Lloyd had it. "He wants to be liked."

"Is that a trait of a good leader?" Adept Sternhaven said, her voice gathering steam. "Someone who leads to fulfill their own vanity? Sounds like the man we're trying to get rid of, not the man we're trying to build as a replacement."

One look from the Grand Adept silenced Adept Sternhaven and gave Lloyd all the confidence he needed to speak.

"It's what he needs," Lloyd said. "If he thinks we like him—and we have to really like him for who he is, not just because he's the guy in the prophecy—he'll grow into his role more. He'll be more ready to learn."

"That should build some trust with him." Adept Birch said. "He'll be more likely to trust what we say and follow our guidance." He nodded approvingly. "That's exactly what we need."

Lloyd felt a fluttering in his chest, a vague nervousness. He felt like he'd somehow betrayed Courtney. "I'm not just saying this is a way to get him to do what we want," he said. "It's just ... something that could help him."

"We do not need to make him do what we want," Grand Adept Serl said. "He will do that anyway, because he is a tool in the

Creator's hand. But what you suggest is in harmony with the Creator's teachings of showing love and respect to all creatures. Well done."

Lloyd beamed, and High Adept Birch smiled gently at him. Adept Sternhaven had stopped trying to inhale her own face and had her composure back, already resigned to a plan she clearly had no liking for. "And how do you propose we all go about ... *liking* the boy?" she asked.

One minute, Aron thought he had been given an important assignment. Sure, Lloyd went to some high-level strategy meeting, but Aron was the one entrusted to stay with Courtney, the chosen one, the tool of the prophecy. That was a pretty important job too, right?

The next minute, he decided that the high adepts saw him as little more than a babysitter with PK talent, and that this assignment was a sure sign that his career within the church had permanently stalled.

Going back and forth on the matter grew increasingly annoying as the minutes passed, but it was still more fun than talking to Whitaker. Whitaker seemed full of questions today, though, and as long as Aron was in the same room with him, conversation seemed inevitable.

"There were six of them at the beginning?"

"Yeah."

"And they were the first PKs ever?"

"No. They were just the first to get away from the testing facility. They were the first we knew about."

"And they were the best?"

Aron shrugged. "I guess, maybe. I mean, it's tough to say. They were the best of their time, and Drauer's clearly one of the best of all time. Plus he kind of got a head start developing his stuff, so he's always a few steps ahead of anyone else. But how can you compare Rachel Kallenbach with someone today? She's been dead for forty years, and she didn't do any spells for the last thirty years of her life. We've learned a lot in those seventy years."

Whitaker stood up. He paced around the room, his head restlessly twisting back and forth, looking for anything in the room that might absorb his attention for a few minutes. But the walls were bare, the weather outside was drab, and Aron hadn't bothered putting any illusions in the room for days. There was a wide selection of church-related literature, but Whitaker didn't seem interested in any of that. *Why read,* Aron thought bitterly, *when you can interrogate?*

Whitaker sat back down on Lloyd's bed, bounced his right foot off the floor three times, then resumed his questions.

"What happened to them?"

"Anderson Drauer became ..."

"Okay, see, I know what happened to *him.*"

"Harriman Ellis ..."

"I know him too!"

Aron was surprised at the vehemence in his voice. There had been nothing at all urgent about Whitaker when he met him a bare few days ago. Now, he was impatient with Aron for not teaching him fast enough.

Aron didn't like it. Personality shifts made him nervous.

"Kale Faltergast is still out there. A lot of people think he's on the Island, others say he's been on the front lines in Latin America the whole time the USNA's been pushing through there. A few adepts think he might have been involved in the whole Antigua thing."

"Antigua? That fire thing, right? Where the church got back the cathedral?"

Another surprise. Aron had been deliberately vague about Antigua, certain that Whitaker wouldn't know about it and Aron could score some cheap superiority points. But it seemed Whitaker had been studying in his time in Hampton.

"Three of them are dead. The Premier Adept passed on a little over twenty years ago. Rachel Kallenbach died of a heart attack in Idaho in '83. Armando Diaz was killed in Austin in '03."

"Killed?" Whitaker's leg started bouncing faster, and a loose piece of linoleum on the floor creaked. "Who could kill one of those six guys?"

Aron grimaced. Whitaker may have been doing some homework, but still had plenty to learn. "Another one of those six guys."

"You mean ... one of the Six killed Diaz? Boiling blood, which one?"

Which one. Aron shook his head several times, to make sure Whitaker saw him doing it. "Which do you think? Drauer, of course."

"Why?"

"It's a long story."

"Sum it up."

"No."

Whitaker's arms fluttered into the air, then dropped, like he was trying to lift himself off the bed through flight. "Why? Why not?"

"The whole *reason* someone says something is a long story is because you can't do it justice by summing it up. You lose the whole essence. It's a long story, it's *staying* a long story."

The sullen expression that Aron knew so well returned to Whitaker's face. Good, he thought. Order has returned to the universe.

There may have been a retort somewhere in Whitaker's throat, but he swallowed it. "What about the sixth one. Who's the sixth one, anyway?"

"Who's the sixth one? Deegan Frau, dammit!"

Whitaker's face was blank.

Aron tried again. "The Frau Foundation?"

"I've never ... wait. Wait. Did they give us some food once?"

"How in hell do I know if they gave you something or not?"

"I think they did. I think they brought by some boxes once. Mom was having trouble finding a job. Like everyone else on the Island. So they brought us some stuff. I think it was the Frau Foundation."

"Your mother is single, right?"

"Yeah," Whitaker said, traces of defensiveness coloring his tone.

"Could've been the Frau Foundation. They do lots of stuff for women, single women, poor women, whatever women need help. That sort of thing."

"And this Frau person is dead?"

"We think so. No one's heard from her in a while. She kind of pulled back and pulled back and pulled back from running things and eventually just faded out of life. Out of public life, I mean. There's been no official announcement, but the only PKs that stay alive for a really long time are the ones with the drive to live, like Drauer and Faltergast. Most people figure Frau lost her drive, so she left the foundation and probably died soon after. The foundation just never got around to telling everyone about it."

"So Drauer's one of the last two?"

"Yes," Aron said, hoping his tone showed enough impatience with the obvious question.

"And I'm supposed to kill him?"

That question wasn't so obvious. Aron had to remove the contempt from his face before he answered.

"I don't really know if you have to *kill* him. You just have to make him ... *fall*. That could mean a lot of things. Just getting him out of power could do it. That would be an 'end,' like the prophecy says."

"I guess. But would he ... do you think, if he was still alive, Drauer would ever let go of his power? Any of it?"

"No."

"So I have to kill him." Whitaker said it one more time, apparently hoping repetition would make the concept more sensible. "I have to kill him."

Since Aron couldn't figure out a way to disagree without contradicting the prophecies of Ellis, he remained silent.

"But you guys want to help," Whitaker said, thinking aloud now. "That's why you brought me here. I mean, if it's a prophecy, it's going to happen no matter what, right? So you could just leave me alone, let me do my thing, and I'd do it. But you guys want to help. You want to be a part of it. So you brought me in here, and you're all going to work with me. You're going to help, right?"

Aron didn't want to follow Whitaker into the USNA. He didn't want to follow Whitaker down the hall. He'd like Whitaker to leave him alone for a long while.

But he, like every other adept in the entire church, wanted Drauer gone.

"Yeah. If you're taking him down, I want to help."

Whitaker nodded, and slowly, slowly, various muscles in his head and neck unclenched. Aron had not meant his remark to be personally supportive of Whitaker in any form, but Whitaker seemed to take it that way regardless.

Interlude: On Friendship

I liked them all. I still like them all. We had our conflicts over time, even severe disagreements, but they were the five most important people of my youth, and we all know what kind of an impact friends at that age have on the rest of our lives. Even though my years have been somewhat extended beyond that which is normal, the impact of my friends remains undiluted.

Harry and I had the longest running disagreement, but I firmly believe it was civil. Even when my government was forced to move against his increasingly belligerent church, we kept the channels of communication open. When he left my territory, he did it voluntarily. I'm not saying every member of his church left under their own volition, but he did. He believed his church could thrive more if he got it established in some areas away from the influence of my nation, so that's where he went. He set up his little earthly paradise on Bermuda. I certainly can understand that decision.

He had his reasons for leaving. Some of those are tied to other disagreements we had, disagreements about the most profitable ways to use the talents we had and about how to lead the people who were subject to us (which reminds me of a particular disagreement right there—Harry would never use the word "subject" in connection with his church members).

I don't mean to minimize the differences between the two of us—they were, in fact, profound—but we managed to stay in touch, to keep talking, and our relationship remained continually cordial. More than that—it was friendly. So I was truly sad when he passed, especially since, as powerful as he was, his death was unnecessary. He could easily have extended his life to the present day, but that was another matter on which we did not quite see eye to eye.

I always harbored a deep affection for Rachel, but she cut all of us off. It was the life she designed for herself, it was her choice, and of course I had to respect that. Still, even though she was isolated, she let us visit if we wanted, as long as we promised not to use the talent in her presence (which, for someone who uses it as constantly as I do, is quite a challenge). I managed to visit her a few times in Idaho, and I was always pleased when I did.

Kale Faltergast remains my friend to this day. As with Harry, we have substantial differences of opinion on several matters, but that's one of the things that keeps our relationship interesting after all these decades. The quality of the debates is just outstanding.

I have tremendous respect for Kale, and have little tolerance for those who describe him as aimless. An aimless person and someone whose goals are not simple or easily understood are two very different things. He is brilliant and vastly talented, and the day I finally convince him to join me in the USNA will be a great one for our nation.

I don't believe I need to expand on my respect for Deegan, as it's a matter of public record. Many public records. I'm very proud of the USNA's continued support of the Frau Foundation, and I believe that organization stands as a lasting testament of the good someone with the talent can accomplish in the world.

And that just leaves Armando, the closest friend I've ever had. The USNA in its present form, or possibly in *any* form, would not exist without him. Even if he had not had a trace of the talent in him, he would have been an incredibly valuable asset to my government.

The course of his life in his last years upset me more than practically anything has in my lifetime. I hope you'll understand if it is not something I wish to dwell on at any length.

His death was a terrible tragedy. Of course there was nothing I could do to stop it. There are things that are beyond even me.

Part Four: Collaborator

Chapter Nineteen

If he wanted to, Kale could make each stomp of his foot echo and resonate like a thunderclap. The whole neighborhood would feel his wrath.

Except it wasn't really wrath—it was just irritation. And making the neighborhood shake with irritation didn't seem fair.

So he settled for making the hallway of his home shake as he walked up and down the hallway. Each time he passed in front of the door to the surveillance room, he stopped and asked Spree a question, being sure to use his curt voice. Each time, she rolled her eyes at his tone, apparently thinking that might somehow calm him down.

"What's Amelia doing?"

Spree's eyebrows were pink today, and the reflected light from the room's many monitors made them glow as she arched one of them.

"Talking at Mira's people. She on a boat on the Sound right now."

"How come she got that job instead of me?"

"Mira don't no hate her."

Kale harrumphed and stomped back down the hall to the kitchen. He looked around the small room and thought about removing the thin coat of grease from the side of the refrigerator. Then he decided he'd rather not and he stomped down the hallway.

"When is Nilda going to report?"

"Tonight, same always. Get to us earlier if something urgent comes. Which hasn't no happened yet."

"Right." And off he stomped again.

He went into his bedroom this time. Maybe he could slip into Nilda's head for a while, monitor what was going on in the acolyte dorms. Though she was miles away, which made the contact a little tricky. Still, he'd done that nearly every day during her first week on the job, then with decreasing frequency as the next two weeks progressed. Watching her wipe down the cinder block walls with a sponge couldn't hold his attention for long, and the acolytes in the dorm had not yet provided much useful information.

He went back down the hall to Spree. "I'm going downtown."

"Hampton?"

"Manhattan."

For perhaps the first time in the day, Spree looked directly at Kale. "Boredom not no reason to go get killed."

"It's not boredom. I've just been putting it off for too long."

He was out the door within five minutes and on his two-wheeled scooter, heading west. When PKs, whether they were chumchas or NArds, were trained in scooter propulsion, they were shown a detailed chart about how reaction time in a crash decreased the faster you went, to make it clear that if you wanted to push the scooter to high speed you'd better have the talent to make a spell that would catch yourself before you reached the ground. Most CMC adepts didn't like to travel faster than 30 mph on the scooters. USNA troops, especially in Latin America, were known to get them up to 50 mph.

Kale was breezing along at 75, and he still had enough concentration to cloak his mind and his physical appearance. And he was only keeping it to 75 because he was bumping over the rocks of the borderlands—on a well-maintained, paved surface he could go 100.

He knew he shouldn't enjoy going into the USNA so much. He shouldn't take so much pleasure in practically walking past the supposed best border security in the world. If he had too much fun, inevitably he'd get lazy, and that was when he'd get into trouble. So this time, he wasn't going to enjoy it. He'd choose the most isolated entry point he knew, he'd put together three more spells than he needed, and he would do absolutely nothing to call attention to himself.

His image was completely removed from existence. The photons that should be bouncing off him passed straight through (a difficult operation—it took most PKs at least half a decade to keep light particles from bouncing off their ribs). His thoughts left no trace. The sound waves of his wheels over the ground, of the air parting to allow him through, of his breathing, were all dampened, completely muffled practically before they formed. There were very few people in the world who would be able to detect any trace of his existence, and none of them were stationed on the wall at the east end of Queens.

Half of a mile away from the wall he turned south, running roughly parallel to it. The skyline of Belmont shrank, first giving way to five- and six-story buildings then disappearing entirely behind the fifteen-meter-tall wall. Then the control tower of Drauer Airport came into view, but no planes. The USNA had trouble finding pilots willing to fly near CMC territory even before Antigua, and the situation had only gotten worse.

He continued south, bumping over the flattened foundations of what had once been several blocks of identical apartment buildings. When the wall went up, the USNA had left the buildings abandoned, but then sent a demolition PK squad to obliterate them once too many border rat squatters took up residence inside.

Then he was outside Far Rockaway. The wall was just as high here, the contingent of guards just as thick. But they were the only people in the area. After Standish Fiske's rebellion of '81 and the subsequent USNA crackdown, the entire peninsula was deserted. Some people said it was cursed, some said it was haunted, but most said it was too isolated, too desolated to be worth recovering.

There were no doors in the wall near Far Rockaway. But the wall only proceeded 100 meters out into the ocean, and Kale knew at least three different ways to get around it, though each came with its own problems. Making a thick coat of ice was probably the easiest, but on a warm day in the bright sunshine it would be far too noticeable. He could ride through the water, making sure only air molecules and no water entered his lungs, but disguising the ripples of his passage was difficult even for him.

That left the option of making the water into a road. There were plenty of tricks to it—hardening the water made in unnaturally smooth, almost as visible as ice, so he'd have to do it one small segment at a time. And water was always shifting, so the piece he'd just made solid may move while he was on it, and one of his wheels would be on actual water, and he'd go down with a sizeable splash.

But it was the best way—assuming he was on two legs instead of four wheels. He'd have to leave the scooter. He altered the air around it so it would stay out of view of the guards on the wall for a good six hours, then continued on his way. He walked to the ocean and stepped onto the blue. His mind was filled with water, with air bubbles, the algae, the swishing flow beneath him, and his concealment spells slipped into the background. They shouldn't be there. They were too complex. He should be picking the air, looking for tendrils of thoughts that may be looking for him, he should be looking at his feet, making sure the light was still going through his metatarsals, but he could only think about water as he walked to the end of the wall.

He was sweating. Radiating heat. The temperature shield around him would keep that concealed, but it was another worry. Hadn't he been telling himself how easy this was when he was crossing the wasteland?

He was around the end and into the USNA. That made him feel a little better, since the guards usually paid closer attention to the opposite side of the wall. And the water on this side felt smoother to begin with, more sheltered from the wind. The worst was over.

Until the cutter passed behind him. He didn't hear it—shield spells often work both ways. He didn't know it had passed until the wake hit him, pushed his solid platform out from under him, and he tilted right.

He tried to catch himself, but he was used to bracing himself with solid ground. He couldn't firm the water's surface in time, and his air support broke over the water just ahead of his body.

The splash wasn't large but it was a splash and it was noticeable. He froze, mostly submerged, as the water around him settled. His eyes and mind fixed on the nearest guard station, waiting for others' eyes and minds to find him.

Nothing came. Ocean water mixed with his sweat and ran down his face.

When he didn't sense any probe coming after him, he waited for a white cap to pull even with him, then he pushed off the sand with his legs, riding in the trough of the wave, using it to help keep him hidden. He reached the break wall and heaved himself up. He did not allow himself to stand still for even a fraction of a second, not wanting the water dripping off him to puddle and leave a trace of him behind. He stayed near the wall until he was clear of the sand, then walked west on the weed-covered ground.

He would have to cover a half-mile before he got to the scooter he kept hidden in one of the many abandoned buildings of Far Rockaway. Once he was on the scooter, he'd head for the train station. The A train hadn't run on the Rockaway branch for thirty years, but the bridge across the bay was still in good shape—at least, good enough for a man on a scooter. The sun was bright, the water sparkling, and Kale was in territory where, if he was detected, hundreds if not thousands of people would try to kill him. It was a wonderful day. The train tracks were bumpy, but that had no impact on his mood.

The train bridge would take him into Queens, where he'd have to be a little more careful. Traffic in the city was never easy to navigate, but it was especially dangerous when you were invisible. His progress would be slow until he crossed the 59th Street Bridge, then be even slower in Manhattan. But he'd get where he wanted to go, and hopefully he'd be dry when he got there.

Chapter Twenty

It didn't seem right that they should be doing normal studies. After the collapse of the tower, all the press coverage, the meeting with Grand Adept Serl and two high adepts, Lloyd didn't think life should just return to banal normalcy so quickly. But here he was, back in his room, staring at his books while his right eyelid slowly dragged downward, trying to pull its twin to the left down with it.

At least one thing had changed—the good-natured moments that used to be more common with Aron had disappeared. Now everything was either resentful silence or resentful argument. Their room had remained undecorated for days, white-painted cinderblocks with their single black-framed window, because Aron and Lloyd couldn't agree on a decorating plan. Actually, that was not strictly true—they'd been too busy arguing about other things to even talk about decorating their room.

Aron had been silent for most of the evening, pretending to study at his desk, though he hadn't turned a page of his text for hours. He was fuming about something, and Lloyd was pretty sure he'd hear about it before the evening was over. Aron was just waiting for a trigger. Since Lloyd was determined not to give him one, the night had been silent.

As it turned out, he didn't need to speak. All he needed to do was shut his textbook, stretch, and stand up.

"Getting ready for bed?" Aron asked. His tone was ice.

There was a trap there, Lloyd was sure, but since he had no idea what it was, he couldn't figure out how to avoid it. "Yes," he said.

Aron feigned surprise. "No high-level councils? No secret assignments from a high adept? How disappointing for you."

"Aron ..."

"I'm just noticing, is all. Wondering if it's tough to come back down to earth with the commoners."

"Boiling blood, Aron, stop being a child," Lloyd said, and instantly regretted it. Aron now had all the ammunition he'd need for a prolonged harangue.

"A child? That's what I am? Well, I suppose it makes sense— only someone of maturity could handle the important jobs around here, while us children can file papers and maybe push a broom on occasion. Never mind if we've been trained like you have. Never mind any skills we have. We're children. You're an adult. Of course. It all makes sense now."

Lloyd lay down on his bunk. He knew he shouldn't do it, but he didn't care—he didn't think Aron could get any madder. He sealed his ears.

Aron noticed it right away. His face reddened. Lloyd was sure Aron was screaming, but no sound made it to his eardrum. Aron was almost dancing in place as his rage shook him, but Lloyd couldn't hear his voice, couldn't hear his footfalls, couldn't hear the sound of Aron's palms slapping on the desktop. It was bliss.

Aron took a step toward Lloyd's bunk, arms outstretched. Go ahead, Lloyd thought. Grab my shoulders. Shake me. The penalty for any sort of attack by one adept on another would guarantee Lloyd a peaceful night.

No contact was made. Aron's head turned to the left and he took a step back. His arms dropped to his side.

For an instant, Lloyd thought Aron had finally started listening to the better demons of his nature. But then he saw the expression on Aron's face, and he knew what was going on. He dropped the shield from his ears and quickly sat up.

"... when other people in the hall are trying to study! You've got problems, work them out! Quietly! You are adepts of the Creator and you must act like it, at all times! Do you both understand?" It was Adept Benzell, the dorm supervisor. He, along with anyone else within a mile of the cathedral, had heard Aron's tirade.

"Sorry, Adept," Aron and Lloyd said together.

Adept Benzell took a deep breath, his brown skin losing its reddish flush. Lloyd thought he could see the grey of his temples actively spreading through his hair.

"Now. The reason I'm here isn't to tell you to shut up, though that quickened my pace on the way to see you. I'm here to let you know there's been a change in assignment. For both of you."

Lloyd and Aron exchanged glances and Lloyd was surprised to discover that, despite everything, he hoped their new assignments would keep them working together.

"What's the assignment?" Lloyd asked.

"You'll report to High Adept Kroll. He has a strict schedule for you, starting at 6 AM. Please report to him promptly. His schedule will completely supersede your current duties."

"What's he going to have us do?" Aron asked.

"You'll see the schedule tomorrow. Any more questions, ask High Adept Kroll in the morning. Six AM, remember."

"Yes, Adept," Aron and Lloyd said together. Then Adept Benzell left.

Lloyd and Aron stood awkwardly with each other for a few minutes.

"What do you think is going on?" Aron said finally.

"I don't know."

Aron gave him a sideways look. "Really."

"Really."

Aron looked back at the door, as if replaying Adept Benzell's brief visit. "Okay," he said, and Lloyd didn't know if that meant that everything was okay, or if the change in assignment was okay, or if Aron was just saying the word to have something to say. Whatever it meant, it was much better than most of the other things Aron had been saying, so Lloyd went with it.

"Okay," Lloyd said.

"I watched! Spree got the USNA feed, and I watched, and I never saw *anything*! How the hell?"

Kale leaned back, probably enjoying Amelia's puzzlement too much. "Do you think I can just explain it?"

"Could you?"

Kale paused. Actually, to a certain degree, he could. But he didn't feel like it. "No, not really."

Spree, at her usual station in front of the monitors, shook her head. "He won't no tell you nothing," she said. "Keep his mojo all mysterious."

"Fine. *Fine.* Don't tell me how. But at least tell me *where.* How do you get past that wall?"

Kale glanced at the wall of screens, which flicked back and forth between over a hundred images of night. "God, Spree, narrow it down a little, will you? I'm getting a headache."

"Not my fault slow eyes can't no keep up. Why not use some mojo?"

Kale just took a step backward, moving the screens out of his direct line of vision. "Fine. Now, I'd love to tell you how I got in, but that's not important right now. The thing is, I got in, and I found the guy, Cain. He didn't say anything, of course, but he's dying to. *Dying* to. So it was all over his brain, and in the studio he didn't think to use blockers. Plucked it right out of him."

All of this was coming at Amelia too fast. She needed to ground herself, but instead Kale kept throwing out whopper after whopper. "You got inside ColumbiaCast studios? How in the *hell* ..."

She watched as Spree and Kale exchanged a private, extremely annoying smirk, then realized what she was asking. How much of a challenge would a netcast studio provide to someone who snuck past one of the most tightly controlled borders in the hemisphere?

"Fine. Never mind. What did Cain know?"

"He knew it was the CMC that brought the tower down. Administration source leaked it to him—on deep background, of course. The source told him that Drauer himself identified the source behind the collapse. He couldn't pin it on an individual, but there was a 'definite CMC character' to it, to use the exact words of Cain's source."

"Group, then," Spree said.

"Would have to be," Kale said, nodding. "Not too many people could do that solo." He puffed out his chest. "Present company excepted, of course."

Spree rolled her eyes, but Amelia seemed ready to believe him. He didn't want her thinking too much about what he could or could not do, though. They'd gotten close to that conversation before, and he had seen the calculating look enter her face, the one he'd seen in so many others before. The expression that wondered just how she could take advantage of all the things he could do.

"So this wasn't a miracle," Kale said. "This was the CMC."

"Huh," Spree grunted. "Damn CMC doin' something 'gainst the NArds *is* a spewin' miracle. Off their asses at last."

"That's what Cain thinks, at least," Kale said. "And there's going to be more. This was impressive, they got some net coverage and all, but alone it's nothing. Plus, they're not taking any credit for it, so it's less than nothing. They've got something else planned. My guess is, the collapse was something to rally the troops for whatever comes next."

"And what's next is ..." Spree asked.

"Beats me. Get on a boat and join the effort in Antigua? Take down more than one tower the next time? Mass cult suicide followed by hauntings that drive Drauer crazy? Haven't got a clue."

The subject was interesting enough to make Kale want to think about it more, but Amelia clearly had her mind stuck on something else.

"Did you go over the wall?" she asked. "Did you climb it?"

"Boiling blood, Amelia, focus! That's not important!"

"But I watched! I scanned the whole wall, I didn't see you leave a trace! Where did you go in?"

"You didn't watch carefully enough," Kale snapped. "You didn't see the splash. That would've told you everything."

Spree's eyes danced. "Splash?"

"It's not important."

"Fell in the water?"

"I said it's not important!"

"What happened? Little fishie get you?"

"The wake of a boat, all right? Tough to hear through a shield. And if you could stand on water for even a *second*, maybe you could mock me about it. But like I said, it doesn't matter."

"Poor Kale. All wet. Lucky today pretty warm."

"Yeah, yeah, lucky. Are we done with this now?"

Something clicked with Amelia, though, and she suddenly sat up straighter. "Far Rockaway," she said. "You went around the wall at Far Rockaway. Just skated around the edge."

"Bravo," Kale said with more sarcasm than he probably needed.

"God, it's so obvious! It's the perfect place! You just have to get past the guards, and then there's nothing! No hyped-up academy students, no paranoid faculty, no damned defense consultants, nobody! The next time you run into people, you're in the middle of Queens, and they're not looking for intruders. It's the perfect place!"

The room was suddenly, oddly quiet. The monitors occasionally made a slight click as they switched from image to image, but that was the only sound.

Finally, Amelia looked up. Spree was staring at Kale. Kale was staring into space. Their mouths were slightly open, but no words were coming out.

"What?" she asked. "What?"

"They wouldn't," Kale said.

"Might," Spree answered. "Got Antigua."

"Not the whole city."

"Got part. All they want here."

"It would be perfect," Kale admitted.

"It's it. They're doing it," Spree said.

"I don't know. After years of *nothing*—it's so *much*."

"Got prophecy. Got God pushing them. Got faith to do it, now."

"Fall of the tower did that, yeah."

"They going," Spree said.

"I don't know. Maybe. Doesn't seem like them, though. They don't seem *ready*."

"They going."

"We have to confirm it somehow. I can't just guess about something like this."

"They *going*." Spree's voice was more insistent than Amelia had ever heard it.

"Where?" Amelia finally asked. "What are you talking about? Who is doing what?"

"Chumchas. Into Far Rockaway."

"*What* in Far Rockaway?"

"Invade," Spree said. "Take it back."

"What? How do you know?"

"We don't," Kale said. "She—okay, we—are just guessing. But it makes sense. They want to make a statement. They want to take something away from the NArds. Far Rockaway would be the best place to go."

"To invade?"

"Yeah. Maybe." Kale considered. "It makes sense."

"So what do we do?"

Spree looked like she had about a hundred ideas that she was going to rattle off all at once, but Kale spoke first.

"We get confirmation."

Chapter Twenty-one

"Good night, then"

"Yeah," the desk clerk said without looking up, He may have scanned her—he was supposed to—or he may have just ignored her. Nilda had barely started her job cleaning the dorms, but as soon as she put on the uniform—dust-grey coveralls—she became practically invisible to everyone she saw. She thought she might be able to attract more notice if she cleaned the halls naked, but even then the sight of a cloth in one hand and a spray bottle in the other might cause the acolytes to look past her.

To be on the safe side, she kept a particularly annoying soap commercial running through her head ("Perk perk perk your head/Dirt dirt dirt is dead"). If the acolyte had scanned her, his head would be infected with the jingle, too, and he wouldn't get anything else. Hopefully.

She kept the jingle going as she walked away from the cathedral, occasionally switching to the conversation intro of "Leader of the Pack." She forced herself to keep her thoughts drowned for an entire mile, then finally decided she could stop forcing the annoying jingle to stay uppermost in her mind. Trying not to think about it took another mile, bringing her close to home.

She practically ran the rest of the way. Now that she could finally focus on what she'd heard during the day, her excitement grew. When Kale had come up with the idea of placing her in the cathedral, she hadn't been sure it would ever bear fruit, so she was all the more surprised to have something to tell so soon.

She walked briskly to her door, entered her home and went right to the phone. She had Spree's face in front of her within seconds.

"Hands okay?" Spree asked. "Keep those gloves on or skin won't no stay on. Cleaners flake it off, leave you nothing but bone."

"Thanks," Nilda said. "I'm wearing the gloves. Hey, is Kale around?"

Spree raised an eyebrow, an effect that was always accentuated by the creases that appeared in the hairless skin on her scalp. "Big news? Straight to the top?"

"Well, I want you to hear it too, of course, but I thought …"

Spree waved her off. "Don't no need to watch my feelings, kay? Know who the bossman is since I started here. Just wait."

She slid off the right side of the screen and Nilda heard her calling for Kale. In a moment, the two of them crowded onto the same screen, meaning all Nilda could see was a half face of each.

"How's work?" Kale asked.

"They're drilling," Nilda said, practically bursting.

Kale smiled sideways. "No small talk today, huh?" Kale asked.

"No, no, sorry, um, it's fine, fine. Boring as hell, but fine, okay? But they're drilling."

"Who's drilling? For what?"

"The acolytes and adepts," Nilda said. "Their schedule changed. They've been talking about it all day."

She'd said the right thing, she could tell. She had their attention now, their foreheads almost pressing together as they leaned in toward their screen.

"What did they say? What kind of changes?" Kale asked.

"No classes. At least, none of the sit-down kind of classes. They've been awake earlier, out of their halls later. I haven't seen anyone studying anything in the dorm—when they're there, they just collapse. And they keep talking about drilling. They're wondering why they're doing it, and one of them said 'Since when did we join the army.' If I didn't know better, it would seem like they suddenly switched from priests-in-training to soldiers in boot camp."

Spree remained close to the screen while Kale sat backward, moving back until he was slumping so far in his chair he was almost lying down.

"Boot camp," Spree said. "Hot damn on a cold roof. Boot camp. You hearin' old man? You hearin'? Confirmation enough?"

"It's a start," he said. He let out a long breath through pursed lips.

"What are you talking about, Spree?" Nilda asked. "Confirmation of what?"

"Theory we had," Spree said.

"Best that you don't know it," Kale cut in. "There's some things we shouldn't put in your brain right now—too risky. We can't have anyone in the CMC knowing what we're thinking."

"Okay." Nilda said, disappointed. Just because she understood Kale's caution didn't mean she wasn't curious about what was happening. "That's everything I have for now."

Kale nodded distractedly. "All right. This is good." He shook his head, then focused more on the camera in front of him. "What am I saying? Nilda, you've exceeded my expectations. This is helpful. I'm not sure exactly what it means, but it's helpful."

She smiled. "Thanks."

"Get some rest. Or do something fun with your time off. We'll be in touch."

"Good night," she said and disconnected the call.

She stood up and walked a few circuits around her small room. She felt like she should be celebrating, commemorating a job well done, but she didn't know how she'd celebrate, and she wasn't even sure why. She was pretty sure what she'd done hadn't helped the CMC. She didn't think she'd helped the USNA. So what had she done?

She'd helped the man who saved her from the borderlands. That would have to be enough.

"Only question is when," Spree said.

"No, it's not," Kale insisted. "Okay, it's *one* question, but not the *only* one. How are they going to go in? How are they going to hold it? Do they think taking Far Rockaway, this little wasted corner of Drauer's empire, is going to change anything? There's lots of questions."

"We don't no have to figure none of them out before we figure when, though. 'When' is the big one."

"There's another big one," Amelia said. Kale had called her in as soon as he was done talking to Nilda. "What are we going to do about it?"

Spree's eyes widened. "What we going to do? Ain't no choice. We help them! They go into Far Rockaway, we help!" She looked back and forth between Kale and Amelia, clearly waiting for one or both of them to agree with her.

Kale tried to keep his expression neutral, but he may have winced at Spree's enthusiasm. "If ..." he started, then stopped, trying to order his words correctly. "It depends on why they're doing it. Sort of. We don't just want to go running after them on a fool's errand."

"Why they doing it?" Spree exploded. "They CMC! They hate USNA! They goin' in to take a little USNA back! That's the why! What more you want? They go against the NArds, we go with them!"

Kale shifted. His face was still blank, but all that did was make his body more expressive. This was why he never played poker. Luckily, he had Amelia to make some of his points for him.

"You're right, Spree," Amelia said. "I'm inclined to help anyone who's putting the hurt on the NArds. That's my gut reaction. But then I have to remember—these are the chumchas. How much better are they?"

"*Way* better!" Spree replied immediately. "Ain't no tyrants! Ain't no gulags! Religious nuts, yeah, but not burning *fascists*!"

"That may only be because they never had the chance," Kale said mildly. "Look, I understand the instinct to prefer the CMC. Heaven knows Harry had far more noble goals in starting the thing than Andy ever did. But it's a powerful organization, and power does funny things. Let's say the CMC someday knocks off the USNA. Will they exile NArd officials just like they were exiled? Will they control their clergy as tightly as the USNA controls their people?"

"They already do," Amelia grunted.

"Right. So it's a matter of caution. Getting into a war where one tyrant replaces another isn't always an advisable course of action."

Spree, unlike Kale, was making no effort to hide her emotions. Her eyebrows—one dyed red, the other green—twitched like hyperactive caterpillars. Her upper lip curled in a sneer.

"Got you all tied in knots," she said. "Thinking so hard. But we not living in the then. We living in the *now. Now* there ain't nothing as bad as the NArds. Don't no matter what the chumchas gonna be someday. Matter what they are now, and now they ain't no USNA. They good guys."

She was right. Kale had a clear understanding of the many faults of the CMC, and many theories about how they could end up being at least as repressive as the USNA. But that was all theory. In the reality that was going on in front of him, he didn't have much of a choice. None of his customary excuses for sitting back, waiting, and seeing what was going to happen were going to hold. He wasn't sure what was the best way for him to take action in what was going to happen. He wasn't sure if he would directly help the CMC or remain on the periphery. But whenever the CMC decided to go into Far Rockaway, Kale knew he would be there, too.

Chapter Twenty-two

Spree was victorious and alone. Kale had left to think and plan, and Amelia had gone off to some meeting or another with one of her contacts. She sat with her screens and, since the Island itself did not seem to be in urgent need of monitoring, she flipped from net to net, getting caught up on the condition of the world in brief, three-second bursts. She always made a point to glance at the net ID in the lower right corner of the screen, making sure she knew what biases were filtering the news she heard.

<<ColumbiaCast: Q. ... reason to try something similar in other areas?

A. No, I honestly don't think what happened in Antigua will really serve as much of a deterrent. The first thing you have to understand is the appeal of martyrdom to the religious mind. The possibility of dying for the cause attracts them to action, rather than repels them.>>

<<AlphaNet: ... and a suburban housewife who killed three of her lovers before being caught in a showdown with her husband and a fourth lover ...>>

<<Atmosphere News: Ontario officials report that the anti-USNA demonstration has now attracted over one million people. If true, this number is more than five times the number of CMC worshippers believed to be living in the province. Officials are not certain if their ranks are being swelled by church members from other areas or by unaffiliated citizens gathering to show their support for the church. Either way, the size of the demonstration is unprecedented ...>>

<<BorderNet: The fact that we don't know what's currently happening in Antigua tells us most of what we need to know. The only people who can put the news in such a state of lockdown are PKs, and CMC clergy would have no reason to keep the news from spreading no matter what happened. Either they're still in control

of the area, in which case they'd want the news shouted from the
rooftops, or they've been kicked out in the USNA's typically brutal
fashion, and spreading notice of USNA atrocities serves the church's
ends. So the area must be crawling with USNA adepts, or possibly
controlled by them.>>

<<Rockefeller Media: … are galvanized by reports of strange
sights and sounds near a small home in Southern California. The
home, believed to be the birthplace of Church of the Miraculous
Creator founder Harriman Ellis, has been flooded by visitors since
the sighting was first reported, but USNA officials caution that
pilgrims visiting the site are likely to be disappointed.
[Sabrina McKey, Associate Minister of Public Safety, Western
District]: People are, of course, free to travel where they will, but I
should note that the amount of tourists visiting the so-called Ellis
Home have far exceeded Public Safety standards. Even if something
extraordinary was happening, which still seems doubtful, odds are
new visitors would not be able to see it through the crowd. In
short, you'd be best served by staying home.>>

<<NANet: … and accounts of increased unrest in borderlands can
be generally regarded as spurious rumors or the agitation of a small
number of mostly powerless dissidents.>>

<<FreeNet: Q. Is there really that much of a CMC presence in
Southeast Asia?
A. Yes, there is, and it really shouldn't be that surprising. Similar to
what happened in most parts of the Western Hemisphere, many
Christians in Southeast Asia made the move to the CMC when it
moved on to the world scene, and the church also gained adherents
from Buddhism and even Islam as people sought a religion that put
the new powers loose in the world into some sort of sensible
context. The CMC is a minority religion in the region, but a
minority that has eclipsed the ranks of other sects, including other
Christian denominations.
Q. But are their numbers over there really anything the USNA
needs to be concerned about? After all, they do have the largest
ocean in the world keeping them away.

A. In traditional thought, no, of course not. A few million believers scattered over several countries would not seem to be of any concern to the most powerful nation in the world. But what you have to remember is you have a good-sized church that is free to train their PKs without the ever-present hindrance of the bordering USNA that the CMC deals with on this continent. There's widespread opinion that the ranks of the CMC in Asia are filled with PKs who put their counterparts in the west to shame.

Q. This brings up the inevitable question of a rumored prophecy by CMC founder Harriman Ellis about help rising from the east …

A. Yes, I've heard reports about that one, too. But the CMC is pretty good at keeping a lid on those sorts of writings, only releasing them when they think they can gain some publicity or other advantage. So that rumor, like so many others about the reputed prophecies, cannot be confirmed.>>

And on and on. It was impossible to watch any news program for more than ten minutes without some mention of the CMC coming up, and usually the news talked about the church's "resurgence" or its "newfound aggression."

It was happening, Spree told herself. It was happening right in front of her as she switched from net to net to net. As the minutes went by, she bounced in her chair faster and faster, flicking through netfeeds with one hand while the other scratched her scalp, rubbed her nose, or just flitted in the air. Kale had brought her in from the borderlands four years ago, and for most of that time since then she had generally been content to watch and gather information. But she heard the messages coming from the nets, and she felt the surge they were talking about, and she wanted to throw herself into the wave and be there when whatever was going to happen, happened.

Chapter Twenty-three

The first week was fun. The air of anticipation made the endless days exciting, and playing soldier was a nice change of pace. They branched into whole areas of spells that the church's teachings rarely covered. The basic skills weren't much different, but the applications—to harm instead of help—were brand new. These were abilities most of the acolytes and adepts had already guessed about in late-night discussions in church dormitories, but now they were real and they were openly taught.

Some of this euphoria carried into the second week, as the fun of setting things on fire or launching them dozens of yards into the air didn't immediately disappear. But the physical demands of the training regimen began to take its toll. There was no time for study, no time for individual contemplation, only time to follow a constant stream of orders from the instructors, who had taken on a gruff air quite different from the calm patience normally endorsed by the church. And since much of the day was given to physical training—jogging, weightlifting, climbing, and more—most of the acolytes and adepts found it harder and harder to wake up when the 6 AM alarm rang.

All this combined to drain most of the enjoyment out of the new schedule by the third week. The new spells were now just so much repetition, and the physical exercise was wearying. Meals were silent, with most of the acolytes and adepts scarfing their food down in five minutes then spending the rest of their time staring vacantly ahead or looking for a corner where they could curl up and sleep.

Lloyd didn't have the luxury of sleep, or even of just sitting and staring. Most of his meals came on the run, as he transmitted an unending series of messages between Grand Adept Serl and Amelia from the ILF. He didn't know if someone in the clergy had requested him to act as go-between or if Amelia had requested him, so to cover all bases he decided to hate them all.

What made it worse was that he was meeting with her more often. She had not become friendly by any means, but she also wasn't stonewalling him anymore. He didn't know how it happened, but whatever the church was doing, the ILF was now helping.

It was a grey, windy afternoon. Drizzle fell like slow leak, a drop here and a drop there. It was never hard enough to make Lloyd bother to put up a shield against it, but enough cold drops caught him to make him feel uncomfortable. He wheeled along on his scooter, traveling the mandatory two miles between the cathedral and Amelia Diaz. Grand Adept Serl had been wary about working too closely with the Islip Liberation Front, not willing to sully the church's good name by connecting it to an organization that some claimed supported terrorism. But High Adept Birch had pointed out that the people who thought the ILF were terrorists were not the ones who thought the church had any sort of a good name, so the association was not likely to do the church any real harm.

He found Amelia in a cramped bookstore with no heat. She shivered in the biography section.

"This is the best you could do?" he asked.

"I've got to keep finding new places," she said. "It's not good to let anyone get too familiar with my face."

Lloyd threw his hands in the air. "Haven't you people heard of *phones*? Just stay at your house and *call* the cathedral."

"You don't think I want that?" Amelia hissed. "Serl and whoever is on top of my damn organization just sit in their homes or offices while I'm running all over the Island waiting for you to show up, and you think I prefer it this way? You've seen Serl with his calm demeanor and his 'The Creator will take care of us' manner, but underneath all that he's about the most paranoid person I've ever met, at least when it comes to keeping an eye on the people he says he's serving. Serl doesn't trust the security of any wires that don't both start and end in your compound."

Lloyd had known there was nothing he could do to change the situation as soon as he'd spoken, but it made him feel better to get some of the frustration out. "Okay, okay," he said. "Let's get out of here and walk. Warm up with some movement."

"Fine."

They walked briskly away from the bookstore, passed mostly empty storefronts, most of which had boarded or broken windows. A few scooters and carts rattled across the pitted road, but no one was out on foot.

"All right," she said. "What've you got for me?"

Lloyd took a deep breath, recalling the exact words of High Adept Kroll's message. "Conventional are limited use. Supply surplus instead." All of the messages were like this—fractured language designed to make Lloyd understand as little as possible about the message he was delivering. It was an imperfect system— as the two parties exchanged notes, Lloyd made some pretty good guesses about what a few things meant. Based on what he'd heard, it wasn't too much of a stretch to figure out that "conventional" referred to conventional weapons. Kroll was telling Amelia and the ILF that it didn't matter if they brought guns on the mission, since the NArds were expert at deflecting that sort of thing and making bullets and other projectiles harmless. Instead of guns, the ILF would apparently offer the most help by supplying what the church forces would need. Though what that was, Lloyd couldn't guess.

He looked at Amelia, but she wasn't looking at him. She was staring at the spine of a book, covered in the red buckram of library binding. Her eyes seemed unfocused.

"Are you going to write it down or anything?" Lloyd said, and regretted it as soon as he did.

Amelia's eyes snapped to him. Her mouth raised into the same sneer he had seen on her face when he had met her in the Islip cabin. "Oh, yeah." She said. "I should write it down. Because the first thing you want to do in things like this is create a paper trail."

"Right, right, it was stupid, I know, sorry," Lloyd said. "I just wanted to make sure you had it all."

"All seven words? It'll be tough, but I might be able to stretch my mind to the job."

Lloyd was ready to leave. His job was done, and Amelia didn't seem to want to be with him any longer than necessary. That was fine with him.

Except all that was waiting for him back at the compound was more training. So he pointed at the red book.

"Is that something good?" he asked.

"What?" she asked.

"The book. You were staring at it."

"I was?" She shrugged. "Maybe I was looking toward it." She lightly touched the book's spine. "I've never heard of this."

Lloyd looked at the book, then at Amelia's eyes. She was looking at him, but she still didn't seem too focused.

"Do you want something to eat?"

That got her attention. Her eyes were immediately more alert. "What?"

"You look like you could use something to eat. I could … we could get something to eat."

"Oh my dear Lord," she said.

"What?"

"A date? Are you out of your mind?" Her voice did not rise above a harsh whisper, but Lloyd felt like she was yelling at him. "What the hell is the matter with you?"

"Date? No, no, I'm just saying you're hungry, we've both been going hard, why not have some food while we're out and away?"

"You're an idiot," she said. "You know we can't just sit at a restaurant and talk."

Lloyd smiled. "Give me a little credit," he said. "I've got a better plan than that."

Kale fidgeted. The air all around him was sticky, and he didn't have enough energy to dehumidify the area around his head. If he had put any effort into it, he might have been able to find a better place to sit than the park. Somewhere cooler, maybe dryer. But the park was empty, and he had too much on his mind to spend time scouting the neighborhood.

And as it turned out, it was probably best to be outside. This Hsu was talented, a pretty good choice to be an errand boy. There weren't a whole lot of USNA spies running around the Island, and most of them weren't highly skilled. Kale knew the CMC would be disappointed to discover how much Drauer and his people ignored what was happening out here. When you had a mortal enemy, you liked to think they were constantly plotting your downfall instead of barely paying attention to you.

Anyway, the point was that Hsu was more than good enough to hide information from the USNA spies on the Island, and even good enough that Kale would have some trouble reading him at a distance—walls and miles of empty space would add a layer of complication to Kale's eavesdropping efforts that he didn't need. He didn't like having to travel toward the eastern end of the Island, but when he came closer to Amelia and Hsu, he had a much easier time finding a path through the twisted holes in Adept Hsu's shield.

He was pretty sure he should have stopped listening by now. Once Hsu started talking about food, Kale's eavesdropping had gone from being sheer business to something a little creepy. But he didn't stop. He'd like to think it was because he had made a promise to Armando Diaz to watch out for Amelia, but he'd never gotten to personally make that promise to Armando. He had intended to make the promise, though, and he figured that counted for something.

He made himself feel better by only half-listening to Hsu and Amelia discuss how they could obtain and eat food without being noticed. He had one more piece of the puzzle with Hsu's latest message, a little more light shed on the CMC's plan. If he had been planning this thing, he would have wanted Amelia and her ILF friends to provide a distraction. He had no confidence that anything they fired at USNA troops near the wall would hit anyone, but at least with guns there would be flashes and noise and other things to occupy the guards while the adepts prepared the real attack. But it seemed the church didn't think they needed a distraction. Where they really that strong?

Maybe the key would be whatever supplies the ILF would be providing. It was strangely worded—"surplus supplies." Like all resistance groups before it, the ILF was accustomed to shortfalls. They fought a jury-rigged war against enemies with bottomless resources and unstoppable assembly lines. They generally never had enough of anything—having too much was an unreachable dream.

The whole Island was like that. The charity boats came by now and then, whenever the other branches of the CMC could put them together, and for a brief day or two the Island was flush with resources. Then it returned to its customary shortages and its long-standing effort to pull as much food as possible out of the sandy ground.

Kale smiled grimly. If Long Island had a surplus of anything, it was sand. The rumors said that Drauer had a special task force whose sole duty was to direct rain away from the Island, keeping it dusty in the middle and sandy on the edges. Kale had never seen evidence of such a squad, and he doubted that any PKs powerful enough to control something as large and unpredictable as the weather would be wasted on an effort of simple spite. Whether the squad existed or not, though, the Island had been dry for a long time, and the amount of arable land on it was shrinking each year, while the sand only seemed to increase.

Sand. Kale closed his eyes. He pictured the wall in Far Rockaway. He thought about sand. Lots and lots of sand. He could picture it going several ways as he plotted reactions and counter-reactions, but in the end there was only so much he could do. There was too much chaos and confusion, too much uncertainty. Which meant that any side that knew about the chaos and anticipated it would have an edge.

Would it be enough? He couldn't be sure. There was a huge gulf, in both numbers and skills, between the CMC forces on the Island and the USNA bulwark in the city. But the chumchas were thinking big, and that meant they thought they had a real chance at success. Which either meant they really *did* have a chance, or they were insane.

Kale, at the moment, wasn't willing to bet on one alternative over the other. But at the very least, the CMC was making him pay attention to what they were doing.

While his mind had been wandering, Amelia and Hsu had moved somewhere else. Kale's sound channel wasn't bringing him anything now except the quiet scrape of books on shelves of the small store. It wouldn't take too much to find them, of course, and resume listening. But he had enough other things to do that he could grant them a few moments of privacy.

Hsu took a small sip at his bottle of lemonade. He had to be careful—Amelia had noticed the chipped glass on the mouth of his bottle as soon as he'd opened it. Pretty much every bottle on the Island had been emptied, washed out, and filled again many times over. Only a few of them were in better shape than the one Hsu had. That's why Amelia carried a canteen with her most everywhere, and why she had told Hsu not to bother getting her a drink.

As soon as the bottle dropped from Hsu's lips, his mouth returned to its small, twitchy smile. He'd been like that ever since he'd come back with the sandwiches he had brought to the small picnic table they'd chosen for lunch. When he'd walked around the abandoned house and handed Amelia her food, he was walking with a straight back and slightly puffed-out chest. She knew what he wanted, and she had no intention of giving it to him. She ate in silence.

He finally lost it when she was about halfway through the sandwich. The twitch turned into a full smile, and his cheeks became even sharper than normal through the force of the grin.

"Come on," he said. "Aren't you going to ask?"

She waited two beats before looking up from her food. "Ask what?"

"Anything! Where I got the food from! Why I picked this house! What we'll do if anyone notices us! Doesn't any of that interest you?"

She looked back down. She wished she had a magazine to flip through just for effect. "Not really, no."

"Come on!" Hsu said. He looked ten years younger than he normally did, which meant that for the first time, Amelia saw his face match his actual age. "Did you know I'm running a spell right now? Simple camouflage. Anyone happens to look over the fence, they'll just see a white table. They won't even see our sandwiches. Isn't that *cool?*"

"It's very impressive," Amelia said without looking up.

"It *is*," Hsu insisted. "I'm out here doing something I'm not supposed to be doing and no one can see me!"

Amelia finally looked him in the face again. She had to work hard not to smile at his expression, the same way it was hard not to smile at a puppy dancing around your legs. "I guess you haven't had much experience with the outlaw thrill," she said.

"No, of course not. Everything at the cathedral is by the book. But the great thing, the great thing is, I'm using the stuff they taught us, and it's working! We're out! No one can see us!"

"You're doing a very good job," Amelia said, laying the condescension on so thick that there was no way Hsu could miss it.

But he did. "Thanks!" he said. Then some of the smile faded, and he lost about half of the youth his enthusiasm had given him. "I guess, though, this isn't new to you. You have to deal with not being seen all the time."

"Right," Amelia said.

"And you do it without the talent."

"Yes," Amelia said. "Which is why I'm so *glad* that this is so boiling *easy* for you."

Hsu remained oblivious to the hostile edge of her tone. "I suppose a group like yours could really use some PKs. It must be tough without them."

"Right. Anyone who might be useful to us is either trapped in USNA borders or locked up in your church. You chumchas have plenty of talent, and most of the time the only thing you do with it is sit around and pray."

"That's not fair," Hsu said.

"The hell it isn't. The ILF is a ragged little splinter of an organization, but we've still done more to hurt the NArds than all of you, with all your talent."

Hsu's face had returned to his full age. He took a bite of his sandwich and chewed slowly. Then swallowed.

"We're doing something now," he said. "Isn't that worth something?"

"We'll see when you're done." Amelia wiped her mouth with a thin napkin. "Look, I'm glad you're having fun playing spy, but this isn't a game to the rest of us. We don't get to skip out of our nice safe haven, play big kid games for a while, then run back to shelter when it gets dark. We do this shit all the time. I'm sorry if you wanted us to sit here and talk about something else, but for most of my life, there hasn't been anything else. This fight is everything. So forgive me for not being enthralled by a bunch of chumchas who are coming to the party late and waiting to be admired before they've even done anything."

Hsu was angry, his brow furrowed, his mouth tight. Amelia watched the struggle for control move across his face. She knew he wouldn't talk until he was under control, which made this a good time for her to make her exit. She stood up.

"It's nice you guys are finally trying to be useful, but you need to be in this struggle for a few years, you need to give up a normal life, you need to watch friends die before you get me to admire your damn talents. So stop patting yourself on the back for doing a simple hide-and-seek trick and figure out how you're going to help in whatever damn fool plan your adepts are cooking up." She crumpled up her sandwich wrapper and tossed it on the ground five feet away from the table. "There. Can anyone see that?"

The wrapper burst into flames. They started orange, then glowed hotter and hotter, becoming a small ball of yellow-white whose heat Amelia could feel. Then it burned out, faded, and was gone, and there was nothing more than a charred spot on the weedy grass.

"Not any more," Hsu said.

Courtney put his right hand near his heart and extended his left. He started with the palm of his left hand open, but then he turned it into a point. But then he remembered that politicians didn't seem to like to point. What did they do instead? How do you make a strong point without pointing?

Then he remembered. The thumb thing. He closed his fist and curled his left thumb up, then moved his hand up and down emphatically a few times.

He looked down. Maybe the right hand was a bit much. He let it drop to his side.

He wanted to practice speaking, but someone would hear him. And he couldn't practice by whispering. Who ever whispered a speech? So he stuck with the gestures for now.

He pivoted. Maybe it was better to use the right hand for emphasis instead of the left. He tried one, then the other, shifting back and forth. Neither position felt comfortable.

He dropped his arms and took a few steps toward the window. It was dark all over. The CMC didn't like to have too many lights on at night. Aron had explained it to him once.

"We can read thoughts and find people by the thoughts bleeding out of their brains," he had said. "Other people can't. They rely more on their eyes to see their way around. So if we turn off the lights, we get the advantage, security-wise. Plus the powers-that-be think it will encourage us to go to sleep sooner if they keep things dark."

Courtney didn't know if there was anyone out there on patrol. If there was, they'd have no problem seeing him framed in his window. The thought made him step back and out of their view.

Maybe he could stand with his hands on his hips. He tried it and felt ridiculous and stiff. Then he let his arms drop to his side, and that was even worse.

He looked at the window again, which from this angle was little more than a dark vertical line. They were out there. He could feel their presence. They were doing all their exercises, running here and there, making different things catch fire. He heard their excited talk in the hallways, saw how they collapsed into their beds when it was all over. And he saw how they looked at him and smiled and sometimes pointed, and he instinctively backed away.

For the tenth, maybe the twentieth time, he resolved to leave in the morning. They didn't have anyone guarding him. For the most part, he was alone and could walk away without anyone looking at him twice. He should do it. He should leave. Before it got any worse, before these adepts did any more to try to make him a leader, he should leave. There was nothing he would be able to tell them, no way to lead them, and if they were going across the borderlands to the wall, he didn't want any part of it. He wanted to be home, by his screen, playing Psychonaut, blowing up the icons of players thousands of miles away.

He would leave in the morning, he told himself. He would go home.

He hoped this time his resolve would last beyond sunrise.

Part Five: Leader

Chapter Twenty-four

The trucks led the way across the barrens. They were all white, most of them freshly painted. There were a few big semis, but most were smaller trucks and vans. There were over a dozen of them, and they kicked up grey dust that looked like it could hang in the air forever.

The sun was setting in front of them, a dark orange disk in the dusky sky. High Adept Birch had hoped it would be brighter, but the plan didn't hinge on that. Those who had organized the attack knew better than to make the plan rely on elements they could not control.

Birch rode in a sedan behind the truck convoy. Like all the other cars, this one was packed, four adepts crammed in the back seat. As a ranking adept, Birch had the front passenger seat to himself.

The night was going to be cool. Birch had warmed the car himself, but once things got going he wouldn't even have the mental energy to dedicate to maintaining a heat spell. So he soaked in the warmth while he could.

He glanced out the driver's-side window and saw a patch of water that was already fading to black in the disappearing light.

<<We've made it to Bannister Bay,>> he sent to High Adept Kroll. <<We will be turning southwest and staying near the coast.>>

Kroll's response was brief. <<Proceed.>> Given how many activities Kroll was monitoring at the moment, Birch was surprised he received any response at all.

He closed his eyes and reached out to scan the area ahead of him. He did three sweeps, one for thoughts, one for spells, one to get a general sense of the air ahead. The first two came up empty. The NArds were out there, waiting, but they hadn't moved forward yet. If they noticed the convoy coming toward their wall, if they cared about it at all, they didn't show it.

The third scan was more complicated. The biggest risk of the plan, the one element they couldn't control no matter how they tried, was the quality of the air. If the wind shifted and came from the northwest, blowing factory smoke into the stifling, treeless air over the Barrens, they might be in trouble. Too many pollutants in the air would throw their calculations off. Birch couldn't measure the makeup of the air with any degree of precision—there were only four or five PKs in the whole world that could do that—but he could get a feel for it, like he was closing his eyes and sticking his hands deep into sand to feel what was under the top layers. His sweep showed that the northeast wind was doing its job. The air felt clean and dry.

He thought about pushing his mind out farther, reaching out until he could feel the cold solidity of the wall, just so he would know it was there and feel precisely how far away it was. He could measure every foot of their progress. And he could also, while he was doing that, broadcast a loud announcement to USNA security that a fairly powerful PK was moving rapidly toward their border. So he kept his mind to himself.

The ground ahead and to the right was grey. The water to the left was a slightly darker grey. And this was going to be the promised land.

When Birch allowed himself a moment to think about what they were about to do, to put it in the scope of history, he felt the coming events looming over him like a giant tsunami, ready to crash down on him and obliterate the landscape of everything he knew. Excitement and fear rose in him in equal measures, so he stopped thinking about broader events and history and anything like it and just looked ahead into the grey, thinking of his next step, and waiting for the wall to get closer.

Amelia had won the right to drive one of the trucks. She could feel its huge weight behind her with every move she made. When she hit the gas, the acceleration was almost imperceptible as the engine labored to move the load forward. When she made the smallest move of the wheel to one side or the other, the inertia behind her kept moving in the original direction, threatening to topple the truck. She took every turn at a crawl, a speed the engine accepted quite readily.

There hadn't been any turns for a while. Once they were off the roads and into the borderlands it had been pretty much a straight line west. The border rats were steering clear of the convoy—groups of people larger than five made them nervous, and this caravan was much, much larger. Amelia imagined them all cowering on the north shore, waiting for the invading train to pass and return their lands to them. She liked the image, since it meant one possible enemy had already been cowed.

Most of the other ranking members of the ILF were behind the wheels of the other trucks on the front lines. Waylon was two cars ahead, driving an ice-cream truck that had been little more than a rusted hulk when the ILF had scavenged it about eighteen months ago. It had been worked on sporadically, and Amelia had never known what the leaders thought they were going to do with it when—if—they got it running. But here it was, serving a useful purpose within two years of the first time the ILF had successfully started the engine.

Her hands drummed a random rhythm on the steering wheel. She had no radio, no music, no way of communicating with anyone. She had been given one simple order—"Follow the truck in front of you"—and that was it. She didn't know what she was supposed to do. She didn't know how driving a truck full of sand furthered the cause of liberation. But it was something to do, and she couldn't help but be excited that she was doing it.

It was easy to keep her eyes on the taillights of the truck in front of her because there were absolutely no distractions. No other vehicles, no scenery, nothing.

Nothing except for an old man hovering just out her window.

When she noticed him, drifting alongside her, no more than ten feet to her left, she almost hit him. The shock of seeing him sitting cross-legged in mid-air while traveling at 45 miles per hour made her jerk her hands suddenly to the left, and the truck lurched. She felt the top shift and lean, gravity reaching out to grab it, and she had images of the old man being ignominiously crushed. But the truck steadied itself, and the old man seemed completely nonplussed. He had noticed Amelia noticing him, and he pointed toward her passenger seat. She rolled her eyes, but she leaned over and unlocked the passenger-side door.

The old man managed to accelerate without moving a muscle, then turned and drifted ahead of the truck. He opened the door and air suddenly roared through the cab, the passing wind flinging the door wide open, but he eased his way into the truck and pulled the door shut without any visible exertion.

"Hello, Amelia," Kale said. "How have you been?"

"Oh," she said, trying to sink to his level of nonchalance, "about the same."

"Good, good." Kale was still sitting with his legs crossed even though he was in the car. "So. This is something, huh?"

She couldn't help but smile. "Yeah. It's something."

"What's in the truck?"

She glanced at him. "Oh, come on. You know that already."

"Okay, okay. I was just trying to make the conversation feel natural."

"Good," Amelia said. "That's good. We're on our way to attack the United States of North America, and you're worried about the pace of conversation. Real good."

"Fine, I'll be direct. Amelia, you're about to attack the most powerful nation on earth with a truckful of sand."

"*Several* truckfuls of sand."

"What do you think's going to happen?"

"I think we're going to piss them off."

"And how do you think Anderson Drauer reacts when he's pissed off?"

Amelia scowled. "Ask grandpa."

"Exactly. You're poking the hornet's nest here. Andy won't like it. And it will be worse if he finds out it's coming from you."

"Nothing's coming from me. I'm a low-level functionary. I'm just doing what I'm told."

"Amelia, listen to me." The kind, avuncular tone Kale normally used disappeared. "If he finds out you were involved, he will come after you. He will try to make an example of you."

"Let him come."

"No, no, no," he said. "Not a good attitude to have."

Amelia looked forward into the fading light. "It's too late to be having this discussion. This is now. This is happening. The consequences will be what they will be."

Kale slowly nodded his head. "All right. All right. I couldn't stop Armando, either."

She turned her head sharply. "You tried to ..." Then she looked ahead again. "This is not the time to talk about it."

"Right. But you have to understand that I'm going to watch over you in this. I have to. I'd appreciate it if you'd let me."

"I can't really stop you, can I?" Amelia immediately regretted the sharpness of her tone. "I won't fight you," she said. "Not now."

"Okay. Good enough."

They rode through the grey border in silence for a few minutes. Kale was eerily still next to Amelia, which made her a little nervous.

"So—you have, um, other things to do in this whole thing?"

"Probably," Kale said. "But I'm going to do them from here as long as possible. For now, I'm with you."

The silver bus was moving a lot slower than the last time Lloyd had been in it. He hadn't looked at the paddles the whole journey—other people were responsible for moving the vehicle forward. At the moment, Lloyd, like most of the other adepts on the bus, was shielding the bus and looking out for signs of USNA activity. There weren't any. The invasion was on the way, but there was no indication the targets knew about it or cared.

Along with assisting with the shield, Lloyd kept busy pulling air apart. He only did it in small pieces, far behind the van. With the normal chaos going on in the borderlands, he didn't figure the NArds would notice some little sparks here and there.

Air ripping was an instinct, something young PKs did without knowing what they were doing. They would just reach their thoughts out into the air and *tear*, ripping air molecules into ions and making small sparks of lightning fly through the hole they created. PKs could be trained to control and enhance their ripping abilities, but very few who hadn't done it when they were young ever learned how to rip when they were older.

Lloyd's parents said he had first made the air pop when he was three years old, one of the many things about Lloyd that made them nervous. He made a spark appear in the air when he was five. He was in CMC Sunday School by that time, learning the discipline he needed, far from his parents who were off somewhere trying to recover their jangled nerves. Lloyd had heard about some rippers whose power grew faster than their control, and they often badly shocked someone (usually themselves) when they were angry, pulling air apart without any control.

Lloyd hadn't ripped the air out of anger in a long time, thanks to the discipline he'd learned. When the drilling started, he wasn't sure he'd remember how to do it. But it came back quickly, and the sound of the pop in the air was immediately familiar. He remembered how easily it came to him, and how fun it was.

<<That's enough practice,>> High Adept Sternhaven sent as he let another crackle through the air. <<Nothing more until the real thing.>>

Lloyd signaled assent without bothering to form any words. He fidgeted a little in his seat, then leaned to his right to try to get a view out the front windshield. There wasn't much to see in the greying light.

He looked at the plain grey walls of the van, at the pedals below him, and the black seats in front of him. He watched his knees bounce for a few seconds. He tried to focus on what he was doing, but he couldn't get a mental fix on it. Like pretty much every kid Lloyd knew, he had played NArds and chumchas when he was growing up, and when young acolytes played, the game took on a strong messianic bent. Lloyd couldn't count the number of times he had redeemed the continent from the evil clutches of Anderson Drauer and his minions. He had imagined his approach in a million different ways, and now all of them felt a million years away. Even with all his pretending and all the drilling of the past few weeks, he couldn't believe that what was happening was real.

His disbelief, however, did nothing to stop the USNA wall from coming closer each second.

The border forces had to know they were coming. The border near Guatemala City was the one most likely to draw attack from CMC sympathizers, but the Long Island border had the most symbolic value of the entire USNA. Until recently, the best and brightest CMC adepts were sent to Hampton, and even though their numbers were ridiculously small when compared to the nearby USNA troops, everyone had always believed that when the CMC made its move, it would start on the Island. But it was an event that seemed a part of the eternal future, a forever distant spot on the horizon. Now that spot was here.

The van turned. Not sharp, but a gradual bend left. Their journey wasn't a straight line any more. That had to mean they were getting closer. It was happening.

And just like that, Adept Sternhaven was all over his mind, using the same mental tones he remembered from his acolyte days.

<<You will now start using everything you have learned in the past few weeks,>> she sent, words that cracked sharply in his brain and in the brains of everyone around him. <<You will send nothing unless it is related to the campaign. You will bury your emotions so deep inside that even *you* won't know what they are. And you will follow any sending you receive from a superior like it was your own thought.>>

Lloyd realized that his hands were numb. He shook them while he looked back and forth out the windows on either side of him, seeing nothing but grey.

But there was something to the front of him. Right now it was nothing more than a hint of purple in the sky, a faint glow. The reflection in the clouds of the bright lights that lined the wall. It was there.

The van was slowing. Everyone had gone quiet. Lloyd could hear the wheels grumbling over the bare hardpan. His hands were tingling now, and he drummed an erratic rhythm on his leg to get the blood flowing.

Then he felt the air change. He couldn't describe it to anyone without the talent—he didn't even know if it was a physical or mental sensation, or both. It was a distant sense that told him the air around him was being pushed and shifted. That people with the talent were active.

<<When the bus stops, leave in an orderly manner and set yourself in your assigned positions,>> Sternhaven sent.

The bus stopped moving the moment Sternhaven's sending faded. Lloyd stood up and fell in behind the other adepts as they quietly marched off the bus.

Lloyd walked exactly twenty paces to the north. Then he turned sharply and faced the east. The other adepts were in a line, standing with about ten meters between each of them. The wind was cold, the advancing breeze of a late-season storm. Lloyd was so used to putting warmth around him every time he walked outside that he had almost forgotten what cold felt like. As he stood facing the wall, he remembered he didn't like it.

He could see the red lights of trucks moving ahead of him. The closest one wasn't far, only about thirty yards away. It turned until Lloyd was looking directly at its rear. Its back lights flashed brighter red briefly as it stopped, then they shut off. It was in position.

Lloyd waited, hands clenching and unclenching at his side. Then he heard several metallic cracks, slaps, and rattles. The trucks were opening.

<<Sparkers, start clearing your path,>> Sternhaven sent.

Lloyd reached out. It was a delicate operation now. He was pushing the air in between the vans and the wall, pushing ions this way and that. He couldn't explain what he was doing in scientific terms, only that he was clearing a path for electricity. He had a particular zone, a space about twenty yards long that was about a

hundred yards in front of the trucks. Working that far from your
body pretty much guaranteed that any half-awake PK in the area
would notice you were doing something. They certainly had the
NArds' attention now. The only question was whether the guards
understood what the adepts were doing and why—and if the
church's shields could keep the guards from doing anything about
it.

A wind kicked up in front of Lloyd. To him it felt like not much
more than a breeze, but he knew it was stronger than that. Adepts
who had ridden in the trucks were calling up dust devils, the easiest
type of wind to summon because it was so localized. All you had to
do was stir the air in a circle, faster and faster.

The trucks had dumped a long line of sand in front of Lloyd and
the other adepts in the rear, and now the dust devils were moving
over it. They weaved back and forth over the long piles of sand,
tossing the particles into the air. Some of the sand flew back to
Lloyd, stinging his eyes, but he ignored it, keeping his mind on his
channel in the air.

And just like that, the time for worries, for reflection, for
waiting, was over. There was no time to pause or ponder. A long
series of things had to happen, and they had to happen exactly when
they were supposed to. It would be a very rapid series of moves and
counter-moves, and Lloyd's final reflective thought before he got
caught up in the flow of events was that it was too bad he'd never
know each and every move that contributed to what was about to
happen.

The wind at his back sprang up out of nowhere and disappeared
as quickly as it came. The moving wall of air slammed into the
hovering sand and pushed it through the fading light toward the
black wall to the west. Sand swirled in the sky, spirals twisting
violently in the impact of the wind, and then a second wall blew
through and the sand moved faster. Lloyd tried to hold his channel
open while the air around it spun. The channel collapsed twice, but
both times Lloyd grabbed the air and pulled the channel back open,
so focused that the sensation of his mind touching the air was no
different from his hands touching a lawn of thick grass. His sight

drained away, his vision fading to a tunnel focused on an empty spot of air twenty feet above the ground and a quarter-mile from the black wall.

Wind hit his face, then his back. He felt psychokinetic energy all around him, coming in waves. The NArds were awake.

Sand came back toward him, stinging his skin. He closed his eyes and listened to the rasping wind and thought only of keeping his channel open. Waves from the west kept coming and the air shivered but Lloyd was not going to lose his grip now. His channel shrank but it stayed open.

Sweat beaded on his brow, making him cold when each burst of air punched into him. His mind started shaking like any muscle shakes when it strains for too long. Either the waves from the west were coming stronger or he was growing weaker as the sand swirled everywhere.

Then he saw the flash. Even with his eyes closed the flash left a reddish slash of afterglow in his eyes. He felt the wave of heat in front of him as every hair he had stood on end. His channel expanded quickly and then collapsed, too fast and too hard for him to control, but it didn't matter any more. He had held it long enough.

The crack of thunder was deafening, the force of the noise physical as much as aural. Then another, and another, the most violent storm of the season erupting in front of the advancing CMC force.

Lloyd opened his eyes in time to see more flashes, two to the left, one to the right, white-hot, charging through channels opened by other adepts. He was already reaching out again, just like every other adept standing in line with him. The lightning flashes had been impressive, but they were only a means. The end result was about to appear.

The air between the CMC forces and the USNA wall was now full of vaporized silicon from the heat of the lightning darting through the sand. Now Lloyd and every other adept who knew how to spark were going to put that silicon to use.

He knew where the wall was. They had drilled from this distance repeatedly so that they could hit the wall without being able to see or sense it. Lloyd set of a spark exactly where he was supposed to—and then he could see the wall.

A glowing ball ignited above the wall, then another, then another. It was almost like distant streetlights illuminating randomly, one by one. Except that with each ball, the crackle and hiss of distant electricity grew louder.

Lloyd was running as the lights came on. Adepts behind him had started pushing the air again, giving him extra speed until the air was carrying him and he was moving his legs mainly to keep his balance. As he came closer to the big black slab, Lloyd could see small fires here and there on the wall. There was a guard station he could see whose windows were cracked. The ball lightning up and down the length of the wall cast eerie flickering shadows, making everything look like it was moving. What USNA forces Lloyd could see looked to be in chaos.

Just how much chaos, he'd know very soon.

Chapter Twenty-five

The lightning had been a thing of beauty.

Kale, of course, was quite capable of making individual bolts of lightning on his own. Even multiple bolts, if he really wanted to. But to produce a line of ball lightning on top of the USNA wall—that was inspiring. Kale had carefully watched how PK energy had ebbed and flowed while the chumchas advanced, and he had been impressed in spite of himself. He had lent an invisible hand here and there—diverting blows sent by the USNA guards, making sure some of the weaker adepts didn't lose the channels they were trying to keep open—but he saw how much happened without him, and he had to admit that to this point, things would have gone more or less the same if he hadn't been there. The chumchas were advancing into the face of a now-disorganized guard force, and they were doing it in a way one PK couldn't do on his own. Kale hadn't been part of a multi-PK attack in so long, he'd forgotten what was possible.

"Are you protecting me?" Amelia asked. She was leaning hard into her steering wheel, practically lying on top of it. The tightness of her grip likely meant that she had fingernail-shaped cuts on her palms.

"Always," Kale said.

"Shut up," Amelia said. "Are you shielding me now? What if the guards attack the truck?"

The vehicle moved a lot better now that its cargo was flying in the air around them. They were rapidly closing on the wall, and the ball lightning, though it had been persistent, was fading. Kale hoped the chumchas had some other follow-up in mind besides a full-on charge.

"I've got you covered," he said, but it didn't seem to help Amelia relax. It didn't help Kale much, either. He'd just been reminded how much more effective PKs were when they worked in packs. He knew could hold off any solo attack the NArds sent his way, but if the guards decided to work as a group—well, he knew how hard Andy's people trained in coordinated assault.

The truck was racing now, piercing the dust clouds kicked up by the vehicles in front of it. Sand was still swirling in the air. Kale couldn't see much more than the dim glow of the taillights in front of him and the fading glow of the ball lightning sparking over the wall. And with the chaos of spells around him, his mind wasn't able to make out anything any more coherently than his eyes.

The tailwind had shifted from the intermittent pulses that had carried the sand west to a steady push moving all of the chumchas forward. There was a quick blur to his right as a black-robed adept passed Amelia's truck on foot, and Kale could only hope that their classes in wind running had included what to do on the off chance you tripped.

He knew the wall was getting closer but he still couldn't see it. He kept staring ahead, looking for a deeper blackness than the dark of the evening. He hoped Amelia would be able to see the wall in enough time to stop in front of it.

That was when the wave hit. It started at his feet and moved up his legs. It felt like his entire body was being lightly scraped, inside and out. He squirmed as the sensation moved up his body, trying to shift the feeling away, but nothing changed.

Amelia was squirming too, finally moving her body away from the steering wheel.

"What the hell was that?" she said.

One glance out the window confirmed what Kale had guessed.

"Strainer," he said. "Look."

Outside the flying sand was changing shape. It was still moving every which way, but it was also condensing. The strainer spell was moving through the air, finding particles of a certain size and composition and pulling them together. Anyone who had swallowed some sand would be experiencing a strange feeling in their gut right about now.

The strainer kept moving, and some areas to the sides were now clear of sand as all the particles gathered in front of the truck.

Kale reached out with his mind and felt massive energy all around him, pulling the sand together. It was the combined strength of at least a half-dozen highly skilled PKs and a large group of lesser minds besides. The USNA guards couldn't miss it.

Kale pushed out even farther, mentally dodging and weaving all around the gathering sand. No matter how bad the guards had been hit, a response had to be coming. They wouldn't lose all of their composure so easily.

There it was. A wave of energy coming from the northwest. No material to it, just a mental blast to scatter the chumcha's strainer and make the sand fly away.

It was strong, too strong for Kale to stop it through brute force. But he had some idea what the blast was targeting, and he knew how to divert it.

A quarter-mile north of the truck caravan, the air exploded. People without the talent wouldn't notice anything, but anyone in the area Kale hit would be hit by a mental hurricane, filled with thuds and screeches that could turn a weak mind into jelly. It was a massive psychic disruption of chaos and mental gibberish, and it was the three things it needed to be—large, loud, and right in the path of the onrushing blast.

The beam from the northwest slammed into Kale's sphere of noise and shattered it. It was Kale's spell so he felt its disruption, his concentration and senses scattering like the blasted spell. He saw nothing but stars and darkness for a few seconds, until two of the stars resolved themselves into the taillights of the truck in front of him and the other stars slowly faded.

"Kale! What's wrong?"

"Nothing," Kale said. "I'm fine."

"I called your names five times! You were just staring at nothing!"

"Oh. Right. Well, there was a thing."

"A thing?"

"It's taken care of."

Amelia looked at Kale and smiled nervously, but she leaned into the steering wheel again, her chest right above the steering column. "The sand's coming together faster," she said.

Kale could see clearer now, and the sand was gathering into a ball. It was starting to look like a solid object, and it was flying through the air as fast as the trucks.

"Lean back, Amelia," Kale said. "You're not going to want to be that far forward."

Lloyd was not moving like the wind—he *was* the wind. The air was pure and driving, carrying Lloyd exactly where he wanted to be. All he had to do was ride.

The ball lightning was gone, but the next phase of the attack was taking shape ahead of Lloyd. The sand was gone. In its place was a large rock, kept aloft by adepts who would need to sleep for days after this exertion. It was flying fast, accelerating even. There was a small red light coming from the center of it, the glow of heat as the strainer kept pushing the sand together, fusing it into a rock. The most powerful nation of the world was being attacked by what was essentially a giant catapult—without the machine.

Lloyd wanted to catch up to it. He wanted to *see*. The ball lightning dancing on the wall had been the most beautiful thing Lloyd had seen in his life, but the giant rock, if it worked right, might be better.

He wasn't sure what he was supposed to do when he made it to the wall. He was pretty sure he had an assignment, but the sand and lightning and general chaos had left his head scrambled. All he knew was that the wall was where he needed to be right now.

Then the air around him erupted in a series of screeches and groans that sounded like metal being ripped apart. No, not ripped—tortured. Lloyd almost stumbled when the noise hit him, and his arms windmilled as he suddenly was looking straight down at the ground rushing under his feet. He managed to steady himself, then he looked for the source of the noise until he realized it was all in his head. The noise was horrible, but it was insubstantial.

Then it was gone. Even the dullest acolyte couldn't miss the pulse of energy that slammed the air near Lloyd and dissolved the cacophony back into nothing. The air around Lloyd was still empty, but the minor battle that had erupted there had twisted Lloyd's brain. He shook his head and tried to keep his vision steady as he came closer and closer to the wall.

The rock flying through the air had grown smaller, the glow on the inside more intense. The wall was clearly visible now, black concrete with sheltered guard posts every quarter mile and lights all along its base and top. The rock was picking up speed, a red-hot stone cannonball traveling at 100 miles per hour, then maybe 150, then Lloyd didn't know how fast. It was sinking like a curveball, diving down in a perfectly planned path and smashing into the wall just above its base. There was a shower of sand and debris after the rock hit, and as it fell away it revealed a hole, a round puncture glowing with heat at the edges. The USNA wall had been breached.

The sight made Lloyd run even faster, courting disaster with each heedless stride, stumbling many times but never quite tripping. He had to get to the hole, he had to get through it. He had to touch the ground on the other side of it.

The trucks were slowing, It was a good-sized hole, but neither low enough or big enough for the trucks to get through.

The guards on the wall seemed to be stunned by the rock's impact. A few of them were running back and forth above the hole, and some of them fired a few rounds out of their rifles, bullets that bounced harmlessly off the shield the frontline adepts had placed in the air above them. One guard was even foolish enough to throw a grenade, which the adepts at the base easily redirected to the hole as it exploded, making the opening a touch bigger. After that the guards still ran back and forth, but they didn't fire anything.

Then, right before Lloyd's eyes, the wall around the hole started to crumble. He could see cracks start to spread through it, then watch chunks crumble and fall. He remembered that part of the plan now—acid from the soil. Wasted lands like the Barrens had plenty of acid, and adepts near the wall had pulled it from the dirt and insinuated it into the wall near the hole. The gap was growing by the second.

The USNA then made their next move. The guards on the wall had been doing more than just running back and forth—they'd been relaying instructions to troops on the ground. On the other side of the wall, those troops were moving forward, jeeps with rows of lights blazing, trucks with canvas covers bringing soldiers to plug the hole. There wasn't any PK energy in the air, but Lloyd was certain something was being readied.

Then he remembered what he was supposed to be doing. Fire. He picked a spot not far in USNA territory and set it ablaze. It didn't last long—the NArds didn't keep a lot of stray fuel lying on the ground—but Lloyd made it as hot as he could so the flames would be high and distracting. When the first fire went out, he lit another one, and he saw other flames popping up on USNA land as other adepts joined him in torching what was supposed to be their promised land.

The fires never came close to touching the advancing NArds. Once the front line of jeeps came close to the wall, frost condensed out of the air and fell onto the fires, extinguishing them. Lloyd felt a sudden psychokinetic chill deep in his skull.

The USNA troops were close to the wall, leaving tracks in the now-frosty ground. Their PKs, wherever they were, were on their guard now, scanning every inch of air near the breach in the wall, waiting for the CMC's next move. Which meant it was time for the spell that made High Adept Birch so proud his eyes moistened whenever he talked about it. Lloyd's only job for the next few seconds would be to put an invisible shield around his ears.

A wave of magnetic energy moved through the breach toward the approaching USNA troops. It was strong enough to make the jeeps difficult to drive and anything metal, like a gun, difficult to hold on to—a minor annoyance, but an annoyance nonetheless. It would be easy enough for experienced PKs to send a canceling wave that would eliminate the magnetism, and so they did. The hidden USNA PKs sent their defense in a brief, strong pulse, and the magnetic wave was wiped away.

But the magnetic counter-wave couldn't do anything about sound. As soon as the CMC's wave was eliminated, the acoustic bomb inside it exploded. Any unprotected eardrums shattered as soon as the whining shriek hit them. Windshield glass didn't do much better, cracking and showering drivers and passengers with small squares of broken glass. A few stubborn drivers kept their cars pointed straight ahead, but most of them swerved to one side or another or even skidded to a stop. Most of the charging troops, along with any nearby PKs, would be out of action until the stabbing pain in their ears faded.

Lloyd could hear traces of the shriek even through his shield, and he was moving ahead as soon as it hit. Once it stopped, he dropped his shield and heard the full tumult around him.

Adepts on foot were through the wall first, punching the concrete (both mentally and physically) as they went through, making the hole wider, creating space for the vehicles. Then the first of the trucks came through on a roaring charge, making the USNA vehicles approaching the hole turn around and flee.

Bullets were flying now, from both the vehicles on the ground and the guards on top of the wall, but few met their targets. Most were swatted from the air by watchful adepts and fell uselessly to the ground. Lloyd couldn't get to the hole fast enough, and neither could anyone else. Adepts were darting in front of trucks, risking being instantly flattened as they dashed toward the hole. Lloyd arrived there behind a white mail truck and ran past it and through, using the truck for cover.

There was a new noise on this side of the wall. It was a lot more pleasant than the shriek; it was a voice, a clear, resonant tenor speaking loudly and clearly.

"You have just made the first successful incursion on to USNA territory in the nation's entire benighted history. You have made history, you make history with each step! But that should only give you a reason to move faster! Finish what you have started! Finish moving forward! Finish it!"

Lloyd didn't locate the speaker immediately; his voice was clearly being amplified, and it sounded like it was coming from everywhere. But then he turned and looked over his shoulder at the hole and saw it.

A truck had stopped just inside the wall, next to the hole. And Courtney Whitaker, of all people, was standing on the truck, gesturing firmly and inspiring the troops moving in front of him.

"Use the trucks!" he was saying. "Any vehicle that is abandoned is ours! Tear it apart and send it west. However fast you can be, you need to be faster. The Creator will help you accomplish what no man could alone! Disassemble the USNA trucks first! Take apart anything of theirs that we can use! Make our fortification out of their ruins!"

His voice was different, and it wasn't just the amplification. It was resounding, it was confident, it was commanding. It was still Whitaker's voice, but only barely—it was the same vocal cords, but with a different personality attached.

And people listened. On the CMC side of the wall, trucks and runners pushed forward to be with him. Each time Whitaker swept his arm across the field, CMC forces surged forward in perfect synchronicity. Bullets were flying faster now, and in the mental war between CMC adepts and USNA security, none of them flew straight. They careened off at crazy angles, bouncing back and forth as each side tried to redirect them to a prime target. But most of them didn't hit a thing.

Lloyd saw a few adepts fall to the ground. His instinct was to go to them, help them, see if they were okay, but the drilling of the past months and the momentum of the charge kept him from doing anything but moving ahead. His balance was so firm, so steady, that his legs were barely moving now. All the air behind him was a rushing wind carrying him deeper into the Rockaways, and he barely had to make any effort to move forward. The wind took him where he needed to go.

Only he wasn't sure where he was supposed to end up. They had to stop somewhere. If the invasion went in too deep, they would be easily cut off from the rear and isolated in USNA territory, and all would be lost.

But the wind behind him served as a guide. It gusted a bit more from the north, turning him gently to the left. When he saw what was in front of him, he understood.

It was a complex of brown brick buildings, each identical to the other. Boxy, four stories high, most of the windows boarded up. Built with nothing more than utility in mind, which made them perfect.

Lloyd focused on the building closest to him. He reached out, mentally touching the surface of the walls and windows, poking gently at the building to see what it was made of. It seemed solid. The board-up job was well done—even a strong mind would need a solid pull to get them off. But there was no reason to remove them.

There was a door, metal, dented in several places. A latch had been fitted on it, and it was securely padlocked. He hoped the hinges were still good.

There were adepts who could slice a lock like that one. At least, that's what Lloyd had heard. They would pull small particles in the air into a knife-edge so fine that it was invisible, then slice through anything they wanted. Lloyd had idly tried that trick when he was younger, but his constructs always shattered when they hit the object they were supposed to cut. And up until recently, Hampton Cathedral had not trained its adepts in anything resembling aggressive spellcasting, so he had never had the chance to hone his abilities, and he didn't know any cutters in the cathedral. Too bad—it was a skill that would come in handy now. Especially since there damn sure would be some good cutters in the USNA forces.

That left him to choose between heat and electricity, and heat was the clear winner. He ignored the lock and focused on the latch where it attached to the doorframe—it looked like the weak link. He started to heat it up and noticed he wasn't the first one there—it was already quite warm. Many minds make light work.

He could still hear Whitaker ahead of him, urging them on. He must be close to the complex now. He'd likely be one of the first ones inside.

Someone else lowered the hammer on the latch before Lloyd was ready. An invisible fist slammed down on it, and the heated metal gave way easily. Then someone else—or perhaps the same mind—pulled the latch entirely away from the frame. The door was unlocked.

But the USNA guards were ready. More dents were appearing in the door as bullets clanked into it. Guards from the west had noticed the converging invaders and were centering their fire on the door.

Whitaker's truck stopped fifty feet from the door. A few stray bullets hit the ground in front of him, but he did not flinch. He wasn't talking now. He just pointed, showing where a handful of guards were hiding and firing down on the invaders.

Adepts responded to Whitaker's gesture immediately. Rubble—pieces of the wall, tires and doors from ruined cars, and any other junk lying out in the borderlands—flew threw the air toward the guards' elevated sniper's nest. A few blows hit right at the top, pushing the guards back into their room. Some pieces of rubble even flew in after them. But most came to the base of the tower, pounding and pounding and pounding. And the base was already starting to glow orange.

Lloyd cursed himself for being so slow to act and joined the other pyros in heating the base of the tower. If any parts of it had been wood, it would already have been ablaze, but instead the metal supports started to soften and twist. Each resounding blow from flying rubble accelerated the damage. The stand on top of the tower had a definite slope to it now, and there was no more gunfire coming out of it. USNA guards were scrambling out of it, some jumping rather than face the blazing heat of the lower levels.

They never completely toppled the tower. Once it was leaning far enough back and to the right, so askew that no one could stand in it and take a good shot, they stopped heating it, leaving it to cool in its distorted shape. There was a good chance the strain of its new shape would eventually bring it down, but for now it remained in its twisted place.

The doorway to the first brick building was clear now, and adepts were already going inside. It seemed as if it only took five seconds from the time the first adept ran into the brick building to the time that same adept appeared on the roof. Once Lloyd got to the door, the whole building had already been shielded. He saw Whitaker by the door, standing in the open (though protected) air, urging his people into the building, a broad smile on his face, his chin up and head held at an angle that made him look nothing like the Whitaker Lloyd knew. Lloyd paused for a moment in front of him and opened his mouth to say something, but Whitaker brushed him along just like he brushed along everyone else, and Lloyd was swept by the CMC current into the building.

He went to the top floor to assist with the shield. It was a shaky construct, already under physical and mental assault from the USNA troops. Lloyd saw dozens of holes appear, holes that could have been fatal had the NArds acted fast enough, but they never did. Each hole was sealed soon after it appeared before the NArds could send anything dangerous through.

Lloyd was in a dark hallway. The only light coming in was through small gaps at the edge of boarded-up windows that he could see through doorways that no longer had doors. There wasn't enough light for him to see his own feet. But it didn't matter. He was focused on the shield outside, and his physical eyes weren't doing him any good. He focused everything on the shield, holding it up continuously, bending his knees under its weight but never, never letting it break.

There were assaults he didn't recognize, new streams of PK thought he had never encountered. He had no idea what they would do if they got through, but he didn't need to know. He just needed to stop them.

There were other people on the floor with him. He didn't know who, he didn't know if they were helping with the shield or just milling around. He didn't know if Whitaker was one of them, or if he was still down by the door. He didn't know where Aron was. He didn't know how long he had been there. He didn't know when the USNA reinforcements would come. He didn't know what else was happening besides the creation and maintenance of this shield. He only knew that the shield would hold until he was told it didn't need to.

The shield kept getting heavier. Had he made it thicker, or was he feeling the weight of the constant attacks? Or maybe it was just Lloyd's legs. Wizard wind at his back or not, he had run a long way. His knees were shaky. If he had bothered to think about it, he would probably realize he was hungry. It was still dark. He thought about sending some eyes out, getting a look at the outside just so he could see *something*, but that would take away from his shield. So he stayed where he was and let his knees get shakier and shakier and didn't see anything and held up the shield.

Then he felt something. By his knees. Were they hands? He couldn't tell. Maybe they were real, maybe they were a spell, but something was gripping his knees. Firming them. He almost gasped with relief—he hadn't realized how much work his legs had been doing trying to keep from buckling. And now he didn't need to. They were braced. He thought about trying to thank whoever was doing it, but the long night and the run through the dust and the time he had spent here, however long it had been, had left his throat parched and closed and he couldn't talk. So he nodded a couple of times and hoped that whoever was supporting him would know what he meant.

The attacks on the shield were still coming. They still seemed fresh. Attack was easier then defense—you could hurl something, take a break, then hurl again. Defenses needed to be held and held and held. You couldn't rest a muscle for a second. Every moment needed to be as strong as the last. Every moment was the same, but every moment was more tiring, too.

There was a rushing sound in his ears, like wind in a tunnel. Sometimes it throbbed. Maybe just his pulse? He didn't know. Maybe there were voices out there saying something, maybe people were yelling. He couldn't tell. It didn't matter, though. He knew his job.

He wasn't aware of his body anymore. The stiffness of his muscles, the dryness of his throat, the noise in his ears—they didn't go away, but they sort of removed themselves from him. Or he removed himself from them. He let them keep bothering his body, which was fine, because he wasn't part of his body anymore. He was the shield. He was the firm air around a plain brick building, and that brick building was his.

Interlude: The Boys

The boys fight because that's what boys do. The secret is not to play their game. It took me a long time to learn that. I would go back and forth between Harry and Andy and explain that it didn't have to be this way. We already *had* enough power to change the world, I would tell them. We didn't need to concern ourselves with acquiring *more* of it. What we had was more than sufficient.

It's all too clear how unsuccessful I was. And as I look back, I consider all the time I spent trying to persuade them to have been wasted. You see, I was just playing their game. It's all a game to them, really. Build the biggest army. Conquer the most territory. Gain popularity points. Just a game. And arguing with me was a game, too. They loved the discussions, loved trying to show me how they'd be making the world a better place, how they would be harnessing not just their own power but the power of thousands of people just like us.

That notion terrified me. The vision of what thousands of people like us could do—well, haven't we seen what horrors people *without* the talent can unleash on the world when they're united behind a misguided cause? How much more damage would thousands of people just like us do?

The past seventy years have answered that question many times over. What happened to those poor Russian people was enough to make me think that we'd been better off remaining as test subjects our whole life and never letting the world know that we existed.

That's why Rachel left, of course. I think she understood even sooner than I did. Andy used to talk to her, describing one of his visions of thousands of people like us all working together, and you could see the horror in her eyes. When she went off to live the way she did, I wasn't a bit surprised. And you know, I was glad. She wasn't ever going to find happiness any other way.

I missed her, though. I still do. She was the only person I had to counterbalance the boys. She was the only one I didn't need to try to explain my position to—she understood it instinctively. And when she was gone, it was just me and the boys.

And yes, I include Kale in that group. People always think that Kale's problem was that Andy and Harry's ideas scared him, that he got a little nervous in the face of the armies they were planning. They make his reluctance to choose a side seem like Rachel's decision to drop out entirely, like he was being cautious about the powers we could wield and the effects they would have.

But that's not Kale. Listen, it was Kale, not Andy, who first figured out that if we used our talent right, we could give ourselves extraordinary lifespans. And once he figured out that trick, he didn't hesitate to use it. He's never been shy about using the power for his own personal gain. He will never, ever shut down like Rachel did.

So I don't think the problem is that Kale doesn't share Andy's or Harry's vision of changing the world at the head of some great army—it's just that he hasn't made his mind up about which one of them was right. Well, that's not fair—I don't think he'll ever believe that Andy was right. Not entirely, anyway. But he also probably will never come totally around to Harry's way of thinking, either. I think what Kale is waiting for is to come up with his own version of how to lead the world into a better tomorrow, and when he's ready with it, he won't hesitate to build his own army. Because he's one of the boys, and that's what boys do.

Chapter Twenty-six

Up was above his head. Wasn't it? The ceiling was up; the ceiling was above his head. The floor was down; his feet were on the floor. Over his head was up.

But that wasn't right. His feet could wiggle. At least he thought they could. He experimented. Left, right. Yep, both could wriggle. The floor wasn't under them. Where was it? Which way was down?

Were his eyes closed? He tried to blink a couple of times. Yes, as it turned out, they were. He should open them. That might make things clearer. They felt sticky, though. He rubbed them, hard, with the back of his hands. Then they opened.

Above him was the ceiling. White plaster, worn here, worn there, pink insulation—how old was that?—sticking out over there.

So there was the ceiling. Above his head. Where it should be.

No, wait. It wasn't. He was looking straight ahead, and he was looking right at the ceiling. So it was in front of him. Not above.

Which could only mean that he was lying down. Was that right? He fidgeted. There was something soft, though a bit thin, under him. Running from his legs to his head. He was lying down, all right.

"What the hell is it about the ceiling?" a voice said next to him. "Do you see a patch of mold that looks like Ellis or something?"

Lloyd blinked a few more times, then decided there was a good chance the voice was speaking to him.

"No," he said.

A face came into view to his left. Pointed chin, mobile eyebrows, sideways mouth. Aron.

"Wow. You're pretty fried, aren't you?"

Lloyd thought. He couldn't think of any reasonable way that he could be considered as being "fried" at the moment.

"I don't think so," he said.

"Right," Aron said. "How long were you on shield duty?"

Lloyd thought for a while. He lifted his left arm and pulled back his sleeve. There was nothing on his wrist. He dropped his arm again.

"Shield duty," he said. "I was doing that." He tilted his head a little. "It was a long time. I think."

"Twelve hours, some people have told me. Through the night and into the morning. And that's after running in here on foot."

Here. Something about that word got Lloyd's attention. All of the sudden his disorientation was wiped away, like his mind had been squeegeed. He sat up straight.

"Here," he said. "*Here.* Far Rockaway. We're here, right? We're still here?"

"Look around," Aron said. "Does this look like any building back at Hampton?"

Lloyd looked around. He saw dusty brick walls, boarded-up windows, and several other adepts sleeping on mattress pads on the floor near him.

"We're still here!" he exclaimed. Then he quickly covered his mouth as a few of the sleeping adepts near him shifted and muttered in their sleep.

"Come on," Aron said. "We'll get something to eat and let sleeping chumchas lie."

Aside from a few pipe-ends sticking out of walls here and there, the apartment building had been entirely stripped. Even most of the interior walls were gone, leaving central hallways and lots of wide-open, warehouse-like space where apartments once had been. One of these large spaces on the first floor had been turned into a field kitchen.

There were a handful of obsessed PKs in the world who could not stop attempting to create food from the matter around them. After all, they surmised, weren't the basic building blocks of nutrition around us at all times, in the ground and in the air? It shouldn't be too difficult to pull those ingredients together and make something edible, even palatable, should it?

As it turned out, it was. There was now an established spell to create what is called "protein paste," which is a bland, slimy grey mass that most adepts found somewhat less appealing than chewing cardboard. The common consensus was that protein paste spells should only be used in the direst of emergencies.

So while popular imagination might picture an invading army of PKs conjuring up all manner of foods from thin air, in reality the invaders of the Rockaways were eating barrels of oatmeal they brought in with them. Their powers had at least some benefit, though—adepts were able to decant fresh water from the ground and heat it, so the oatmeal could be cooked without benefit of a real kitchen.

Aron and Lloyd found an empty corner in the dining hall (another large empty room next to the field kitchen) and sat on the floor, holding their plastic bowls. The oatmeal lacked seasoning, and Lloyd wondered if it was that much better than protein paste. But after the first bite hit his stomach, he knew he might be able to polish off an entire barrel by himself.

"Who knew a shield spell was so draining?" he said to Aron.

"Everyone," Aron said. "That's why we drilled so hard on the boilin' things."

"Oh. Right."

He took another bite of his food. He was squatting on a floor in a drafty building, eating tasteless food, and far from any of the basic comforts he was used to. And he had never been happier in his life.

The invasion of the night before came back to him in flashes, and he had trouble sorting out what had actually happened and what he had just dreamed. Though he had a strange suspicion that his sleep had been dreamless, and all these images in his head were real.

One image kept coming back to him, perhaps the most surprising thing he had seen that night.

"Whitaker," he said to Aron. "Did you see him yesterday? Riding that truck?"

"I *know*!" Aron said, and Lloyd could not detect a trace of his usual sarcasm and scorn. "That was incredible! It was like ... it was like ... oh, hell, I have no idea what it was like! I'd say King Arthur rallying the troops or something, but I don't want to go *that* far. But still, wasn't it *something*?"

"Where did that come from? How did he just turn it on like that?"

Aron shook his head. "Beats me. He must have been saving it up. Hey, but remember that one guy? Transferred down to Brazil a while ago? What was his name, Robinson?"

"Kevin Robinson," Lloyd said, nodding.

"Right, that was the guy. Quietest guy ever, remember? Didn't speak during class. Didn't speak to anyone after class. Didn't *speak*, as far as most of us knew. So introverted, always seemed to be on the verge of turning himself inside out. And then we heard he was going to be guest lecturer for a day, right? European history? And we figure we'll be bored to death. Or maybe we'd get to class, and Robinson wouldn't be able to say more than two words, and we could all leave. But he gets up there, and holy *hell* was he good! Funny, lively, resonant voice, the whole package! That was one of the best classes I had *ever*. Then it was over and he sat in a chair at the front of the room and folded into himself again and watched us all file out." Aron shrugged. "Maybe Whitaker's like that, you know? He's not on much, but when he's on, he's *on!*"

"I didn't ..." Lloyd shook his head, then looked down at his oatmeal. "I didn't believe it. Sometimes. I know how we found him and all, I know all the signs but sometimes ..." He looked at Aron. "It was hard, right? At first? To believe he was the one?"

Aron agreed. Lloyd could see it in his face. They had both struggled, even though neither had said as much. But Aron wasn't about to admit to it now. His eyes narrowed, his smile twisted, and he looked very much like himself.

"I don't believe it," he said. "Lloyd Hsu, the most faithful man on the planet, had a moment of doubt. So what hope do the rest of us have?"

"Hey, I doubt," Lloyd said. "I doubt all the time!"

"You doubt yourself," Aron said. "Not the same thing."

Lloyd started to protest, but Aron waved him off. "Look, it doesn't matter," Aron said. "Why are we talking about doubt now, when God's stepped in pretty clearly to show us which side He's on?"

"Amen," Lloyd said. "So where's Whitaker now?"

"Sleeping," Aron said. "He was up as long as you were, walking around, talking to everyone, giving directions, boosting spirits. He did it all night long, and High Adept Sternhaven practically had to drag him to bed. They've got him in a well-guarded room."

"Keep him safe from the NArds?"

Aron snorted. "More like keep him safe from the long line of adepts and acolytes who would keep him awake all day, worshipping him and kissing his feet if they could. They think we have a real leader now."

Lloyd smiled at his oatmeal. "I guess we do."

"FreeNet," Spree said. "All *over* FreeNet. They all talk about it, they all have words about it crawling underneath them. You watch, you can't no stop hearing and reading about it."

She pointed to another screen. "AlphaNet. AlphaNet *loves* it. Figure hey, could be end of the world. Get people all apocalyptic and shit. They hooked it in to boilin' *Nostradamus* already."

A third screen. "Even Atmosphere's on board. Quieter, of course. Restraint, dignity. They don't no make it as big a deal. But they talk about it. They know it something."

Kale looked at the screens. When the story was mentioned, it was mainly news anchors with a still or two over their shoulder. They didn't have a lot of video to show—only one reporter had been on the scene, and she'd been trying to do everything herself, without help from a crew. And shooting the footage might have been the easy part—getting it to the media outlets undamaged was its own giant labor.

"What about the others?" he said. "ColumbiaCast, NANNet, Rockefeller?"

Spree scrunched her eyebrows. "You crazy man," she said. "Won't no NArd stations show any of this. Won't even no mention it."

"Right, right," Kale said. "I always keep hoping for a streak of independence to pop up somewhere."

"You just keep hoping."

Kale leaned forward. There was one piece of video AlphaNet seemed particularly fond of, and he could understand why. Slane Olsen had taken a beautiful shot of the chain lightning darting through the sand and blasting away at the guards on the walls. The flashes were so bright they entirely washed out the picture a few times, and the bolts flying all over the place, so close to the ground, gave the video a hallucinatory feel.

If Kale was pressed to say what it looked like, he'd say it resembled nothing more than God's wrath.

He leaned back as the picture switched to the AlphaNet anchor. "Andy's watching this," he said. "He's probably watching this right now."

"Don't no need to watch it *now*," Spree said. "Been on every few minutes. He already had chance to see it plenty times."

"But I'll bet he's still watching it. Letting the images sink in. Making sure he gets good and angry and stays good and angry."

"How long you figure they got? Before Drauer come back at them?"

"I don't know," Kale said. "Not long. Every day they're there—every time this story is repeated, even—he's taking a hit. Not that he can't afford it. He and his nation could take hits for an awfully long time without getting hurt. But Andy will be watching this video because it'll make this whole thing feel personal. No matter how much actual damage the chumchas did—and it wasn't much, they just took a square mile or so of unused land—he'll get himself all worked up about it and take it as a matter of personal pride, and he'll come back and hurt them good."

"So how we stop him?"

"What?"

"How we stop him from hurting them?"

"Who said we will?" Kale said.

Spree threw up her hands. "You still like that?" she said. "You still pretending you on the fence? Ain't no fence for you any more! You jumped off the fence, then you burned the fence down and danced on the ashes! You *helped*! You helped get them there! Now you say you can't make them stay? No. Uh-huh. You don't no get to play that game no more. You picked a side. You on a side. You got to help now."

"I'm not on their side! I'm not CMC!"

"You not CMC," Spree said. "But you got them there. Maybe they be there without you, maybe not. But you helped. You help like that, you don't no get to leave them. You got to keep helping."

Kale rubbed his temples. "You should have explained this to me beforehand."

"Case you hadn't no noticed, old man, you no not so good at listening."

"You've been talking to Amelia, haven't you?"

"Just 'cause two people be right at the same time, don't no mean they been talking to each other. Just mean they both right."

"All right, fine," Kale said, then sighed. "Show me their wall."

The image of a junk wall appeared immediately.

"USNA security feed?" Kale asked.

"Yep," Spree said. "They cameras never stay broken for long."

"They're already watching, then," he said. "Probing for weakness."

He looked at the wall. It was a mess—a pile of bricks, broken concrete, twisted metal, and unidentifiable refuse. The metal, melted by pyros, was the mortar that held it all together. It was twenty feet high, at least that wide, and no more than a quarter-mile long. It connected to brown brick buildings at each end.

"What's to keep the NArds from just going around the damn thing?" Kale asked.

"Nothing," Spree said.

"Then what's the point?"

"Keep them from charging in a straight line," Spree said. "Keep them from throwing things directly at them. Give their shielders a few spots they don't no have to cover."

"Still plenty of work for whatever shield squads they have. And most of them are rookies, only been shielding for a few weeks." He shook his head. "We gotta shore up those defenses somehow."

Chapter Twenty-seven

There were plenty of stories to be told, but Slane complained that none of the adepts were very interested in telling them. Sure, they'd been happy to have her come along, they'd loved how she'd managed to get footage of them out and tell the world their story, but now that they didn't have an immediate need for coverage, their helpful spirit went away. Everyone was too busy to help her.

Except for this new leader, the one who had come out of nowhere. Slane told Amelia that she had never seen anything like this Courtney Whitaker guy before. Young kid, just a teenager, with sloppy bangs that were always falling in his eyes. By all accounts, a kid without even a trace of PK ability in him. But here he was, walking around Far Rockaway, giving orders, and when he spoke, everyone listened. Where he pointed, people went. He was in command, but neither Amelia nor Slane could find anyone who had any idea of who he was and why people were listening to him. Slane had asked a few adepts about Whitaker, but they'd just smile and be on their way.

This meant that Slane was increasingly anxious to get an interview with Whitaker, and she turned to Amelia for help. Slane had the luxury of being the only media person of any kind on the scene. The chumchas weren't letting anyone else, no matter who they were, come within a mile of their stronghold. The story, at least this side of it, was hers alone, and she was grateful. But it would help if they would talk more. Amelia used what little influence she had, but mostly she got the same results as Slane—the adepts would give her a beatific smile and do absolutely nothing to help.

It was quite a shock, then, when Slane and Amelia were sitting in front of Amelia's tent and the young man with the floppy brown hair emerged from one of the buildings and walked straight toward her.

He was unescorted. No assistants, no lackeys, nothing. It was a little unnerving. Amelia and Slane stood, getting ready to intercept Whitaker before he passed them, but then Amelia realized he was there to talk to them.

He stuck his hand out as he approached, and they shook it. He had a good grip, firm but not crushing.

"Hello," he said. "I'm Courtney Whitaker."

"I know," Slane said.

"Listen, I know that you're responsible for getting some images of this whole affair here to the world, and I can't thank you enough for that. You probably have no idea how many people your images have inspired."

"No, I ... well, thank you."

"And I've been thinking, there's probably more of this story that you'd like to tell. I would imagine you have plenty of ideas running around in your head, lots of stories you could tell, so I don't mean to step on your toes and act like I know what you want to talk about. But I thought I'd come to you and see if an interview with me would be of any interest. If it's not, I certainly understand. I just thought I'd make myself available."

Amelia smiled as she watched Slane quickly compose her face into calm. She could imagine Slane's surprise—nothing like this had likely ever happened in her journalistic career, or possibly in anyone else's. It was as if D.B. Cooper had strolled into a news bureau, offered himself up for a no-holds-barred interview, and then asked if anyone would like to touch the briefcase full of money that he was carrying.

"That ... that would be excellent," Slane said.

Whitaker smiled. "Great! I'll give you some time to prepare, then we can talk."

Slane opened her notebook to the section where there were five pages covered front and back with handwritten questions. "I'm ready anytime," she said.

"About three months ago," Whitaker said.

"Are you serious?"

Whitaker smiled. Once his hair was out of his face, he turned out to have broad, pleasant features and a very warm grin. "Completely," he said. "Well, I suppose I went to a few other churches once or twice, here and there. Never regularly, though. And the first time I went to Hampton was three months ago."

"And you don't have the talent?" Amelia interjected. Slane glared at her each time she spoke, but Amelia didn't care.

"No. Not one bit."

"All right," Slane said. She crossed her legs, trying to get comfortable on the plastic milk crate that was serving as a chair. "So how does someone completely without the talent, a non-churchgoer, walk into Hampton Cathedral and three months later emerge as a leader of everyone there?"

"God," he said.

"That's it?"

"What else could there be?" Whitaker said. "I certainly can't explain it any better than that. Can you?"

"Not with what you've given me so far, no," Slane said.

"And I'm telling you everything there is." Whitaker leaned forward. He was sitting cross-legged on the dusty ground, which helped him look like some sort of ascetic philosopher—except for his hair, of course. "Look, I know how all of this sounds. Most of the time, I didn't believe it either. I know I don't have the talent. I know I don't have any special skills. I know I've never led anyone anywhere. Most of the time I spent at Hampton, I kept telling people this. 'How can I be your leader?' I said. 'How can I be this chosen one? I don't have anything to offer you.' But they all believed in me, they kept insisting I had a role to fill. And" —he spread his arms— "here we are. It seems pretty clear who was right."

"So how did you know you were this 'chosen one'?"

"I didn't really—that's what I'm saying. Not until we got here. But if you're asking how they found me, it was through the power of the Creator. The leaders of the cathedral sent two of their adepts, Lloyd Hsu and Aron Nesbitt, to find me. They had little to go on, nothing more than a few lines of Harriman Ellis' prophecies.

But thanks to the Creator, it was enough. He led them to me, and they brought me to Hampton. When this is all over, you should talk to them. I imagine their account of those events would be interesting."

"You keep saying you didn't believe you were the chosen one, but now you do. Can you pinpoint what happened that changed you?"

"This happened," Whitaker said. "This is why I think your images will do so much good—who could not see what has happened here and not recognize the hand and power of God? I was rushing to the wall along with all the others, feeling terror and adrenaline, wanting to run toward the wall faster while also wanting to run away, when I understood. All at once. I understood my role, I understood why I was here, I understood what I would do. I was filled with a desire to see this work, to watch these people strike a blow against oppression. I wanted that more than anything in the world. So I started encouraging them. I spoke, and my voice became louder and louder. Words came easily to my mind, and it seemed everyone within a mile of me could hear them. Now, I know this will sound immodest, but I could see them take energy and inspiration from my words. I could see how what I said pushed them along. And I realized that I could keep doing that forever. I could push them on and encourage them to do this great thing, and I could watch history. I just kept talking and talking. And the people here, they seem to like hearing what I have to say."

"So you believe this whole invasion has God's support?" Amelia said. She ignored Slane's glare again, because she firmly believed this was a question that needed to be asked.

"I think the fact that we're here, doing what no one believed could be done, is proof enough of that."

"But what if you're repulsed?" Amelia said. "What if the USNA launches a counterattack and you lose what you gained?"

Whitaker smiled serenely. "What if I turned water into wine, then left the wine unbottled, and it went bad? Now, don't get me wrong—I'm not saying I'm any sort of miracle worker. Not hardly.

The point is, though, that a miracle has occurred. Right here, in front of us. Perhaps we should appreciate it for what it is."

Amelia wasn't going to let the question go that easily, even though she could hear Slane's teeth grinding.

"But if you lost this ground here, if you end up right where you started, why would God bother with this miracle at all? It seems like a lot of chaos and destruction to go through just to end up with nothing to show for it."

"Seeing the handiwork of the Creator is not what I would call 'nothing.' The Creator has shown us the He is on our side. Isn't that a good thing to know? Regardless of what happens next, isn't that something that should give us comfort?"

Slane sighed loudly and then spoke quickly, re-asserting her control of the interview.

"Okay, so you've made it this far. What's next?"

"Whatever God wills."

"Right. Any thoughts on what that might be?"

"I don't claim any privileged access to the mind of God. I'm not a prophet, after all. Just an instrument."

"But you're sitting here, in what yesterday was USNA territory, you've led the CMC to an historic victory—surely you'll take steps to capitalize on it?"

"If that is the Creator's will."

Slane slammed her notebook on her leg. Amelia jumped—she didn't think reporters usually liked to show anger to their sources. Whitaker jumped too, but his expression didn't change.

"This is bullshit," Slane said.

"Really?" Whitaker said mildly.

"Yeah. This 'I'll do what the Creator wants' nonsense. You're talking as if you don't have a plan, like God will tell you what to do and when. But you people prepared for this day, hard. The adepts drilled for months, learning new skills. You made an alliance with the ILF to help out your attack. You crated a few tons of sand across half of Long Island, for God's sake. You planned, you prepared. You didn't just sit back and wait for the Creator to bring the walls down so you could stroll through them. You worked and worked and then you marched over here and brought the damn wall down yourself."

"Yes," said Whitaker.

"So you worked and worked to get here, and now you're here, and you're not going to do any work any more? You're just going to sit here and wait for your marching orders from God?"

Whitaker chuckled softly. "When was the last time you did anything on faith?"

"What the hell kind of question is that?" Slane snapped. "This isn't about me."

"Actually, it is," Whitaker said. "As long as you're picking which questions to ask, and as long as you're indulging in a theatrical outburst in an attempt to shake me up, this conversation is about both of us. You're angry at me because you don't think I'm giving you good answers, and because you don't think I'm planning adequately. I'm content, because I've watched the Creator carry me, and I know He will continue to do so. But I can't help you understand that unless you have some idea what it means to live by faith. So I'm asking—do you know what that is?"

"Of course I do."

"And when was the last time you did it?"

"What do you want, a date? You think I keep track of these things?"

"No. But I think if you had any practice at all in living by faith, the question would not bother you so much."

"What bothers me is that you've made history and don't seem to care! It's like landing at Normandy on D-Day, then pulling back to Dover immediately afterward! You can't just get a foothold and do nothing with it!"

"I never said we weren't going to do anything."

"Then what are you going to do?"

"I'm going to have faith."

Slane ran both hands through her hair, lightly rubbing her scalp as her hands moved. "God, you're annoying."

"Probably," Whitaker agreed. "Just don't tell everyone else. They haven't figured it out next."

Slane was quiet, glaring. This gave Amelia the chance to say something that had been nagging her for the entire conversation. "They're going to kill you, you know."

"Who?"

"The NArds. Who else?"

"Really?"

"Yeah. They're working on a plan now. They're getting ready to strike back."

"You've seen this plan? You know what they're doing?"

"No!" Amelia said. "Since when has Drauer ever made his moves in the open? I haven't seen anything. But I still know." She smiled crookedly. "That's acting on faith, isn't it?"

"Yes," Whitaker said, as placid as ever.

"And you know it too," Amelia said. "You know they'll be coming for you. You know it'll be bad. And you don't have any plans except to wait."

And then it finally made sense. As she kept talking, she saw a small, amused smile appear on Whitaker's face. Slane and Amelia looked at each other, and Amelia started talking first."

"Of course you know they'll counterattack," she said. "Of *course* you do. I'm trying to figure out what the next phase of the plan is, and that's it. The next step is to be attacked."

Whitaker didn't respond.

"And you think you'll win," she continued. "You know that whatever Drauer comes back with will be stronger than what he had here yesterday. You know it'll be big. But you think you'll hold it off. It was one thing to surprise the guards and sneak into a piece of land no one really cares about. It'll be something else when Drauer tries to land a haymaker and you guys take the punch and don't move a step. That's what you think is going to happen. He's going to come back at you, and he's going to fail."

"God willing," Whitaker said.

Chapter Twenty-eight

It was always difficult to help people who didn't want to be helped—or who at least didn't want *your* help. Having been on both sides of that particular equation, Kale knew it well. So he didn't approach any of the high adepts and see how he could help, he didn't ask for any advice, and he didn't offer any of his own. He arrived at the new CMC enclave in Far Rockaway, he watched what the adepts were doing, then he did whatever he thought would be useful, all while staying on the fringes of the invasion.

That also kept him out of Malvoin Serl's way, which was probably for the best.

It had been three and a half days now. The CMC had taken up residence in the USNA half a week ago. Yesterday had been Sunday, and they held a service in their gutted brick building. None of the regular parishioners from Hampton made it out, of course, but Slane Olsen and Spree both recorded the whole thing and then showed the video back at Hampton Cathedral. The sight of CMC rituals taking place in USNA territory was enough to pack the chapel and send several parishioners into a state of religious ecstasy. They'd repeated the showings of the service all day long in the chapel. New people, some of whom hadn't attended church in years or even decades, kept arriving, while some stayed the whole day, memorizing every last detail of the service.

The Sabbath day had improved the morale of the invading army, not that it needed much of a boost. Kale had never seen a group of people happy to be living on plain oatmeal while taking shelter in totally stripped apartment buildings. Any given adept walking around the area looked ready to break into a hymn of praise pretty much every second of every day.

That was another good reason for Kale to not even attempt to talk to them. Aggressive cheerfulness made him uncomfortable.

He hadn't attended the Sunday service; there was too much work to be done. He had several decades of trickery to call upon, and he used it all in the spaces that the CMC's makeshift barrier didn't cover. Those areas were minefields now, with all sorts of unpleasant surprises ready to jump from the ground as soon as anyone walked across it. While Kale didn't directly coordinate with the adepts, he made sure they saw what he was doing. They should know that there were some areas to avoid.

He'd slept about three hours the night before and felt guilty about taking even that much time off. A distant, removed section of his mind kept mocking him for doing so much to help the CMC, even going so far as to throw together a mental image of Kale in full high adept regalia. Kale quashed that image as soon as it appeared. He told himself that he was fighting *against* Andy, not *for* the church. He'd spent enough time in Andy's kingdom. He knew what he was fighting. He'd seen the camps Andy had built for the PKs that wouldn't adapt to his system. He'd listened to voices that attempted to offer dissent fall suddenly silent. He'd watched as roving bands of PK soldiers amused themselves by toying with mere citizens who didn't have the talent and who had no way to complain about their treatment at the hands of the military. And he'd been there when Armando died.

He remembered how it felt when Armando's shields had been shattered. It was a devastating assault, a keening wail that seemed pitched to shatter inch-thick glass combined with the cold sting of an ice pick in the neck. Kale had felt Armando's shields give way immediately, disintegrating like a thin sheet of ice over a suddenly boiling lake. Both of them had fallen to the ground as a crowd gathered around them, a crowd that couldn't hear or feel the attack that had them reeling. Kale had waited for something worse to come, and it wasn't until he felt the wave of heat to his right that he knew it had already started.

Armando's skin was all red, with blisters forming everywhere. His hands were covering his eyes, which had likely already been destroyed. He looked like he was screaming, but Kale couldn't hear him over the high screech that still filled his mind. Armando thrashed and thrashed for an eternal few seconds, then he stopped. Steam raised from him when he was still.

Boiling blood. Andy's landmark invention. *A signature punishment*, he had called it. *The worst thing we can do to you.* To Andy, it meant more than death. It was a symbol of the superiority of the executioner over the accused, a final expression of contempt. It was the manifestation of the worst fears he exploited to keep his people in line.

As he lay there, watching Armando's body cool, Kale waited for the moment when he would feel his own blood heat up. He waited and waited, even after the shriek was gone. He stayed down on the sidewalk and braced himself. But it never came. Andy left him alone. Armando was a traitor, and so needed to be punished. Kale had never chosen sides, so he could be left alone.

Since that time, Kale had invented thirty-seven defenses against a boiling blood attack. People could question his commitment to just about anything in this life, but not his desire to hold on to it. He would not let Andy catch him like he had caught Armando. Defense number thirty-seven was perhaps the simplest, a bio-chemical trigger implanted in Kale's brain. If his body temperature ever got above 115 degrees, a major vessel in his head would erupt. He'd have a blinding moment of pain, then be dead of a cataclysmic aneurysm. Kale had no idea how he'd eventually die, but once he watched Armando boil, he knew he would never allow that particular death to take him.

He grew more and more nervous as Monday went along. Three and a half days seemed like a long time to wait. It wasn't as if Andy needed to call in reinforcements—Manhattan was only a few miles away, and it was as well stocked with PKs as any place on Earth, with the possible exception of Austin. So Andy wasn't waiting for more reinforcements to arrive. The more Kale thought about why Andy might be stalling, the more nervous he became.

He kept shuttling back and forth between the front of the encampment and the rear. He didn't put any mines or traps in the back of the camp so he could leave an escape route open. But there were other things he could do, from setting up unmanned gun nests on the broken wall to tricky little particle arrangements that would turn into mist when hit by certain common PK spells, thereby providing both a warning and a bit of cover. He'd do a few of these, then wander back to the frontline to lay a few more traps, then return to the rear. He kept this up all day.

He didn't eat. Too busy. The lack of sleep would catch up with him, but not while he had all this adrenaline flowing. He would keep working as long as he was able, and he knew enough tricks to keep him going for a good long time. Unless Andy was delaying simply to mess with Kale's head, using this invasion as an excuse for a good joke.

That wasn't it. Lying on the street next to Armando help Kale realize how peripheral he was to any of Andy's plans. In this affair, just as in the previous one, Kale was certain he was barely an afterthought.

He was back at the front now. Once, a few hours ago, he had stopped and looked, and marveled that he could see the Manhattan skyline without the wall cutting off the bottom part of it. He had seen it plenty of other times, of course, on his various illicit excursions into the city, but now he was standing in open air, without any concealing spells on him at all, looking at a city that could just as easily look back at him. He enjoyed the feeling.

Then he remembered that he had more important things to do than enjoy himself, so he went back to work. But he still glanced at the skyline from time to time. The last purple colors of the sunset were fading behind it, and the wizard light from behind Kale had taken over from the sun. If you worked at wizard light enough, you could make it as warm and natural as sunlight, but if you were lazy or unfocused it came off harsh and too bright.

The lights around the camp now were almost as harsh as the glare of burning magnesium.

There were no more mines to lay. No more traps to bury in the walls of nearby buildings. Not really much space left for any sort of defense. But he had to do more. He couldn't stop until the attack actually started.

He decided to weaken a few buildings on the USNA side of the wall. There weren't any troops right on the border—had the CMC wanted to, they could easily have pushed on another mile or so through the abandoned Rockaways. But that would not have increased the symbolic value of their assault, and working right under the eyes of watchful USNA guards would greatly weaken their strategic position. They were wise to have not overreached.

Kale looked at a building on the other side of his minefield, one of the three dozen or so brown brick buildings that had once been part of this complex. He sent his mind out and poked carefully around the wall that faced the street. He found the spots securing the wall to the frame of the building and applied some heat, melting them down until the connections were either very weak or completely gone. Then he sent out a tight sonic beam at a frequency that would grind up some of the mortar while doing little damage to the bricks. He moved the beam up and down the building (unconsciously moving his head up and down, back and forth along with it), undermining the integrity of the entire front wall.

When he was done, the wall didn't look that much different, aside from a little dust in the air around it and a few chips of mortar on the ground. Any heavy impact near the building, though, would cause the bricks to collapse like—well, exactly like a ton of bricks.

Kale repeated the same procedure on a building across the street from the first one, and he was about to move on to the third building when he felt it. It was like a distant tickle, a small, forgotten itch, buried far back in his skull. As soon as he felt it, Kale forgot about the building and kicked up a wind behind him so he could go east as quickly as possible.

Every time he thought about that day for the rest of his life, Kale wondered why he didn't raise an alarm as he sped through the CMC encampment. Had he been too successful in convincing himself he wasn't really one of them? Was it a subconscious way of undermining his own defense efforts, his mind taking steps to ensure that he wasn't really choosing sides? Was it the lack of sleep? Or was he just too caught up in the moment to think about anything besides moving east?

If these thoughts ever came with a twinge of guilt, he consoled himself with a simple thought—even if the chumchas had a few extra seconds of warning, it would not have made a difference.

It only took him a few seconds to make it to the breach in the old wall, but the tickle in his mind had already grown stronger (though as soon as he had turned east, it had moved from the back of his skull to just above his eyes). He reached out, pushing his senses across the borderlands. How many had come out this way? Was anyone out there? Was it just a mental attack?

He only sensed two people within two miles of the wall, and from their gibbering thought patterns he was all but certain they were border rats. But the tickle in his mind had advanced to a full-fledged itch. Whatever was coming would be there soon.

He tried to see what kind of attack was coming. But they had filled the air with noise, the whole atmosphere crackled and popped. Kale couldn't sense anything, except that it was getting closer.

He put up a wall. He didn't know what kind of barrier he'd need, so he tried an all-purpose shield, one that would hold out heat and cold and electricity and actual substances all at the same time. As he put it up, he knew it wouldn't be enough. One of the things he'd learned early on was that the more things you tried to do at once, the worse each of those things were.

But he tried anyway. He had a huge barrier up, going from the ground to three hundred feet in the sky. If they were bringing their attack in any higher, he'd just shift the damn thing up in a single piece.

A few nearby adepts sensed what he was doing, though his mechanisms were so old-fashioned they probably weren't sure what he was up to. He saw them out of the corner of his eye, looking at each other, taking a step or two toward him, then stopping, looking at each other again, then looking at the sky.

It was coming closer. Close enough for Kale to find it. It was moving up from east-southeast. They must have brought it in over the Sound, maybe launched whatever it was from a boat. He could sense its shape now, a huge oval in the sky. The static around it fell away. It was a pod. A carrying case. They'd wrapped up something in a container of air and were trying to fly it into the CMC camp.

It was one thousand feet in the air but dropping. He'd have to raise his barrier a little, but not much. He strained, pushing the weaving complex of his thoughts even higher from him while trying to keep it intact, keep the mesh of particles he was knitting firm and solid.

The oval screamed out of the sky toward him, and Kale closed his eyes. When it hit, it felt like he had been punched inside his skull. He stumbled backward, almost fell. His vision blacked out. He focused every thought on the barrier, keeping it up, keeping it strong.

After a few seconds he could see again. He looked up. The barrier had held, but it wasn't invisible anymore. It glistened, something on it reflecting the harsh white lights of the camp. The substance oozed down Kale's barrier slowly, and he knew instantly what it was.

"Spark it!" he yelled at the adepts near him. "Someone set that on fire!"

Most of the adepts looked confused, but one stepped forward and did as he was told. He focused on the now-slick barrier and threw a spark into it.

All of the ooze ignited it seconds, flashing bright yellow and orange in the sky. Kale felt the heat of it as it burned into nothing. His vision was purple after the fire was gone.

He looked at the adepts who were staring at him with their mouths wide open.

"Napalm," he said. "Get ready for more."

As soon as he said it, he felt another tickle, then another. Then more. They were coming from the same direction as the first.

Kale could handle it, though. Now that he knew what they were throwing, he could modify his shield. Make it an anti-napalm barrier, not an anti-everything barrier. It would be bigger, stronger. It would hold against a dozen napalm pods, assuming they had that much napalm available.

He waited for the arrival of the next assault, bracing himself, leaning a little forward as if he were physically holding up the barrier he had erected. The air was still too filled with static for him to know for sure how many ovals were on the way. He tried to make his barrier a little broader, since he assumed they wouldn't be dumb enough to launch all their attacks in a single-file line, and he was ready to keep his barrier moving for side to side if he needed to. He could be a lot nimbler with the napalm barrier than he was with the everything barrier.

He was so focused on the wave of ovals coming at him that he never sensed the arrow.

It was long but had an incredibly sharp tip, and it flew faster than sound. The rush of wind it made didn't reach Kale's ears until well after it had ripped through his barrier and made him fall to his knees in pain. The arrow kept widening from its tip, becoming broader and broader until it shredded every last bit of Kale's barrier and left him with a black hole of pain in the middle of his head. He wrapped his head in his arms, twisting in pain, but still managed one conscious thought.

Just like always. The first part of Andy's plan is to push me out of the way.

Lloyd was on shield duty, standing in his familiar corridor on the top floor of the brick building, when the assault hit. He knew it was coming—the psychic buzz the NArds put into the air was impossible to miss. Even though he was waiting for it, though, he was not prepared for how heavy it would be. Something hit the top of the shield and just sat there, and the shield sagged under its weight. Lloyd could feel the strain on his mind like there was a rubber band in his head, and someone was stretching it down to the small of his back. Then something else hit the barrier and sat on it. Then more and more.

Lloyd felt like his head was being crushed, like he was slowly being pressed to death, when he felt the shield collapse around him. Minds across the complex gave way, and Lloyd fell with them.

Once the main structure was breached, the integrity of the whole gave way.

The immediate effect was an odd slurping sound, then quiet. No screams. No explosions. But Lloyd knew enough not to stay where he was.

Orders started coming before he even reached the stairwell. It was High Adept Kroll, his thoughts sharp and bracing.

<<Adepts and acolytes! Servants of the Creator! The expected assault is here! Napalm has fallen across the encampment. Cover all your skin—save your spells for more serious matters. Prepare for firefighting! If you are in a building, get *out*! *Now!*>>

When Lloyd came out, the fires had already started. To the west, flames flared along their ramshackle wall and across the empty streets. As quickly as the flames went up, though, ice came down, blanketing flames here and there, never putting them all out, but keeping the whole camp from going up at once. Lloyd threw ice where he could, though he was better with heat and lightning than frozen water.

There were more objects flying through the sky, more wet splats as the jellied gas hit buildings and coated the ground. Everything glistened now, as if the camp had been hit by an ice storm. The air was becoming unbreathable—it was clear but suffocating. The gel was evaporating, choking off the oxygen supply near the ground.

There was a rumble to the west, a shaking like a minor earthquake that traveled up through the ground and into Lloyd's legs. It grew deeper and more intense with each second. Lloyd tried to see if anything was approaching, but his eyes were burning. He had to stop creating ice and focus all his energies on creating a zone of clean air near his head so he could at least breathe and maybe see. Others around him must have been doing the same—fires were springing up faster and faster.

Lloyd tried to stabilize the spell scrubbing the air around his head and push it to a low level of his brain, trying to make it almost subconscious. He ran west, dreading what he would see.

They weren't exactly tanks. They were lumbering metal vehicles with walls that had to be a foot thick, but there were no guns or any other weapons on them. The metal teeth of their tracks tore up the road beneath them as they ground forward at speeds that were no faster than ten miles per hour. It was a slow, implacable charge. The vehicles looked so heavy that very few PKs in the world would have been able to devise a spell to slow them down, let alone stop them. Lightning, ice, and fire would bounce harmlessly off the thick walls that were undoubtedly buttressed by the combined minds of the many PKs sheltered inside.

The rumbling was stronger now, and Lloyd's legs were beginning to feel like jelly. As the transports passed one building, the façade crumbled and gave way, covering one of the transports in bricks and leaving obstacles for the others to traverse. The vehicles cut their speed by maybe a quarter and continued traveling forward.

A wave of heat hit Lloyd's left side. He turned to see a wall of flame advancing toward him, white-hot at its base. All he could do was run.

He fell twice, the ground shaking hard beneath him. Each time he waited for the flames to overtake him. Each time his legs and arms scrambled so quickly that he was up before he was engulfed. He shot out ice and water where he could, but for the most part his volleys evaporated before they touched the flames. Each breath burned his insides. Once he caught a glimpse of the back of his hands and saw blisters bubbling over red skin. He couldn't see the building that had briefly been their headquarters. He couldn't see either the old wall or the new wall. All he could see now was flame.

He reached out with his mind as far as he could, hoping to hear someone rallying the troops, or at least giving some sort of instructions. But everything was chaos. Most of what he found was wordless, instinctual fear. The discipline of the adepts' training days was almost entirely gone.

Lloyd kept running, dodging the fire, once even coating himself briefly in ice to leap through a sheet of flames. He tried to get clear, but everything, everywhere, was burning.

But there was an opening. Something. To the left. There was ground that was not on fire. Lloyd ran to it. It wasn't even charred. Fire hadn't touched it. He kept running, then dove, rolled, and got back to his feet when a jet of flame leaped out at him. He panicked—would the clear spot still be there when he got up? Would he see it?

There it was. Still clear. He ran, gasping, straining, then finally falling to the ground and sucking in air. He wanted to stay down, but the heat behind him was too intense. He crawled forward, pulling himself with his elbows since his hands were too raw. He didn't know how far he went, but eventually he felt he could stop.

He wanted to sleep forever on the barren ground he had crawled to. He wanted to cry, but it didn't feel like there was any moisture left in his body. He didn't want to look behind him, but he knew he didn't have a choice.

He somehow managed to stand and look around. He was outside the wall, in the border wastes. The whole area they had taken, the entire encampment, was ablaze. He wasn't alone here, though. There were other adepts not too far from him, gasping on the ground. The rumbling had stopped—the transports were no longer advancing.

The air around Lloyd was now relatively clear—he could breathe it without having to filter it. He dropped the spell he had been running since the gel had fallen, and dedicated his full energy to reaching back into Far Rockaway with his mind. Could anyone still be alive in there?

Surprisingly he found people. There was plenty of life. Some of them were NArds, slowly advancing with perfectly shielded minds. Others, though, were adepts and acolytes, running from the flames, looking for safety. Lloyd picked one fairly close to him, then focused a powerful wind in the adept's direction. The gale separated the flames, and Lloyd sent a terse command—<<This way!>>—on the heels of the wind. The adept saw immediately and ran to Lloyd. In a few seconds, she was clear.

Lloyd looked for more and more targets, helping them come out. A few of them thanked him on their way out, but most of them just collapsed silently, thoughtlessly, on the ground next to him.

Not all of them made it out. Flames came from unexpected directions and claimed them before they could get clear. Once, Lloyd's wind faltered, and the flames closed on the desperately sprinting acolyte before he could make it out. The acolyte's screams echoed in Lloyd's head, the noise pushing him to get more people out, more and more and more.

One of them, maybe the fifteenth, was Aron. The left half of his face was charred, but when he came out, he refused to fall to the ground. He tottered, possibly unconscious on his feet, but he didn't go down. Stubborn defiance radiated from him, seeming more powerful than even his life.

<<We're going to need to defend ourselves,>> Lloyd sent, even though he wasn't sure if Aron could hear or understand him. <<When they're done in there, they'll come after us.>>

Aron's reply took a while in coming, and when it did it was covered in mental static. <<Right,>> was all he sent. He remained standing and shuffled slowly, turning to face the Rockaways.

Lloyd kept working until he could no longer find any traces of life besides the NArds. A few others had helped him once they were safe. Lloyd didn't know how many had come out. He didn't know how many were lost. All he knew was that he couldn't do any more.

He was sitting down. He didn't know when he had done that. He was facing the Rockaways, watching flames that already seemed to be fading. He sometimes spotted white shapes moving through the flames, NArds in their fireproof gear, chasing out each and every chumcha. Soon they'd regroup and come after the ones on the border. Lloyd hoped he would be able to offer at least a token resistance.

But they never became more than indistinct shapes. The NArds never came out of the fire. When the flames faded and it was dark, Lloyd couldn't see anyone moving on the other side of the breach of the wall. Most of the buildings on the other side were gone, now nothing more than heaps of charred brick. The ground looked all black—but maybe that was just because it was night. There were no bodies in sight, living or dead.

Aron was still standing near Lloyd, his legs slightly spread. Waiting. Then, without a word or an external thought, Aron started walking back toward the seemingly empty Rockaways.

<<Wait,>> Lloyd sent, but Aron didn't respond and he didn't stop. He kept moving toward the breach in the wall.

Lloyd looked around until he found a fist-sized rock. He grabbed it, ignoring the pain in his hand, and threw it as far as he could. He knew that wouldn't be far enough, so he tried to summon enough energy to push the rock through the air, hoping it would make it.

It almost didn't. It hit the ground about a few feet in front of the breach in the wall. It landed on something hard, hitting it in a way that the rock made a large skip toward the wall. It hit the ground again, made a second hop. When it hit the ground a third time, the rock was even with the wall.

The air around it lit up, a violet spark in the night air. It was a brief flash, then it was gone. And the rock was gone with it. Not a trace of it remained.

Aron stopped walking, freezing in mid-stride. Lloyd tried to read what he was thinking, but either Aron was shielding himself or he wasn't thinking anything. Lloyd was afraid Aron would start moving again and walk right to the wall and take the wall's invitation to oblivion. Aron stood frozen for a while, a long time, until suddenly his legs gave way, collapsing under him like they were made of sand and a wind had popped up out of nowhere. Aron drifted slowly to the ground and stayed there.

Chapter Twenty-nine

Nilda watched them come back, her eyes growing wider each minute. She hadn't received much direct information—Kale had gone off somewhere, and all Spree knew was that he was "watching over them chumcha asses." And Nilda hadn't spoken with Spree for almost a day.

So when the first of them arrived back at Hampton, practically falling out of a dilapidated van, she was stunned. What were they doing back here? She could not miss the scorch marks on their clothes, on their hands, on their faces. The singed hair. The limps, the scrapes, the open wounds. There had obviously been a fight. But only a few had come back. Maybe this was just the wounded. Maybe the rest were still fine, still fighting.

But as the sun rose and people kept coming until Nilda knew that there couldn't be anyone left holding on to Far Rockaway. The counterattack had finally hit, and it had been devastating—but she couldn't find out *how* devastating, since no one spoke to her. They just shuffled or limped by, their eyes empty, their shoulders slumped. She saw one car, an old grey sedan, drive onto the lawn and pull up right next to the door of Grand Adept Serl's residence. She couldn't see if the Grand Adept himself was one of the people who crawled out of the car and into the building.

Most of the adepts who arrived walked. Some of them had a numb look about them that made Nilda think they wouldn't stop at the cathedral—they'd just keep going until they reached the end of the island and walked into the sea. Some of them used their abilities to bring them home—pushing themselves with breezes, or even floating to the cathedral on a cushion of air—but most of them seemed too drained to attempt anything. Nilda saw three of them who collapsed on the grass outside the cathedral, too weary to even go inside.

She wanted to ask them what had happened, but she knew she would get no response. They didn't tend to notice her even in the best of circumstances. Besides, she could see it on their faces—they didn't want to talk. Or think. Some of them didn't seem convinced that they wanted to keep living.

She did what she could. She tidied hallways, made beds, cleaned restrooms, and hoped the adepts and acolytes who made it back to their dorms found them comfortable. She knew it wouldn't be enough, not nearly, but there was nothing else to do. She cleaned and waited for Kale or Spree to call, or for someone to talk to her and let her know what had happened out there.

This would have been the time for Whitaker. Lloyd had talked to a number of adepts, both at Far Rockaway and on the way back to Hampton, and they all agreed that Whitaker had been inspiring. When they heard him speak, they had gained energy and hope. Something Stel had said stuck with Lloyd.

"The High Adepts were great at convincing us to try to invade," she said. "But Whitaker, right there on the day, was the one who convinced me we would actually do it."

Stel freely admitted that she didn't like Whitaker much before the invasion, seeing him as a lazy interloper. But she had seen what Lloyd had seen, what everyone else had seen. Whitaker had risen to the occasion, had been transformed by it, and had helped transform them all.

And now he was gone.

The NArds, hidden behind their new barriers, had sent only one message to the retreating CMC troops. It had been brief, but was sent widely enough that no adept or acolyte could miss it.

<<Whitaker is ours,>> they sent.

That was not the only loss of the day. High Adept Kroll was gone. As Lloyd had worked from the east side of the wall, trying to pull survivors out to him, Kroll had worked from the west, finding anyone he could and urging them to safety. By all accounts, the suffocating air and the flames hadn't caused him much trouble— he'd arranged his defenses and was able to clear a path for himself through the flame at will. But with all his attention on the fumes and the fire, the High Adept apparently had not placed an adequate physical shield around himself. Something hit him in the head—a brick from a falling building according to one witness, a rock thrown by one of the white-suited NArds according to another—and he went down, unconscious. His shields dissolved as his mind went blank, and no one was able to reach him before the flames did.

Grand Adept Serl had decided to hold a memorial service on Tuesday evening, less than twelve hours after the first adepts had staggered back to Hampton Cathedral. Stragglers had continued arriving throughout the day, and there were likely more still coming, pushing their way through the border wastes and the intervening towns. Lloyd could see them wandering around the halls, still wearing the same robes they had worn in Far Rockaway, soot-covered garments with frays and burns. It made him feel strangely guilty that he had been back long enough to have cleaned up, to even have grabbed a few hours of restless sleep. As long as some of his fellow adepts were still out wandering, he probably should be out there too.

It took forever for Lloyd to fasten the clean robe he had put on. Only the tips of his fingers stuck out of the bandages on his hands. Archie Gwin had set up shop in the common room of the dorms, giving medical help to whoever needed it. Lloyd felt guilty taking any of Archie's time or effort—he was far from the most seriously injured person there, and only a few parts of his hands had advanced to third-degree burns. But Archie had waved him over, insisting on having a look at his hands. He couldn't completely rebuild them—that required substantial time and effort, along with a chunk of bio-material to synthesize into the flesh—but he began the restorative process and tried to lessen the pain.

"The skin on your hands is going to be quite raw," Archie said when he was done. "Keep them covered until me or someone else can give you the full treatment."

Now Lloyd's hands felt okay, except for when he moved them. The pain was an unfamiliar sensation—in Hampton, there were too many ways to remove pain for anyone to have to deal with it for long. Now he'd have to deal with it for at least the rest of the night, since he remained woefully ignorant of the workings of most med spells.

It seemed fitting, though. After what had happened, he *should* be in pain.

He looked at Aron's bunk. They had returned to Hampton together, and Aron had immediately went to sleep. He hadn't been to see Archie, and Lloyd dreaded seeing what Aron's face looked like now.

"It's time," he said quietly, not wanting to wake Aron if he was sleeping. But Aron moved immediately, sitting up and climbing off his bunk.

The left side of his face was covered with black skin and grotesquely swollen. The burnt skin covered his forehead, his entire left cheek, and a good portion of his nose. It trailed off under his left ear, leaving his chin red and blistered, but at least not black. There was no hair on the left side of his head.

"Are you—" Lloyd started, then stopped himself. "Does it—" he tried again. Then stopped again. The questions seemed trite, the answers obvious. Aron shuffled quietly toward the door, and Lloyd decided silence was appropriate.

They arrived at the chapel half an hour before the service was supposed to start, and the building was packed. Lloyd could see the black robes of CMC clergy dotted throughout the congregation, but most of them were laypeople. Word had spread across the island quickly, and the people that had been celebrating together for the past three days had now come looking for comfort.

Lloyd had trouble believing they would find any.

There were no empty seats. Folding chairs had been brought out and placed in every available square foot of the chapel. All of them were full. Lloyd sighed. He was too tired to stand, but he would do it. He looked at Aron to ask him where he wanted to stand, but Aron's back was to him. He was headed toward the stairs up to the balcony. He sent the passcode to the door, and it swung open. Lloyd, moving as fast as he could, followed him through.

A few other adepts had the same idea. Stel was up there, along with Robin Vranes and a few people Lloyd didn't know. He didn't greet them. They didn't greet him. There was a bench lining the back wall of the balcony. Aron and Lloyd dropped down on it and sat wordlessly while they waited for the service to begin.

Lloyd didn't do anything while he sat. He didn't scan the crowd, either with his eyes or with his mind. He didn't talk to anyone. He didn't think. He occasionally wiggled his fingers to make sure his hands still hurt.

The beginning of the service caught him completely by surprise. There was no light show. No descent of the speaker, no chorus of praise. When Grand Adept Serl walked to the podium, it's likely that most in the audience either didn't see him or didn't recognize him. He was dressed in his usual white, but it didn't glow like it normally did, and there was no halo of light around his head. Still, when he spoke, his voice carried the normal levels of resonance and amplification for a church service.

"The miracles of the Creator," the Grand Adept intoned. "They are what unite us. They are what call us here today. They are the continual manifestations of his power and grace. Amen."

The "amen" he received in return was staggered and weak.

Lloyd had already mapped out the speech in his head. There would be an expression of sadness at the cathedral's loss. But then a reminder of the miracle they had seen in Far Rockaway. An urging to not give up hope, to remember that the Creator still watched over them. A call to rally again around the cause, no matter how hopeless it seemed.

Lloyd hoped the speech would work better in reality than it did in his head, because when he imagined it, it failed to produce an ounce of feeling in him.

The Grand Adept had fallen silent since the ritual greeting. He stood with his hands at either side of the lectern, slowly surveying the congregation, looking right, then left, then right. But not speaking.

People in the congregation stirred a bit, looking at each other. Lloyd could feel confusion in them. Still, the Grand Adept didn't speak. There were a few murmurs now, people whispering back and forth, one or two of them pointing at the Grand Adept. One woman looked at the balcony with an inquiring expression. Lloyd looked past her while next to him, Aron only shrugged.

It was uncomfortable now. The Grand Adept's expression was impassive, unreadable. Had he forgotten what he was supposed to say? Had his mind collapsed after the strain of the retreat from Far Rockaway? The murmurs grew louder each second. People were turning around, looking at the door. In another moment they'd head out.

That was when the Grand Adept spoke.

"I will not comfort you," he said. His voice was deeper and louder than usual.

Then he was silent again. He let his words echo through the cathedral, and that was the only noise in the building. All voices fell silent when the Grand Adept spoke—some people had started in surprise due to the loudness—and they remained silent after the echoes died away.

There was a brief second of total silence before the Grand Adept spoke again.

"I will not rebuild your faith," he said. "And I will not tell you that everything is going to be okay.

"In fact, this is what I would like to say to those of you who are feeling downcast, discouraged, and disheartened. To those of you who feeling like giving up. To you I say: leave. Go home. If you do not have the strength to continue, if you do not have the memory to recall the miracles and the goodness of God, then there is no place for you here.

"I will not comfort you because no one who is here should be in need of comfort. No one should be any less committed to performing the works of God today than we were yesterday."

The longer the Grand Adept spoke, the more scathing his tone became. "The Creator has no need of people who only demonstrate devotion when things are going well. He has no need of those who require sign after sign, miracle after miracle, to inspire them onward.

"There is work to do. Territory to reclaim, and a man to rescue. A man who is waiting for us, confident we will come, because he will not lose hope. His confidence in all of us was the crystal-clear miracle of Far Rockaway. He is waiting for us, and we will come. If you do not have the stomach for that fight, or if you need to be coddled each step of the journey, then this effort is not for you. For the rest of you, the next stage in the journey begins immediately."

He did not ascend back to the ceiling. He did not even bother to extinguish the wizard light above the altar. He just turned around and quickly walked away, robes flowing behind him, out of the cathedral.

Lloyd was shaking. His right hand was in a fist. He was going to hit someone, and it might well be the Grand Adept. He'd come here from comfort, and the Grand Adept had spat in his face. He should take him up on his offer and walk out. The Grand Adept didn't want people like him? The Grand Adept thought he was weak? Fine, then. He was gone.

But he didn't move. Where would he go?

He stayed in the cathedral. Not everyone did. Some people had been ready to leave during the Grand Adept's long silence, and his words did nothing to change their mind. They walked quickly out the back doors, some scowling, some crying. Some people gathered in small groups after the Grand Adept left, talking in whispers that sometimes rose to normal tones and once or twice to yells. But just when shouting matches threatened to break out, people looked around and remembered where they were and calmed themselves.

They were a confused, distraught group down on the floor of the cathedral, but they were still there. Grand Adept Serl's words hadn't brought Lloyd any comfort, but the sight of all those people down there, struggling together, did. Those were the kind of people Lloyd wanted to be with. As long as they were still there, he could stay.

Chapter Thirty

Every time he tried to treat an injury, Kale told himself that he probably should have made a more detailed study of human biology. He treated himself the same way he did everything—by feel, by instinct, by doing what seemed to be the right thing at the right time. When he thought about it, he realized that there probably shouldn't be that much guesswork involved. This was his body he was talking about, a delicately balanced machine, and monkeying with things in the wrong way could have some unpredictable and potentially disastrous effects.

But so far it hadn't. He'd been doing this for many, many decades, and so far, so good. If he completely understood the way the body worked, if he had some knowledge beyond the most basic medicine, his solutions might be more efficient, and the time he took to discover them might be shorter. The solutions wouldn't be more effective, though. Kale knew Andy had studied biology in detail, and in his opinion Andy didn't look any healthier than he did. They had just taken two different roads to the same destination.

The trickiest part had been the burn on the back of his right hand. He didn't like to think of how it looked—charred black with the skin entirely burned away in some parts. Speeding the body's natural healing process was one thing—trying to regenerate things that normally wouldn't re-grow was considerably more complicated. The skin could be replaced with the help of some bio-material, but the muscle and especially the nerves required extra work. In some ways it was like talking to a stubborn child, convincing the old, singed nerve endings that the new material he was attaching to them really was a part of it—yes it was, yes it *was*, until finally the nerves agreed and started letting him feel again.

He had been the last person out of Far Rockaway, staying put until all of the chumchas were either escaped or dead. Fortunately, far more were the former. It had gotten quite complicated at the end, since the NArds that came in on this wave were far more competent than the ones that had been guarding the border during the initial invasion. Most of the disguises and camouflage he attempted were pierced, and he found himself having to dodge a number of quick, subtle attacks. He'd lost an adept or two while he was saving his own skin, and it bothered him. He should have been more prepared, he should have been better than he was. But it was over and done with now.

The sun had already come up when he arrived at his compound, and he had retired directly to his quarters. He didn't want to talk to Spree, because she'd just ask him questions, even though she'd probably seen a lot more of what happened than he did. He'd be ready to deal with her when he felt better.

Addressing his most serious wounds took most of the day. By nighttime, he wasn't all better, but his body was doing what it needed to so that he eventually would be back to normal. He had some aches and pains, but nothing that would prevent him from functioning. He still didn't feel ready to talk to Spree, but he knew he had to.

It didn't take much to find her. She was pacing outside his door, waiting for him to come out.

"They gonna kill him," she said. "Three days. Whitaker got three days left."

Kale walked quickly, leading Spree to her watching room. "Are you sure?" he said. "Are your sources good?"

"Are my sources good," Spree snorted. "Don't no need sources. Didn't no put work in. Just watched, boilin' NArds tell me everything."

"They've gone public?"

"They everywhere. Every newscast, every talk show, everything. They got people, they got footage, they telling they whole story all day."

"Footage? What kind of footage?"

"They taking high road for a change. Didn't no put up pictures of burning chumchas or bodies or nothing. Mainly showed NArds back on the wall, guarding they border, with a few shots of burnt earth and buildings. Make everyone feel good, give them pictures of the big strong NArds on the wall, let them go to sleep thinking the good guys won. Or if they secretly chumcha supporters, make them think they can't win."

"What about Whitaker?"

"Don't no show him at all. They put up Kravitz, the AG, and have him get all frowny and stern and talk about how the crimes of Whitaker cannot be ignored and have to be dealt with in a way that will be an example to Whitaker and all his people and anyone that might want to be one of his people someday."

"Which is why they have to do it quickly without any semblance of a trial."

"They say they got all the video they need to show he guilty. Trial would just waste public money. So they passing the savings on to the people by building a big execution box for the boy."

"Execution box?"

They had made it to Spree's viewing room, and she slid into her chair while Kale took his customary place behind her.

"Be patient, it'll come up soon. They run the AG thing every few minutes."

"You could just tell me about it."

"Don't no want to do AG's work for him. There he is. Cain's setting him up now."

Edison Cain, wearing his trademark beige suit, was finishing a question.

"... ensure that this execution will have the impact you are looking for?"

Kravitz frowned extra deep, putting furrows in his brow and mouth. "What we must remember is that this is not a simple crime—this is war. We have been invaded by members of the outlawed church, and extraordinary actions demand extraordinary responses.

"We need to be certain that the punishment we are administering will be witnessed by all who need to understand how serious we are, particularly by those who joined Whitaker in his invasion. Thus, we will be executing Whitaker on top of the wall dividing the United States of North America from the independent territory of Long Island."

Several reporters raised their hands and started speaking, but Cain was still on his feet and managed to put his voice above all the others in the room.

"You can't mean this execution will take place in the open air?"

"Of course not. We will be taking all precautions needed to ensure that the execution will take place as scheduled. Whitaker will be enclosed in a secure chamber that is bulletproof and has other protective measures. The execution will be carried out through psycho-kinetic means."

Boiling blood, Kale thought.

"I should add," Kravitz continued, "that we are forced to take the unfortunate step of showing the execution across all available networks. What happened in the Rockaways cannot happen again, and Whitaker will serve as an example for all who would follow in his footsteps. The execution will take place in three days."

There was another flurry of hands and voices, but Kravitz had said everything he intended to say. He walked away from the podium without giving another glance to the reporters.

Spree turned down the volume. "*That's* how NArds take care of crisis," she said.

"That's nothing new," Kale said. He sighed. "We need to get the word out."

"You no not listening," Spree said. "They show this every few minutes. Word is *out,* is *all* out. Called Nilda, let her know what's coming down, she already knew. Already heard, they all knew."

"If they already know, then they're already doing something," Kale said. "We should know what."

"Nilda already looking," Spree said. "I told her." She leaned a little closer to Kale. "Three days. You be ready?"

"Of course I'll be ready."

"You don't no look ready for anything."

He looked at the screens. No one had any pictures of Whitaker, so the nets used various sketches based on whatever descriptions they'd managed to cobble together. None of them looked alike. The world would not know what Courtney Whitaker looked like until they saw his face in his execution chamber.

"I will be," he said.

Moving west across the Island was like moving backward in time. Civilization thinned and then disappeared, leaving only hardpan and scattered weeds, a world where life had barely taken hold. Or maybe it was the future, when life had run its course and mostly faded away.

Kale's compound squatted on the hard ground, it's vinyl walls dull, its shape ungainly. Kale hadn't designed the building for looks, comfort, or efficiency. He'd designed it to do what it needed to do. Appearance was secondary.

It had been a long walk. No cab wanted to take Amelia this far, and she hadn't wanted to use any ILF vehicles to get here. She'd managed to get a driver to drop her off about a dozen miles away, and she'd had to walk the rest. It was late now, very late, and the city glowed purple just to the west, blotting out the stars. Amelia knew she'd have to rest soon, but she was at that peculiar stage where she felt too tired to sleep.

Walking up to Kale's compound was always an eerie experience. Between Kale and Spree and anyone else who might be staying there, the grounds were well monitored. If you weren't supposed to be there, one of any number of defenses would activate long before you came near the building. If you were welcome, however, everything was made easy for you. Gates and doors swung open on their own. Lights turned on to show you what path to travel. No one was visible, and there was no other sound beside the compound letting you in. Amelia always found herself shuddering a bit until she finally happened upon either Spree or Kale.

This time, she found Kale first. It wasn't hard—he came running down a hallway shortly after she had passed through an interior metal door. He didn't stop until he caught her in an uncomfortable, almost bruising hug. He didn't say anything for a while.

Finally he let her take a step back. He dropped his arms, then awkwardly touched her shoulder before letting his hand fall again.

"I knew you were okay," he said. "You know ... well, you know that I keep an eye on you. So I knew you got out of there okay." He smiled, and his lower lip shook a little. "I didn't even have to help you. You got out of there entirely on your own. I was impressed."

Amelia looked at her feet. "Thanks."

"So I knew you were alive, and well enough to get away, but that's all I knew. I didn't know if you were hurt, or if there was anything else wrong. I'm glad to see you ... whole."

Amelia didn't know what to say. She hadn't expected the conversation to go like this.

She was still looking down, but she could feel Kale still looking at her.

"I've made you uncomfortable," he said. "I'm sorry. Didn't mean to be so emotional. I was ... I'm glad to see you. But you're here for a reason, and I should stop interfering. What brings you out here?"

She could look at him now. She had one hand in her pocket, leaning back on one foot while she lightly scraped the toes of the other foot on the ground ahead of her. "The ILF is giving up."

Kale's eyes widened. "They're folding?"

"No, no. Not giving up on everything. But on this operation. On the invasion, and on Whitaker. They're done."

Kale puffed his cheeks and blew. "Okay. Well, I guess it got a little hotter than they thought it would."

"The chumchas haven't given up."

"Of course not. There's no way they could. The investment they have on this—well, they've put everything into it. Backing down isn't possible, not when they think their entire destiny is pushing them forward."

"And you're going to help them."

Amelia had known Kale her whole life, and he had not aged a bit the whole time. But now, when she asked that question, he seemed to age a full quarter century or more in an instant. His shoulders sagged, and wrinkles of all sorts appeared across his face.

"I thought I might," he said, and his voice was strangely small.

Amelia knew that if she asked him why he wanted to help them now, after keeping the Church at arm's length for so long, he might crack and change his mind on the spot. So she didn't ask.

"I want to help you," she said. "Whatever you're going to do, let me help. Make me part of your plan."

"I can't …"

"Don't try to protect me!" Amelia said. "I got out of Rockaway without your help, and I'll just go right back in without you. So let's cut the crap and use the next couple of days to do something useful."

The wrinkles were still on Kale's face, but some of them were smile lines.

"Okay," he said. "Okay. One more person on the team. One more to go against the most powerful nation on earth."

Chapter Thirty-one

A few times, just before the invasion, Lloyd had been up in the early hours of the morning. It was the first time he'd been outside of his dorm between 10 PM and 6 AM for years—adepts kept to a very regulated schedule, and Lloyd had never felt the need to deviate from it. Once he was out, though, he noticed there wasn't much difference between the middle of the night and the rest of the day, except for the level of light. Adepts and acolytes drilled, security patrolled, and there was a general sense of bustle about the whole cathedral.

That had been during the training, though. That was over now, the intensive schedule they had followed before the invasion had been abandoned. The grounds were still, quiet enough that Lloyd could almost hear the dew beading up on the lawn. Most of the lights had been dimmed—cathedral security preferred it dark, in case any intruders without the talent tried to stumble around at night. The brightest light came through the cathedral itself, royal-blue light streaming through the tall stained glass windows. From a distance, the windows hovered alone in the air.

Lloyd walked past the cathedral to the cluster of cottages behind it. All of them were dark, including his destination. But he knocked on the door anyway. The summons had hit him hard enough that it was still bouncing around in his skull. So while High Adept Birch's cottage looked dark, Lloyd was quite certain its occupant was awake.

<<It's open,>> Birch sent as soon as Lloyd knocked. Lloyd walked in.

The cottage wasn't as completely dark as it looked from the outside. There was a low-level dim light in the living room. It didn't come from any single source, but rather seeped out of every bit of air. It was enough light to keep Lloyd from bumping into anything, but that was about it. The tables, bookshelves, and chairs were dark blobs.

High Adept Birch was sitting on the other side of the room. Lloyd couldn't tell if he was still wearing his adept robes or if he had put on some sort of nighttime clothing. All he could see was his round face, and there wasn't even enough light to reflect off his bald scalp.

"Adept Hsu," High Adept Birch said. "Thank you for responding to what I know was a quite unusual summons. I have resigned myself to the fact that I won't be getting any sleep tonight, and I made the probably unwarranted assumption that others were in a similar state."

Lloyd wasn't sure what to say—he had, in fact, been quite asleep when High Adept Birch's summons had exploded in his head. He smiled awkwardly, even though he didn't know if the High Adept could see him.

"Why don't you sit?" the High Adept said, and Lloyd reached in front of him and touched a chair that was slightly fuzzy. He walked to the front of it and sat down. The chair was stiff.

"I've been thinking," High Adept Birch said. "Mostly, of course, about what we will do tomorrow. But also about what will happen afterward. And there are some things of which I think you should be aware."

Lloyd fidgeted, and the chair creaked. "Okay," he said.

"Courtney Whitaker earned himself a large number of admirers during our time in Far Rockaway, but I wouldn't say that many of us know him. Of all of the adepts, you and Adept Nesbitt were the closest to him."

"I'm not sure about that ..." Lloyd said. He didn't like to think about how annoying he had found Whitaker before the invasion. He wouldn't think of himself as Courtney's friend—he'd only known him for a few weeks.

"I've been encouraged by the amount of faith the clergy and our congregation has shown in the past few days, yet I worry perhaps we have gone too far. That we have faith in things that are not possible."

Lloyd could not recall any of his superiors at the cathedral ever even suggesting that there was such a thing as too much faith. His mouth struggled to say what he was thinking. "What ... what things? What is not possible?"

"When we get Whitaker back"—Lloyd noticed High Adept Birch did not think there was room for doubt on that issue, at least—"he will likely be different. Changed."

"How do you mean?"

"When we rescue Whitaker, we will be taking him from a box intended to kill him. I've reviewed our plan several times, along with our best estimates of when Drauer's people will begin the procedure, and the rescue will be a narrow thing. It's quite possible that we will save him at a moment when he has become convinced he is about to die. And that will come after days of being held captive by the USNA and being subjected to who knows what kind of treatment."

"Do you think they ..."

"Long experience has taught me not to put anything past USNA officials. I wish I didn't have to say this, but there is no limit to what they may have inflicted on him."

Lloyd lightly scratched at the fabric on the armrest of the chair. It was mildly abrasive.

"There are people who think that the Whitaker we rescue will be the same as the Whitaker who roamed around Far Rockaway. I think they may be in for a disappointment," Birch said. "He will need time. He will need to recover. There may be impacts to his mental health that will take a long time to manifest and a longer time to heal. We should not expect to rescue him and immediately have him lead us triumphant to the heart of Manhattan. This may be a longer-term effort. We need to be patient."

Lloyd nodded. "Whatever it takes, however long it takes, I'm sure we'll be ready."

Birch chuckled lightly. "I appreciate your dedication. Especially because I think you have a significant role to play in helping Whitaker recover from whatever the USNA has done to him."

"Me? I do?"

"As I mentioned, you and Adept Nesbitt are Whitaker's closest friends in the cathedral. You will be in the best position to help him talk about what he needs to talk about, and to use your friendship to help him heal."

"But I ... isn't there someone else? I mean, Whitaker had a life before he came here, didn't he? There's his mother, and he must have had some friends. Friends he's known longer than he's known me. Wouldn't they be in a better position to ...?"

"The Whitaker we know—the Whitaker we will have to deal with—was born the day you discovered him." High Adept Birch's voice had become raspier. "His mother will be helpful, of course, but she doesn't know what he is. What he became. You do. You were there for the whole evolution Whitaker went through. You will need to be there for whatever evolution lies ahead."

Lloyd wanted to say that he had no idea how Whitaker's evolution had occurred. He had abruptly shifted from an annoyingly shallow, ignorant boy to a confident, eloquent leader. It was a drastic, immediate switch, and Lloyd had no confidence he could play any role in accomplishing another such change.

But he didn't say that. "If there's anything I can do, I will do it," was the only thing he said.

"Good. That is as it should be." High Adept Birch moved a bit, and he may have smiled a touch. "But it is late, and there is much to do tomorrow, and there is always a chance that you will sleep more than I. Thank you for coming by."

Lloyd stood, unsure of the formalities of ending a casual conversation with a High Adept. He bowed slightly, but it felt awkward so he stopped, then turned to leave.

"Good night, High Adept," he said.

"Good night, Adept Hsu."

When Lloyd was at the cottage's door, the High Adept spoke again. "It's curious," he said. "We know, of course, that the prophecies of First Adept Ellis are the stepping stones that will take us to the destination we desire. But we persist on believing there is only one step between each stone, that we will skip lightly from one stone to the next. In truth, we may be required to occasionally take several steps on our own before returning to the comforting guidance of the First Adept's path."

There did not seem to be any response required to High Adept Birch's musings, so Lloyd didn't offer any. He stood quietly at the door for a moment, and when the High Adept did not offer any more thoughts, Lloyd opened the door and walked back to his dorm.

There was no way Spree could enter Kale's quarters if he didn't want her to. He hadn't survived as long as he had without learning how to keep some spells and wards running in his sleep. His door was locked in ways that none of Spree's electronics could affect, and had she been able to get it open she was sure there were other alarms and unpleasant things that would make her sorry she had made the attempt.

That was unfortunate, because what she really wanted to do was walk up to him and shake him awake. She was pretty sure he was asleep—if he was awake, there would probably be questions popping into his mind every few minutes so that he'd have to keep bothering her about something or other. She hadn't heard from him for over an hour, though, which generally could only be explained by Kale being away from the compound or unconscious.

She wished she had some way to wake him up. She needed someone to talk to. Everything was crazy here. The things they'd been doing pretty much since Spree came on board—arranging aid shipments, committing minor acts of sabotage, rescuing exiles—now seemed like nothing more than spinning their wheels waiting for something real to happen. And now it was real, and it was here—again—and Spree couldn't sleep. Didn't want to sleep. She wanted to drink and eat and tell stories and talk big and get ready to spit in Anderson Drauer's eye. She wanted to make someone fall in love with her and then dump him or her, all a single night (not Kale, of course—there were more problems involved in trying to seduce Kale than she cared to count).

She had one trick up her sleeve. Kale had entrusted her with the maintenance of each piece of electronic equipment in the compound, and she had found it easiest to control everything from the room where she did everything else. Which meant she could quite easily take over Kale's screen whenever she wanted.

He wouldn't be happy when he woke up, of course, and he'd know she was responsible for waking him up. But as long as he was up and Spree had someone to talk to, it didn't matter how angry he was. He could spend the rest of the night yelling at her, and she'd find that preferable to sitting up all night alone and watching a whole bunch of screens that all showed nothing much. Except for the box.

The NArds had put the box up just after sunset. It was in two pieces right now, the roof sitting next to the rest of the box. The roof was a simple black pyramid made of some black plastic composite, the box was clear with walls that were several inches thick.

Spree was pretty sure she knew how the whole thing would go down. They'd get Whitaker to the top of the wall, drop him in the cell, throw the roof on top and then sonically weld it to the cell. Then they'd damn sure shield the cell and make sure nothing on the frequency that could shatter that weld would get through. Once everything was secure, the show would begin—Spree didn't figure there would be any reason to wait. Every second that Whitaker stayed alive was a second that maybe Kale and the chumchas could pull off a miracle.

The display of the cell, swinging in front of the wall, was impressively dire, but Spree thought it might be a mistake by Drauer. Maybe, by looking at footage of it or even by sneaking through the borderlands and getting a look at the box in person, the chumchas could figure out a weakness in the cell's structure. Maybe it would be enough.

The stared at the box for another moment, but then remembered that it had distracted her from what she had meant to do. She had to close her eyes for a moment to block the box out of her mind so she could focus on annoying Kale.

She opened her eyes and flicked a few switches. Kale's screen was now on. She tuned it to AlphaNet, because it was loud. Kale would be awake soon and stomping down the hall to yell at Spree.

She sat back in her chair, pointedly averting her eyes from the one screen that was dedicated to a non-stop showing of the cell. She waited to hear Kale's door slam open.

After a few minutes, nothing had happened. So she turned up the volume in Kale's room. But more time passed, and Kale didn't come out.

Stupid old man, she thought. He was either deep asleep or avoiding her. Either way, it didn't look like she was going to get what she wanted.

She turned his screen off. How could he sleep so much? How could he sleep at all? She'd been keyed up before the Rockaway invasion, but this was even worse. She really didn't know anything about this Whitaker, but she knew the chumchas really wanted him back and the NArds really wanted him dead. That was enough for her to know this could be a big clash, the kind of thing she'd been waiting for ever since Kale dragged her out of the borderlands and gave her a place to stay. She'd been waiting for the USNA to pay for everything they'd done to her and to everyone like her, but Kale always talked about being patient and waiting for the right time. And now, maybe, finally the right time was here, and Kale was asleep.

If she wasn't going to wake Kale up, there was no point to being in the screen room. She stood up, walked out, and wondered where she should be.

After walking back and forth through various dark hallways, she ended up in the kitchen. She wasn't hungry, but she was there, so she slapped some peanut butter on a piece of bread, bit down, and chewed slowly. Maybe she could make it last all night. It would give her something to do.

She heard a creak, and then another one. She walked to the doorway, looked down the hall, and saw a light under a door that hadn't been on before. Amelia was awake, too.

Spree thought about knocking on the girl's door, but she never really knew how to talk to her. That girl was always so angry about something or another.

But at least she was awake. She had to be at least as keyed up as Spree, maybe more. She had a lot on the line in this thing, too.

Everyone did. Everyone was risking something. Everyone on the Island should be awake tonight.

But Kale, despite everything, was asleep.

Interlude: The Mouse and the Hawk

From *The Collected Speeches and Stories of Harriman Ellis*

There once was a mouse walking through a field of tall grass, gathering seeds for his evening meal. As he came near a spot in the ground that was a hill to him but would only be a small bump to larger creatures, he stopped cold. He had heard something that chilled him to the bone.

Then he heard it again. It was a snapping sound, a quiet, clean break. It was coming from the other side of the hill.

He knew better than to go anywhere near that sound. He backed slowly away from the sound for several paces, then turned and dashed away.

But the prairie winds had fooled him. The sound had not been in front of him, but behind. He saw it in front of him, white-and-grey feathers in an inverted arc, spread into a fan. Then the pure, dark grey feathers on the sides, cloaked over the ground. The head was low, out of view, and the shoulders jerked up and down with each snap.

The mouse knew he should flee, run as fast as he could, but he was frozen with fear. The sight and sound of the hawk ripping apart its victim overwhelmed any sense in the mouse's head.

But the hawk was too busy with its meal to notice the mouse, and eventually the small creature was able to recover his senses and start moving away.

Then the hawk spoke.

"You may stay if you like," the hawk said. "I have my meal in front of me, and I'm not looking for anything more." There was another snap as soon as the hawk finished talking.

"If it's all the same to you," the mouse said, "I'd rather be on my way."

"Whatever you wish," the hawk said. "But I have always enjoyed a good conversation with my meal."

The mouse knew he should run, but he found himself drawn to the opportunity to learn a bit more about one of his mortal enemies.

"Your meal," the mouse said. "Is that ... is he ..."

"Another mouse?" the hawk said. "A family member? No. It's a robin. Chubby and rather slow, I'm afraid."

"And how long will that last you?"

The hawk tilted his head as he swallowed his latest bite. "Today," he said. "You won't need to worry about me until tomorrow."

"Do you ... prefer to eat robins instead of mice?"

"That's a good question," the hawk said. "You definitely have different flavors, but I don't know if I could say I prefer one or the other. What I like is to switch back and forth."

"So tomorrow ..."

"Tomorrow we won't be having this conversation," the hawk said.

The mouse fell silent and once again thought about leaving. But the hawk spoke before he left.

"I know why you were asking the question, though. You were hoping I would say I would prefer robins. Then you would have a new way to escape me if I ever had my sights on you. If you do not have an escape hole nearby, all you need to do is run toward the nearest robin and let me eat it instead. Trade its life for yours."

The mouse was quiet for a moment. "I'm ashamed to admit that you're right, that I was indeed thinking that. But I appreciate you setting forth my thoughts in such clear terms, because you have helped me realize how wrong I would be to do what I was thinking. Should we meet on the field, I will try to escape you. But I will not live at the cost of another animal."

"How admirable," the hawk said. "However, I'm afraid the question is academic."

The hawk turned, facing the mouse directly for the first time. His beak was terribly sharp and spotted with blood. "It turns out this robin didn't have as much flesh on its bones as I expected, and I am still rather hungry. And while I like to alternate meals of mouse and robin, what I truly love is to combine them in a single meal."

The mouse was already moving away, but he knew he wouldn't be fast enough. He knew how hawks gave pursuit, and he knew he would be caught.

But he heard a strange noise behind him, a guttural sound followed by a light brush on the grass. And when he cautiously turned around, he saw the hawk lying on the ground, twitching. He was choking on a bone he had neglected to swallow or spit up properly.

There was nothing the mouse could do even had he wanted to. The hawk expired in short order, and the mouse went on his own way.

The moral is simple. Sometimes, the desire to be good is, by itself, enough. Because sometimes, evil cannot help but choke on its own foul deeds.

Chapter Thirty-two

There could be no sneaking in this time. No surprise. The USNA expected them to come—invited them, even. That was the only reason to execute Whitaker on top of the wall. The NArds wanted to dangle him in front of the church, to force them to make an effort to save him. There were plenty of ways they could kill him and allow the public to witness the execution, but only one that would be certain to draw the adepts of the church back to their front door.

Just like the last time, the sun was setting as Lloyd crossed through the borderlands. Just like the last time, the border rats knew enough to stay away.

There was at least one change, though. A screen, a giant screen, visible for miles. Lloyd had seen the glow from a distance, and knew immediately what it was. Screens gave off a glow like nothing else. What he didn't know was what it was there for or what it was showing. But that became clear soon enough.

The cameras must have been built right into the cell walls. They displayed a live image of Courtney Whitaker, his head looming over the borderlands, possibly larger than the main cathedral. His hair had been cut, trimmed to stubble, for no apparent reason other than to make him look more like a prisoner.

He was scared. His eyes darted around, his head wouldn't stay still. He looked up, down, back and forth, and twitched and twitched and twitched. The confidence he had possessed in the Rockaways, the lifted chin, the almost regal bearing—all were gone. He looked like the Whitaker Lloyd had first met after his blind journey across the Island, only every last bit of self-confidence had been stripped away. His mouth opened several times, it was clear that he was yelling, but no sound came from the screen. It did not require any talent for lip reading, though, to see that all he said was "Let me out!" over and over.

High Adept Birch's words from the night before now fully sank in. Lloyd didn't know how far Whitaker had buried his confident persona, but he knew it would be a devil of an effort to drag him back out again. He knew Whitaker would be relieved at his rescue, and Lloyd was anxious to see his face when it looked less fearful, but the confidence would be a long time in returning, if they could get it to return at all.

But that was a job for another day. Whitaker's face loomed before the advancing CMC army, asking again and again to be let out, and Lloyd dearly wanted to grant his request.

This assault was led by Grand Adept Serl himself, who sent crisp, curt directions to the adepts as if they were in the middle of mass

<<They do not want to keep us away,>> he sent as they approached. <<They want us there. They want to world to see us there. <<All we have to do is advance. No defenses, no caution. We just need to get there.>>

So they were advancing, most on foot with powerful winds at their backs, charging forward. To this point, the Grand Adept had been proven right. The NArds were content to let them come.

Lloyd felt nervous coming in sight of the wall without a shield around him. It was like those dreams about being naked in church, right down to the panicky feeling that disaster was just around the corner. But the orders had been given. Adepts were to save as much strength as possible, because they were going to need it.

As he ran, Lloyd kept an eye on the screen and Whitaker's face. The execution was not supposed to take place for another half hour—Grand Adept Serl had wanted to arrive in plenty of time to stop the procedure, but not before they had loaded Whitaker into the cell. His timing looked to have been perfect, but Lloyd was not convinced that the NArds wouldn't just go ahead and move the execution up a bit rather than deal with any possible inconveniences. But while Whitaker still appeared petrified, he didn't look like he was in pain. It hadn't started yet.

For perhaps the fifth time, Lloyd was startled by a brief "whoosh" sound that came from behind him. This time, he didn't turn around. He had looked before and got a quick glimpse of a man moving behind the frontline adepts, running back and forth doing who knows what. Lloyd recognized him because he had seen him a few times before—the first time was the day he met Amelia Diaz in her underground bunker, and he had seen the same old man lurking around the Rockaways after the invasion. He had asked around, and while no one seemed to know who the old man was, no one was concerned about his presence. Lloyd was surprised that some unknown outsider would be allowed to roam in their midst, but he assumed the church leaders had their reasons for letting the man stay with them.

The wall was now only a half-mile away. The breach they had made barely a week ago had been repaired. The surface of the wall was smooth, but they hadn't been able to match the color exactly, making the new wall a few shades lighter than the old section. When he saw the jagged "V" that he had run through not long ago, Lloyd felt a surge of pride and confidence. They had done the impossible once—doing it a second time should not be a challenge.

The wind behind him died, and Lloyd's feet made more regular contact with the ground until he was running at a normal pace, then jogging, then walking. The CMC lines were contracting as the adepts and acolytes pulled together, massed in a group facing Whitaker's cell. And Whitaker saw them.

His eyes widened, and for a moment he stopped yelling. There was almost a smile on his mouth, and then he started yelling again. As before, it was not difficult to make out what he was saying.

"Hey! Hey! There they are! Come on, come on! Get me out of here!"

Without thinking about it, without knowing what he was doing, Lloyd raised his arm in a sweeping wave. He didn't know if Whitaker could see him, but it felt like the right thing to do.

The entire CMC force had gathered together now, and Lloyd couldn't help but notice how small they looked without the support of the ILF. The strange old man was still there, darting back and forth before the motionless clergy, hopefully doing something useful. There was still no attack, or any activity at all, from the NArds on the wall.

<<Gather all your strength,>> Grand Adept Serl sent. His thoughts were firm but calm, soothing as cold water streaming over hot rocks. <<Remember your role. Use everything you have and then reach for more.>>

Lloyd pulled in force. It was one of those things adepts did without knowing just what it was they were doing. He was not gathering any sort of molecules of material, he could not explain what it was, but he knew when he unleashed it, it would have the force of an avalanche. Or so he hoped.

<<Now, as instructed,>> Grand Adept Serl sent. <<Spike first at the center, then disk at the top.>>

Lloyd was supposed to help make the disk, so he had nothing to do for a moment or two. A good number of adepts and acolytes, more than half of the total number, combined the force they had gathered into an invisible spike, like the head of a spear with a point whose width could be measured in molecules. Then they thrust it forward, hurtling it through the air, right toward the heart of Whitaker's cage.

There was no chance it would reach Whitaker. There was, undoubtedly, a tremendous shield around the entire cage. Should the spike penetrate the shield, or should the shield for some unfathomable reason not be in place, the adepts and acolytes would let their spike collapse on the wall of the cell.

<<The spike is away,>> Grand Adept Serl sent. <<Launch the disk!>>

Lloyd threw the force he had gathered into a giant disk, where it joined the force of several other adepts. They started the disk spinning and then threw it forward. It was aimed slightly above the cage; the idea was that if the spike did not penetrate the shield, it would at least weaken it around the edges, and the disk could shave away a good portion of it.

The disk was moving now, flying with great speed, and Lloyd knew something was wrong. Or rather, something was miraculously right. The disk had power in it that he had never felt before, and it was flying at speeds the adepts could not have obtained on their own. Someone was helping them out.

He didn't know what was happening with the spike; all his focus was on the disk. He hoped it wasn't moving too fast, since it would do no good if it hit before the spike. Its whirl was so fast that Lloyd thought he could feel a breeze from it where he was standing. It flew closer to the cell, its sharp edges looking for a shield so it could cut it to ribbons.

Then, in an instant, the disk shredded.

It was like a tire hitting road spikes at high speed. The disk simply fell apart, force dissolving to the air, and the sensation of it was like Lloyd's mind was being torn in half. His hands reached for his head and his knees buckled.

He managed not to collapse, though. He rested his elbows on his knees briefly, then stood up as soon as he could. His stomach was heaving.

Other adepts had not stayed on their feet. They were on the ground, in the dust, some writhing, some twitching. The ones that were still standing looked disoriented and confused.

Grand Adept Serl's voice cut through the pain in Lloyd's head like a fan blowing on mist. <<We must recover! We cannot let our efforts slack. The shield is not breached, but it is damaged! Saws, now!>>

Acting on reflex more than conscious thought, Lloyd gathered a thin line of force and send it toward the shield. He pushed it forward cautiously, not wanting to charge this time. Before long, he felt it. It was solid, dark, seemingly undamaged. It was power with its own gravity, a force that seemed like it could rip Lloyd's mind out of his skull if he pushed too far into it. It had the form of a shield, but it felt like pure destruction.

Lloyd hated the feeling of it, hated having a part of his mind so close to it, but he could not withdraw. He set his small line of force to moving, a back-and-forth sawing motion. He made the edge of it rough so his force would cut into the shield and gradually pick it apart.

His wasn't the only saw. Every adept, every acolyte, was cutting away at the shield. If they were doing it right, if they were applying enough pressure, the NArds were feeling it, the cutting motions working into their brains. The more they cut in, the deeper they went, the more it would hurt and the weaker the shield would become.

Lloyd pressed his saw ahead. The progress was slow, but it was happening. It was moving deeper. He wanted to look at the screen, to see if Whitaker noticed any of this and took comfort from it, but he needed to concentrate fully on his saw, pushing it deeper and deeper, cutting through the shield.

He leaned forward, as if the saw was a physical object that he could force ahead with his weight. He heard grunts and groans around him as the others pressed ahead too, working their saws. Cutting through. Making progress.

Then he hit something. Something different, just as dark but harder. It stopped his saw in his tracks. He tried to get it moving again, but the new layer, the hard layer, was expanding. Pushing him back. Accelerating. Moving fast now, then faster, his saw losing all the ground it had gained and then some. It was then thrown back, his saw flying through the air as it dissolved completely, and once again Lloyd nearly fell to the ground.

He blinked through the sweat that was streaming into his eyes. They had been anticipated. The NArds had the perfect counter for their first two attacks. They could really use the element of surprise, but so far they didn't have it.

Lloyd looked at the screen and saw Whitaker shaking his head and crying. He must have seen what was happening below him, adepts falling to the earth, and he must have known the time of execution was drawing nearer as his rescuers helplessly collapsed.

The strange old man was there then, helping adepts to their feet, looking intently at each one as he pulled them up. He was clearly sending them something, but Lloyd didn't know what.

The old man ran by Lloyd and saw him standing—his knees were weak, but Lloyd had remained upright. The sending came in a brief, urgent burst.

<<Hit the cell's supports,>> he said. <<Bring it down. I'll catch it.>>

Lloyd nodded curtly even though the old man wasn't looking at him anymore. He had already started to focus on the beams holding the platform on which the cell was mounted when a sending from Grand Adept Serl arrived.

<<All of you, do what the old man is telling you. Do it fast!>>

Lloyd knew he didn't have time to reach out and do any sort of analysis of whatever the supports were made of. He would have to go in fast and crude.

He started with sound, sonic waves no one would hear but would excite the molecules of the support. It was a tricky operation, using one part of his mind to try different frequencies while another monitored the support to see if he was making any difference. He waited for a sign of heat, any sign that what he was doing was making a difference.

But he couldn't even put a solid wave together. There wasn't a shield around the supports, but the NArds kept tossing waves of interference through the area, breaking up anything he organized.

So he switched tactics. Microwaves. Easier to organize, didn't need to be quite as sustained. He could send a burst here, a burst there, and hope for the best.

He managed to get a number of pulses through, once even collapsing one of the interference bursts the NArds sent. But when he checked, he couldn't detect any difference in the support. Damn thing must be microwave safe.

He threw more bursts, hoping others were doing the same. He heard noises around him, but he didn't know what they were. Were people yelling? Crying? Or was there just some distant pack of dogs, or maybe geese, blathering away?

But he couldn't pay attention to the noise, or anything beside the support. The support had to give. Something had to happen.

Sound wasn't working. Microwaves weren't working. He needed heat, he needed it fast, he needed it *there*. He needed ...

Atoms. Collisions between atoms. Hydrogen.

There wasn't much in the air, trace amounts, but he could find enough. He put out a filter, dragged it through the air, pulling all the hydrogen he could to the supports. He kept waiting for the NArds to scatter his collection, but they weren't looking for that tactic. The hydrogen soon hovered around the support, ready to float away without Lloyd keeping it down.

He had never done this before—for all he knew, no one had ever done this before. But it had to be possible. It had to. All it took was a collision, right? Densely collected atoms, a high enough speed, and heat that could melt anything.

He tried to get the atoms moving, sending them around at high speeds, then faster, then faster, and there were some collisions, there had to be, but not fast enough. Not enough heat.

So he accelerated them. Got them moving faster and faster. And he crushed them down, moving them together, and it almost seemed like he could feel the atoms bouncing around, like billions of tiny marbles.

He had no idea what was going on around him, except that the NArds had finally noticed him. He felt them trying to interfere, brushing at the edge of his collection, but he must have made the walls too strong, because the efforts fell away without any real impact.

It was happening. Or at least, it was going to. He had a feel for it now, just like the feel he had developed for fire and electricity. He would keep the speed increasing until hydrogen became helium, until there was a minor sun by the support, and the cage would come down.

His mind was vibrating, shaking, like the atoms were inside his skull, and he kept them moving ever faster. NArds attacks came more frequently, but they were too hesitant and he was too confident. He swatted them away with barely a thought. It wouldn't be long now.

Then something hit him. A crushing blow to his left side. His breath fled from his lungs as his feet left the ground. There was something wrapped around his midsection, and something hard in his stomach, and he was falling. He had lost sight of the support, now he could only see the sky with its small collection of stars.

He'd lost it. As his back hit the ground, he knew it was gone. He'd lost his concentration, and the hydrogen was gone, floating away. Slowing back down as it left him.

Something—someone—was on top of him. The person was breathing heavily and climbing off Lloyd. He lifted his head and looked.

It was the old man. The goddamned strange old man had tackled him.

Lloyd struck, first with his fist, then with his mind. The old man turned both blows away without much effort.

"You can't!" the old man said. "You can't do that!"

Lloyd had no idea what the old man was talking about. All he could do was shake his head.

"You can't control it," he said. "You start what you were trying to start, it doesn't stay localized. It goes everywhere. You would kill us all!"

Lloyd wanted to argue, but then he remembered what he was supposed to be doing here. And he looked.

Whitaker had moved back. He was leaning against the back wall. His head was wobbling back and forth, his face a mass of twitches. He looked flushed.

The old man made a sound, an animal scream, and ran off. Lloyd looked away from the screen and toward the cell and threw whatever he could think of. More microwaves, needles, lightning, whatever. The air around the cell lit up, but nothing got through. Nothing helped.

Whitaker wasn't standing in his cell anymore. He was on the ground, twisted in the small confines, writhing. Lloyd knew he shouldn't look at the screen, knew there wasn't anything there he should see, but he looked, and he saw the burns and the blisters on Whitaker's skin, and he knew it was because he was burning from the inside. Whitaker had fallen, but Lloyd could still see his face, because the bastards had chosen the camera locations carefully because they knew this would happen, and they didn't want anyone to miss any part of it. Whitaker's mouth was open and there was no sound from the screen but Lloyd could hear him anyway, a scream that split Lloyd's skull, and he wanted to look away from the screen and do something else, try one more thing, but there was nothing more to do, and Whitaker's movement was already slowing down because smoke was rising from him, there were parts of him that were blackened on the outside and the parts Lloyd couldn't see would be worse, and then Lloyd knew, he knew that wasn't Whitaker anymore, that wasn't anyone anymore in there, it was just a corpse, because the chosen one, the one Harriman Ellis had prophesied would come, was lying on the bottom of a USNA cell and was completely, irrevocably dead.

Part Six: Heretic

Chapter Thirty-three

Lloyd drifted. He floated through currents of the church that he didn't really know existed. Hampton was an important part of the church, but it was also isolated. There were thriving congregations, crowded chapels across the hemisphere. There were churches across the ocean, too, but Lloyd hadn't made it that far. Not yet. The currents so far did a better job carrying him north and south instead of east or west.

The first current took him north and east to Nova Scotia. Halifax. A city with multiple parishes, the first time Lloyd had been to such a place since he was eight. A city that became noticeably darker each day as warmth slid away from it.

When Lloyd was there, he kept wondering how he had gotten there. Had he applied for reassignment? Had he just been transferred? He couldn't remember. He had no memory of anyone at Hampton telling him "You're going to Halifax." He was just there one day, and he wasn't sure he was supposed to be. But people at his church treated him like he belonged and gave him duties to perform, so he reasoned he must be in the proper place. It didn't matter how he had gotten there as long as he was expected and had something to do.

He had some vague notions that he had tried to get in touch with his family at some point. He might have even made a phone call, something he did very rarely in Hampton due to the lack of secure lines. He had a recollection of talking to a series of people who had been supportive but distant, the way you might talk to a total stranger you saw sobbing on a street corner. If Lloyd's recollections were correct, the conversation was pleasant enough and even buoyed his spirits, but only briefly.

He stayed in Halifax for a time, and then he left. He couldn't remember why. He didn't think there had been a problem, since he couldn't remember fighting with anyone and he couldn't remember anyone telling him he was in trouble. He was in Halifax for a while, and it was cold but it was peaceful enough, and then he wasn't there. He was on a boat, and it took him to a town called Stephenville. A few thousand people, a single church, and water everywhere. Very picturesque—Lloyd didn't have too many memories of his time in Stephenville, and most of it involved sitting on rocks and watching waves while pretending it wasn't cold.

Then it wasn't. It was warm, quite warm. He washed out of Canada and moved to independent Mexico, the one sliver of the former nation the USNA didn't control, mainly because the nation had ignored the little northern outcropping on their push south. Lloyd found himself in Cancun, where hotels that had once catered to tourists were stuffed with refugees who had arrived years ago, just ahead of the USNA troops, and still hadn't found a permanent place to go. And why should they move on when the hotels they were staying in weren't too bad? The air conditioning even worked in some rooms, at least when the power was running.

There was plenty of work in Cancun. In some ways it reminded Lloyd of Hampton, cut off and isolated from the rest of the church, but smuggling goods to Cancun was easier, mainly because it was closer to the parts of Central America where the church still held sway. Still, there were shortages, questionable reception of network signals, and everything else that Lloyd thought about when he thought about Hampton. Which he did as seldom as possible.

The weather was nicer in Cancun than in had been in Stephenville, but it seemed like Lloyd had more time in Stephenville to just wander around aimlessly and look at things. In Cancun there was always something to do—every minute could be scheduled for Lloyd if he wanted it to. People threw work at him from all directions, and all he had to do was make sure he ate and slept. The rest was just following orders.

But it seemed he didn't do that well enough. Lloyd seemed to remember whispered remarks about how slowly he moved. Sometimes people would try to make excuses for him—"Shh," they'd say. "That one, he was there when ... he was there ..." and their voices would trail off as they explained why he couldn't be expected to do anything quickly.

Eventually, though, the explanations weren't enough. Some people—Lloyd didn't know who they were, but they seemed like people in authority, High Adepts or something—sat him down and told him they appreciated his efforts very much and thought he was a bright and clearly very talented young man but that Cancun was likely not the best fit for him. There were places, they said, not too far away where the pace of the work might be better suited to Lloyd and he might have more chances to indulge in his contemplative nature. So they sent Lloyd south.

He rode in the back of a mostly empty fruit truck that smelled like decay and was filled with the buzz of flies even when the truck engine was roaring. Once again, he was infiltrating USNA territory, but Lloyd felt no thrill at the prospect. He also didn't feel any fear, nervousness, or anything else. He wanted to get out of the truck because it smelled bad, but that was the extent of his emotional involvement in the journey. The truck took him south without incident, and when it unloaded him he was in Guatemala City.

And he felt something when he was there, though he wasn't quite sure what it was. He remembered a time back in Hampton when he had been sitting in a room with some other adepts and High Adept Birch had just strolled in and started talking. Birch was not the most talkative man Lloyd had ever met, but on that occasion he had been giddy and the words would not stop.

"We have seen prophecies be fulfilled before," Birch had said, starting at what sounded like the middle of a discourse. "They started being fulfilled shortly after the First Adept made them. And the non-believers, they always dispute it. They cannot see what is plain. But how will they ignore this? How will they not see the hand of the Creator in this?"

Then he recited the prophecy.

Justice will burn
Fire in the old cathedral
Sorting the righteous
Purging the wicked

"How can anyone not see? How can anyone not believe? There had been confusion about this in the past, of course, because of the world 'old.' There are so many old cathedrals, how would we know which one he was talking about? How could we prove that the event, when it happened, was the one the First Adept predicted?

"But it happened in Antigua Cathedral. Antigua Cathedral! Old cathedral! What more to the doubters want? How much more specific would they like the prophecies to be?"

It took Lloyd and the others some time to get Birch to say just what had happened, but when he did they were as impressed as he was. It felt like something was in the air, like all the talk from CMC leadership over the years was going to lead to something. And for a few brief months, it had.

More than a year later, Lloyd had arrived where it all started. Maybe that was a good thing, maybe it was a bad thing, but being in this place drew some response from him, an itch of curiosity. It was possible that he wanted something from this place, which would be the first time in almost a year that he felt like he really wanted anything.

The trick, though, was that he wasn't at all sure what it was he wanted. But he had some idea what he wanted was tied to what happened in Antigua, so it gave him an avenue to follow. Something to do besides following orders.

The church in Guatemala City was far less chaotic than the congregations in Cancun. When he'd arrived in Cancun, he'd been shuttled around town by people who were mainly concerned with making him someone else's problem. He bounced around from building to building until he was finally directed to a cot in a long, narrow room. He had a place to sleep, but he hadn't found anything to do until the next day.

When he arrived in Guat City, on the other hand, Lloyd was taken to a broad concrete building next to the city's cathedral and told to enter the glass double doors in the middle of the building. Once he was inside, a friendly woman in acolyte robes beamed at him from behind her desk.

"Welcome to Guatemala City!" she said—in English, to Lloyd's mild surprise. "You must be Adept Hsu."

"Yes," Lloyd said.

The woman stood. She was barely taller standing than she was sitting, and she had round, glistening cheekbones. Her black hair was pulled into a small bun.

"I'm Acolyte Violeta Guerrero," she said, grabbing his hand with both of hers. "We are *so* happy to have you here. We've heard so much about you."

"Really?" said Lloyd. He tried to keep his tone light, but he could tell from Acolyte Guerrero's expression that he failed.

She patted the back of his hand while she smiled reassuringly. "Only good things, of course," she said.

"Of course."

"I'm not sure how much they told you in Cancun about the routine here."

"Very little," Lloyd said, because he thought saying "nothing" would sound too harsh.

"Then that just gives me the chance to tell you whatever I want. Come, walk with me," she said. Lloyd followed her down a hallway to an elevator.

"We ask every clergy member who is new to the city to stay here for the first few months. You will be based out of the cathedral, where of course there is plenty of work for everyone. When they get a better understanding of your skills and abilities, the High Adepts will decide where you should be stationed."

"That sounds fine."

The elevator doors opened, and Violeta led Lloyd in and pressed the button for the third floor.

"The quarters here are comfortable, of course, but I hope you'll understand if they're plain. Once you have a place where you can really get settled, it will be a little bigger than the rooms here."

"I'm sure whatever you have will be fine with me."

The elevator doors opened and Violeta walked about halfway down a long hallway. She stopped in front of a door marked "312" and pushed the door open.

"This will be your room," she said. "It will be up to you to lock it however you want."

"Thanks," said Lloyd. He wandered in. There was a single bed, a plastic desk and chair, and a window that looked at another grey concrete building.

"This looks like a great place for private contemplation," Lloyd said and hoped he didn't sound sarcastic.

"That's what we try to provide," Violeta said. "I'll give you a little time to get settled, then I'll come get you and we can start your orientation."

"Okay. Thanks," Lloyd said, and Violeta left.

He took a look around the room, then pulled open a closet door. He took off his backpack and tossed it in, and it fell to the closet floor with a solid thunk. He closed the closet and sat heavily on the bed.

There, he thought. Settled.

As disorienting as Cancun had been with its lack of organization, Lloyd wasn't really looking forward to being oriented here. Starting over in a new place took energy, and Lloyd didn't feel up to it. He'd already started over twice in the past year.

But if he cut out on the very first assignment they had for him, they'd probably have him either on kitchen or on babysitting duty in the very near future. As bad as starting over was, those would be worse.

So when Violeta knocked on his door, he quickly stood to follow her.

The orientation took the rest of the day. He spoke with Violeta, High Adept Crissella Flores, and Adept Estaban Blanco, High Adept Flores' assistant. They regaled him with plenty of facts—the history of Guatemala as it related to the church, the number of church members in the city, the responsibilities of different adepts, and even the major festivals celebrated in this part of the world.

But throughout the afternoon and evening, no one said anything about Antigua. High Adept Flores highlighted over a dozen important events in the recent history of the church in Guatemala, but none of them had anything to do with fire in Antigua.

The orientation process made Lloyd feel a lot like he was a first-year adept again. He had to do a lot of tests to show what he knew, both about doctrine and about PK spells (he deliberately underperformed on most of those), and they occupied him with lots of busy work that did very little to affect anyone's life in any way, including Lloyd's.

On the positive side, this meant Lloyd had plenty of time to think and, when he felt so inclined, to talk to people in the city. Some days, when he felt up to it, he'd finish his tasks as quickly as possible, leaving him time to wander in the city near the cathedral. There was lots of adobe and stucco, white buildings and light concrete making midday blindingly bright.

While the city was attractive, Lloyd thought the people seemed somewhat guarded. Part of that might be because his Spanish was still developing—he'd learned some on the fly in Cancun, but he was fairly certain he spoke it like a four-year-old. Whatever limited affability he managed to coax from the people he met always disappeared when he mentioned the church in Antigua. They would just shake their heads and act like they didn't understand what he was saying, even though "Catedral de Antigua" was one of the earliest Spanish phrases he had learned.

The clergy in Guatemala City wasn't any more helpful. In Hampton, Lloyd had been surrounded by acolytes and adepts in the same position he was, people he could ask questions about anything that was on his mind. Here, he was the only new arrival as far as he could tell. There were other people in the building, but whatever they were up to didn't involve Lloyd. He exchanged cordial hellos with them when he could, but they always seemed to be hurrying to some place or another, a place that invariably was away from Lloyd.

He tried, though—probably too much. He had developed a habit of bringing up Antigua as soon as he could in conversation, and he often didn't bother to remember if he had already quizzed the person he was talking to on a previous occasion. Once, when he was coming in after a long day of having his PK skills tested, he found Violeta behind the desk and talked with her for a bit. When he mentioned Antigua, she tilted her head and frowned.

"I think you've mentioned Antigua every time I've talked to you," she said.

"Really?"

"Yes. And you seem kind of anxious about it. It really makes me wish I had some idea what you were talking about so I could be helpful."

"You've really never heard of the miracle of Antigua?"

"Like I've told you before, I'm afraid I don't know what you're talking about." She then smiled brightly and changed the subject.

Lloyd didn't like the fact that people might think he had a one-track mind, but he supposed that was inevitable. And he cared a whole lot more about getting some answer about Antigua, any answer, than he cared about what people thought of him.

His single-mindedness, however, didn't bring him anything besides puzzled stares for weeks, until most of his interest at being in Guatemala had faded. He still mentioned Antigua to anyone and everyone, but his hope of finding even a small tidbit of information had started to fade.

It was quite a surprise, then, when his questioning finally drew a response besides blankness. It happened when he was at a market, buying guabilla. He almost didn't say anything to the fruit vendor once the bartering was over, but he stopped walking away after a single step, sighed, and turned back to the vendor.

"Usted sabe qué sucedió en Antigua?" he asked.

The vendor was rearranging his fruit, and he didn't look up. He didn't speak for a moment, and when he did, it was in English.

"You want to know about Antigua," the man said. It wasn't a question, and he placed the emphasis on the word "you."

It was all Lloyd could do from grabbing the man's shirt and pulling him close. "Yes. Yes! What do you know?'

The vendor looked directly at Lloyd. He had small, round eyes with heavy lids that could open no more than halfway. "No sé nada," the vendor said.

Lloyd lowered his voice to a whisper. "I need to know!" he said. "I need to know something! Please!"

"No sé nada," the vendor said again and returned his attention to his fruit.

Lloyd walked away dejected. Why should a fruit vendor, of all people, be different? Why should that one man provide what the rest of the population of Guatemala City could not offer?

It wasn't until he was undressing that evening that he saw a small piece of paper fall out of his pants. He unfolded it and saw an address: 2, 2 Ave., San José Villanueva.

He went to the computer room, and within minutes he found where he would need to go. It would be a long walk down Calz Raul Aguilar Batres to get there. He'd go tomorrow.

The sun was setting by the time he was finally able to make it away from his dorm. It was a pleasant evening, warm and not too humid, and the sky glowed orange with scattered clouds and hovering dust. The streets were filled with so many pedestrians that cars had difficulty getting anywhere. A few bikes weaved in and out of the slowly moving walkers, occasionally clipping people's hips with their handlebars.

Lloyd stayed to the edges of the crowd, moving as fast as he could near the buildings and doorways. His black robe got the attention of a few passers-by, and one or two of them nodded at him and smiled. Others looked away.

The farther southwest he traveled, the sparser the crowd became. He passed the markets and multi-level apartments and walked through neighborhoods of scattered, low houses and weed-strewn lots. Lloyd occasionally heard the sounds of people walking or running, but he seldom saw anyone. The streets near the cathedral had been full of voices, but here, no one spoke.

He crossed a small creek that had no buildings near it, only flat expanses of concrete. Whatever had been here was gone, ripped away.

In order to get to 2 Avenue, Lloyd had to cut across one of these brownfields. At some points weeds were as high as his knees, but for the most part the concrete was still solid, with few cracks

for plants to push through. The empty space made it easy for Lloyd
to see his destination, a small cluster of wooden buildings gathered
around a handful of dead-end streets. He became concerned as he
drew closer to the buildings—many of the windows were either
broken or boarded up. He'd walked all this way without using the
talent, not even bothering to scan the minds of the crowd to check
for pickpockets or other possible threats. In fact, the only things he
had used the talent for since he had arrived in the city was getting
through his orientation exercises and locking and unlocking his
door. As he approached the seemingly empty buildings, though, he
reached for the talent and felt a sudden surge of worry that he
wouldn't remember how to make it do what he wanted.

But it hadn't really been that long—a few months of letting his
exercises slide could not compete with his years of rigorous training
in Hampton. The talent responded to him immediately, ready to do
whatever he wanted it to.

He pushed his mind toward the buildings, scanning carefully.
Building after building was as empty on the inside as on the outside.
He suddenly wished the man who had slipped him the note had
bothered to include a specific time with the address.

But then there was someone. A very calm mind in the first floor
of a building hidden from Lloyd by other structures. There was no
trace of a shield on the mind—the person must not be a PK. The
individual might be asleep, since Lloyd had trouble pulling any
conscious thoughts from the mind. Out of instinct, he slowed
down, giving himself time to find whatever he could about this
mind.

The sending, when it came, surprised Lloyd so much it might as
well have been a thunderclap going off right behind him.

<<You can take as much time as you like,>> the sending said,
<<but the quicker you get here, the quicker we can be done with
this. For whatever it's worth, I can guarantee your safety.>>

It's worth nothing, Lloyd thought, but buried the notion deep
down where it couldn't be read.

He kept walking slowly. He checked the surrounding area and
didn't find anyone else, so he focused all his energies on the one

person he'd found. There was neither a shield nor any readable thoughts. Lloyd couldn't detect a trace of a threat or hostility, but that didn't mean much because he couldn't detect anything else. So he spent the rest of the walk preparing defenses against physical and mental attacks. It was a good refresher course.

No. 2, 2 Avenue was a dump, a two-story building that sagged on its southern end. The front porch of the house was three feet off the ground, but there was only an empty space where the steps up to it should be. Lloyd took a running start and leaped, feeling somewhat proud that he made the jump easily without any PK assistance.

<<Come on in,>> the person inside the building sent. <<Glad you made it.>>

Lloyd pushed the door open without touching it. The push was a little too hard—the dry, splintered door nearly ripped off its hinges. It swung around fast and slammed into something inside the building, then almost bounced closed.

"You seem very enthusiastic," a woman's voice said. It had the same dry, calm tone as the sendings.

Lloyd stepped cautiously toward the doorway. "It's not ... I'm a little out of practice."

"That explains why I could practically feel your fingers rubbing my brain when you tried to read me," the voice said. "Now come on, come in, you've been dallying out there long enough."

Lloyd walked into the dark house. The sun had completely set, and inside the building was as dark as night. When wizard light flared near the ceiling, Lloyd blinked several times before he could see anything.

When he finally could focus, he saw a short, squat woman sitting on a chair whose upholstery was little more than fraying ribbons.

"Hola, adepto joven," the woman said. Her voice was heavy and thudding.

"Hola," Lloyd said, and his mind refused to remember any other Spanish words.

Fortunately, the woman continued the conversation in English. "You have not been here long," she said. "There are some things you do not know."

"There's a whole hell of a lot that I don't know," Lloyd said.

The woman acted as if he hadn't spoken. She continued to sit placidly, hands folded on her lap. "Antigua is not discussed. Anyone who discusses it for long soon finds out that it is not a suitable topic for conversation."

"How do they find this out?"

Again, the woman did not respond to him. "You have two choices on the matter. One is to stop asking. Most people here have chosen that solution. Stop asking, stop talking. It is safer."

"And the other choice?"

The woman looked directly at Lloyd for the first time. Her eyes were difficult to see behind heavy eyelids and thick, round cheekbones. "The other choice is to learn quickly. Find out what you can before anyone stops you."

"That one," Lloyd said. "That second one. That's what I want."

The woman sat quietly for a moment, staring at Lloyd. On impulse, he reached out with his thoughts, a sharp, quick stab into the woman's mind. She was talking about Antigua—there was a good chance some thoughts about the place were bubbling into her conscious mind.

It was like trying to read the air. He came up with nothing—not only was she not thinking of Antigua, she did not seem to be thinking of anything at all.

"I am here," the woman said, "because I am suited to be here. I have a small bit of the talent, enough to send thoughts to you and let me hear thoughts you send to me. I also have an ability earned through meditation—I can completely empty my mind. It comes in handy." Her cheeks widened in a smile.

"Fine," Lloyd said. "I can't read you. So just tell me. Tell me what happened in Antigua."

"That is not for me to say. If you are going to hear that story, you should listen to the right people."

"Which people? What do you want me to do?"

"I want you to say that you understand that if you learn what you want to know, you will be making your life more difficult."

"I understand," Lloyd said. "I'll deal with whatever consequences come my way."

The woman nodded. "I hope you were not planning on sleeping much tonight."

Chapter Thirty-four

Lloyd was not allowed to know where he was going. At least they didn't blindfold him, though there wasn't much to see in the dark besides the headlights of oncoming cars.

The woman from 2 Avenue had led Lloyd on a short walk to a truck that had to be at least fifty years old. Lloyd was directed to sit in the back and told that if he tried to read the mind of the driver his trip would immediately end and he would be left stranded wherever he happened to be at the moment he decided he was too important to follow directions.

So he rode quietly and kept his mind to himself. He had been scanned at least twice during the ride. Both were clumsy, fumbling efforts, like a child playing piano after only two or three lessons. Lloyd didn't bother trying to shield himself—the only thought anyone scanning him was likely be able to read was that he really, truly wanted to know more about Antigua. He didn't know why he trusted these people or what made him think that they would bring him anywhere he wanted to be. The simple fact was that they were the only people offering what he wanted.

The truck drove and drove, then finally stopped somewhere where there was only one visible light, a yellow glow coming from a small window on top of a rise to Lloyd's right. He couldn't make out much of the surrounding landscape, but judging from the roadside it was a broad, patchy meadow. Here and there, Lloyd could make out a few silhouettes of clumps of trees.

The driver of the truck had already exited and was walking down the road. Lloyd couldn't begin to guess where he was going.

He scrambled out of the back of the truck. "Am I supposed to follow you?" he said.

The driver turned. He lifted his shirt a bit, and the glimmer of moonlight was enough to tell Lloyd that he was seeing light bounce off gunmetal. Lloyd took that as a "no." The driver dropped his shirt, turned, and continued on his way.

A quick scan told Lloyd that someone was in the building on top of the rise. He could always start the truck and go back home (sparking an auto engine to life without a key was a simple trick for any PK who worked with electricity), but he had been taken out here for a reason, and he guessed that reason was sitting near the yellow light.

He walked through the meadow, hearing dry grass crackle under his feet. Crickets chirped in front of him, falling silent as he passed.

Lloyd thought about getting a reading on the person waiting ahead, but he did not know how much PK ability these people had access to. Encountering one rogue PK already was unsettling enough; he did not want to attract the attention of others.

He opted for a quick, broad scan, mainly to discover if anyone nearby meant him any harm. He didn't find a trace of hostility, so he pushed ahead.

The light turned out to be coming from a small, square adobe home. The window with the light was the only opening on the side of the building Lloyd approached. He found a door on the side opposite him.

He knocked on the door, and it rattled. There was no response, no movement from inside. Lloyd reached out quickly and found that the person was still there and seemed awake. So he knocked again, and again got no response.

There was no lock or knob on the door, so Lloyd reached forward and pushed. It opened easily. He stood in the doorway, looking forward, and all he saw was an empty room with a dirt floor. There still was no response or movement from whoever was there.

Lloyd took a hesitant step forward. Then another. Then he saw the person who was waiting for him—a thin, wiry man with the look of a marathoner about him, the kind of person who could probably run for days on end. His skin was weathered, especially the crinkles that surrounded his eyes. He looked neither hostile nor friendly.

"Hola," Lloyd said. "Soy ..."

The man cut him off with a quick wave of his hand. "Silencio," he said.

Lloyd stood still, listening. Was someone coming? He made a quick scan and still didn't detect anyone besides the man. The driver of the truck seemed to be long gone. There was nothing at all threatening in the air.

Then Lloyd understood.

He laid a static blanket over the room. Aron had helped him learn this trick, since Aron was especially good at spells that involved avoiding detection. Now, any PK—or at least, any PK of approximately Lloyd's skill level—would notice nothing but silence in this building, no matter how much noise Lloyd and the other man made.

"Acabado," Lloyd said when the spell was ready.

The man nodded. "Good," he said. "Now, I will tell you what I have to tell you and then you will leave. You will not ask any questions. Do you understand?"

Lloyd nodded. He knew he could overpower the man easily if he wanted to, maybe force him to give as much information as Lloyd wanted. But that was not the way he wanted to do things.

"I was at Antigua," the man said. "When the fire fell. I was one of the first to hear about it, because my cousin watched the border for the military. He told me about the miracle, and about the people who were risking their lives to sneak across the border. Soon, that trickle would become a flood that pushed the USNA guards back, but I went in before that happened. I cannot imagine that their guards did not sense me as I passed, but for whatever reason they decided to let me through to see the miracle.

"It was the most beautiful thing I had ever seen. It was brilliant orange fire, cascading slowly down from the ceiling of the cathedral. It looked like molten metal being poured at a foundry, only it fell slower and with more grace. When it hit the altar, it scattered sparks like a new galaxy was being born in the cathedral.

"I saw the first person who put his hand into it. It was Pablo Benalcazar, a good but simple man. I think he just reached to touch it because it was pretty. People tried to pull his hand back, but they were too slow. It didn't matter, though. Pablo stuck his arm into the fire, and the fire passed right through it. He said it did not even feel warm.

"Once Pablo had waved his arm around enough to show us that the hairs on his hands had not even been singed, we all took turns. I placed my arm in the fire, and I felt like I was touching God. I was in the presence of His glory, witness to proof that He had not forgotten us. My eyes blurred with tears.

"So it was that I did not see Samuel Rincon climb on the altar. No one liked Rincon. He was a petty braggart, one who could not listen to conversation without trying to make it center on him. He was also known to be cruel to anyone weaker than himself.

"I assume that Rincon climbed on the altar to outdo the rest of us. If we stuck in our arms, he would insert his entire body. And so he took a running jump, apparently hoping to leap right to the top of the altar. He overestimated his own abilities, though, and only placed his torso on top while his legs struggled and kicked to move the rest of him into place.

"He never made it all the way on. I heard the scream first, and I wiped my eyes. When I saw Rincon, his legs were sticking straight out and shaking. I did not know what to do. Others were faster. They grabbed his legs and pulled him off the altar. But it was too late. The top half of him, from head to waist, was completely charred. He was already dead.

"And so we knew that the miracle was more than a light show. We knew this was the true power of God. We could only assume that Rincon had died while none of the rest of us had suffered because that was God's will. From that point, it was easy to make certain assumptions about the fire, especially when Emmy Diaz, who went to church every day of her life, remembered the prophecy and recited it to us."

Lloyd's mouth moved involuntarily as the man recited the prophecy in a low rasp.

"Justice will burn
Fire in the old cathedral
Sorting the righteous
Purging the wicked

"How many mortals had ever had such a tool in front of them?" the man continued. "The judgment of God, right there in the cathedral, waiting to be used! The greatest judicial system the world would ever see—fast, efficient, and completely accurate. With such a tool in front of us, would we not be ungrateful if we did not use it? So the word spread, and the flood of people arrived.

"The judgment lasted a long time. Hours, going into days. Person after person thrown onto the altar to be condemned or exonerated. Some of the guilty were punished with death, others received painful burns while their lives were spared. Praises to the Creator filled the cathedral.

"Then came a moment I did not expect. A friend of mine, Adrian Suarez, was brought to the altar. Those who were serving as judges—a pair of villagers who had found some inquisitor robes in the back of the cathedral and had put them on for fun—said what he had been accused of.

"Adrian was thought to have robbed the bank where I worked. He had a long history of petty theft, and one day he was seen running out of the bank. A quick check showed that one of the tills was missing some money. Everyone believed that Adrian had snuck up to the till and snatched the money while no one was looking, then run as fast as he could. There was no proof, however, so the police never brought any charges against him, and Adrian always maintained his innocence. God, though, would tell us the truth.

"I was not anxious to see the truth revealed, however. You see, I was the one who had stolen the money. I saw Adrian running out of the bank that day—most likely to get to a suddenly remembered appointment, just as he eventually claimed—and had an idea in a flash. I could snatch a bundle of bills and blame it on Adrian. No one would ever suspect me—I was a loyal employee of the bank and had been so for eight years. I would secure for myself a small bonus while making sure blame never came in my direction.

"Once the Creator exonerated Adrian, however, I would be in trouble. When everyone knew he was innocent, they would look elsewhere for a suspect. The till that was stolen from was the one next to my station. The woman who had been operating it was known to be careless but unfailingly honest. How long would it be before someone thought of suspecting me?

"There wasn't anything I could do, though. The men dressed as inquisitors were already putting Adrian in the fire.

"His screams came quickly, though they did not last long. True to the Biblical punishment for thieves, Adrian's hands had been burned. The Creator was merciful, though—He did not burn them all the way off. Adrian still has his hands, though they are permanently damaged. Manual labor, which had been the only way besides thieving that he ever earned money, was no longer an option for him. He relies on the kindness of strangers. I myself have offered enough assistance to him to repay the thousands of pesos I stole several times over.

"But I am becoming distracted. As soon as Adrian's hands were burned, it became impossible for me to believe that the fire had anything to do with the Creator. I thought, briefly, that perhaps Adrian was guilty of some other crime, and the Creator was punishing him for that. But I was not comfortable with that idea. The inquisitors had specifically accused him of the theft from the bank. That, and only that, was the crime he was accused of in the church. For the Creator to punish him for some other crime at the moment seemed random, willful, and petty. I had no desire to believe in a God like that. That meant I was left a choice—either believe that the fire in the cathedral did not emanate from God, or stop believing in God entirely."

Lloyd listened in silence. At the moment, he could not have asked a question if he wanted to. The evening was warm, he could feel sweat on his brow, but he was shivering like he was back in Stephenville.

"I chose the former option, and as time passed I gathered evidence that I had made the correct choice. I found others whose circumstances were similar to mine, people who had reasons to know that some of the individuals judged to be guilty by the flame were in fact innocent. It was a difficult task—the individuals with whom I spoke seemed to be subject to an inordinate amount of street crime—muggings, random beatings, and worse. More than once one of the people I had sought turned up dead before I found them.

"Then I found Miranda. You have already met Miranda earlier this evening. Miranda has a small degree of your talent, enough so that she was recruited by the church. She never wanted to be part of that organization, though, and her talent was so scant she would have had little opportunity for advancement. She fled the grips of the clergy over a half-dozen times before they finally gave up and decided her small talent was not worth the effort to keep her. And so they tolerate her as a rogue PK, as long as she does not go about using her abilities openly.

"Though Miranda did not enjoy her time as part of the clergy, she learned some valuable things. And one of those things is that she claimed there was indisputable proof that members of the Church of the Miraculous Creator were behind the fire and the killings. That it was the judgment of two adepts, randomly, even whimsically made, that condemned people to death. The so-called Miracle of Antigua was a manufactured lie. And it was murder.

"That story was occasionally whispered through the streets of Guatemala, but few tell it any more. There have been too many accidents, too many disappearances. But even though we do not often talk about it, there are many of us who know the truth."

The man fell silent for a time. Lloyd wished there was another chair in the building so he could sit. If he had to listen to much more, he would likely just drop down and sit in the dust.

Then the man sat again. "That is all the story that is mine to tell."

Lloyd waited for the man to speak again, but he did not. The silence became uncomfortable.

"So what now?"

"That is up to you," the man said.

"But what am I supposed to do with what you told me?"

"That is up to you," the man said again. Then he was silent again.

Lloyd wanted to grab the man. Forget attacking him with the talent—Lloyd wanted nothing less than a full physical attack. He wanted to grab the man's thin neck and shake it. He wanted to squeeze the neck until the man's eyes bulged. He didn't really want more information from the man, he didn't want to make him talk. He wanted him to hurt.

He could feel power gathering around him, even though he hadn't willed it. It was electricity, the ions in the air shifting and organizing and waiting for a spark. A spark that could blow up the entire building, if Lloyd wasn't careful.

The wiry man sat in his chair, his posture unchanged. He looked tired, but he had looked tired when Lloyd walked in. He had probably looked tired for a long time.

Lloyd's shoulders sank. He let the power around him go, slowly. It bled out harmlessly through the air. Maybe the wiry man felt the hairs on the back of his neck tingle from it, but he likely never felt a bit of the threat that had gathered so close to him.

Without another word or glance, Lloyd turned to the door and slowly shuffled away.

The next day Lloyd was next to useless. He went through the motions of his day, discussing doctrine with his theology teacher, performing little demonstrations for his PK teacher, and making sure he ate a bite or two whenever food was placed in front of him. But he paid only the barest amount of attention to his day, and when it was over he had formed no new memories of what he had done.

The second day, the anger he had felt back in the adobe house returned. It started as anger at the man, but Lloyd knew that was misplaced. So he was angry with everyone else around him, including himself. He wanted to go away, leave everything behind, find something else in life. There had to be something else. But when night fell, he was still in his dorm in Guatemala City.

On the third day, he was still angry when he woke up. It was a good anger, a righteous anger. Vengeance was his, or at least it should be. He was on the side of truth and honesty, while those who had angered him were liars and deceivers. There was nothing wrong with being angry at those people.

And so when an adept Lloyd didn't know made the mistake of talking to him outside of the dorm building that night, Lloyd prepared to unleash his full fury on him. The fury of the righteous.

The adept was medium height with dark, nearly black hair that was slightly sliver at the temples. He had rough bangs, a triangular jaw, and a strong Mayan nose. He had the gentle shield around his mind of someone who had lived among PKs for a long time.

"Excuse me, Adept, but can I have a moment of your time?" He spoke English with a strong accent.

"If you'd like," Lloyd said.

"I hope you don't mind me saying this, but you seem angry."

"No, I don't mind you saying it."

"May I ask you what you're angry about?"

"Who says I'm angry?"

"You just admitted you were, didn't you?"

"No," Lloyd said. "I said I didn't mind you saying that I seemed angry. It's part of my training—I'm trying to appear angry while I'm actually quite content. I'm practicing hiding my real emotions enough so that people believe what's fake."

"Ah." The adept nodded. "You're lying, of course."

"As far as you know, I'm telling the truth."

"Except I've been through many, many training programs, and I don't remember any that required that sort of deceit. The church tends to emphasize honesty a little more than it does deceiving others."

Lloyd snorted.

The adept raised an eyebrow. "You believe differently?"

"No," Lloyd said, not bothering to conceal his sarcasm. "Of course not. The church is wonderful. The High Adepts are perfect. Everything's great."

"I think all I said was that the church emphasizes honesty. I didn't make any of those other claims."

"Good for you."

The adept was quiet for a moment. His right foot tapped on the ground.

"I think it would help us a bit if this conversation were a little more private. So you could speak freely, if you wanted to." Lloyd felt a static wall spring up around them. "There," the adept said. "So, it turns out you really are quite angry."

"Oh, am I?"

"Generally, when adepts speak with each other, the claim that the church teaches honesty is not enough to draw a bitter reply."

"I guess I must be in a pissy mood, then."

"Yes, you must," the adept said, and there was a light tone to his voice. "You seem to be at that stage of anger where you're not sure who to be angry at."

"You're wrong," Lloyd said. "I've got plenty of people to be mad at."

"Including me, it seems. Why me?"

"Because you're intruding into my business. No one invited you."

"True," the adept said, "but maybe I could help you."

"I didn't ask for your help."

"Also true. But we are talking, so perhaps we should continue. Maybe we can understand your anger better if we look at your specific targets. First, you're angry at me."

"Right."

"But that's mainly because I showed up at a bad time. I clearly am not the cause of your anger—I'm just an innocent passerby caught up in it."

"If that's how you'd like to think of yourself, fine."

"It probably doesn't help that I'm an adept. I saw the way you looked at me as soon as I approached you. I'd venture to say you're angry at most of the clergy at the moment."

Lloyd looked at the adept suspiciously. He strengthened the shield around his mind and tried to keep his conscious thoughts as empty as possible.

"I'll take that expression for a yes," the adept said. "Now, being angry at the entire leadership of the church is a big thing. And it usually goes right up to the top of the command chain. Let me ask you this—are you angry at God?"

"What the hell kind of question is that?" Lloyd snapped. "And what makes you think I would answer it?"

The adept, though, no longer seemed to be paying direct attention to Lloyd. He was nodding slightly and looking past Lloyd, at some distant object.

"You see," the adept said, in a quiet tone, "anger is a sign of a struggle, or of questioning, but the real sign of a lack of faith is apathy. If you really don't believe in God, you stop being angry at Him, because anger at a nonexistent being is ridiculous. It's like holding a grudge against the Easter Bunny. You are angry and want answers, but that means you think there is someone to be angry at, and that answers are possible." He nodded. "That should be enough."

"What are you talking about?" Lloyd said.

The adept refocused on Lloyd. He was no longer smiling. "Your orientation is done," he said. "You will be assigned to your new duties tomorrow, and you will report to the church in San Jose Pinula. May the light of the Creator shine upon you."

Lloyd did not offer the standard reply. He said nothing as the adept walked away with long, smooth strides.

Chapter Thirty-five

"Who drives that truck?"

Lloyd had taken three steps into the street, watching the blue truck disappear north, when he remembered there were other cars in the road. He quickly jumped back as an ancient horn wheezed at him.

"What truck?" said the adept who had met him at the bus stop. Her name was Calla, she was almost as tall as Lloyd, and she had clearly been outside for a while. The sweat on her face made her skin gleam like obsidian.

"The old blue Ford! The one that just passed by! Whose truck is that?"

Calla shrugged. "I don't know. Everyone down here drives a beat-up old truck. I haven't met them all yet."

"You haven't been here long?"

"A few months. Just transferred over from Santo Domingo."

"Dominican Republic?"

"Yeah. Moved back there when I was eight, once Drauer's boys finished their push through southern Florida. One of the only times I know of when a flood of refugees led to an economic boom for a town."

Lloyd looked at her curiously. She shrugged. "A lot of us knew what was coming, and we were prepared. We got out of there with plenty of solid assets."

Now that the truck, the one that looked just like the one Lloyd had been in a few days ago, had gone, he followed Calla as she walked a block down the highway and turned down a dusty road. He scrambled to keep up with her so he could hear what she was saying.

"Santo Domingo was fun, because a lot of the 'refugees'—that might not be the best term for us, come to think of it—were treated like royalty over there. They loved what we did for the place, so they loved us. But it got a little surreal sometimes, especially once they funneled me into the church. There were a lot of games over there, you know? People one-upping each other, trying to prove who had brought the most out of Florida and had done the most to help the city. Once the church started selling choice pews to the highest bidder and doing everything except command the congregation to bow to the people in the front rows, I figured it had gotten out of hand.

"But here, it's all different. It's all pure *work*, right? We've got medical aid to distribute, we've got the Re-education Center to deal with, and around here there's never any shortage of poverty-related problems. I felt like I've made more of a difference here than I did in thirteen years of work in Santo Domingo. It's nice to be useful, you know?"

"Yeah," Lloyd said. The lie was better than the alternative.

The church stood in front of him. It was a humble compared to both Guatemala City and Hampton cathedrals, a white building with two spires that couldn't be more than twenty-five feet high flanking the entrance. The entryway, though, was spectacular, a double wooden arched door with a grand mosaic exploding over it. Two tile doves hovered just above the door, and images of vines and flowers flowed up from the door all the way to the roof of the building. The bright greens, yellows, and reds shone like they had been freshly painted.

"That's the HQ," Calla said. "We live right next door." She pointed to a long, two-story building, whose walls were the same bright white as the chapel. The building had a crook in the middle, forming a very obtuse angle. "The quarters are pretty nice, if small, for adept dorms, but if you do things right while you're here, you'll barely be in them. I'll take your stuff to your room, number 207. The lock's got a simple password in it. Just send the word 'sarabande' and it'll open right up, then you can set it however you like. You should go to the chapel first, though so High Adept Alfonzo can get you oriented."

The interior of the chapel was as well kept as the exterior. Unpadded wooden pews gleamed darkly, and the sunbeams slanting through the windows showed only a small amount of dust hovering inside. The altar at the front of the chapel was a simple white block.

Behind the altar and to the left was a wooden door, and light shone underneath it. Lloyd walked back to that door and knocked.

"Come in," a soft voice said.

High Adept Alfonzo looked like she was one hundred years old—or more, if she'd used any of the talent's life-prolonging capabilities. Her wrinkled face reminded Lloyd of a potato left out for too long, wrinkled everywhere. Her hair was thick and completely white. She had it pulled in a bun that lay at the base of her neck. Her arms were very thin and shaky, and Lloyd wondered if the weight of her robe would be too much for her.

"You must be our new relief adept," she said in a wavering voice.

"Yes, High Adept. I'm Adept Hsu."

"Yes," she said. "Yes. Of course." She fell silent. "I believe you were requested by Guatemala City."

"No, High Adept. That's who sent me."

"Oh, yes, of course, excuse me," she said. "You *came* from Guatemala City. You were requested by ... by ..." She shook her head. "Oh, what's the sense in my trying to remember when I have things written down for me?" She slowly pushed a few papers across her desk until she found the one she needed. "Here it is. You were requested by Adept Diego." She shook her head. "That young man has been a great blessing. I've never seen such an active recruiter before. I don't know what I would do without him."

Lloyd didn't have any reply.

"So you will be with Adept Diego, which makes you—you're going to work as a relief adept, aren't you?"

"Yes, High Adept."

"Wonderful. I hope someone has taken your belongings to your room? Good. Now, I could try to explain a thing or two to you, but why make you listen to my old voice when Adept Diego knows what he has in store for you? He can probably explain everything better, or at least faster, than I can. Let me see where he is."

She closed her eyes, but only briefly. She opened them back up in surprise. "Good gracious, he must be anxious to meet you! It seems he just walked into the chapel. You may go speak with him there if you'd like."

Lloyd nodded. "Thank you, High Adept." He walked out, wondering how High Adept Alfonzo could run things as efficiently as Calla had claimed.

There was an adept waiting for him in the chapel. He was walking forward, and was at first too backlit for Lloyd to see him properly. But when the adept came into the sunlight, Lloyd saw ragged bangs and an aquiline nose.

He tried to hide his surprise. "I guess this is how you knew I was leaving," he said.

"Yes," Adept Diego said. "I requested you."

"Why?"

"Because I saw the results of the tests conducted during your orientation. Your skills are in line with what we need here."

"Really? Did they tell you I'm especially good with fire and electricity? Are you planning an offensive against someone?"

"Perhaps you could learn that there are other uses for your talents besides violence."

Lloyd didn't reply for a time. The chapel was dark and cool. Lloyd found both of those conditions comforting.

"So that's the only reason you requested me? My skills?"

Adept Diego smiled. "Mostly," he said. "There is one task in particular I need you for. We'll have to leave early in the morning. Let me show you around a little, then you should get some rest."

Lloyd awoke to the sound of waves early in the morning. He blinked and rubbed his eyes and tried to remember where he was. Back in Cancun? What would he be doing there?

He looked around at the room he was in. Dark wood furniture, white walls, just like the interior of the chapel at San José Pinula. That's where he was. San José Pinula. Without an ocean anywhere nearby.

Then he understood. It was a sending. A soothing, gentle wakeup call from Adept Diego. It was 5:30—he was supposed to be on the road in half an hour. The sun hadn't cracked the horizon yet, but it was close.

The ocean noise died away, replaced by words from Adept Diego. <<No robes today. We're going undercover. I'll be in front of the chapel in half and hour with breakfast.>>

Lloyd didn't need half an hour. He washed quickly, threw on a t-shirt and olive green canvas pants, and was ready to go. He was sitting under a palm tree in the plaza in front of the chapel fifteen minutes after Adept Diego's wake-up call.

The air was cleaner and drier than it had been the night before. It felt like a storm had swept through, but Lloyd couldn't remember hearing any thunder. It could very well be uncomfortable by the middle of the day, but for now the breeze that glided by the chapel had a cool edge to it.

Lloyd looked around, hoping Adept Diego would be early, but there was no sign of him. He thought about sending a message to him, letting him know that he was ready, but an unsolicited sending to a superior adept was a significant breach of etiquette. So he'd have to wait.

He sat for a few minutes, but he was too jumpy to just sit and wait. He stood up, looked for somewhere to go, and decided the chapel was the place most likely to be open.

The doors were unlocked, and Lloyd walked in. The interior was just as empty as it had been yesterday, and he didn't see a light under High Adept Alfonzo's door. There was probably someone in the building, maintaining this and tidying that, but they weren't anywhere Lloyd could see them, and he didn't want to startle anyone by doing a scan.

He walked to the pews. Like every church Lloyd had ever been in, there were small shelves in the back of the pews holding hymnals and scriptures. Without really thinking about it, Lloyd reached out and grabbed one of the scripture books. It was hardbound, like a library book, with several dents and scratches in its black cover. All of the book's content was directly tied to First

Adept Harriman Ellis—the First Adept's favorite books from the old Christian Bible, in Ellis' favorite translation; Premier Adept Eliazer Dugwu's account of the life of Harriman Ellis; and, naturally, *The Sayings of Harriman Ellis* and *The Prophecies of Harriman Ellis*.

The prophecies. Lloyd slammed the book shut. He didn't need to look at it now.

He walked back outside, returned to the bench beneath the palm tree, and made himself wait until Adept Diego arrived.

It didn't take long. Adept Diego was in a loose white shirt and khaki pants, and he carried a brown paper bag. He shook the bag as he approached Lloyd.

"Breakfast," he said. "*Pan fraces* and plantains. Let's go."

A few minutes later, Lloyd was sitting in a small blue car, biting into one of his rolls. Adept Diego was working the long, thin stick shift lever like it was a pump that needed to keep moving for the car to roll. The car was given to sudden lurches and hiccups that Adept Diego accepted with a silent, grim determination.

"If we just hold on," he said after a few minutes, "the car will calm down. *Dios mediante.*"

Traffic was light, giving the car plenty of time to find its bearings. They were heading west, the sun at their backs, and the mountains ahead were dark green, except for the brown tops of the volcanoes. Lloyd had no idea where they were going or why they were going there, but the bread was good, the plantains were fried to a brown-tinged gold, and the sun was out. If Lloyd forgot about everything else in his life, he could almost be content.

Adept Diego was not a talkative companion. The engine was buzzy at any speed over sixty kilometers per hour, which would have made conversation difficult if there had been any. But Adept Diego was focused on the road, and Lloyd had no desire to talk. Silence was fine.

They skirted south of the city and then went further south still, then turned back west. Then they were heading northwest, then due north.

Lloyd finally spoke. "Are we going to go around in a circle?"

Adept Diego smiled. "We're getting closer. In fact, our first big test is coming up in a few kilometers."

"What's that?"

"Border crossing."

Lloyd felt a sudden chill. "I don't … I don't want to …"

"I know. You won't like it. Not any of it, really. But it must be done."

"How are we going to get across the border? After everything, after everything, aren't they … won't they be …"

"Of course they will," Adept Diego said. "So we'll be careful. Which reminds me—you should call me Rafael for the rest of the trip."

Lloyd nodded. There was a cold knot inside him, under his sternum.

"Listen to me," Adept Diego said. "Both sides, we have been playing games with each other for a long time. We are rivals. We are convinced that we must beat the others, to show that we are better than them. We must be stronger PKs than they are. So everything we do is about shields, and scans, and anything else we can do to out-muscle them. We have been different from each other, in competition with each other for so long that we have forgotten how to just be."

Lloyd was grabbing the sides of his seat, and he felt like he was in danger of punching through the upholstery, thin and brittle as it was. The border was approaching, and Adept Diego was caught up in philosophizing.

"Do you like music, Lloyd?" Adept Diego said abruptly.

"What?"

"Music. Who do you like?"

"I haven't gotten the chance, recently …"

"But you have some time in your life. Everyone has a favorite song, Lloyd. What's yours?"

"I haven't heard anything recent, really," Lloyd said, speaking slowly but trying not to, since he knew there was a bit of a rush. "Where I've been, the libraries haven't had much, and I don't buy

... well, anyway, there's older stuff, last century stuff that I listen to and ... the Beatles. I like that Beatles group."

"Good, good!" Adept Diego said. "Wonderful! What song?"

"I've always liked 'Penny Lane.'"

"That will do. That will do just fine. Now, all you need to do is close your eyes, lean back, and think of 'Penny Lane.'"

Lloyd stared at Adept Diego. Adept Diego glanced quickly over at him.

"Your eyes are not closed," Adept Diego said. "Come on, come on. Don't make me pull rank."

Lloyd wasted one more minute trying to show his confusion and lack of confidence, then he leaned back, closed his eyes, and thought of "Penny Lane."

"Try to think of the first time you heard it. Remember when that hook hit you and you thought to yourself, 'Now *this* is a song.'"

Lloyd obeyed. He hadn't heard the song for a long time, over a year at least, but the lyrics came right back to him. He could run through the whole song, beginning to end. He should get a copy of that song someday.

The car was slowing. The fist in Lloyd's stomach tightened, and he started to open his eyes.

"The song, Lloyd," Adept Diego said. "The song. Eyes closed, think of the song."

The car stopped. Adept Diego said something, and another voice spoke as well. There was a quick rustle of papers, then the engine buzzed, and the car was moving.

Lloyd kept his eyes closed and thought of the song right up to the end.

"Can I open my eyes now?" he said.

"Yes," Adept Diego said. "But it's not a bad idea to keep thinking about Beatles songs."

Lloyd thought about turning around and looking behind them, but he knew he didn't need to. "We're through," he said. "We made it through."

"Without having to go through the trouble of making a shield that the guards would not detect," Adept Diego said. "A nice, simple approach. It helps, of course, that you have the mental training of an adept. Your mind, when it focuses on something, locks out any other thought. All that the guards got from you was 'Penny Lane,' nothing more."

"And the papers?"

Lloyd wasn't sure, but he thought Adept Diego flushed a little bit.

"The work here sometimes requires unusual accessories," he said. "Remember, though, that the USNA does not have an unlimited number of elite PKs at their disposal. No matter what their press says. There are better people closer to Antigua, but an outpost like the one we just went through does not attract the finest the USNA has to offer."

Lloyd smiled, but then he remembered where he was. "What happens next?"

"There is a town ahead—Santa Maria de Jesus. We will stop near there and abandon the car."

"And then?"

"We hike."

A hike in the USNA. The small trace of contentment Lloyd had felt earlier was entirely gone.

They left the car parked behind an abandoned store and walked toward a volcano. It rose to a perfect cone thousands of feet above them.

"Up there?" Lloyd said.

"Up there," Adept Diego said. He was wearing a large, brown backpack that was bigger than his back. Lloyd only carried a small knapsack. "But not all the way."

It wasn't steep, not at first. There were plenty of trees and shade on the lower portion of the mountain, and they were able to plunge straight ahead. Or at least it felt like straight—once they entered the canopy of trees, Lloyd lost his bearings. But each step felt like he was going higher, and he became winded very quickly. He blamed the altitude.

"Is there any chance of this erupting?" he said when he could gather enough air.

Adept Diego did not turn around when he answered. "It is a volcano," he said. "There is always a chance."

Lloyd took his next steps carefully, testing the ground for any minute shifting or shaking. But when he looked ahead he saw Adept Diego was quickly leaving him behind, so he went back to his normal pace.

As the day advanced, the hike became steeper, and they started having to cross the face of the volcano instead of assault it directly. Occasionally Lloyd thought he saw traces of a path that they might be following, but those impressions didn't last long. He heard occasional rustling in the undergrowth, and once or twice he saw the droppings of animals that must have been human-sized or larger.

"Should we be scanning?" he said. "For animals, I mean?"

"No. They don't want to hurt us. And the less we use the talent while we're on this side of the border, the better."

The sun was nearly directly overhead when Lloyd, panting, saw the trees thinning ahead and becoming shorter. Then he was in bright sunlight, walking on the dark rock of the volcano's cone.

Below him was the USNA. There were a few towns and then a bigger city to the north. Antigua. Lloyd almost darted back into the trees when he saw it. They were so exposed here—anyone looking up from the city would surely see them.

But then, the streets were very distant to him, and he could not make out any people walking in the city. He steeled his will and followed Adept Diego.

It wasn't much farther. After another few hundred feet, Adept Diego stopped, shrugged off his backpack, and let it clunk to the ground. He was looking ahead, across the mountain, not down at the city that made Lloyd so nervous. He stood for a moment, hands on his hips, still looking west. Then Lloyd saw Adept Diego's shoulders heave for a moment, and he turned and faced north.

He stood still for another few moments. Even though the sun was overhead and slightly behind him, he was squinting, his eyes almost closed. His jaw was clenched, occasionally shifting.

"That is Antigua," he said. Then he was quiet again.

Lloyd waited. Below him, birds called and a gentle breeze blew through the leaves. The unstable ground beneath him was completely still.

Adept Diego shook his head quickly, then bent down and grabbed his backpack. He pulled out a long black tube, opened one end of it, then removed a telescope as black as its case.

"Now you get to see."

Lloyd's heart raced. No image of the Antigua Cathedral had been seen outside of the USNA for over a year. Ever since the miracle occurred. Back at Hampton, Lloyd and his friends had contented themselves with images of how the cathedral looked before the miracle, imagining what had happened when the people of Guatemala took it back. Lloyd liked to think of red and black bunting draped down the broad white exterior, announcing the return of the church and the rededication of the grand old building. He imagined the three double doors in front flung open, letting streams of worshippers in and out. He imagined standing there, looking at the carvings of the ancient saints, and wondering if they had any conception of the miracles to come. Then he imagined himself going inside and watching the fire fall.

As soon as that last memory returned, Lloyd felt a wave of nausea. The fire had started it all. The fire was the first major miracle. And it was a complete fraud.

Adept Diego reached out, handing the telescope to Lloyd. He grabbed it quickly.

"You can see Santa Maria de Jesus below us, to the right. Highway 1 is easy to see there. Look through the telescope and follow it."

Lloyd did as he was told, moving slowly up from the small town, occasionally losing sight of the road when his arm bobbled and made his view shake.

"The highway will take you straight into Antigua."

"I'm there," Lloyd said. He saw buildings now, most of them looking old but well kept.

"Continue north. The street will end."

Lloyd did as he was told, keeping his hands as steady as possible. Then he found the end, and at the end of the street was a church.

"I see a church, Rafael," Lloyd said, and he heard how quickly he spoke.

"That is Santa Clara," Adept Diego said. "Not the cathedral. Proceed two blocks west and you will find another."

It didn't take long. "I see it," Lloyd said.

"San Pedro," Adept Diego said. "Now, move to the street just west of San Pedro. Follow that street north. Stop when you find a park that covers the entire block west of the street."

"Found it!"

"Plaza Mayor. The center of the city." There was a pause. Lloyd waited.

"Look across the street from the Plaza," Adept Diego finally said. "The block to the east."

Lloyd looked—and saw nothing. In the middle of this well kept, cobblestoned city, there was an empty block. There were weeds growing, and stones scattered across the lot. Some of those stones were white.

"That is Antigua Cathedral," Adept Diego said.

The empty lot shook, bouncing up and down violently. Then it fell away, disappeared as Lloyd dropped the telescope.

He whirled on Adept Diego, who had moved quickly and caught the telescope because it hit the ground.

"There's nothing there! Nothing!"

Adept Diego nodded. "Yes."

"It's ... they ... it's gone! They, they destroyed it. They didn't just take it back! They destroyed it!"

"Yes."

"What happened ... the people inside. Where did they go? What happened to the crowds?"

"The cathedral was packed when it was destroyed. What is left of the worshippers who were there lies in the rubble."

Lloyd fell to the ground. He looked up at the sky, willing his eyes to stay open as the sun burned into his vision. Then he closed his eyes, clenched his hands into fists, and curled into a tight ball. He wanted to scream. He wanted to send out a wave of power that would light the forest below him on fire. He wanted to crack the cone of the volcano and fall deep into its heart. But he could only bring himself to clench his fists tighter and tighter.

"It was the most unusual time of my life," Adept Diego said, talking even though Lloyd sat curled in a ball. "I discovered the miracle was a fraud early on. Perhaps I was the first one who discovered that. I happened upon the adepts who were generating the illusion of fire, who were working the machinery of death. I witnessed how cavalier they were, how little the decisions of life and death meant to them. And I staggered out of the cathedral and walked home. For that brief period, you could walk from Antigua to Guatemala City freely.

"When I left the cathedral, I had every intention of leaving the church as soon as I returned to Guatemala City. But it was a long walk. I had time to think. And I did not leave.

"I did not return to the cathedral in Antigua. Everyone else was begging for a chance to visit Antigua, and they thanked me repeatedly for covering for them while they wandered away. I had not left the church, but I was not going to return to the site of that blasphemy. I remained in Guatemala City throughout the week of the miracle, and so I am alive while many of my fellow adepts are dead.

"It was not easy to find out what happened to them. One day, they simply did not come back. By the time we started worrying about them, the blockades had already been erected. The USNA had returned to their original border without a word of what they had done to our people who had been in Antigua.

"I wanted to find out what had happened. I spoke with many of my superiors, presenting idea after idea for infiltrating Antigua, for discovering what had happened to our people. Every idea was rejected. The High Adepts, they had no desire to launch an investigation of any sort. For if people started looking into what happened in Antigua, how long would it be before they uncovered secrets the High Adepts did not want revealed?

"But I was persistent. I kept asking about it. And so they transferred me to San Jose Pinula, serving under High Adept Alfonzo, who is a very good woman but has been practically running her own independent church for well over a decade. She does not talk to the other High Adepts much, and that is how they like it. They sent me there to isolate me.

"It was not difficult to mount my own investigation from my new location. I worked for a time on presenting myself as a person without any PK ability, and once I knew how to do that I was able to cross the border, as long as I did not attempt it too often. The USNA cannot erect a wall here as they did where you are from— the border is too long and too variable. And building a wall would be a concession that the USNA's plans for southward expansion have ceased, and no one believes that to be the case.

"The people in Antigua did not speak openly about what had happened to the cathedral, and there were no official records or news stories about the event. But the truth was not hard to uncover, once I was over there. They wanted to talk about it. They took a certain pride in it, many of them. The religious zealots had tried to invade, and they had been put in their place. They viewed the destruction of the cathedral the same as the victors regard almost any battle in a war—as a glorious triumph, with the loss of life being a mere footnote.

"Once I knew what had happened, I was as angry at the USNA as I had been at the church. Almost. The USNA has been responsible for much more violence in its time than the church. But I held the church to higher standards. I still judged the church to be the better of the two organizations, but it was not as glorious as I had thought, and the pain that fact caused me was deep.

"So I returned to San Jose Pinula with a question. What do I do next?"

Adept Diego fell silent. The day was warm now, but the altitude kept it from becoming hot, and the air flowing down the mountain was cool.

Lloyd sat on the ground, still curled in a ball, still gouging his palms with his fingernails. He waited for Adept Diego to continue his story and provide an answer to the question he had left dangling.

Adept Diego finally spoke. "Only a handful of people outside the USNA have seen what you have seen. You now know everything I can tell you about Antigua. That means it is time to leave."

Adept Diego shouldered his backpack and started back in the direction they had come. Lloyd was left with little choice. Part of him wanted to do nothing but stare at the town below him, to find the empty, blasted patch of land with his naked eyes and just look at it. Another part wanted to stay on the ground and keep his eyes closed and never see the valley, the town, the ruins again.

But in the end he did what was simple, and what he had to do. He stood and followed Adept Diego down the volcano.

Interlude: The Prophecies

If I were to speak with complete honesty, I would be forced to say that sometimes I find the attentions the prophecies receive to be somewhat disconcerting. Please do not misunderstand me—I am quite appreciative of the fact that people take the prophecies seriously and spend significant amounts of time and effort studying them. Anything that comes to us from the Creator is worth our attention. What concerns me, though, is the amount of speculation that people put into their studies of the prophecies. They try to guess what they mean, when they will happen, who will be involved, and so on and so forth.

As a side note, I find it interesting and somewhat amusing that church members continually approach me to ask about the prophecies. They act as though I know in great detail the events the prophecies describe, and that I encoded my descriptions in obtuse language to befuddle the general membership, though they do not seem clear about why I would want to do such a thing.

One of the sad truths about my position is that I know no more about the prophecies than anyone else. When I am inspired to write a prophecy, I put down the words the Creator inspires, nothing more, nothing less. Thus, when the prophecies are published, members of the church then know exactly as much about them as do I.

It concerns me that people believe I would hold back information from them. I hope that my leadership record demonstrates that I want nothing more than to pass any knowledge and understanding I have to the people I serve. I do not lead them on wild goose chases or down blind alleys. I take them where the Creator wishes them to go.

Since the Creator has decided not to give us the details of the prophecies, the only reasonable conclusion is that we do not need to know those details to serve His purposes. The prophecies are to serve as landmarks—when we see them fulfilled, we will know that the course of events is proceeding along the path that He has ordained. We will know that He is in control, and the ends he has established for us will inevitably arrive.

Thus it disturbs me that people dwell at such great length on what might be termed the trivia of prophecy—the whos, whats, and whens. Their time would be much better spent focusing on what the Creator wants us to be so that we may be ready when the prophecies arrive. The prophecies, taken together, portray events that are overwhelming and earth-shaking in their scope. Are we, as a people, prepared to endure those events and emerge, refined and purified, on the other side? Are we faithful enough? Are we strong enough?

These are the questions we should ask. We should look into ourselves more and into the future less. The question is not when are these things going to happen—it is how ready will we be for them?

I believe this tendency is connected to how we think about the talent. It is so easy to find destructive ways to use the talent, and people's minds seem to gravitate in that direction. Thus, when they think of the future and of the prophecies, they think of conquest and triumph, not of humble efforts to help their fellow men. Those who can make fire think of burning their enemies, not of providing warmth to people who are cold. Those who have talents with electricity imagine ways to make lightning split the sky, rather than channeling their abilities to help people in times when the power grid might be down.

We are interested in the prophecies when they speak of destruction, but we ignore the fact that in their aftermath, we will inevitably have to build. To create.

Chapter Thirty-six

The drive back to San Jose Pinula was as quiet as the drive to the volcano. At the border, Lloyd sang "Ob-La-Di, Ob-La-Da" to himself, and they once again passed through without incident.

It was late afternoon when Adept Diego dropped Lloyd off at the church. "Take the rest of the evening to get yourself situated and take a walk around town to get your bearings. Tomorrow you'll be on relief duty. Adept Calla will be at your door at seven to help you get oriented."

Lloyd stepped out of the jeep slowly. He almost spoke, then didn't. Then again. Then he turned away.

"Was there something you wanted to say, Adept Hsu?" Adept Diego asked.

Lloyd turned back. "No. Well, it's just … is that it? You take me to Antigua, and that's it?"

"What more do you want there to be?"

"I don't know. I can't … I haven't figured anything out yet. But what if I want to talk to you? Can't we talk or something?"

Adept Diego laughed. "We're not in the USNA anymore, Adept Hsu. We can talk anytime you want. You know how to get a hold of me." He smiled, waved, and drove away.

Lloyd stood in courtyard in front of the church for a while. Then he slowly walked back to his dorm.

The next morning, Adept Calla showed up as promised and put Lloyd to work. She kept him busy all day, and he was exhausted by bedtime. He did not send a message to Adept Diego the whole day.

The next day was similar. Lloyd thought about Adept Diego more often, but he still did not reach the point of sending him a message. The third day after his visit to Antigua was the same.

By the fourth day, Lloyd felt a little different. Some of the numbness he had felt when he looked at the broken lot from the volcano had faded, and it was replaced by raw anger. Raw enough to overcome his normal reluctance to bother people with his petty concerns. For the first time since their trip, he communicated with Adept Diego.

His question was promptly and gently answered. Lloyd did not immediately follow it up, instead taking some time to think over Adept Diego's words. The next day, though, he had a new question, so he asked it.

It continued like that for a long time. It was a single conversation, but it stretched over days and weeks. The answers Adept Diego sent always caught Lloyd's attention, and it took no effort to remember what he was doing when he received them. So his memory of his time in San Jose Pinula became a series of images, bright snapshots of the unending work serving as a backdrop to the ongoing dialogue with Adept Diego.

An afternoon thunderstorm (a daily occurrence) while Lloyd unloaded dozens of boxes from the Red Cross off a dark green truck.

<<Why are you still working in this church when you know how corrupt it is?>>

<<Because I've been trying to learn how to separate the corruptions that humans introduce from the purity of the Creator's teachings.>>

Morning in the church kitchen, eyes stinging as Lloyd cut onion after onion after onion.

<<But the problem is more than corruption. The church was wrong. The First Adept was wrong. He prophesied Whitaker would deliver us, and Whitaker's dead. It's just wrong.>>

<<That's not really a question.>>

<<Okay, how about this. You said you can stay in a church that's corrupt—but what about a church that's just plain wrong?>>

<<We're all wrong sometimes. Was the fault the fault of the Creator or of humans? Was the prophecy wrong, or was our interpretation of the fulfillment of the prophecy wrong?>>

Sitting in the rain, surrounded by mud, after the last survivor had been taken out of a mudslide to the south of San Jose Pinula.

<< So the way you figure it, every time the church is right, God gets the credit, and every time it's wrong, it's man's fault. Do I have that right?>>

<<Yes.>>

<<That seems a little pat. How do you know the Creator's not screwing up?>>

<<Because I believe in a Creator that doesn't screw up.>>

<<That's not an answer. That's circular reasoning.>>

<<Yes.>>

Late in the evening, the last bit of sun fading into an indigo sky, strings of lights all around the courtyard in front of the church as music played and everyone but Lloyd danced. Even Adept Diego danced, answering Lloyd's questions without missing a step.

<<If we can't count on the Creator to show his hand in a way that makes it clear that He exists, how do we even know He is there?>>

<<Can you think of a way for the Creator to do what you say that would convince everybody?>>

<<I don't need everybody to be convinced. Just me.>>

<<What would it take to convince you?>>

<<A personal visit would be fine.>>

<<Not too many people get those. And the scriptures give us examples of people who received such a visit, or something close to it, and still had trouble believing.>>

Under the warm sun in the fields, acting as a human sprinkler, taking vats of water dropped on the ground by villagers and spraying the contents across the bean fields.

<<If the Creator is not going to give me direction right from his mouth, and I can't count on the church to be honest or honorable, where do I get direction?>>

<<Why do you need someone to give you direction?>>

<<Because I don't know what to do!>>

<<Okay. Go climb the Volcan de Agua and jump inside.>>

<<No!>>

<<Why not?>>

<<Because I'm angry, not suicidal!>>

<<See? You know how to hear advice from others and evaluate it on your own. Do you think the Creator wants robots who always need instructions, or thinking beings who have developed their wills and learned how to tell what is good and what isn't on their own?>>

Late at night, when a cool breeze came through the window, and an owl sat in a tree in the courtyard, hooting gently.

<<Adept Diego? Are you awake?>>

<<Yes.>>

<<I don't want to disturb you. You can tell me to leave you alone if you'd like.>>

<<No, it's fine.>>

<<You weren't trying to sleep?>>

<<I will be if you keep stalling.>>

<<Why didn't you leave the church?>>

<<I might ask you the same question.>>

<<But I asked you first.>>

<<Because I cared for it too much. Because I had given too much of myself to it to allow it to fall completely under the control of deceivers and murderers. Because I believe there is something worth rescuing.>>

<<And how are you going to rescue it?>>

<<What would you do?>>

Lloyd stayed up for a long time after Adept Diego asked that question, but he did not send an answer, because it took him a long time to come up with one.

The next day he was back in the kitchen. This time, he was rolling dough for tortillas.

<<I'd go public with what I know. I'd expose them for what they are.>>

<<Then why haven't you?>>

Lloyd rolled out a dozen tortillas before he answered the question.

<<No one would believe me.>>

<<Or at least not enough people would. And think of the culture we have in the church that helped create the leaders we

have. If you remove those leaders now, would their replacements be any better?>>

<<Dammit, is this thing even worth saving?>>

<<What do you think?>>

It was nearly a week before Lloyd communicated with Adept Diego again. He spent most of that week composing what he wanted to send. When he finally got around to it, he was walking alone through the streets of San Jose Pinula. The rain had just stopped, so the air was clean, the dust beaten back down to the ground.

<<When I became an adept, it was the best day of my life. I put on the black robe, and I understood what it meant. Not just that I had the talent, not just that I knew how to do stuff, although that was all cool. But I knew what an adept could do. I knew how adepts worked with their congregation, how they helped people who need helped, and gave advice, and did all the good things people are supposed to do. When people told stories that needed a hero, the hero was usually an adept, because an adept was the person in position to do the most good. That was what I wanted, and that was what I thought I had become. The person who could do the most good.>>

Adept Diego did not reply instantly. He may have been waiting to make sure Lloyd was finished.

<<I felt that way, too,>> he finally sent.

<<That's worth saving.>>

<<I think so, too.>>

The next day, out in the fields again, scouting the beans for traces of anthracnose. There was a line of adepts and other townspeople, walking through the field together.

<<This is worth saving, too.>>

<<What?>>

<<All this, here. The work in San Jose Pinula. The bean harvest we'll get. The medical supplies people keep sending. All of it.>>

<<Yes.>>

<<But how do we do it?>.>

<<Didn't you ask me that once before?>> Adept Diego sent.

<<No, you asked me.>>

<<Right. Do you have an answer yet?>>

The next day was a clinic day. Lloyd was still learning the spells of the healers. He had been so good with fire and lightning, he'd never given much focus to the subtle arts of encouraging veins and tissue to reform. He still needed to be watched carefully when he worked, and he had to concentrate completely on what he was doing. He couldn't send to Adept Diego until he was on his way home.

<<I would try to change the culture of the church from the bottom up.>>

<<How would you do that?>>

<<Find people who understand what the church should be and ensure they don't forget. Keep them thinking about serving and doing good instead of the power games with the church's hierarchy and the USNA.>>

<<Then you know why you're here.>>

<<I already know you asked to transfer me here from Guatemala City.>>

Lloyd could feel amusement surrounding Adept Diego's next sending. <<It was a larger effort than that. Unlike what happened in Antigua, the execution of Courtney Whitaker was quite public. As soon as I heard about it, I knew there would be people I should look for. You were the first name on my list. When they sent you up to Canada, I was worried about reaching you. But I finally got one of my friends in the right place, and they brought you to Cancun, which paved the way for your entry to Guatemala City.>>

<<You have friends in good places?>>

<<I've been at this for over a year, and I have a good group of people to work with. You know that, Lloyd. You know as well as anyone the problems the church has, but you also know how many good people are in it.>>

<<What about the others?>>

<<Others?>>

<<From Hampton. Couldn't you bring anyone else down here?>>

There was a pause. <<I tried,>> Adept Diego sent.

The next idea came to Lloyd after a few weeks' thought. He couldn't believe he actually thought of it, but as he turned it over in his mind it made more and more sense. He finally sent it to Adept Diego when he was walking toward the chapel as mist rose from the streets following an afternoon rain. <<Can I go back?>>

<<Where?>>

<<The Island. Hampton.>>

<<Why?>>

<<To do there what you're doing here. To help people understand what the church should be. I have friends there—I want to help them.>>

<<I thought it would come to this. I hoped it would, actually. Yes. I think you should go back to Hampton. There are a growing number of us now—we're not really an organization, we're just a group of adepts and acolytes allied to the same cause—but we don't have anyone in Hampton. It would be good for you to go there.>>

Hope, even something like happiness flared in Lloyd. But then faded, when he thought of actually returning to where he had been. To the town where he had found Courtney Whitaker. Going back to Hampton still seemed like a good idea, but it didn't seem like an easy one.

<<I'm still mad at God, you know,>> he sent to Diego. <<For helping me find Courtney, then letting him die. That was mean.>>

<<You can be mad at the Creator all you want, as long as you're willing to do His work.>>

<<I don't know if I want to do *His* work,>> Lloyd sent. <<I'm just trying to do good.>>

<<Same thing,>> Adept Diego sent.

Chapter Thirty-seven

The hardest thing would be the lack of communication. For the past few months, Lloyd had been able to reach out the Adept Diego whenever he had wanted to, and the response had always been instant. Now, the distance would be too great. They could try e-mail, assuming Hampton's cables were intact and the USNA was not messing with any attempts at communication. But even if it worked, it wouldn't be the same.

"The sooner you get in the habit of answering your own questions, the better," Adept Diego told him as he took him to the ship that would take him north. Once they had made the decision that Lloyd should go back to Hampton, it had taken a month to arrange passage. Finally they found a ship taking produce to Long Island that would provide a bunk in a dark corner for Lloyd as long as he stayed out of the way. Lloyd and Adept Diego didn't figure they would get anything better than that, so they secured the berth for Lloyd.

He was excited, nervous, worried, and just about any other emotion he could imagine. He both dreaded and looked forward to his first step back on the Island. It had been more than a year.

The good-byes had been quick. Lloyd felt like he was on the verge of getting emotional, but Adept Diego would have none of it.

"We've only known each other for a few months," he said. "You're going back to the people you've known for years. Get on the boat. No reason to linger here." He then practically pushed Lloyd onto the ship.

It was a long trip. Lloyd read a lot. He thought. He made half a dozen plans of what he would do when he got back to the Island and then discarded them. He thought about adepts who were dead, adepts who were missing. He thought about Whitaker and justice.

He knew what his main goal was—the long job of trying to build a different culture in the church. But maybe there was a shorter-term job he could try. Something to figure out just what had gone wrong with Whitaker. There had to be a story there, and maybe it was a story that would help show people why things in the church needed to change.

In his berth, it was difficult to tell day from night. Someone occasionally brought him food, but it came irregularly and the contents, generally beans and rice, didn't help Lloyd determine what meal it was supposed to be. He ate fruit he had brought with him to supplement the meals, he slept when he wanted to, and for a few days completely lost the rhythm of normal life.

Then, just like that, the ship had docked, his bags were packed, and he was walking off the ship and onto Long Island. He immediately spotted the pair of black-robed adepts waiting for him. They were young—he didn't know either of them.

"May miracles guide your way," one of them, a tall, thin woman with straight red hair, said as Lloyd approached.

"As the Creator wills," Lloyd responded, working hard to keep the words from catching in his throat. "Hello. I'm Lloyd Hsu."

The woman beamed. "We know who you are, Adept Hsu. Of course we do. We're very glad you're back. I'm Adept Colleen Friel, and this is Adept Nashiv Rawat." The other adept, who was a good six inches shorter than Adept Friel, waved tightly and smiled.

"Glad to meet you. You have a car, I hope?"

"Of course. We'll be at the cathedral within an hour."

Lloyd's stomach twisted at the thought.

He had told Friel and Rawat that he could just go to his quarters, that he didn't need to disturb High Adept Birch, but they were adamant.

"Everyone wants to see you, of course, but High Adept Birch was especially anxious. He made us promise that we would bring you to him first."

"Isn't it a little early for him?"

Adept Rawat turned and looked at Lloyd curiously. "It's ten in the morning," he said. "It's not early for anyone."

Lloyd glanced at the grey sky. "Oh. I kind of lost track of time while I was on the boat."

"We understand." Adept Rawat opened his mouth, then closed it and looked forward. Then he turned back around again.

"I just wanted to tell you, Adept Hsu. I—well, we, all of us—appreciate everything you did for the church."

"You do?" Lloyd wondered what they thought he had done. What stories were they telling about Whitaker and the Rockaway invasion?

"Yes. That's why we're all happy to have you back. Because we know your dedication."

Lloyd just nodded and thought of Beatles songs.

He stood outside High Adept Birch's door for several moments after he arrived. It looked the same. The paint was still chipped, the linoleum was a little thinner, and the only thing written on the door was the number 133.

He knew that whoever was on desk duty was already aware that someone was waiting outside. They were probably wondering why he was just standing there.

Well, what was he waiting for? He took a deep breath and opened the door.

Again, it was an adept he didn't know. A large woman with a stern face but a friendly voice.

"You're Adept Hsu aren't you?"

"Yes. Is High Adept Birch expecting me?"

"I don't no know if he ..." She stopped herself, then spoke slower. "I do not know if he is expecting you this second, but he wanted you to be sent in when you arrived. Go ahead."

Lloyd nodded and walked back into High Adept Birch's office.

The first thing he noticed was that the High Adept had unpacked. There were no boxes in the room. Every book was on a shelf, every paper was in a drawer or folder. And in the middle of it all, High Adept Birch sat at his desk. His face seemed a little rounder, the creases were a little deeper, but when he stood his smile and his grasp were as warm as they had ever been.

"Adept Hsu!" he said. "I can't tell you how happy I was to hear you were coming back. I understand why you left, of course, as I told you at the time."

Lloyd tried to think about what the High Adept had told him when he left, but he couldn't remember. He couldn't remember saying good-bye to anyone, or packing, or even how he had left. Was it a car? Train? It had to have been a boat, didn't it? What kind? He tried and tried, but all he could remember was showing up in Canada. His departure from Hampton was a blank.

"I appreciated your support," Lloyd said.

"But I'm truly glad your back. There have been—" he stopped. "There have been changes. How was your arrival?"

"Fine."

"Wonderful. We can always use qualified help here, and you have proved your mettle here. We have plenty for you to do."

"I'm glad to hear it. But I was hoping ..."

"What?"

"There are some ideas of my own I'd like to work on. Some initiatives. I hoped I would have time for them."

"Of course, of course! Whatever you need." High Adept Birch's face grew serious. "Listen, I want you to know that I understand that an adjustment process will have to happen. I don't want to pretend that the past didn't happen, and I'm sure you don't, either. So if some time on your own would be helpful to you, then I'm happy to provide it."

"Thank you. I really appreciate it."

"Not at all." He stood. "If there is anything I can do for you, or if you ever want to talk, my door is always open."

"Thank you," Lloyd said. He thought for a moment. "How is Grand Adept Serl holding up?"

Birch's mouth twitched slightly. "How do you mean?"

"I remember seeing him before I left. He seemed—tired. The whole affair took a toll on him. Has he recovered?"

"Grand Adept Serl continues to lead the cathedral and the Island in his normal dynamic fashion."

"Right. Of course," Lloyd said. "But is he better? Back to normal?"

Birch's chin fell toward his chest. "Adept Hsu, we seek to serve the Creator as best we can and continue his work, but I do not believe anyone here will tell you that the cathedral is back to normal. Not normal as it used to be, anyway." He smiled again, though it was thin. "But you are just back. You do not need to hear all of this now. You should go to your quarters and get settled. We can talk more whenever you wish."

"Thanks again," Lloyd said, and he shook the High Adept's hand.

He walked out of the office feeling dizzy. The High Adept had been warm and welcoming, and Lloyd had no reason to believe he was anything but sincere. He was given everything he wanted, but he didn't want it. He didn't want to be welcomed here. He didn't want to be comfortable. He wanted to be in surroundings that kept him angry, and High Adept Birch had not helped.

The woman behind the desk was still in the reception area, and she smiled again as soon as Lloyd appeared. She grabbed a piece of paper and wrote a quick note.

"This is where you'll be living," she said. The note said "Hamilton Building, No. 5."

Lloyd blinked. "Hamilton Building?"

"Yes. You know where it is?"

"Yes. It's behind the chapel and—yes, I know where it is. It's just—aren't those guest quarters?" He paused. "I mean, the *good* guest quarters?"

The woman's mouth wavered a little. "Yes, it—I think it is. I haven't no—haven't been here long. But not many people staying there. Not many visitors lately." Her smile firmed again. "Should be nice, though, right?"

Lloyd smiled back. "Should be," he said.

Lloyd had been living in some kind of CMC dorm as long as he could remember. He seldom had a room to call his own (his solo room in Guatemala City was a rare exception), usually living in a single room that he shared with another acolyte or adept. He usually had a narrow bed, a plastic desk, and a dresser—those were the limits he was used to.

Now he had a set of rooms. An apartment. A living room that was bigger than any of the dorm rooms he'd lived in. It had a couch, a love seat, a few other chairs—seating for at least six. Who did they think he was planning to entertain? It also had a large screen, the kind you used just for entertainment, like watching netcasts. Like he could just sit in the living room and be entertained and do nothing else.

There was a bedroom with a bed twice as large as Lloyd was used to, covered in a burgundy and green comforter. There was a closet as wide as one of the walls, and the room also had two light-brown wood dressers. He'd have to spend a week shopping to acquire enough clothing to fill the space he now had available.

And there was a kitchen. A big kitchen with clean wooden countertops and shiny metal appliances. There was a nice set of knives and a sink and a bunch of things Lloyd wasn't sure how to use. He'd performed kitchen duty in Guatemala, but he hadn't cooked a meal for himself in—well, ever, really. He'd never thought about having to live without a cafeteria. He hoped he'd still have food service privileges while staying here.

And there was a den. A little office with a portable screen, floor-to-ceiling bookshelves filled with more church literature than Lloyd knew existed, and a wooden desk. Not plastic, not chipboard. The drawers opened and closed so smoothly and quietly that Lloyd entertained himself for a good five minutes pulling on them.

This was now his place. His home. The blue couch, the leather recliner, the wooden desk, the large bed. They expected him to live here.

After his quick tour of his new home, he moved his bags to the bedroom and then left. It would not do to get too comfortable.

Outside, the air was humming. Lloyd hadn't noticed it before. The day didn't seem like it had gotten any warmer, but the area around the cathedral seemed more active, the molecules moving faster. Lloyd heard cars moving here and there, and he thought he heard occasional shouts. And there was energy in the air, PK activity. Lloyd reached out a little, tried to sense what was going on, but the energy didn't seem active. It was just hanging in the air, waiting.

He walked toward the west edge of the of the cathedral campus, coming out between the dorm building he used to live in and the classroom building where he'd spent months drilling. There were two adepts ahead of him, milling around on the sidewalk, trying to look casual but too obviously keeping an eye on anything that came near them. One of them had Lloyd in his sights, and he smiled and nodded as Lloyd came closer.

"May the light of the Creator shine upon you," the adept said. He had a mild voice that didn't suit his bulky frame. Lloyd just nodded in reply. "Where are you off to?"

"Just a walk," Lloyd said. "I've been away for a while. Thought I'd re-acquaint myself with the Island."

"Yeah, that sounds like fun. Were you going to take anyone with you?"

"No. I don't really know anyone here right now."

The bulky adept exchanged a glance with his companion. "You were just going to walk around town on your own?"

"Yes," Lloyd said. "Is there any reason I shouldn't?"

The bulky adept shifted from one foot to the other. "You're Adept Hsu, aren't you?"

"Yes."

"Welcome back. I should probably let you know that things have changed a little since you were here last."

"How so?"

The bulky adept looked at his companion again. The other adept, a tall woman with straight black hair and a serious face, took a step forward.

"Our relationship with the residents of the Island is not what it used to be. Last year's events unnerved many of them, and many of them are scared and angry. Since the church is a convenient target, they often choose to turn on us."

"Just because we're convenient," Lloyd said.

"Yes," the woman said.

"Not because we did anything wrong."

Neither adept replied.

"How bad is it? Do they attack us?"

"Sometimes," the woman said. "Not often. But sometimes."

"And so we have adepts watching our borders—sometimes? All of the time?"

"All of the time."

Lloyd nodded. "There's a lot of energy in the air. Is that you guys or your backup?"

"I don't think we have to ..." the bulky adept started, but his companion cut him off with a wave of her hand.

"Those are monitoring spells from adepts stationed inside," she said. "We're trying to be as thorough as possible."

"That's it? Just monitoring?"

"Yes," the woman said. "Monitoring and shielding."

"Shielding? Do the townspeople have their own PKs now?"

The woman winced. She apparently hadn't meant to let that out. "There are adepts who were here a year ago who are unaccounted for," she said. "There are concerns that they carry hostility for the church."

"Have any of them actually done anything?"

The woman spoke slowly and carefully. "There are no official reports of rogue PK action against the cathedral."

"Okay," Lloyd said. He looked at the cars passing by. He saw people turning their heads and looking at the cathedral. Maybe it was a trick of the light, maybe it was a trick of his mind, but all of them seemed to be glaring at the church or at him. Beyond the street, the buildings looked unfocused and dim.

"I suppose I don't need to go out yet," Lloyd said, and turned back to the interior of the campus.

About an hour later, he walked out again, down the same path.

"Adept Hsu!" the bulky adept said. "Good to see you again. Where are you—are you leaving?"

Lloyd smiled as he approached the two adepts but he didn't say anything. He walked faster.

"You may go wherever you like," the woman said, "but you need to understand that the Grand Adept has determined that it may not be safe for adepts and acolytes to wander off the grounds by themselves. Perhaps you would be advised—"

At that point Lloyd walked by the two adepts. They took a few steps, but they couldn't leave their station.

"If you spoke to High Adept Birch, you could be assigned a chaperone. There are arrangements that can be made to—Adept Hsu? Adept Hsu?"

He walked off the campus and straight out into the street, running through traffic. Cars honked at him, long and loud. Hopefully that would be the worst they had in store for him. He made it across the street, and he was off.

He didn't take a direct route. It had been a year since he had walked around the Island, but he still knew the neighborhood. He stopped a few times, walking into a couple of stores to browse, and each time he noticed the hostile stares his black robe drew. There were even a few muttered comments, generally along the lines of "Go back to church." Nothing all that threatening.

Eventually he made it out of town, farther east on the Island, near a long string of large beach houses. He didn't see lights on in any of them.

At one point there was a clump of trees marking what had once been a property line. Lloyd ducked into the trees, then did a quick scan. He didn't sense anyone behind him, so he moved through the trees down to the shoreline.

The waves were gentle, and even the sand looked grey under the cloudy sky. Lloyd walked quickly, wrapping himself in a small warming spell as a cool breeze ran down the shore. He didn't have far to go—once he emerged from the trees, it was only a few hundred yards until he saw the low, flat beach house.

There wasn't a light on in that building, either, but Lloyd walked up to the front door and pushed. It opened.

The room inside was mostly empty. There were a few windows, but they were boarded shut for the winter. Furniture was pushed against the wall except for two nylon folding chairs. Amelia Diaz sat in one of them.

He wondered how she'd react. He kind of hoped she'd be happy to see him. But she just gave him half a smile.

"So," she said. "Lloyd Hsu. Back on the Island."

"Amelia Diaz," he said. "Still here."

"What do you want?" she asked.

"No small talk?"

"Has there ever been any?"

"I wanted …" A sudden thought struck him. "Did I say goodbye to you when I left?"

"What?"

"My memories of leaving here are kind of hazy. Splintered. I don't know if I said any proper goodbyes. Did I say goodbye to you?"

"Why do you care?"

Lloyd let his heat spell drop, because he suddenly felt too warm. "I don't know. We just, you know, talked a lot during the whole thing. We ate stuff together. We were like friends, right? And if we were friends, I should have said goodbye."

"We worked together, Hsu. We were on a mission. The mission ended, and we did other things. That's all. I wasn't expecting a hug goodbye, or even a call. So if you dragged me out here because you're feeling guilty, you can stop. Are we done?"

"No. That was just the first thing. There are others."

"Are they more significant?"

"I hope so."

"Then go ahead."

"Has anyone tried to find out what really happened?"

Amelia crossed her hands behind her head. "What are you talking about?"

"We thought we had a prophecy about to be fulfilled, and then the person who was supposed to be the chosen one died. Has anyone tried to figure out what went wrong?"

"I thought it was what you just said—the chosen one died."

"But that wasn't supposed to happen," Lloyd said. "So what went wrong—the prophecy itself or just the way the church followed it?"

Amelia idly rubbed her leg while her eyes wandered around the room, looking anywhere but at Lloyd. Then, abruptly, she focused right on him.

"Why should I care what went wrong? Sounds like a church thing."

"You came with us to the wall. The rest of the ILF stayed behind, but you came with, and you saw Courtney die." Lloyd's voice caught slightly at the words. "You cared then. I'd think you want to know what happened."

"I already know. You guys got in over your heads, and Whitaker paid the price. It's not that complicated."

Lloyd leaned forward, elbows on his knees, and lowered his chin a little. "I think it is," he said. "I think it's a lot more complicated."

Amelia kept rubbing her leg, then she smiled. "So that's you being intense, huh?"

"Yeah. I guess."

"It's not really your thing, is it?"

Lloyd sat up straight. "I'm still working on it."

"So that's why you came back. You really think there's something to find, don't you."

"Yes. I do."

Amelia sighed and looked at the ceiling. "You might be right. There was—something off. The way Whitaker came out of nowhere, turned into this leader, and then was gone just like that."

"Yeah."

"So what do you plan to do? I hope talking to me isn't your entire plan."

"No. That man. The older man. The one who helped us at the Rockaways. You know him, don't you?"

Amelia smiled. "The older man?" she said.

"Yeah."

"You really don't know who he is, do you?"

"No."

"Okay." She stood. "Then it's probably time you met. Formally, this time."

Chapter Thirty-eight

The next day, Lloyd left early in the morning, rushing out past a different set of guards and making his way west. He thought about generating a wind behind his back and running, but then decided he'd rather take the bus.

He had to endure a few hostile stares, but it was still early and the buses were never crowded anyway, even during rush hours. There were plenty of places Lloyd could look so he didn't have to make eye contact with anyone.

The bus didn't take him as far as he needed to go. Once it dropped him off, he had another fifteen miles to walk before he was far enough from the bulk of civilization to satisfy Amelia. Fortunately, the day was brighter and drier than the previous one.

It took him a little over three hours to arrive at an empty cul-de-sac. There were plenty of weeds and even a few tree saplings trying to poke through the old concrete foundations around the circle. Any building material, from bricks to wires to wooden beams, had long been stripped from the area. This was almost the borderlands—close enough that the rats made regular excursions to the area, so the land now mostly belonged to them.

Lloyd strolled around the cul-de-sac, looking for any sign of non-plant life. He didn't see any. Some of the weeds were taller than his knees, with thick stems that resisted the day's slight breeze. They were spiky and ugly.

Then Lloyd heard a noise, a distant sputtering to the north. He thought he saw a cloud of dust, and he hoped it was Amelia.

The sputtering grew louder, and there definitely was a dust cloud. Lloyd thought about performing a scan, but he remembered what the guards had said about adepts who had left and never come back. He probably didn't need to be announcing his presence. He put up a small shield and waited.

The sputtering kept approaching, and Lloyd finally saw the source of the noise. It was a dune buggy, a metal frame with two seats mounted on it. Amelia was behind the wheel, and she pulled up next to Lloyd.

"Hop on," she said.

He did. "A dune buggy?" he asked as he fastened the seat belt.

"Not really," she said. "An easy-to-make junkyard vehicle. It saves a lot of time and effort when you don't have to worry about a frame." She bounced a little in her seat, and the vehicle creaked. "I wouldn't trust this thing on the sand."

She hit the gas and the buggy leapt forward. A number of parts had gone into this vehicle, but it seemed none of them were shock absorbers. They were driving on dirt and hardpan, and every bump in the road traveled all the way through Lloyd's body. Occasionally, some especially springy weeds managed to bounce back and whip his legs. If he had been wearing shorts, his legs would have been slashed bloody in minutes.

There wasn't any chance for conversation on the drive because the engine was too loud. Lloyd watched the waste ahead of him and hoped the journey would be worthwhile.

After a while, Amelia's mouth moved, and she pointed. Lloyd didn't hear what she said, but he could follow her arm, and it pointed to a lump on the horizon. It looked like a large, brown boulder, uneven and ungainly. As they drew closer, it resolved itself into the shape of a building. Sort of. In some places the roof was flat, in others sloped. The building, at different intervals, was one, two, two and a half, and three stories. It had only a few windows, and all of them were shuttered. Lloyd looked at the building for a few seconds, then blinked and looked away. The building practically glowed with psycho-kinetic energy.

Amelia stopped the buggy a good hundred yards away from the building. Lloyd wasn't sure he saw a door—there was a dark corner where the outer wall of the building made a sharp turn, and he thought he saw the dark outline of a doorway in the shadows.

He climbed out of the buggy and tried to catch up with Amelia, since she was already twenty feet ahead of him. But after a few more steps, she stopped and put her hand up.

"You'll probably want to stay where you are for a moment," she said.

Lloyd started to ask why, but then his mind was filled with someone else's thoughts.

<<Adept Hsu,>> the thoughts said, and Lloyd knew they came from the old man. <<Amelia clearly thinks you must be trustworthy, but now you have to convince me. What are you doing here?>>

<<I came to see you,>> Lloyd said. <<Amelia thought it might be a good idea.>>

<<I didn't mean what are you doing at my house. I meant what are you doing *here*, back on the Island? You left once—why did you come back?>>

<<It's—kind of a long story.>>

<<Then show it to me,>> the old man sent. <<Open up.>>

Lloyd reflexively took a step backward. He'd been trained in defense for so long that the prospect of voluntarily opening up a part of his mind unpleasant. But he braced himself and did it anyway.

The old man's touch was extraordinarily gentle—Lloyd didn't feel a thing. A few seconds, he received another sending from the old man.

<<You want to find out the truth of what happened,>> he sent. <<What do you think that truth is?>>

<<I have no idea,>> Lloyd sent back. <<All I know is that something went wrong.>>

<<What if that something is your church? What if the church is wrong?>>

<<Then it's wrong,>> Lloyd sent back promptly. <<You already got my story. I already know the church has been wrong. I want to change it.>>

His mind grew silent.

Ahead of him, Amelia had her arms folded while she stared at him. "Are you done yet?" she asked. But before Lloyd could answer, she jumped a little and stood up straighter.

"I guess you are," she said. "Come on, we can go in now."

Lloyd walked through several crooked hallways with worn black linoleum on the floor. The walls had been off-white once, Lloyd guessed, but they were making a journey toward brown—or even darker colors in spots with water stains. Most of the hallways were dim, and Amelia led him by several closed doors. Lights shown beneath a number of them, and at one point Lloyd heard what sounded like a news netcast. But Amelia didn't stop at any of these doors or offer any explanation about what was there.

Finally she stopped at a light brown door and knocked on it. The door opened smoothly, and Amelia walked through. As soon as Lloyd followed her in the next room, the door glided shut.

The room was cluttered. The walls were covered with unframed photos, a large map of the Island, some newspaper front pages, and a handful of pieces of small, framed artwork. Every horizontal surface, including part of the floor, was covered with open books, scattered papers, and file folders. The paperless revolution hadn't made it to this room yet.

The old man was there, sitting behind a large wooden desk. He didn't get up when Amelia and Lloyd entered. He had the grey eyes Lloyd remembered from the first time he had met the man, but his face looked strangely younger. His dark hair and beard had many grey streaks, but his face was smooth except for hints of wrinkles around his eyes. He was clearly older than Lloyd, but the word "old" didn't really seem accurate when he got up close.

Amelia sat in a tan chair near the desk, and Lloyd dropped onto a brown armchair just a shade off every other color in the room.

"So," the man said. "Well. Adept Hsu. I think the first thing I should tell you is that I appreciate you listening to my admonition regarding Amelia the first time we met. While she did some rather ... unadvisable things since that encounter, I can't blame them on you."

"Thanks," Lloyd said.

"Now, having said that, let me say this. I don't care much for adepts. I live in this part of the Island for a reason, and that reason is to keep away from your church and your people. I'm not pleased that Amelia decided to bring you out here, and I'm certainly not thrilled to have you in my house. But she did what she did, and here you are."

A year or so ago, the old man would have left Lloyd speechless. He would have stammered out a few syllables without forming any words. But that was then. Now, it didn't matter to him if the old man disliked him.

"Sorry to put you out," he said. "I wanted to meet you for something I thought was important, and I thought it might even be worth inconveniencing you. These things happen sometimes."

The man sat quietly for a minute. He looked at Amelia, then back at Lloyd. The hints of wrinkles around his eyes had deepened into lines, but Lloyd couldn't tell if he was amused or angry.

"All right," the man finally said. "I suppose we should start with proper introductions. Adept Hsu, I'm Kale Faltergast."

"Hi," Lloyd said. "Are you a relative, or are you just named after him?"

The man said nothing, but the lines by his eyes got even deeper.

"Are you a close relative? A cousin or nephew?" Still no response. For no good reason, Lloyd started to flush. He sent out a quick scan that was thoroughly blocked—if he hadn't seen the man sitting right in front of him, he'd have thought Amelia was the only other person in the room. "You can't be a son. I've never heard about a son existing. I mean, I know people can have children that no one knows about, but not generally ones that have the same ... the same ..."

The man waited.

"Oh my God," Lloyd said. Now that it had been pointed out to him, the resemblance of the old man to the painting of the Six back at the cathedral was clear. He had aged, of course, but the eyes were almost the same.

"Don't do anything rash," Faltergast said. "No worshipping."

"No what?"

"Worshipping."

"Why would I do that?"

Faltergast grimaced. "I don't know, but that's what chumchas like you seem to do."

"Really? We don't even worship Harriman Ellis—why would we worship you?"

"I don't know. No reason. You shouldn't," Faltergast said. He shuffled a few papers around his desk without looking at them. No one spoke.

"So. I should tell you why we're here," Lloyd finally said.

"What?"

"I thought you wanted to know why Amelia brought me here."

"Yes, yes, I do but—is that it? You don't have any questions? About Harry, and Andy, and the early days? Usually, once people know …"

"Yes, I'm sure you're an interesting person with lots of interesting things to share, but unfortunately that's not what I need right now. You can tell me stories some other time."

Faltergast leaned back. "You're not the same Adept Hsu I met last year. You've changed."

"Shouldn't I have?"

Faltergast didn't move for a moment. Then he slowly nodded. "Yes, I suppose so." He turned to Amelia. "Okay. Whether I like it or not, you're here. Why?"

"You need to know what Adept Hsu wants to do," Amelia said.

Faltergast looked back at Lloyd. "What do you want to do?"

Faltergast had put a map into Lloyd's mind, and Lloyd followed it. He didn't bother with the bus this time, instead putting a cushion of air under his feet and a breeze at his back and sailing along. He noticed a lot of angry stares from people he passed, but he didn't care.

The directions took him through a dilapidated neighborhood. Most of the houses looked abandoned, and still more didn't have electricity. But when he approached the end of Faltergast's directions, the house in front of him looked well kept and had lights glowing behind all windows.

Lloyd felt an odd combination of anger and excitement. He couldn't believe that the church had been infiltrated, that someone had been watching them while they drilled and prepared for their invasion of Far Rockaway. What if the spy had been from the USNA? How much worse could it have gone?

Lloyd almost laughed. In all fairness, things probably couldn't have gone any worse.

The house ahead of him was a small brick ranch that had been divided into two homes. He headed toward the door on the left, still gliding on his air cushion.

The door of the home flew open when he was still a hundred feet away. A woman with straight black hair and a narrow, sharp face came running out of the building.

"What the hell is wrong with you?"

Startled, Lloyd let his spell drop. His feet slapped the ground.

"Are you talking to me?"

The woman—it must be the Nilda Yashie that Faltergast had told him about—looked left and right, back and forth, keeping an eye on everything besides Lloyd. "Get inside," she said. Lloyd walked into the home, with the woman behind him, still looking back and forth.

The interior of her home was small but tidy. There was a pink floral comforter on the small bed, a white sofa without any stains or dust, and a small plastic desk with a screen and keyboard on it. Yashie gestured toward the couch, and Lloyd sat on it while she perched on the bed.

"You've been gone a year," Yashie said as she closed the door. "You don't know how things have changed."

"I've heard popular support for the church has decreased."

Yashie let out a short, barking sound. "That's what they say at the cathedral. Here's the truth—if the people here weren't so wary of the talent, they would have burned the whole complex down months ago."

"It can't be ..."

"If anyone saw you come in here, I'll have to move. If they knew I worked at the church, they'd run me back to the barrens. Don't tell me what can and can't be. You haven't been here."

"Why are they so mad? What did we do?"

"Are you joking?"

"No!"

Yashie shook her head. "You took someone off the Island, some kid who didn't know any better, filled his head with ideas about him being the chosen one, the person who would lead the church to victory, then you not only failed to win a victory but you got this kid killed. It was one thing when they saw you as somewhat powerless against the USNA, but it's something else when you drag Islanders into your fight and get them killed. The pro-USNA voice on the Island used to be quiet, but they've gotten much louder lately. Whitaker's mother is pushing them—ever since he died, she has blamed the church as much, or even more, than the USNA. Said they set him up to die, that the USNA wouldn't have killed him if the church hadn't egged him on first. And lots of people are ready to listen to her. They say they'd be better off under Drauer than under Dugwu, and they think the adepts in the cathedral are the only thing between them and a better life. So they wouldn't mind seeing all of you gone."

"They think the USNA would provide them a better life?"

"They'd at least have regular power and water."

"Sure, those things are great," Lloyd said. "Who cares about freedom?"

"You don't have to tell me," the woman said. "I used to live on the other side."

"That's right. High Ad—I mean, Adept—I mean, Mr. Faltergast said that. He said you were an exile."

"Yes. I used to be one of them."

"A citizen?"

"A government worker," Yashie said. "Human Services. I was a deputy secretary, five heartbeats away from the head of the New York department. Meaning I was approximately six thousand heartbeats away from the presidency."

"That's impressive. So what happened?"

"I partnered with an organization that I found was very efficient in delivering services—counseling, emergency funds and clothing, that sort of thing—where they needed to be. I made sure this organization received plenty of government support, I championed them in several meetings." She sighed. "Then it came out that the organization had direct ties to Mira Corwin."

"Ah," Lloyd said. "I've heard of her."

"Everyone in the city has. I don't know how that fact slipped through the initial vetting process—unless Corwin influenced that process. Anyway, no one believed that I did what I did in ignorance. Everyone thought I was secretly supporting Corwin. They hurried me through a plea bargain, making it clear that if I didn't accept exile they would probably try to sentence me to death, and most likely succeed. And here I am."

"So we didn't just have any spy in the cathedral," Lloyd said. "We had a bona fide USNA spy."

Yashie laughed. "They threw me to the border wastes to die. What loyalty do you think I have for them? Anyway, I can do for you what I did for Kale. I'll open my mind all you want. Search it. See what you find."

Lloyd looked her over. She sat on the edge of her bed, her hands gripping the mattress as she leaned forward. There was tension all through her shoulders, and her eyes blazed.

"That's all right," he said. "I'm going to have to trust Mr. Faltergast for this to work. If he said you're okay, you're okay."

Yashie snickered.

"What?" Lloyd said.

"'Mr. Faltergast,'" she said. "He'd blow a brain vessel if he heard you call him that."

"Well I can't just call him—you know who he is, right?"

"Yes," she said. "He's a man who likes to be called Kale."

Lloyd knew he couldn't call him that, but there was no point in discussing it here. "So, you've been working in the cathedral for more than a year."

"Yes," Yashie said. "I even got a few promotions—a lot of non-clergy quit in the months after Whitaker died."

"Does that mean the information you get is better?"

She shrugged. "The information a custodian gets is about the same as the information a shift supervisor gets. I know a little more about when the other custodians are working, but I'm pretty sure you're not interested in that."

"No. There's some people I need to find. I wondered if you knew where they had gone."

"Go ahead and ask."

"Stel Grant?"

"Transferred to Brazil."

"Archie Gwin?"

"Transferred to Canada. Quebec, I think."

"Silvia Krilow?"

"I don't know. I'm not sure anyone knows."

"What do you mean?"

Yashie waved one hand in a vague, circular gesture. "I mean I've heard some people say they wonder where she went, and no one seems clear on it. I can't know this for sure, but even the high-ranking adepts don't seem to know. She's just gone."

Lloyd felt a churning in his stomach. "Did she disappear during the invasion? Or after?" Had Silvia died in the Rockaways without Lloyd even noticing it?

"No one seems to know that, either."

Lloyd had to strain to say the next name. "Aron Nesbitt?"

Yashie tilted her head. "Why do you want to know about Nesbitt?"

"Because I want to know where he is!"

"Nesbitt left. There's been talk about him from time to time. About whether to go after him, to try to bring him back. A few people went out and didn't succeed. Now, most people don't want to try."

"Go out where? Bring him back from *where*?"

"The border wastes," Yashie said. "Nesbitt stayed around for a while after you left, but he didn't do much. Stayed in his room most of the time. The High Adepts' patience started to wear thin, and they became more and more stern with him. Finally he just took off, went rogue. Some people have tried to bring him in, but never with any luck. And Nesbitt—Nesbitt's not gentle with the people who try to bring him back."

Lloyd felt himself sinking deeper and deeper into the sofa. "Aron's a border rat?"

"It seems so. I guess that's what he wants to be right now."

"Yeah," Lloyd said. Then he sat still and didn't say anything for a while.

Yashie fidgeted a few times, but stayed silent. Lloyd let her wait.

"Are you going to do something?" she finally said.

He looked at her. "What do you mean?"

"I mean that I've been working as a custodian for a year. Not my first choice of jobs, but I've been doing it because Kale wanted a spy. I've fed him plenty of information, but God knows what he's done with it. Not much has happened, except the Island around us has gotten angrier and angrier. So if I'm going to keep cleaning your rooms, I want to know—are you going to do something?"

"What did you have in mind?"

Yashie leaned forward. "*Anything.*"

Lloyd nodded. He stood up and brushed the wrinkles out of his robe. "Yeah," he said. "I'm going to do something."

Chapter Thirty-nine

He was at the wastes the next morning at dawn. The red light behind him gave the only color to the bare ground stretching miles to the west. Grey rock covered grey dirt, and the blight the USNA had imposed on the land kept anything green away.

The border wastes were large enough that even a PK would have a tough time finding a specific individual there, especially one who did not want to be found. Lloyd could try to scan the spaces he crossed, but he could only cover so much area. And if Aron was moving, there was no guarantee that Lloyd would track him down.

But Aron had the talent, and Lloyd could not imagine that he had suddenly become shy about using it. If Aron had stayed in the wastes the past year, every other border rat would know about him.

He went south to the ocean. The hard rock of the wastes carried to the edge of the water, slightly relieved by thin deposits of dark sand washed up by the waves. The beach wasn't pretty, but the ocean was, plus the sun was up and the air already felt warm. It would be a good day to be near the water.

Lloyd walked along the shore and kept his eyes on the sky. The border rats knew how to make fires with very little smoke, but occasionally they were in a hurry or they got sloppy. He hoped they would be especially careless in the morning hours.

He had to walk for an hour and a half, but then he saw it, a thin plume of smoke rising maybe half a mile ahead. If they hadn't seen him yet, they would soon.

Lloyd kicked up a wind behind him and sprinted ahead. He had barely taken a few steps when he saw sparks flying at the base of the smoke column. They were kicking out the fire, and they would soon be on the run. But they couldn't run faster than him.

He saw three of them. The furthest one away ran the fastest because he was unencumbered. Another, a man who wore only tattered pants, labored with a bucket of water. A third, a woman with patches of close-cropped hair across her scalp, carried a something that looked like a large, battered tin pitcher. That would be their still—the one possession they couldn't afford to lose.

Lloyd ran toward the woman and caught up to her easily. She lashed out as he approached, swinging the still and baring her teeth, but Lloyd stayed out of her reach. He gathered the air around her and pressed it in tight, until her arms were bound tight to her side. The still fell to her feet.

The other rats hadn't turned around. They would keep running until they were caught, regardless of what happened to the others. Though one of them might come back for the still.

Lloyd looked at the rat in front of him. He hoped he had made the right choice. She was snarling at him, and her eyeballs kept rolling around until he only saw the whites.

"There's someone like me out here," he said. "Someone with the talent. Where is he?"

The woman snarled louder.

"Where is he?" he said louder, then pressed his mind to hers.

He quickly recoiled in horror. There was no sense to her thoughts, only a swirl of hunger and hostility. There was also a too-vivid picture of her ripping his throat out with her teeth.

But there was fear, too. If he let her go, she wouldn't attack him. She knew what he could do to her.

He cut off the spell. The woman dropped to all fours and let out a sharp bark, then turned and loped off, leaving the still. Lloyd picked up the pitcher and followed her.

It took another hour, but eventually the woman, with Lloyd trailing behind, came to a large rock. She disappeared behind it.

Lloyd slowed. The woman might be wary of his power, but that didn't mean she wouldn't try an ambush.

Then someone came out from behind the rock. Then someone else. Then five other border rats. They held weapons, though nothing more than broad sticks or metal rods. All seven of them charged forward.

Lloyd didn't waste any time. He hardened some air into a beam and moved it forward. It caught most of the rats around the shoulders and laid them out flat.

Lloyd started to run. He didn't think he could maintain seven separate restraining spells, so it would be better to just get around them. But after he took five steps, he hit a wall and fell to the ground himself.

It hurt, but he jumped up quickly since the border rats were already on their feet. He brought them down again, then cursed the USNA for keeping the land barren—some wood to fuel a fire would be handy right now.

He felt a spell coming at him, an air ram like the ones he had made, and he shattered it. He briefly sensed the surprise of his attacker, and he knew who it was.

"Aron!" he called. "Aron, come out! I brought back your still! I just want to talk."

Thoughts abruptly entered his head. <<I thought you all had given up,>> Aron sent. <<Who is it this time? What do you want?>>

<<Aron, it's me,>> Lloyd sent. <<Like I said, I just want to talk.>>

There was a pause, and then Aron's thoughts came with fury. <<Who are you really? Lloyd's gone! He *left*! Who are you? You can't trick me!>>

<<Aron, it's me,>> Lloyd sent. <<You know it's me. I came back.>>

Then there was nothing. No sendings. The border rats who had charged Lloyd were on their feet but not moving. They stood, waiting.

Then the order came, and they moved. Away from Lloyd and back behind the rock. All seven of them disappeared, and Lloyd was left alone.

"Aron?" Lloyd called. <<Aron?>>

There was no reply. Lloyd took a few cautious steps toward the rock, then a few more. Nothing happened.

He walked slowly until he was at the rock. Carefully, he moved around it. No one was hiding there.

He looked around. The ground was hard and grey, like everywhere else in the wastes. There were scuffmarks in the dirt, but no other sign that anyone had been there. He looked up and down, but he couldn't find any trace of the rats. Aron must have learned some new tricks.

Then thoughts entered his mind, thoughts with the dry, sarcastic tone he knew very well. <<Lloyd, if you want me to come out, you'll have to stop standing on top of me.>>

<<What?>>

<<Just move back a few steps, okay?>>

Lloyd did as he was told. When he did, a square crack appeared in the ground. Then it swung open, and Aron crawled out of a trapdoor.

He looked surprisingly good. He moved with a sense of tension and tightness. His hair was even shorter than Lloyd was used to, barely more than stubble. And his eyes were bright, their blue pulling color from the sky. Rough skin around his left eye was the only trace of the burns he had suffered near the wall.

"I know what you're thinking," Aron said. "'Lord, at least he doesn't *look* crazy.'"

"You're not supposed to be reading me!"

Aron smiled crookedly, without much warmth. "I'm not an adept," he said. "Those rules don't apply. But I didn't have to read you. It's all over your face."

Then there was silence. Lloyd shifted his feet, and their scrape across the ground was loud.

"So," he finally said. "How are you?"

"I'm living with border rats underground. You?"

Lloyd started to laugh, but the hostility in Aron's face choked it off.

"Aron, what are you doing out here?"

"I'm doing the only thing I *can* do. I'm not going to the USNA to be one of Drauer's lackeys. I'm not going back to that joke of a church. This is the only place that will have me right now."

"Aron, the church would have you if ..."

"I don't care!" Aron shouted. "I don't care what the church wants! I'm not putting that robe on again, ever!" He pointed at Lloyd's chest. "How could you be wearing that? How *could* you? You know how fake it is! You know what they did! How can you bear to be with them, live with them? It's all a lie, and you're helping tell it!"

Lloyd got angry, then he got confused, then he thought of several things to say, each going in a radically different conversational direction. Then some words weaved their way through the crowd and made it out of his mouth. "I should have been here with you."

That took Aron aback. "What?"

"I should have been here with you," he repeated. "The past year, time and time again, I tried to build up enough courage to leave the church. Because you're right, I know what they did. I wanted to leave, but I couldn't. I didn't know what else to do. So I just stayed and became one of the worst things in the world, a clergyman who doesn't care. I would have been better off leaving. Better off here."

"So that's what you're doing here? You came to join me?"

"No," Lloyd said. "That's how I felt a lot over the past year, but not now."

"If you're about to tell me a conversion story, I'll drop this big rock here on your head."

"I'm not going to tell you any story. I just wanted to let you know what I'm going to do."

"Which is?"

"Find out what went wrong. Find out why something everyone thought was a prophecy turned out to be nothing."

Lloyd thought he saw interest flicker across Aron's face, but then his expression hardened. He chuckled, low and harsh.

"You're an idiot," Aron said.

Lloyd's fists clenched, but he didn't say anything.

"You're still playing their game. Still thinking about the church. You want to know what went wrong? People acted like what all those old men say and do *mattered*. We treated them like they had a connection to God, when all they were hearing were their own delusions. It's no surprise something went wrong—only that the whole mess held together as long as it did. It's a bunch of nonsense, all to control skills that should be ours. So I'm not playing their game any more."

"This isn't a game," Lloyd said, keeping his voice level. "This is finding out what happened to Courtney."

"I don't care what happened to Courtney," Aron said. "I didn't like him much anyway."

"So what are you going to do?" Lloyd said, his voice heated. "Stay out here? Live underground with the rats? Is that any kind of a life?"

Aron smiled. "I'm just here for now," he said. "It's a place to be until I go somewhere else. I'll get on a boat. Go to Europe where you can be a PK without being part of a government or nation. Do my own thing, leave all this shit behind."

"You haven't left yet, though," Lloyd said. "I could use your help while you're here."

Aron took a quick step to the trap door, then started climbing down. He looked back up at Lloyd as he descended.

"No," he said. "I'm out."

Lloyd took the long way back to Hampton, and he didn't feel like doing anything other than walking. He traveled through the late afternoon, into the orange evening, and to the night. It was a pleasant night, warm and with a breeze from the northeast. People were out, talking and occasionally laughing, and none of them seemed to care that Lloyd was around. He walked toward them, by them, and away from them, and they didn't give him a second look.

He was walking through one of the nicer areas of the Island now—houses were inhabited and lit up, roads were almost entirely paved, and most of the lawns had been mowed in the past year. Lloyd looked in a few of the front windows of houses he passed, but most of the time all he saw was curtains and blinds.

When he was about three miles from the cathedral, his legs grew heavy. He wasn't sure how far he had traveled, since he didn't know how deep he'd gone into the borderlands to find Aron. It had taken most of the day, though, and his desire to walk was gone. Maybe he could find something to eat or drink, or a place to sit down.

But he'd started to notice some stares. People were looking at him, then looking away. Turning to their friends and muttering something. He had been noticed, and no one was happy to see him. He should hurry home, but he didn't have the energy for it. Just thinking about walking through three miles of hostility made him even more tired and slow.

He sensed the rock as soon as it was thrown. He used the talent to swat it away without turning around, and the stone clicked a few times on the road behind him.

He felt anger surge around him, felt it like something was being cinched over his gut. He'd used the talent in front of them, and they didn't like it.

There were more rocks flying through the air. He batted a few aside, mainly just to show he could, then set a shield around him. Everything they threw at him, rocks and bottles and shoes, bounced harmlessly to the ground. He easily stepped over the rubble that landed in front of him.

Their complete failure didn't make them give up. A group, something less than a mob, was following him now, yelling. They might have been throwing more things at him, but he didn't notice.

He kept walking, they kept yelling, and the noise built to a harsh buzz, like a mosquito whine but lower. He could have shut it out, or at least most of it, but he didn't.

But as he continued on, he thought maybe it was a mistake. The noise behind him became more harsh, more grating, and he heard some individual words, all directed at him, all rough. These were people he had served for years, people he had ministered to, and they were calling him the worst things they could think of because he hadn't let himself be hit by a rock.

None of the people behind him had the talent. Not one of them. They didn't know what he could do, they didn't understand. A group like that ... he had so many options. So many ways to cause chaos, or to cause pain if that was what he wanted. He could shoot a spark through them—not lightning, of course, not that harsh, but a shock, something that would make all of them jump. Or he could put up a moving wall and knock them over like bowling pins. It could even just be a wind that would stop them in their tracks. So many ways.

And why shouldn't he do something? They weren't stopping. He'd given them every chance. They were louder than ever, more annoying than ever, and he could easily stop them. So easily.

He turned. There were objects, mostly rocks, flying toward him, and they all stopped a foot in front of him and dropped to the ground. He didn't know how his face looked, if he was impassive or if his mouth and brow was twisted. He thought about raising his arms for effect, but there was no reason to. He could cast the spell without moving a muscle.

He gathered power reflexively, without thinking about it, without knowing, at first, what kind of power he was calling. It was electricity. Electricity had always been easy for him. He could gather enough to make himself glow, then hit them with it. Hard.

He saw their twisted faces in front of them, their anger and hate, and imagined how they would look when he unleashed the lightning. He saw their surprise and their pain, mostly their pain. He imagined many of them falling to the ground.

And he let the power go. He released it slowly, dissipating it into the air. The crowd around him wouldn't notice anything about what he had just done. They wouldn't even have felt so much as their hair standing on end.

He had to move. They were circling him. He ran, no wind behind him, just natural speed. The sudden movement caught them by surprise, and they didn't close fast enough. He made it through them and sprinted east.

After only a block his lungs felt tight, his legs dragged. They were behind him, chasing, and he felt their elation. They thought they'd put a scare into him, and they loved it. But he kept going, running at top speed even though he felt like his legs would seize up any minute.

But they didn't. They moved, and the people chasing didn't feel like traveling too far from home. A few of them went over a mile in pursuit, but they finally gave up, and then Lloyd was alone.

His legs and lungs didn't feel any better, but he made himself run all the way back to the cathedral, and he did it without a wind at his back.

Part Seven: Conspirator

Chapter Forty

Lloyd had planned on doing this with Aron, on having Aron to bounce ideas off of. Now he didn't have anyone. He couldn't bring Amelia in, even if she'd wanted to come—outsiders weren't welcome in most areas of the cathedral even in the best of times. There were other adepts around, but none that he trusted. There was a nagging thought in his brain saying that he couldn't fully trust anyone who'd stayed at Hampton.

Without the help he counted on, he had to rely on the help that was available to him.

He was back at the top of the staircase that led down to the archives. The staircase had not changed a bit. It was still dim, still grey, and Acolyte Terrin still sat at the bottom of it. Lloyd walked down the stairs alone and in silence.

Acolyte Terrin was unchanged, and he sat hunched over the books on his desk as if he had been sitting there reading continuously for the past year and beyond, which may well have been the case.

Lloyd spoke without introduction, without preamble. "All of the prophecies were supposed to be fulfilled," he said. "They're not."

"Of course they are," Acolyte Terrin said, his voice little more than a wheeze. His mouth was the only thing that moved when he spoke. "The fulfillments have continued and will continue."

"Even after the chosen one died?"

"The fulfillments continue," Terrin said. "November 23rd, the white branch prophecy. January 1st, the year of light prophecy. March 8th, the burning sky prophecy ..."

"Whitaker is dead! The chosen one is dead! Why are you keeping track of all of this when the chosen one is dead?"

Terrin looked at Lloyd above his ancient, dirty glasses. "I am the archivist," he said. "I collect information. Others decide what it means."

"You've got all this information about which prophecies have been fulfilled and you haven't thought about what it means?"

Terrin was already looking at his books. "It means the prophecies are being fulfilled."

Lloyd sighed. It was like talking to a recording. "All right, Terrin. Help me out here. The prophecy about the chosen one. How does it go?"

"*Walking from a white field*
Comes the fall.
The oppressor will meet
The one who is his end," Terrin recited without looking up.

"That's the one," Lloyd said. "Did we get the wrong chosen one?"

"You brought the chosen one to us, and he was widely recognized as such. Were the signs of the Creator insufficient?"

"Seeing as how the chosen one is dead, yes, they were! I'm trying to find out what went wrong, and you're sitting here acting like nothing did!"

"I have information," Terrin said. "I have facts. That is all."

"Then give me the fact that tells me what went wrong with Courtney."

"That is not fact," Terrin said. "That is analysis."

Lloyd shook his head, turned quickly, and stomped up the stairs.

By the time he was at the top of the staircase, though, he was walking at a more normal pace. He hadn't been down there for long, and he hadn't really gotten what he wanted. But there was a chance he had gotten enough.

When Lloyd made it to the study room, Nilda looked very nervous. Kale, by comparison, was slouched on one of the black chairs and looked like he may be asleep.

"I just came up from the archives," Lloyd said.

Kale blinked. "Yeah."

"Right now. I was just down there, talking to Terrin."

"Right," said Kale.

"Do we have to talk about this here?" Nilda said. "If Lloyd is done in the archives, can't we go some place else?"

"I like it here," Kale said.

"But if someone finds us ..."

"If someone finds us, you're fine," Kale said. "You're supposed to be here, the boy is supposed to be here, I'm the only one who's not. And I can take care of myself."

"I'm not supposed to be *here* here, though. I don't work over here. People will wonder why I'm here. Can't we just leave?"

"No," Kale said. "Lloyd was talking. Go ahead, Lloyd."

Lloyd still had trouble with the fact that he was suddenly on a first name basis with Kale Faltergast, but he was at least learning how to respond when he was addressed.

"We talked about the prophecies. Acolyte Terrin and I. It wasn't an easy conversation—he was ready to list all sorts of prophecies and ..." Then he noticed that Kale was barely concealing a laugh. "What?"

"You remember why I'm here, right?"

"Of course! You were going to monitor the conver—oh. Okay. So I won't summarize what happened."

"Good idea. Let me tell you what I found out," Kale said. "There's nothing in Terrin's head."

"I know!" Lloyd said. "He's got all those facts and information, but he doesn't seem to have any idea what to do with them, or even that anyone *should* do anything with them. It's strange."

"It's not just that," Kale said. "He's got enough of a mind to control basic motor functions, to keep him alive and all. But anything else—" he shook his head "—there's nothing else. He's not really a person. He's a puppet."

"I don't understand."

"The reason it seems like Terrin never leaves the archives is that I'm fairly certain he never does. He has no will of his own. If he doesn't have an outside mind controlling him, he doesn't do anything but sit and breathe. He's comatose, only in a sitting position."

Lloyd didn't know how to respond. Terrin was a regular presence in the cathedral. Lloyd hardly ever saw him, of course, but every time he came near the archive, he knew he was there. He could feel it. And that presence he had been feeling was—a puppet?

"I didn't think—I didn't know that was possible," Lloyd said. "I didn't think we could pull off that kind of control."

"*You* can't pull off that kind of control," Kale said, his chin lifting slightly. "And most of the time, no one else can either, because the other person's will gets in the way. It's very difficult to overwhelm them from the outside. Unless there's nothing there. I don't know how they got Terrin to this point—if they found him this way or if they made him. The point is, Terrin's words aren't his own. Someone else is writing his material."

Lloyd took a deep breath. He waited for his legs to shake, or his stomach to heave, but he felt steady. He kept telling himself that this was what he had come back to do.

"So who is doing the writing?" Lloyd said, pleased that his voice sounded calm and level.

"It was a sending. Very strong, very distinct. You know, of course, that each sending has its own signature?"

"Of course."

Kale looked at Nilda. "This is going to make your life difficult," he said. "You've already heard enough that will be difficult to keep hidden. What I'm about to say will be even harder to bury in your mind."

"Should I leave?" she said.

"No." Kale said. "You're going to need to know this. We'll need your help. But I want you to know that you're going to have to control your thoughts more than you ever have. Even if you think what we're talking about now won't be in your conscious thoughts, this is the kind of thing that can pop up out of nowhere and be read. You'll have to be incredibly careful."

"All right, all right, I'll be careful. So what is it?"

"I've been on the Island for a while," Kale said. "Most PK signatures blend into the background, like bird chatter. You're stronger than average, Hsu, from what I've seen, but I wouldn't recognize your signature if you were standing in front of me casting with four other adepts. Most of the time I don't pay any attention to signatures.

"But there are a few adepts here who are quite powerful. Not bad at what they do, really. They've been around a while, like me, so I've learned to recognize their signatures. Just like the handwriting of an old friend. As soon as I sense it, I know who's behind it.

"I'm not saying I know who controls Terrin all the time. But this time, while you were down there, the signature was obvious. Terrin was being controlled by Grand Adept Serl."

Chapter Forty-one

There were a few adepts who would never speak to the person cleaning their quarters. Some stayed quiet due to shyness, others due to snobbery. But there were plenty others who were happy to chat when they saw Nilda.

She hadn't been very good at it at first. They would greet her, she would nod or say "hi," and that was it. But cleaning was not stimulating work, and after a few months on the job she became anxious for distraction. She became better at small talk almost by necessity.

She'd made some friends since Whitaker's death, adepts that Lloyd didn't know. Of their small group of conspirators, she had the best connections now. The whispering campaign had to start with her.

Her first attempt was terrible. She was in the women's dorm when Acolyte Carmen Pujo, a young recruit whose PK abilities greatly outweighed her piety, walked in.

"Hi, Nilda," Pujo said. "Anything I can do for you? Any dust I can blow out of hard-to-reach spaces?"

"If you can clean your room with the talent, what am I doing here?"

"Serving as a reminder. I keep forgetting I should clean my room until I see you."

"Glad I'm serving a purpose." Nilda paused. "Can I ask you kind of a strange question?"

"Is it more interesting than my homework?"

"Maybe."

"Then go ahead and ask."

"Have you ... do you ever think about all the things that happened last year? The whole thing with Courtney Whitaker?"

"What do you mean?" Adept Pujo wasn't smiling anymore, and Nilda was all too aware of how strange the question must have sounded.

"I don't know. I just think about it still. Even though it was kind of a while ago. I wonder about all that stuff. Don't you, sometimes?"

She could see Carmen flinch slightly and lean away. "No, not really. There's, you know, enough to do without worrying about that stuff."

Nilda let it drop. She went back to work and resolved to be smoother next time.

She got better. A lot of it had to do with listening. If she paid attention, she could hear the acolytes and adepts talking about the invasion and the capture and execution of Whitaker and things like that. She learned how to stay out of the way and let the people she was talking to open up.

The next conversation she had on the subject with Acolyte Pujo, five weeks after the first one, went considerably better. She saw the acolyte rushing out of her room one morning, holding a stack of books in one arm while trying to get a black headband on straight. One of her shoes wasn't on right—the back of the shoe was being crushed under her heel.

"The room's a mess this morning," Carmen said as she hurried by. "I'm sorry." She turned and walked backward quickly while she talked. "You can leave it alone if you want. I'll tidy it some later."

"Don't worry about it," Nilda said.

Later that afternoon, after the room had been cleaned (it had been cluttered but was not really in terrible shape), Acolyte Pujo returned, walking slower and looking calmer. Lloyd had found the acolyte's schedule, and he gave Nilda the information she needed to be in the right hallway when Carmen returned.

"You're still here?" Carmen said when she saw Nilda.

"I'm here again," Nilda corrected. "Nothing ever stays clean for long."

"I know. And the way the schedule's been ..."

"Has it gotten busier lately?" Nilda said.

"Yeah. It's almost like we're drilling again. But it's different. I don't think we're going to invade again, or anything like that. I think ..." Carmen trailed off.

"What?"

"Oh, I don't know. It's just a guess. But I think the Grand Adept still thinks our security isn't good enough. He keeps his calm appearance and everything, but you can see the way the parishioners are acting bothers him. Everyone out there, even the ones who come to church, glare at us. And more. Mrs. Whitaker has them pretty riled up. I hear they've been throwing Molotov cocktails at us some nights. It doesn't do anything, of course, but they're getting more aggressive."

"I've heard that," Nilda said. "I don't know why they're getting angrier, though. The church hasn't done anything to them."

"Yeah, but we haven't done much to help them, either. There's this antagonism that we can't get over, and I'm not sure the Grand Adept's even trying." She closed her eyes. "Whoops—I've just said enough to get me midnight guard duty."

"Who am I going to tell?" Nilda said, and she laughed lightly.

But later that day she did, in fact, tell someone what Acolyte Pujo had said. Lloyd received all the details of the conversation, and she told him to add Acolyte Pujo's name to the list he kept in his head.

About two months after his conversation with Acolyte Terrin conversation, Lloyd returned to High Adept Birch's office. As Lloyd expected, the High Adept was once again enthusiastic and welcoming, making sure that each and every aspect of Lloyd's life in the cathedral complex was satisfactory. It made Lloyd's job simple.

"There is one change I'd like to make, now that you ask," Lloyd said at one point. "I don't want to be presumptuous, of course, and I know the adepts already have a strict schedule ..."

"No need to beat around the bush!" High Adept Birch said. "What can I do for you?"

"Well, I had just been thinking, there were a few things, some spells, that I've always been good at, and I was wondering if there was any way I could get together an informal group ..."

"You'd like to lead a study group?" The High Adept smiled, a thin line that was barely an arc. "That's an interesting idea. What kinds of things would you like to cover?"

"Nothing specific," Lloyd said. "I thought I could let the students set the agenda. You know, see what they're having difficulty with, and find out if there's any way I can help them along."

"I see," Birch said. "Well, the students certainly would do well to learn from your habits. Between you and me, you were one of the best students we've had here in recent years, and it would be a tremendous blessing if some of them absorbed your example."

"That's very kind of you."

"However, the Grand Adept has been rather reluctant to add extra duties or responsibilities to the students. The extra security work has them stretched a little thin."

"Of course. Do you think it would help if I spoke to the Grand Adept directly?"

Birch's face fell into blankness, and Lloyd could almost feel the shield settling over his mind. "I don't believe that it would," he said. "The Grand Adept's ... extra vigilance has resulted in a bit of a separation between himself and the rest of the cathedral. So that he may better look after security concerns and think about the big picture." Birch spoke in a carefully neutral manner.

"Then what can I do to make this happen?"

High Adept Birch sat very still, expressionless. "I think your idea is a good one. I think there are things that need to change. Perhaps your class could be a step in the right direction." He smiled, and this time it was more natural. "Find some acolytes and adepts you think could use your help. Start having your class. If the Grand Adept decides it's a bad idea, he can let one of us know."

Lloyd smiled with relief. "Thank you, High Adept Birch."

The plan took time, enough time that Lloyd often felt like the nervous energy building up in him was enough to push him around the whole Island, on foot, three or four times. But at least things were happening, which was better than his first few weeks back in the cathedral, when he had spent far too much time in his ridiculously large apartment trying to decide what he should do with himself. It was also considerably better than the year after Whitaker's death, for a wide variety of reasons.

It was better, but not easy. Sundays were particularly difficult, listening to the Grand Adept's sermons in a mostly empty chapel. Whenever the Grand Adept spoke on subjects like honesty and integrity, Lloyd felt like throwing away all his slow work and jumping to his feet to denounce the Grand Adept then and there. But then he would look at one of the members of his study group frowning or leaning over to another member and whispering a comment, and he knew he could be patient.

It helped when he heard from Rafael. The messages from Guatemala were erratic—there was no reliable postal service, of course, and any electronic messages that went over cables running near the USNA generally did not make it to the Island. But Rafael was becoming more and more experienced at using relays, sending messages across the ocean and halfway around the world before they bounced over to Lloyd. One cold February morning, a terse message from Rafael made Lloyd send out a quick message of his own and then jump up from his desk and run out of his room, leaving his breakfast to cool and congeal.

Leaving the cathedral complex had not become any easier. While the Islanders still had not inflicted any real damage to the cathedral, their aggression had steadily increased. Some acolytes and younger adepts, still learning the intricacies of shielding, had been hit by rocks and batteries on journeys out of the cathedral, occasionally receiving wounds they could not easily heal on their own. The Grand Adept and the other leaders had conferred on multiple occasions about the possibility of covering the whole complex with a shield and leaving it at that, but in the end they decided that the continual expenditure of energy that would necessitate would be too much.

"High Adept Sternhaven, bless her charitable soul, had also said something about a shield further isolating us from the remaining friendly Islanders who like to visit the grounds," High Adept Birch had told Lloyd once. "But there are so few of those people that we didn't really need to take them into account."

So the Grand Adept had updated the security procedures, and he now insisted on even more rigorous questioning of those leaving the cathedral, along with a written log of who left when and with whom they were traveling. Unaccompanied trips were strongly discouraged.

This morning, however, Lloyd was fortunate—a member of his study group, Adept Vic Hart, was on duty at the east checkpoint. He let Lloyd go with a minimum of hassle, despite the disapproving glares of other adept on duty.

Once he was free, Lloyd made his way into town. He wore a long wool coat, and he didn't bother with his adept robes. He traveled to one of the few places left that accepted the business of adepts, a bookstore that had three rickety tables where they served hot drinks and muffins. When he arrived, Amelia and Slane Olsen were waiting for him. Neither one of them was looking at the other.

This time, Lloyd didn't bother to attempt any small talk.

"How would you like to go to Guatemala?" he said to Slane.

"Hi," she said.

"Hi, how are you, right, fine," Lloyd said. "How would you like to go to Guatemala?"

"Are you kidding? What for?"

"You're going to be the first reporter to tell the world the true story of what happened at Antigua almost two years ago."

Slane's face, which was pale anyway, lost what little color it had. "You can't be serious." She pointed at Amelia. "She doesn't even believe anything happened down there!"

"I believe it now," Amelia said.

"You changed your mind about something?" Slane said. "What's going on here?"

"I have a friend in Guatemala," Lloyd said. "He's spent a lot of the past two years gathering any evidence he could about the events in Antigua. It wasn't easy—you know how the USNA can cover their tracks. But he's got a good collection of witnesses and evidence now. And he's willing to show it to you."

Slane slumped back in her chair. Air slowly whooshed out of her. "Antigua," she said. "The whole story."

"The whole thing," Lloyd said.

"How would I get there?"

"My friend has arranged for that. You can ride down on a ship that's docking here in two days.

Slane recovered enough from her surprise to raise an eyebrow. "This friend of yours seems a little too resourceful. How can he get me on a ship?"

"He's developed a good network over the past two years," Lloyd said, "and he's managed to get quite a few people to owe him favors."

"That's it?"

"He can tell you anything else when you get down there."

"Look, it's a great story, but I'm not in the habit of putting my life in the hands of people I don't know. I barely know if I can trust you, let alone this friend of yours."

"I understand. That's why Amelia's going with you—to help you any way she can, and to make sure your trip is safe."

Slane looked at Amelia. Amelia smiled.

"Sunshine and beaches," Amelia said. "It's a dream assignment."

"Still, this will take a while. I won't be able to do anything else when I'm covering this thing. It'll limit the number of pieces I can sell to ..." Then Slane shook her head. "Shit, what am I saying? If I get this story, it'll be the only one I need all year." She looked at Amelia. "Okay. You helped me get good coverage of all the fun in Far Rockaway. And this is a story I've wanted to tell for a long time."

Then she pointed at Lloyd. "Your friend better have good stuff. If I come back with a bunch of stories from a guy named Luis about how his mother's butcher's second cousin heard that Anderson Drauer took apart the cathedral by hand, I will come back here and lead a citizen attack on your cathedral myself."

Lloyd grinned. "Just you wait," he said.

Lloyd thought about going out again that evening after he got back, but the winds were too cold. He could keep himself as warm as he wanted, but every bit of energy he spent on warming would be a distraction from his shield. It was for his own safety, he told himself. Besides, he had plenty of time to go out again. He'd make it out, someday.

He waited a week, then another. He had more sessions with his study group, and listened with pleasure as their questions became more thoughtful, more probing. It had taken some time to get them to focus on the ideas of Ellis rather than his personality, but they were getting there.

Lloyd wished he had the excuse of being too busy to travel to the wastes, but that wasn't the case. He had time to read (though he stayed away from the archives), to think, to write messages to Rafael that he hoped would get through, and to perform other contemplative tasks. There was hardly a day that went by that didn't present an open block of time for Lloyd to make the journey he had been thinking about. A few times he even made it to the door of his apartment, ready to leave. But each time he stopped. He couldn't imagine what he would do or say when he got there.

So even though Lloyd thought about visiting Aron almost every day, he didn't go. He thought a few times about having Kale or Spree look into what Aron was up to, but he didn't want to bother them. Weeks and months passed. News started to trickle in, while Lloyd's study group grew. Lloyd led the group and waited.

Chapter Forty-two

There was a knock at the door. Lloyd probably could have been summoned through a sending, but everyone was being extra cautious recently. The High Adepts always paid more attention to sendings than to speech, so most of the planning had been done through oral conversation.

Lloyd opened the door a crack. Acolyte Pujo was on the other side, her arms folded.

"Yes?"

"It's happening."

Lloyd nodded "I'll be there," he said, and closed the door.

He went into the bathroom, smoothed his hair, and made sure his robe was straight. Then he looked at his face, and for the first time in more than a year he didn't think he was looking at a stranger. The changes he had earned where still there—the lines by his eyes, the first hints of grey at the temples—but he recognized those features as part of him now. That didn't make him feel any better about his appearance, but at least he didn't walk away from the mirror feeling disoriented.

It was quiet inside the dorm. There was some murmured conversation, but the noise didn't rise above a whisper. But every face turned to Lloyd as he walked by, and some of the clergy pointed at him. He smiled and waved, knowing he looked uncomfortable.

A few acolytes and adepts stood and walked behind Lloyd. Once he had a crowd of five behind him, Lloyd realized he'd better figure out where he was going. Walking back and forth through the halls would be awkward with a trailing crowd.

There were only two rooms in the dorm building that would hold a group of more than four people—the cafeteria and the study room. The study room felt more appropriate, so that's where Lloyd went.

There were already eleven people in the room, and none of them were studying. They had pushed tables and chairs out of the way and were sitting cross-legged on the floor. They all turned and smiled at Lloyd when he entered, and they shifted to make their circle bigger.

Lloyd would have preferred a chair, but he was not so blind to visual symbolism that he would sit above the acolytes and adepts like a regent above his subjects. He dropped to the orange carpet, leaned back against a metal bookshelf, and smiled at the gathered students.

"No class today, huh?" he said.

A few of the students laughed, then repeated the phrase. "No class today! No class today!" The words echoed in the room and down the hall. Soon the building was vibrating with the chant. "No class today! No class today!" They got louder and louder, yelling now, some of them beating fists or feet against the floor. They smiled as they chanted, and Lloyd looked at their eyes and saw the energy this would need. When they were done chanting, they broke into a round of applause for themselves.

Lloyd crossed his legs and rested his hands in his lap. He would have to be careful about what he said if he wanted to keep things simmering instead of boiling over.

He thought he should probably let Slane and Amelia know what was going on, but it wasn't really news yet—it was only a bunch of students cutting classes. It would be bigger news later.

The students in the circle with Lloyd talked back and forth about what to do now, their tones bright and excited. They talked about compiling a list of demands, or making signs, or marching around the whole campus. They rejected the march, because if they stayed put they might be able to control the dorm building. If they walked out into areas the High Adepts were watching more carefully, their short-lived protest might dissolve quickly. And as long as they were safe in the building, they could start working on their demands.

At a few minutes past nine o'clock, Adept Wallace Dorn walked into the study room and looked around cautiously. He often taught High Adept Sterhaven's class first thing in the morning, and his sharp nose twitched, like he was sniffing out his students.

"You're all in here," he said. "Why are you all in here?"

The chant restarted instantly, at full roar. "No class today! No class today!"

Dorn stepped backward and raised his hands in front of him. "Wait, wait, wait," he said. "What? What is this?"

And then everyone looked at Lloyd, and he took a deep breath and stood up.

"No one's going to class today," Lloyd said, and everyone around him cheered.

"Oh," Dorn said. "What—what's going on?"

"There's some things we need explained, and some changes we need made," Lloyd said. "In the light of some information that has come to light and discussions we have had, we've all decided it doesn't make much sense to continue with the education of these students until these things are taken care of." Lloyd cursed silently—he needed to make better speeches if he was going to keep up with this role.

"What should I tell High Adept Sternhaven?" Adept Dorn said.

"Tell her we're here and that she can come by anytime she'd like," Lloyd said, and the group in the study room cheered. *That was a little better*, he thought.

Adept Dorn backed out of the room, staring at the group, shaking his head. Then he turned and practically ran out of the building.

The festive atmosphere of the sit-in continued throughout the morning. They had donuts and cereal from the cafeteria, and everyone had plenty of energy from not having to go to morning classes. The good spirits of the morning kept anyone from noticing, or at least caring, that no one other than Adept Dorn seemed to notice that a large number of students were skipping their daily routine.

The lack of contact from the leaders continued through the first hours of the afternoon. The High Adepts hadn't acknowledged the sit-in in any fashion—except a single sending from High Adept Birch.

<<I trusted you,>> the sending said, and the disappointment and sense of betrayal that came with it was almost enough to make Lloyd regret what he was doing.

As the afternoon grew later, much of the energy left the room. The students had taken action, but nothing was happening as a result. It was like a long trip—once the initial euphoria of travel fades, you realize just low long it will take to get where you're going.

Lloyd figured there would be no activity the whole day—no media attention, no visits from the higher-ups in the cathedral, nothing to galvanize the students. Lloyd wasn't worried that they'd quit, not this soon, but if their attention flagged they may not be ready for the long haul. He needed to keep them focused. So he spoke.

"I didn't like Courtney Whitaker much," he said. He used a normal tone, speaking off-handedly, but the room immediately grew quieter. "I'd grown up with the prophecies, and I knew about the white field prophecy. Like pretty much any adept, I thought about ways the prophecy could describe me. Maybe I'd be on a farm on a snowy day, walking through the blinding white, and the voice of the Creator would tell me I was the one. Or some High Adepts would come tell me the same thing. And I would be at the head of an army of adepts that would sweep past the walls and into the city, and our exile would be over."

Students must have quickly sent messages to those in other parts of the building. They came through the doors by twos and threes, looking for seats in the already crowded room. Lloyd kept talking.

"I worked hard to learn the ways of the talent for a lot of reasons, but one of them was so I would be ready just in case I walked into that white field.

"Then I found Courtney. The chosen one. I'd spent hours learning about the lives of the Six, and Courtney didn't know their names. I felt awed and inspired every time I entered our cathedral, while Courtney looked like he wanted more screens and videos in there. I was fascinated by every aspect of life here. Courtney was bored.

"I didn't think he was worthy, I didn't think he was interesting, I didn't think he was charismatic. But I had been told he was the chosen one, and I had been waiting for the chosen one my whole life. I would follow him if I had to.

"Then he actually became a leader, and I thought there might be something to this whole chosen one thing. I saw the hand of the Creator at work. I saw the miracle happening.

"Then he died.

"I don't know what happened in Far Rockaway. I don't know how Courtney found enough in him to be a leader for a few days. What I know is that I saw him in the cage where they killed him, and I saw the terror in his eyes, and he was totally alone.

"I hadn't been wrong about him. He wasn't ready to be a leader. He wasn't the chosen one. He was a poor kid who was forced into a role he wasn't ready for because the leaders of the cathedral here thought they could play God. They were tired of waiting for the Premier Adept's miracles so they tried to make their own.

"I imagine that all of you have read Slane Olsen's reports from Guatemala, so you know adepts were playing with miracles before I found Courtney. And I've told many of you what we learned about Acolyte Terrin in the archives. But I didn't tell you everything about how we learned everything about Acolyte Terrin."

He took a deep breath. Mr. Faltergast would hate him for what he was about to do.

"The sendings controlling Terrin were intercepted by a man who has been helping me. He also helped us in Far Rockaway, though he liked to stay behind the scenes and out of sight as much as possible. His name is Kale Faltergast." He waited while gasps echoed through the room. "*The* Kale Faltergast."

That did it. The room buzzed. Students talked, laughed, even danced a little. They had one of the Six on their side! They were more convinced than ever about the rightness of their cause.

Of course, if Kale was here himself to talk to them and share his thoughts on the church, they might not be so pleased to have him as an ally. But for the time being, his name would be enough to keep them happy, so they didn't need to know the rest of Faltergast's opinions.

Then a knot tied itself in Lloyd's stomach. He was telling half-truths to advance his cause. But his cause was to make things better than they were. He was supposed to be doing things differently.

"Mr. Faltergast is a great friend to have," he said, trying to make himself heard in the now-noisy room. "But I don't want you to take it as a sign that the Creator is with us. Mr. Faltergast thinks the church is about as inspired as the USNA. But he's willing to help us, and I'm happy to have his assistance."

The enthusiasm in the room didn't decrease. Lloyd leaned back in his chair. His stomach felt better.

The media arrived the next day. Or at least, one reporter did, but it was a start.

"Thanks for coming, Slane," Lloyd said. "Welcome to the compound."

Slane looked back and forth as the walked through the building, taking in the cinder block walls, orange carpet, and wizard-light sconces.

"I guess you save the nice stuff for the cathedral," she said.

Lloyd laughed. "Pretty much. But you should see my place." Then he remembered High Adept Birch's sending of yesterday. "Might not be mine anymore, though."

They made it to the study room, and Slane took a look around at some adepts who had started to look a little grungy.

"So this is the heart of the glorious revolution, huh?" she said.

"It's what we've got for now."

"Hmmm." She rubbed her chin. "I was going to ask about the possibility of getting video footage out of the compound, but at the moment this is not the most compelling visual I've ever seen. I'll start with print."

"Do people still read news?"

"Of course they do, as long as it's electronic and mean. And I can make it mean."

Lloyd looked at her in alarm and started to open his mouth, but she quickly waved him off. "Mean to them, not you."

"Okay. What do you need from me?"

"Nothing at the moment," Slane said. "Turn me loose, let me talk to people, and we'll see what happens. I'll need some stuff from you, too."

"Just let me know."

Word that a reporter was covering the sit-in traveled quickly, and students were practically lining up to get a chance to share their thoughts with Slane. Lloyd felt edgy watching them talk to her without monitoring what they were saying. Trying to encourage freedom without being a hypocrite wasn't always easy.

Slane did her job, pointed her recorder here and there, talked to Lloyd for a time while he tried to sound eloquent and bold, and then she said she was done.

"I'll call you if I need any clarification on anything," she said. "Hopefully, there will be enough interesting stuff going on that I can do a follow-up." She looked around the dorm that once again was going quiet in the late afternoon. "I hope something happens."

"Thanks. Me too."

Then there were more reporters, and then Lloyd started hearing about the story hitting the nets. Not the big ones, but FreeNet and BorderNet had small pieces about it. Then they stopped coming—word came through that the cathedral campus was under lockdown. Lloyd had to find other ways to get the word out. With Kale and Spree on the outside, though, it wasn't hard. Words got out, and coverage grew.

Official communication from the leadership of the cathedral did not come until the fifth day of the sit in. Lloyd was in his customary place in the library when the sending from Birch arrived.

<<I'm coming over there. I'm assuming your people will behave appropriately.>>

<<Of course,>> Lloyd replied. <<All we've been asking for is a chance to talk and work some things out.>>

Birch didn't reply, but a few moments later Lloyd heard a commotion in the hallway and he knew the High Adept was there. Students in the hallway made room for him as he walked by.

Then High Adept Birch entered the study. "Adept Hsu," he said.

"May the Light of the Creator shine upon you," Lloyd said.

The High Adept's expression didn't flicker, and his mind was tightly shielded. "Is there a place where we can talk privately, or will we have to do it here?"

"Do I still have access to my apartment?"

"No," he said.

"Then we're staying here."

Lloyd dropped and sat cross-legged on the floor. Birch looked around for a moment, then joined him, moving with agility.

"I assume all this has come about because you and the others here decided to believe the worst about the church," Birch said.

"I can honestly say that I wouldn't be on the Island anymore if I believed the worst," Lloyd said.

"You are having a crisis of faith, which is understandable," Birch said. "I only wish I would have realized it sooner. I've always wanted to believe the best about you, and I was so happy to have you back here that I trusted you too much. I should have talked to you more myself, but I hoped that by following your own plan you'd continue healing and build your faith rather than break it down. The mistakes I made are quite clear in retrospect."

Lloyd didn't need to look around the room, or reach out with his mind, to know that everyone was listening to this conversation. He wished he had mentally prepared some appropriate remarks.

"This isn't that complicated," Lloyd said. "This isn't about my faith or my path or anything about me. There's a lot of questions we could ask, questions about Whitaker and the invasion and even Guatemala if we wanted to press the issue, but we'll settle for one.

One answer. You've got a puppet watching over the archives. Terrin can't even move himself, let alone speak. The Grand Adept was controlling him on at least one instance, and who knows who else has been in his head. All we want to find out is—why? Why put someone like Terrin down there? Any explanation we can get will help resolve our concerns."

"And that's it?"

"Not quite. There are a few other matters—making the cathedral leadership more transparent, re-establishing the trust of the students, things of that nature. But explaining what's going on with Terrin would be a good start."

"You are aware that the allegation that Acolyte Terrin is anything other than a dedicated worker and servant of the Creator is ridiculous."

Lloyd stared at Birch for a few moments. His expression was easy to read—his lips were white and thin, his jaw was clenched, and his arms were folded.

"You either know about Terrin and are lying or you didn't know about him—until now," Lloyd said. "I don't know which is worse, that the leaders of the cathedral are all in this together or that they can't even trust each other with the cathedral's secrets."

"You didn't used to speak like this," Birch said.

"That was a shame," Lloyd said. "But if you don't know anything you should probably just take our request to the Grand Adept. We'll wait for his answer."

"I can't imagine that the Grand Adept has anything to discuss with you."

"Well, all of you should think it over," Lloyd said. "We'll wait here for you." He stood quickly so he could help Birch to his feet.

The High Adept stood and brushed his robe in one quick motion. Then he walked out of the room, down the hall, and out of the dorm. He did not stop, he did not slow down, and he did not once look back.

Chapter Forty-three

Kale would have been more unhappy about the task Hsu had proposed except for the fact that it would be kind of fun. It seemed odd for the adept to be issuing any instructions, but when Hsu said what needed to happen and that Kale was the only one who could pull the task off, Kale, in all modesty, had to agree.

There was an appealing cloak-and-dagger element to the whole scheme, too. Hsu was getting more and more cautious with his sendings, not wanting the High Adepts to learn anything. So he had taken to passing notes along to Kale, and the latest one had him meeting an adept who was even younger than Hsu. This one had red hair, freckles, and a mouth that seemed permanently set in a diagonal line. Her talent glowed like a torch.

"You're Angie," he said when he walked up to her.

She nodded. "Yes. And you're ... you're really ..."

"Yes, I'm afraid I am. Come on, let's go. You can marvel at me as we walk."

He tried to keep his mind out of her thoughts as they made their way to the cathedral, but her shielding was so poor and her thoughts were so open it was tough for him to ignore them. It was the sort of questions he'd heard millions of times—"Was Rachel Kallenbach really as nice as everyone says?" "Could you tell that Drauer was evil and the Premier Adept was good right from the beginning?"—and he had no desire to answer them again (even though he could have just said "yes" to the first one, "no" to the second and been done with it). So he walked quickly, made Angie keep up, and kept her too worried about walking fast and taking care of the task at hand to say anything.

When they made it within two blocks of the cathedral campus, Kale stopped. "You need to work on a spell. It shouldn't be a shield, because you're shields aren't that good. How are you at cooling?"

"Pretty good," she said, "but the cathedral's always a little cool anyways ..."

"We'll walk quickly to warm you up. Get your spell going."

The plan Hsu had proposed showed a decent understanding of the mechanics of psycho-kinesis. Kale wouldn't have much difficulty shielding both his appearance and his thoughts, but it wouldn't be at all easy to hide the fact that PK activity was taking place. The High Adepts, and especially the Grand Adept, were too skilled at spotting PK activity for Kale to slip into the cathedral unnoticed, no matter how good his shielding was. But if he shielded himself and walked in next to someone the High Adepts knew, they would likely just attribute any PK activity to that person (as long as he disguised his signature, of course). That should be enough.

They walked at a brisk pace to the edge of the campus. They came up on the south side, as Hsu had instructed, picking their way through a group of reporters and residents who had set up a sort of camp, and they passed the dorm building where Lloyd and his people were set up.

Entering the cathedral would be harder than walking onto the campus. In one of his notes, Hsu had confessed that he hadn't really learned how to read other wizards' signatures, so he could only guess about the security plan for the building. High Adept Birch's office was on the west side of the building, so Hsu had surmised that's where Birch's attention would be focused. There was a side door on the west wall, and Hsu had told Kale that going in there would be his best chance to do what needed to be done.

The door was dark, banded wood set deep in the grey stone of the cathedral. Angie the Adept slowed down when she came close to it, stepping slowly, waiting for Kale to go ahead of her. She couldn't see him anymore, so she was just guessing that he was still there and wanted to go first.

He reached out tentatively and checked out the door. It was locked. The mechanical part wouldn't be a problem, but he had to make sure the High Adepts hadn't put any special measures on the lock.

It was clear, but he had Angie open it anyway. The tumblers inside the door clicked and clanked, and the door creaked open.

Kale felt the PK energy immediately. It was a simple screen, barely enough for Kale to get a sense of the signature. But he knew it would either be Serl, Sternhaven, or Birch—at this point, they weren't about to trust anyone else to keep an eye on their central building. Those three had very different signatures, and he could tell the screen belonged to Birch. The chumchas didn't much go for disguising their signatures—they generally felt that if you couldn't put your own stamp on a spell, you shouldn't be casting it. This particular spell had a thick, detailed feel, the type of screen that wouldn't let a mouse through without Birch knowing about it. Either the cathedral was remarkably rodent-free for an old building, or Birch was regularly disturbed by the stream of alarms going off in his head.

So now Birch knew they were there. They moved forward into the dim vestibule, waiting for his response. Nothing came.

There was a door to the left, a gothic arch with a smooth metal handle. Angie opened it, and Kale followed her through. A dark stairway went down.

Angie lit a wizard light around her, and Kale saw she was writing quickly on a notepad.

Birch sent msg, she wrote. *Said lower levels closed. I sd I wntd to stdy in annx.*

Kale nodded, but Angie was already writing more.

He's glad I'm not w/ the othrs, but scrty tight right now. Espclly on A.s they hvn't seen recently, like me. I have to leave. She was already turning to walk back up the stairs.

Kale grabbed her pad and wrote with a furious scribble. *Don't turn around. Keep sending. Get emotional.*

Angie's eyes opened wide, and she shook her head.

Kale wrote faster, trying to keep his words legible. *You missd being here. Need to stay longer. Rmbr how it's imprtnt to you.*

She nodded and turned back down the stairs. Kale nudged her gently, pushing her into a run.

The hallway they were in was plain, dark shadows all around a circle of dingy tan lit up by Angie. Their footsteps were loud, but Birch already knew they were down there. They could be as loud as they wanted.

Angie was writing again. *Not buying it. Sez we nd to leave or he'll snd alrt and come get us.*

Kale didn't bother grabbing the pad. He just ran, and Angie followed him.

The door was up ahead, but it was a long way down to the archives from there. Kale reached for the lock and started fiddling with it when they were twenty feet away, hoping to have it open and waiting for him. But it was more complicated than he thought it would be.

They weren't going to have enough time. Kale needed to buy some.

<<Birch, if you could wait on that alarm for a moment, that would be for the best,>> he sent while he fiddled with the lock.

<<Who's that?>> Birch sent, including some surprise with the thought.

<<We're going downstairs,>> he said. <<If you keep watching, you'll see something interesting.>>

<<Why should I listen to you? I don't know who you are.>>

<<You know me,>> Kale sent, and accompanied his thoughts with a picture of himself in Far Rockaway.

<<I saw you!>> Birch sent. <<You were running all over the place, but no one knew who you were! What are you doing here?>>

Kale didn't answer. They were at the bottom of the stairs. Acolyte Terrin's desk was covered with papers, like someone had just been working there, but there was no light. Terrin wasn't there.

Kale looked around. He'd seen into Terrin's mind—this was not the kind of person who just wandered off. So where was he?

He directed Angie to one side of the front room while he looked at the other. The large, square entry to the archives was in front of him, holding a darkness he could practically feel. There

were shelves on the wall next to him, books and papers thrown
haphazardly all over.

Then he got back in touch with Birch.

<<Yes, I was in Far Rockaway,>> he sent.

<< We appreciate your help there, but that does not mean we
are inviting anyone to the archives now. I have to ask you to
leave.>>

<<Of course,>> Kale sent while he looked frantically for any
sign of Terrin. <<We'll be leaving shortly.>>

<<We need you out sooner than that.>> There was a slight
pause, then Birch's sending came with new urgency and anger.
<<You're in the archive! You broke into the archive! That is
impermissible!>>

<<No!>> Kale looked at Angie. She was gesturing frantically,
waving her left arm. Kale ran toward her. <<You need to see
something!>>

It was too late. The alarm ran through Kale's mind, a keening
shiver that would wake the others from the deepest sleep. In
normal times, a half-dozen adepts would be on top of Kale in
moments.

But at the moment the only adept nearby was Angie, and she
was pointing into a small closet. Inside was an off-white globe on
top of a tower of dark fabric. It was Acolyte Terrin, stiff and
motionless, standing in the closet where he apparently had been put
away for the night.

His eyes were open, but he was motionless. Kale thought about
waving a hand in front of his eyes, but he had already seen into his
mind, and he knew how little was there.

He didn't like what he'd have to do next, but he hadn't found
any way around it. He reached into the closet, grabbed Terrin, and
hoisted him on his shoulder. Then he ran like hell up the stairs.

He didn't have to worry about staying concealed now, so he
spent some energy making Terrin a little lighter on his shoulder. It
helped that the acolyte didn't weigh much in the first place—his
bones might have been as empty as his mind.

He met an adept at the top of the stairs, running toward him, casting a simple trip spell toward Kale's feet. Kale shattered it easily.

<<Stay behind me,>> he sent to Angie. <<Stay *right* behind me.>>

He pushed the adept out of the way, then layered a thick plank of heavy air on top of him. That would keep him occupied for a few moments.

He dashed down the hall, skidding at the stairs leading to the first floor. He went up, taking stairs three at a time, and there was a wall in front of him, thick and interlaced, the work of at least two adepts. He threw a counter to break it apart, and his effort shattered on the wall.

He didn't have time to find another way out, so he sent a scream, a high-pitched signal that ears couldn't hear but that would bounce around the skull of any PK in range.

Behind him, Angie fell immediately to the floor. The scream was working. It wouldn't buy him much time, but he only needed a second. He blasted the wall again, and this time it gave way. He ran ahead, dragging Angie after him. He cut off the scream so she could move better.

She staggered up the stairs behind him while he worked on a new spell. It was a simple one, a sort of PK helmet for himself, Angie, and Terrin. It worked like a mask, so that on a quick scan the adepts wouldn't be able to tell which one of them was which.

He was near the top of the stairs when the next attack came. It was aggressive, a hard rake across Kale's mind. All three helmets he had constructed shattered immediately, and PK fingers dug through their heads. It was disruptive, jumbling up Kale's thoughts, briefly making him feel like he'd just woken up from a disorienting dream. He lashed out at the adepts' spell and it disintegrated.

He had fallen to the steps without realizing it, and the feather-weight of Terrin was still on his shoulder. He could almost feel a sense of surprise hanging in the air, and he knew he had done what he was needed to.

"Come on," he said to Angie. "They'll pull themselves back together pretty quickly. Let's move."

They came to the top of the stairs and entered the vestibule at the top. There was a small bench in the room, and Kale laid Terrin on it. He briefly hoped he would be comfortable, but then remembered that Terrin wouldn't notice. Still, he patted Terrin's hand briefly before he walked away. He hoped the person Terrin had once been would appreciate what Kale was doing for him.

He led Angie out of the cathedral and toward Lloyd's dorm building. She kept pace, but every few steps she turned and looked back at the cathedral.

"It's still there," Kale said after the fifth time Angie turned around. "It's not going anywhere."

"No. No, it's not that. It's—how did we get out of there? So easy?"

"Easy? There was the wall, there was that rake spell ..."

"They're High Adepts," Angie said. "I know who you are, but still. Three of them, one of you—I thought it would be harder."

Kale thought about letting her believe that he was, in fact, more than a match for three High Adepts, but she would likely find out what had happened soon enough.

"Two of them," he said. "In the end, we were only against two of them, and they were too confused to mount a good defense. Birch was supposed to take the lead in the defense of that part of the cathedral. But Birch stopped defending."

"What do you mean?"

"I mean he stopped defending!" Kale snapped. He took a breath and made his tone level again. "It was the rake. I knew something like that would be coming after I did the scream—if you get in someone's head, they usually want to get in yours. Human nature. Once I talked to Birch, I knew he'd want to target me, so I put the helmets on us. Birch and the others did the reasonable thing and went after all three of us, blowing up the helmets, stirring up our thoughts. And when you do that, you usually notice what it is you're stirring."

"So?" Angie said.

What are they teaching these kids? Kale thought. "So Birch noticed Terrin's thoughts—or the complete lack thereof," he said aloud. "He saw that Terrin was nothing. That the story Lloyd had been putting out there was true."

Angie stopped. They weren't back to the dorm building yet, and Kale still couldn't be convinced the other two High Adepts wouldn't come after him. He grabbed her arm to pull her ahead, but her feet were glued in place.

"He is a High Adept," Angie said. "Didn't he already know?"

"No," Kale said. "Birch hadn't been brought in. This Terrin thing—it's not his style. Birch is a straight arrow."

Angie tilted her head. "When you say that—are you making fun of him or complimenting him?"

"Hell if I know," Kale said. "Come on, I imagine Lloyd is anxious to hear how we did."

Interlude: Ellis on Drauer

Anderson Drauer is capable of great things. Is *still* capable of great things. He will remain capable of great things until the day he dies.

I do not say that to in any way acquit Andy of anything he has done. He will have to answer for his treatment of the church. He will have to answer to the Creator, and he will have to answer to himself. I say that because I have enough faith in Andy's intellect that I believe he will eventually understand the full extent of what he chose, and how it affected millions of people, and he will be decent enough to regret it.

It concerns me that many church members will react with surprise when I use a word like "decent" to describe Andy. He has been demonized by our clergy to an extent he does not deserve, at least not in my opinion. I have heard him described as "the greatest force of evil on earth today," "a power-hungry devil who will not rest until the church is dead," and "the enemy of the truth."

I find these all interesting, especially the last, because it attempts to force Andy to live in our terms. Many of us want to believe that his objection to us is theological in nature, that he fights us because something in him wants to fight good. Which is nonsense, of course. People commit evil acts all the time, but there are few people indeed who are actively dedicated to the cause of evil. Most evil that happens occurs incidentally—accidentally even, committed by those who want to do good but were severely misguided as to how to accomplish it. Or who mistook things that were good for them as individuals as being "good" in the absolute sense.

Andy never fought the church because he is some demon figure, or because he wants to tear down the truth that we teach. Andy outlawed us because we did not fit in with his vision for his nation. Nothing more. Andy always had a deep interest in control, and he knew the church would not be easy to manipulate if he was not a part of it, directing it. And so we had to go.

I have not been able to hate him for it. I have been angry with him, true, and I have spoken harshly about his actions. He has, in fact, acted unwisely, unkindly, and harmfully. He has criticized the church for its dogmatic character, but his nation has been at least as strident as any church member in fighting to establish the truth as they see it. But even with this streak of hypocrisy, I have not been able to hate Andy.

I imagine many people have difficulty imagining the world into which we first emerged. We had been isolated, separated from the rest of the population, treated like laboratory animals. We were living experiments, not humans, until Andy led us out of the facility and introduced us to the world. We were all a little worried about what would happen when we got out. What would the world think of us? Would they be scared? Would their first reaction be to throw us right back where we had come from? We were all worried—except for Andy.

Andy said they would love us, for no other reason than that we would show them that we deserved their love, their admiration, and their loyalty. And from day one, that's what he sought, and that's what he got. We went from lab rats to leaders, and it was because of Andy.

He took it too far, of course. Power corrupts, and few people in history have possessed as much power as Andy. No one should have the ability to do whatever it is that comes into their head, as it prevents them from subjecting their thoughts and ideas to rigorous analysis about what should be done. There is no "should" to Andy any more, and there hasn't been for a long time. There is just "is."

The Creator has shown me, and I have recorded it, that Andy will rediscover humility at some point in the future. I hope the Andy that led us out of the Area, who told us we could be anything, re-emerges, to replace the Andy that persists in the mistake that all people must be like him.

Chapter Forty-four

The next time High Adept Birch came to the dormitory, his gait was much slower. He seemed to be pulling a great weight behind him, each leg dragging as he leaned forward.

It took a long time for Birch to make his way to the study. The adepts in the hall didn't fall into the reverent hush like they did during his previous visit, but they still watched him and waited to see what would happen.

Birch arrived at the door of the study and stopped. Lloyd didn't blame him—the sit-in was in its eighth day, and the room had had a certain musky aroma coated by an overlay of pizza.

"Can we talk somewhere?" Birch asked.

<<If you want privacy, we can send,>> Lloyd said.

"I'd rather find somewhere we can talk," Birch said.

Lloyd thought about talking here, letting all the adepts around hear whatever Birch had to say, but then he saw the dark circles under Birch's eyes and the emptiness in his face, it reminded him what he'd seen in the mirror the year after Whitaker's death.

"We'll go upstairs," Lloyd said. "Come on."

They found a small, tidy room. Lloyd sat on one of the hard plastic office chairs in the room, and Birch took the other. Birch's back had the same firm posture he'd always had, but his neck was bent so Birch could stare at the floor.

"I still find many of your claims to be incredible," Birch said. "I didn't read anything this Slane Olsen person had to say about Antigua, but some of the details reached me anyway. It seems nonsensical to me. It makes a mockery out of one of the greatest miracles of our time. It borders on blasphemy."

"I thought Whitaker's death was an even worse mockery," Lloyd said.

Birch looked up, and there was anger firing his eyes. "It was a tragedy that had nothing to do with God."

"That was the problem. It was supposed to."

Birch's head dropped again. He didn't talk for a minute or two, and Lloyd was content to stay silent.

"I went down to the archives three days ago," Birch finally said. "One of my regular visits. I've been researching the prophecies quite a lot in the past year. I've seen Acolyte Terrin more frequently, become more familiar with his quirks and oddities. I'd even started to look forward to talking to him, because his mannerisms, his bluntness, his lack of propriety was so—*him*.

"When I was there three days ago, I was returning Ned Carline's analysis of the Five Pillars prophecy and checking out a series of essays on the Six Days of Night prophecy. I smiled when I asked for that book and said the prophecies were easiest to tackle in numeric order.

"Acolyte Terrin didn't react. I'll admit that my remark wasn't all that amusing, but he did not even make a grimace to show he didn't like the joke. His face remained impassive as ever. It was Terrin being Terrin, I told myself.

"But then, two days ago, I felt his mind. I expected to feel his thoughts swirling around, but I felt nothing. It was like reading a head of cabbage. Now I know that Terrin is never just being Terrin—there's nothing to him. Every conversation I had with him was part of an elaborate lie whose purposes I can't guess.

"I don't think everything you've said about the church is true. I don't think we are killers. But I need answers, and although you may be misguided in some things, you haven't been lying to me. So at this point, I'm here with you."

Lloyd nodded. "I'm glad you're here," he said, fully aware of how inadequate the words sounded.

Birch did not look up and did not smile.

With the arrival of the High Adept, the building took on a new energy. A few students put on impromptu light shows above the dorm every night, and the party atmosphere of the first day returned, but now redoubled. The media presence outside the cathedral campus grew, and even though Birch refused to talk to any of the press and Lloyd didn't talk about him, the story got out, and soon all the nets were carrying the story about a high-level defection in Hampton cathedral.

That led to a new element—Islanders, members of the congregation, gathering with the media. Birch's defection told them there was weakness in the cathedral's power structure, so they took advantage. They sided with Lloyd and the students and took their anger out on the High Adepts. While she did not appear near the grounds, Courtney Whitaker's mother issued a statement supporting the dissenting students.

One day there was a handful of them milling around the reporters, the next there was a full-scale march, with signs and chants, walking around the campus. The next night there was another, larger march. When they walked by the north end of the campus, the part closest to the actual cathedral, some of them threw things, rocks or whatever else was handy. These items couldn't have hurt the church even if the Islanders' arms were strong enough to reach the building, but the regular shower of small missiles kept clattering on campus sidewalks.

"They want to storm the cathedral," Carmen told Lloyd one afternoon, a little under a week after Birch arrived at the dorm. "With Birch and Faltergast on our side, no one thinks the High Adepts can stop us."

"So we storm the cathedral, overwhelm the High Adepts, and then what? Throw them in a dungeon somewhere?"

"No. Of course not. We—I don't know, we convince them to step down."

"That's why we're here," Lloyd said. "Same purpose. Only no one has to storm anything."

"But we have to wait, and people don't really want to do that any more."

Birch's thoughts then filled Lloyd's head. <<The Grand Adept would like to talk to you,>> he sent.

Lloyd smiled at Carmen. "The wait may be over."

An hour and a half after Grand Adept Serl made contact with Birch, Lloyd and Kale walked through the front doors of the cathedral. Grand Adept Serl and High Adept Sternhaven were sitting on one of the pews in the back. Neither of them turned when the doors opened.

The cathedral was dark, no wizard light at all, only some traces of sunlight coming in through the stained glass windows about the south door. Lloyd's footsteps sounded unnaturally loud.

He and Kale sat on the pew in front of Serl and Sternhaven and turned backward, draping their arms awkwardly over the back. Lloyd opened his mouth to speak, but his training made it hard for him to speak before the Grand Adept.

"Mr. Faltergast," the Grand Adept said with forced courtesy. "You haven't set foot in our cathedral for quite some time."

"I thought we had decided that would be for the best," Kale said.

"Only because you refused to …" Serl stopped himself. "My apologies. There is no point in rehashing a very old argument. We have other issues at hand."

"Of course."

There was silence again. Serl's cheeks puffed in and out a few times before he spoke. He looked like he hadn't been keeping up with his anti-aging maintenance—his hair had grown noticeably thinner, and his round face now had jowls.

"I want you to understand," the Grand Adept finally said. "I want you to understand what we were doing here."

"I'm going to assume a lot of it has to do with following orders," Lloyd said.

Serl's eyes narrowed. "It's always easier for people with little rank to take something like obedience lightly. But you do not become Grand Adept without understanding that the church works because people are willing to listen the people who are above them."

"I thought it worked because everyone in the church tried to do good things."

"And what do you think obedience is?" Sternhaven snapped. "It's the effort to do good by those of us who are humble enough to admit we don't know everything."

"Perhaps this meeting would go faster if the boy here was quiet for a bit and you gave whatever explanation is was you wanted to give," Kale said.

Serl did not directly reply. Lloyd wondered if the Grand Adept was trying to decide just how much respect he needed to show to the First Adept's friend.

When he spoke again, he looked at Lloyd the whole time, not once at Kale. "Terrin was not my idea," he said. "A long time ago, we had a series of acolytes and adepts who worked in the archives. It was on the regular job rotation, and that system worked fine. Then, however, Acolyte Terrin was transferred to the cathedral, along with orders that he was to be permanently assigned to the archives."

"Did he have a mind when he arrived?" Lloyd asked.

"No. He was like he was now." He paused. "When Terrin arrived, he came with quite detailed instructions on how to ... operate him."

"Where did he come from?"

Serl hesitated before answering. He glanced at Sternhaven, but her expression was rigid.

"He was transferred from Bermuda."

Lloyd leaned back and almost fell to the floor before he remembered how he was sitting. He had too many questions to know which to ask first.

Kale didn't have that problem. "The folks in Bermuda have been working on mind control, have they?"

"It's Terrin," Serl said quickly. "He doesn't have a mind. Controlling his mind is nothing like trying to control a fully functional, sentient mind."

"That's not entirely true. It teaches you the basics of how to make a mind do what you want, which is what mind control is about."

"Still, the complications involved in trying to make an average person ..."

"What did you do to Whitaker?" Lloyd said, in a voice that echoed across the large, empty room.

"Beg pardon?" Serl asked.

"Mind control on Whitaker. Some of the tricks you learned by practicing on Terrin. What did you do to Whitaker?"

Sternhaven opened her mouth, but then her head jerked back and she didn't say anything. The heat of Serl's sending to her almost left a smoke trail in the air.

"Whitaker was the chosen one. He would have developed as he needed to. But time was short, and his development needed to move a little faster. The changes were not drastic, and it was very different than what I do to Terrin. Without my presence, Terrin is nothing. Whitaker did not need the same constant guidance. It was a matter of shifting some parts of his brain, raising the levels of certain chemicals, and then he was the leader he was destined to be."

"But in the cell on the wall ..."

Serl looked left and right quickly. "The effects I instilled were not permanent."

"You manipulated him," Lloyd said.

"That's what I was told was needed."

"By whom?"

"Bermuda."

"And the guidance I received to find Whitaker?"

Serl nodded once, stiffly.

Lloyd looked at Kale, hoping he would have a decent idea of how to react to these revelations. By his expression, Lloyd guessed he did.

"These instructions from Bermuda," Kale said. "Sendings?"

"Yes," Serl said.

"From Bermuda?" Lloyd said. "That's more than 700 miles!"

"Yes, but it's over water," Kale said.

"Still—who can send anything 700 miles?"

"The Premier Adept."

Jason M. Hardy

"And it's pretty much only from there to here. They figured out the right path a while ago." Kale shrugged. "It's one of the reasons the headquarters moved out there when things in the USNA went bad."

A thought struck Lloyd. "Poulsen Tower," he said. "Did that come from Bermuda? Did they bring the tower down?"

"That was a genuine miracle!" High Adept Sternhaven snapped, then fell silent after Grand Adept Serl raised his hand.

"The information about where we should be and when came from the Premier Adept," Serl said. "But I can assure you that neither anyone in Bermuda nor here had anything to do with the tower's collapse. It was the will of God."

He took a ragged breath, like he had pain in his ribs. "I've now told you everything I can tell you," Serl said. "Can you end your sit-in now?"

"Yes," Lloyd said, and what he should do started to become clear as he spoke. "At least, the part here is done. I think we'll be leaving."

"Leaving? Who?"

"All of us at the dorm."

"You're leaving the church?"

"No, we're leaving the cathedral. We could discuss whether you're willing to leave your position of leadership, but I'm not convinced you are, especially with the support of the Premier Adept. So you may stay here, and we will leave."

"If you're not at the cathedral, you're not part of the church," Serl said.

"What do you think makes someone less a part of the church?" Lloyd asked. "Changing their physical location, or constantly going against the things we're supposed to hold sacred?"

"I was—"

"Under orders, yes. How well has that excuse gone over in the past? We'll be on our own for a time, which means you can have the run of the cathedral to yourself. And High Adept Sternhaven, I assume."

Lloyd stood. Serl and Sternhaven remained seated, watching him carefully. Lloyd tried to keep his body relaxed, but his mind was busy weaving every shield he could think of. He felt a tingle to his left that told him Kale was doing the same thing.

Lloyd and Kale walked out of the cathedral without another word.

Kale started talking as soon as they were out of the doors.

"I have to say I'm a little confused," he said. "I didn't think—"

Lloyd raised a finger to his lips, and then pointed back to the cathedral.

"Oh, please," Kale said. "Do you think I can't hide whatever it is we want to say? What do you take me for?"

"Sorry."

"What I was going to say was, I didn't think the point of your protest was to get you to leave the church. If you wanted to do that, why not just leave at the beginning? Hell, why not leave a year ago?"

"We're not leaving the church."

"But you're leaving."

"And taking the church with us. Serl's not the church. And if he's been taking directions from Dugwu, Dugwu's not the church. We're just going to have to move the church away from the cathedral for a time until the situation at the top works itself out."

"'Works itself out'? And how do you think that's going to happen?"

"You'll have to give me a little time to answer that," Lloyd said.

The move away from the cathedral came with a few hitches. While some students were willing to protest, they didn't want to walk away from the campus, even after Lloyd explained how they were taking the church with them. Still, a good-sized group followed him out, which only led to more questions—where would they stay? How would they eat?

Between Kale and the parishioners on the Island, though, things came together quickly. The townspeople, happy to have clergy they believed in, let Lloyd and his students use two abandoned warehouses on the north side of the Island. They put benches in one and called it a chapel, and the other became the new dormitory. Kale helped connect the warehouses to the net and the electric grid, and the locals were quite generous with their food.

Much to his embarrassment, people in the makeshift warehouses started calling Lloyd "High Adept Hsu," which he corrected any time he heard it. Still, no matter what they called him, few decisions were made without being run by him first. He could dedicate as much time as he wanted to administering church affairs and still leave many tasks undone. And none of that work included figuring out what to do about the leadership left behind at Hampton.

He'd had one idea, but he didn't like it. He kept hoping that he'd come up with something else to do, anything else, if he thought about it more. But he had come back here to find out what happened to Courtney, and he felt he only had part of the story. As it happened, the next step in that process might also help do something about the cathedral's old leadership, one way or another. It didn't make him like the idea any more, but he wasn't sure he had other choices. And he had gotten decently far to this point by acting instead of dithering.

He arranged for business of the warehouse church to carry on without him for a time, then he told Kale what he was going to do.

"Are you sure?" Kale said as they stood on the roof of the warehouse dorm.

"Yes. And it needs to be more. The longer I wait, the more tied up I'll get. I can't delay it any more." He looked at Kale and tried to look casual. "So do you think you could come along?"

Kale took long enough to respond that Lloyd started sweating. Finally he spoke. "All right. I'll see this thing through to the end. Besides, I haven't talked to Eliazer Dugwu in a long time. It would be good to get caught up with him."

"That's what I was hoping."

Chapter Forty-five

Before he left, Lloyd finally made the trip to the border wastes he'd been putting off for so long. He wasn't sure he would be able to find the rock he had been to before, but the location, as it turned out, was imprinted strongly in his mind. He was able to walk almost straight to it.

It was a grey day, like most days in the wastes. The USNA had developed a simple solution to the problem of air pollution over New York—push it all east. It made the sunsets on the Island red and the days dim.

He found the rock, but he couldn't find the entrance. He was on his hands and knees, digging through the dry dust, when he heard a voice to his right.

"No robes," the voice said.

Lloyd jumped to his feet, brushing off his knees. "Not today, no," Lloyd said.

Aron looked him up and down. "I've seen you without your robes plenty of times," he said. "But it still doesn't look right."

"I'm on leave," Lloyd said. "At least, that's what the official records say."

"Why do they say that?"

"Because Serl thinks that's the best way to keep a lid on what's going on here and not have the media go crazy on him. Besides, he doesn't really need us—with no active parishioners, there's not much of a reason to have any active clergy on hand."

"So he's shacked up with Sternhaven and Birch at the cathedral?"

"Birch is on leave. With us."

Aron smiled, and even though his face was weathered and covered in uneven stubble, the expression was familiar and welcome. "You turned Birch?"

"No. Kale just showed him a little bit of what was going on, and that was enough."

"Quite a group of leaders you've got out there," Aron said. "Liars and cowards. That's one hell of a clergy."

"It gets worse. It looks like problems go all the way to the top."

"Dugwu?"

"Right."

Aron shook his head. "Man, what are you still *doing* hanging out with those people? Why do you still bother?"

"Because I can't let them have it." Lloyd was surprised at the sudden swelling in his throat. "They can't keep doing this to the church. This isn't what it's supposed to be."

"You're still caught up in what you thought the church was when you were a teenager," Aron said, with less scorn than Lloyd expected. "You still want to be a white knight, saving the world."

"Yes," Lloyd said. "I do."

"Well, nothing wrong with your ego," Aron said. "Good luck with that."

"Come with me."

Aron laughed, but it was brief. "I just told you I thought you should get out. And now you're asking me to get back in?"

"I'm going to Bermuda, where it's warm and sunny. I thought that alone might interest you. But I'm taking Kale Faltergast with me, and we're going to meet with Eliazer Dugwu, and we're going to see what we can get settled. I know you don't want to come back to the clergy, and I'm not asking you to. At this point, *I'm* barely part of the clergy. All I'm saying is that we're going to Bermuda, and it's going to be interesting, and I thought it's the kind of thing you might want to see."

Aron slowly rubbed his uneven beard. "It might be a good show," he admitted. "But you're not just going to let me tag along. I'm sure there will be something or other you'll want me to do."

"Probably," Lloyd said. "You go to the show, you have to pay admission. But do you want to sit here in the wastes waiting to hear about it, or do you want to be there when it happens?"

Aron was silent for a while. He scratched his head, and dust drifted out of his hair.

"We roomed together too long," he said. "You know too much about which buttons to push."

Lloyd smiled. Then he almost laughed.

Kale walked up and down the dock, scowling. His right hand occasionally shot up in the air, emphasizing some silent point, and his mouth kept moving as he muttered words under his breath. He was alone, which meant there was no convenient target for his wrath.

But then someone approached the dock, and it was the exact right person. The very individual he most wanted to yell at. He pointed at a boat floating nearby.

"Do you know how much this thing costs?"

"Stupid-ass question," Spree said. "Bought by me, no? I saw it, I bargained for it, I paid. Course I know what it cost."

"You wiped out almost a whole year's worth of income!"

Spree was still a good twenty feet away, and she did not seem to be inclined to move any closer. She folded her arms and sat on one of the wooden support posts holding the pier up.

"Income. Like you work. Don't no do nothing for that money. Interest. You get money sitting on you ass. You miss the money this year, you wait till next year, you get it again. You ain't never spent more than you got coming in whole time I know you."

"Of course I haven't! That's how you save money, by not spending more than you take in! And now I can't do that."

"One year out of one hundred or whatever ain't no going to mess you up. You survive. Ain't no way to spend all that money out here anyway. You ain't no going broke."

Kale turned to look at the boat. "And I don't see how that thing is going to hold all of us."

"You ain't no moving in!" Spree said. "Bigger than a van, and all you could fit in a van. One or two you could even sleep. Ain't no reason to complain."

Kale disagreed. There were barnacles on the hull, grease and oil all over the stern, and the whole thing smelled like low tide. Or maybe that was just the ocean.

Kale shook his head and climbed onto the boat. It was white—beneath the grime—maybe about twenty-five feet long, and could probably seat all of them above decks, with more space below. He knew Spree was right. They were lucky to have this—there were no more boat dealers left on the Island, just people here and there selling used craft or whatever salvage they could put together. The fact that this had turned up was just short of a miracle.

But that didn't make him happier in the here and now. Kale became even angrier with the boat as he tried to put the canvas roof over the top deck. He fumbled with one side as the other side came unattached, moving back and forth and making no progress while Spree laughed.

"Just magic the damn thing," she said, wiggling her fingers in the air. "Abracadabra, poof, roof's up."

"You've lived with me this long and you still don't know how it works?" Kale said. "It's all about motion, and the talent's never been entirely useful for making small movements with big things. It would be like trying to thread a needle using only the breeze. Only slightly easier."

Spree sat back and laughed.

"You could help, you know," Kale said.

"Could maybe," Spree said. "I'm building up energy."

Kale didn't bother to glare at her, focusing on the canvas until it was about two-thirds done. Then he stopped, because he sensed the rest of the group coming.

They walked down the pier, two men and a woman, all of them young, like they were going out on a weekend jaunt. That impression disappeared as they came closer. Amelia had worked so long to keep her expression unreadable that now she did it by reflex, Hsu looked serious as always, and the friend he'd managed to drag along with him looked like a prophet who had been stranded in the wilderness.

"Hsu, could you get the other side of this secured?" Kale barked when they came closer.

"Sure," Hsu said. With another set of hands, the job went quickly.

When it was over, Kale turned to the boat's controls. He'd paid a bundle for it, and he wasn't too eager to let anyone else have the helm, which meant he needed to learn how to operate the thing. As he scanned the controls, he felt some eyes on his back. He turned and saw Hsu's disheveled friend staring at him.

"What?" Kale said.

"So," the friend said. "Kale Faltergast, huh?"

"Yeah," Kale said, then turned back to the controls.

"I thought you'd ..." the friend started.

"... be something else?" Kale said. "I thought about becoming something else, but I haven't yet. Maybe someday I will be."

He felt the friend look at him a bit longer, then disappear. The next time Kale turned around, Spree and Hsu were sitting on the above-deck benches, while the other two were somewhere out of sight.

"Where are the others?" he said.

"Below," Hsu said. "Do you have it figured out yet?"

"Yes," Kale said. "I'm just going to set up a wind behind us and blow us in."

"Then you should have bought a sailboat."

Kale frowned at Hsu, mainly to keep from smiling. Hsu's sense of humor was a well-concealed attribute, but he seemed to be giving it more free rein recently. Kale gave the instrument panel one quick look, then turned back to Hsu and snapped his finger. The engines started right up.

"The snap was a little unnecessary," Hsu said.

"I guess they don't teach showmanship in church," Kale said. Then, without waiting for a reply, he asked "Is everything packed and ready?"

"Only hold-up is you," Spree said.

"Then do whatever needs to happen so this moves."

416 Jason M. Hardy

Spree stood and untied the boat from the pier. "You ain't no been floating much ever, no?"

"There's always been too much land around me to worry about it." He pulled the handle he assumed was the throttle, and the boat moved forward.

"You got some spell or something 'case boat wants to go over? Keep it from tipping too far?"

"We don't need a spell," Kale said. "We've got me at the wheel."

"Helm," Spree said.

"Whatever."

"I'm going down below," Spree said, "see if anyone there knows how to keep our asses afloat.

After ten hours at the helm, Kale decided it was time to see the rest of his boat for the first time. The cabin was cramped, but Kale had to admit it had a certain charm. When he descended through the hatch he found himself in a small kitchenette, and the main cabin was in the fore section of the boat. A long, cushioned bench ran along the entire bow wall, with a small table sitting in the middle. Amelia was curled at the very front of the boat, Hsu a few feet away from her, leaning forward with his elbows on his knees, and Hsu's friend sat across from him with his feet propped on the table. Kale thought about telling him to get his feet off the furniture, but they still had a day and a half left to go—if Hsu's friend had found a way to be comfortable for part of the trip, more power to him.

Kale walked over and sat on the steps leading down to the fore cabin. "I didn't get your name before."

"Aron Nesbitt," the friend said. "You told me to be nice to Amelia a while back."

Kale squinted. "That was you?"

"Yeah."

"Oh," Kale said. "So. Why are you here?"

"'Cause I was invited."

"Just because you're invited somewhere doesn't mean you have to go."

"True."

"So why are you here?" Kale said again.

"Because I want to see the show."

Part of Kale wanted to smile at that remark, part of him wanted to scowl. "You think this is a show?"

"I think it's going to be."

"What do you think you'll see?"

Nesbitt smiled, tight-lipped and hollow-cheeked. "Why are you asking me?" he said. "This is your show, yours and Lloyd's. You guys should be the ones who have an idea about what's going to happen, not me."

"I'm at a point in my life where I don't do things unless I'm unsure of the outcome. I've had enough of predictability."

"Is that why you came with us to Far Rockaway?" Hsu said. "You wanted to see what was going to happen?"

"That was part of it," Kale said.

"What was the rest of it?"

Kale tilted his head and scratched just above his right ear. "I'm not sure," he said. "Maybe it's that Andy has been too successful for a long time. He needs to get taken down a peg."

"Didn't quite happen, did it?" Nesbitt said.

"Not quite," Kale said. "But you people gave it a good shot."

Hsu nodded, but his face was creased in a deep frown. Kale thought about reading him, just to get a hint of what he was thinking about, but that wasn't the way you were supposed to treat friends.

"It wasn't a good shot," Hsu said. "We weren't ready for it, and we went in under the supposed leadership of a guy who wasn't ready to lead. Courtney died. High Adept Kroll died. This was Dugwu's operation, if we can trust Serl, which means Dugwu's got some explaining to do. I think Aron's about as interested as I am in hearing that explanation."

"He's not going to explain anything," Kale said. "He's not going to meet with you. With any of us."

"Not even you?"

"I know Dugwu. I first met him a long time ago. It's safe to say that he holds me in lower esteem than he does his clergy."

"Why's that?" Aron asked.

"It's a succession problem," Kale said. "When you have a charismatic founder like Harry, it's tough to find someone who has all the elements that made that person so special as a leader. You need someone who's powerful, who's a good manager, who can inspire his people, and who truly cares for those people. There aren't many people good at all four of those things."

"And Dugwu?"

"He got three out of four. All the stuff you want in someone at the top—good managerial style, power to spare, and even a good public speaker. But you never got the sense that he cared for the members of his church like Harry did."

"When you say 'you,' I assume you're actually talking about yourself," Nesbitt said.

"Assume away," Kale said. "Look, here's the thing. Harry made the church and moved to the head of it because he thought it was the best way to help people. Dugwu came through the ranks later, and he rose partly because he wanted to. Harry was the First Adept because he wanted to do good; Dugwu became Premier Adept because he wanted to be Premier Adept. I never liked that in him, and I'm usually not good at hiding it when I don't like people."

"You don't say," Nesbitt said.

"Harry always hoped I'd join his church, but then when Dugwu took over I made it pretty clear I never would. That didn't make him too happy, and he still holds it against me."

"So we're not headed to a reunion of old friends," Amelia said.

"Right. I'm going to rest for a while. When I wake up— assuming I make it to sleep—we'll have to figure out what we're going to do when we hit land."

"Does that mean we can't stay up and talk?" Aron asked.

Kale rolled his eyes. "Two out of three of you are PKs. Haven't you figured out any ways to communicate quietly?" Then he lay down and tried to find a way to make the overly firm cushion comfortable.

They had been at sea for more than thirty hours and were less than one hundred miles from their destination, when they were noticed. Nesbitt had been pestering Kale to have a turn at the helm, and since the skies were clear and the sea was level, Kale let him steer—though he stayed right behind him the whole time. He had to protect his investment.

He heard it first, a high whistling sound followed by a sharp slap. About fifty feet off the starboard side of the boat, a column of water splashed five feet into the air, then fell.

Kale leaned forward and did a quick scan. There wasn't any trace of a large animal there, and the splash didn't look like whale spray.

Before he could think more about what it might be, there was another whistle, another splash. It was closer, only twenty or thirty feet away.

Kale looked up, and his eyes widened.

<<Hsu, get up here!>> he sent, so forcefully that Nesbitt felt it too and jumped. Kale put a shield over the boat, just before the first rock hit. It was traveling at a great speed, and it bounced off the shield and flew far from the boat. Three more skittered off in rapid succession.

Hsu scrambled up through the hatch. He didn't have time to ask what was happening before five more rocks hit Kale's shield.

Kale felt Hsu's shield join his, but it didn't last long. There was a blast, a wave of power from the east, and it scattered both shields like dust hit by a tornado.

More rocks hit right after the shields fell apart, driving into the aft section of the boat, punching holes and splintering wood.

<<Fix the holes!>> Kale sent, then set up another shield. It wasn't strong, though. He didn't have time to put the molecules in the right places, to gather everything in the right way. A few more rocks made it through, and this shield fell apart even easier when another blast came from the east.

<<Get below!>> he sent. It would take several hits to do real damage to the boat, but one rock making contact with a human would be very, very messy.

Nesbitt, Hsu, then Kale dropped down the hatch, Kale pulling the cover shut after him.

<<Support the ceiling,>> he sent. "Ceiling" was probably the wrong nautical term, but luckily Spree wasn't the target of the sending and couldn't correct him.

A few more rocks came through, but then they stopped. Making a shield using actual solid material was a hell of a lot easier than throwing one together out of thin air. Rocks were still landing, and the upper deck wouldn't look good once this was all over, but at least they weren't getting through. The hull should be sound—unless some of the earlier rocks had punctured all the way through.

<<Either of you any good at physical scans?>> Kale sent.

<<Aron's better at it than me,>> Hsu replied.

<<Check the hull, especially the rear,>> Kale sent. <<Make sure we're not taking in any water.>>

The patter of the rocks was slowing, like the final pops in a batch of popcorn.

"They must be running out of ammo," Kale said. Amelia and Spree both nodded. Both of them looked calmer than Kale felt.

"There's a few leaks in the back, one of them is a decent hole," Nesbitt said. "I'm shifting some things around to plug it."

"Okay. I'll get the pump on."

"Pump?" Amelia said. "How pedestrian."

"It can't all be magic," Kale said. Then he climbed back up to make sure the boat hadn't drifted too far off course during the shower of rocks.

Kale took the boat to within ten miles of the island, then dropped anchor. The highest points of Bermuda were visible over the rolling waves, along with a few distant lights. The sun had set half an hour ago.

The boat couldn't go any further. Kale knew more about concealment techniques that almost anyone on earth, but concealing an entire boat, along with five passengers—and not just their appearance and noise but anything else a PK could sense—was beyond him. He'd been thinking about this for most of his waking hours on this trip, and he finally had the beginning of a plan.

"We're going to sneak by them in a way that ensures they see us," he said.

"Oh, good," Nesbitt said. "We should make sure they know just where to aim their rocks."

"That was just a warning," Kale said with a wave of his hand. "The thing is, we're not going to sneak onto the island without them noticing. That's one of the reason Dugwu moved the headquarters out here—he knew it could be a controlled environment. If we fool ourselves into thinking we really can get in unseen, then we've pretty much already lost. We need to mess with their expectations, and the first way of doing that is to let them think that we don't know they're watching us."

"Is this a plan or just a way of screwing with their minds?" Amelia said.

"Who said it has to be one or the other?"

"So how are we going to get to land?" Hsu asked.

"Good question," Kale said. "I think the first thing you all should know is that the water temperature here is a very comfortable 77 degrees."

Chapter Forty-six

Moving currents of water is a lot trickier than moving air. Water is heavier and more assertive about continuing in the direction it wants to go. When you put a current of air behind you, it often acts as its own wall, turning aside any small breezes that attempt to interfere with it. Water is more insistent—currents that have been flowing for hundreds or thousands of miles do not want to change their course simply because a wizard in the middle of the ocean wishes it.

Still, despite the fact that the flow behind Lloyd broke up a half-dozen times in his first half hour in the water, he made progress. He wrapped his arms around his life vest, kicked his legs, and rebuilt a stream behind him that would take him to shore.

Kale wasn't much better at controlling the water than Lloyd, a fact that made Lloyd oddly cheerful. Several times he saw Kale bobbing up and down in the ocean, looking behind him and cursing at the water until Spree told him to shut up and move forward.

The water was, as Kale promised, fairly comfortable. It would have been better if Lloyd had been wearing a wetsuit instead of soaking his clothes, but the boat hadn't come with any diving gear. The clothes he was wearing were wet, along with the single change he carried in a pack on his back, and the sun wouldn't be up to dry them off for a good eight hours. But his comfort and appearance were not high priorities.

Spree had been the most worried about getting in the water. She provided a long list of the gear she had brought along that would be destroyed by salt water, and she had made Kale lay an extra spell on her already waterproof pack (which might, Lloyd had to admit, be contributing to Kale's difficulty in the water). Once that had been settled, Spree slid into the water and swam ahead quickly and smoothly until Kale yelled at her to wait for the rest of them.

After the first half hour the land ahead didn't seem to be any closer, though the boat was rapidly vanishing behind them. After another hour, the boat was gone from sight, and the lights of the shore still were unaccountably distant. Waves, many of them much higher than Lloyd's head, bobbed him up and down, making him lose sight of his destination. He suddenly wished they had decided to sleep on the boat and set out in the morning.

Lloyd's legs were tired and he wasn't kicking much anymore, but his current was becoming better organized. Then a new current from the side swept in, making Lloyd want to slap the water, until he realized what it was—a shore current. He was getting close.

His feet finally hit sand after about three hours in the water. He stood up, coughed out some salt water, and breathed deeply. Then something hit him from behind and he was full of water again.

He turned as quickly as he could to see that the tackle had been delivered by Amelia. She glared at him.

"We're supposed to be pretending to sneak in," she said. "Standing up without any cover and stretching is *not* sneaking."

"Sorry," Lloyd said, and was glad it was too dark for Amelia to see his face.

The ground Lloyd had stood on was a sandbar a quarter-mile from shore. Lloyd didn't bother much with currents at that point, as the waves carried him in. Soon, he was lying on a sandy beach at the east end of Bermuda. There was no sign of anyone else on the sand.

A puff of sand flew in his face. It was Kale, scuffing his feet as he ran by.

"Come on, get up," he said. "No lying in the open." Kale walked quickly to a clump of trees behind the beach, and Lloyd followed.

"Okay," Kale said once all five of them were together. "Another reason Dugwu decided to set up shop here is that the whole place is pretty open and visible. We're not going to have too many wilderness places to hide, especially between here and Hamilton. But we don't want that, so it shouldn't be a problem."

"So what do we do now?" Aron asked. "Walk to Hamilton and wait for them to intercept us?"

"No. Spree's going to make sure her equipment is in good shape—which I'm sure it is, since I was protecting it—and you and Hsu are going to find us a cable. Preferably one that's not buried."

For about ten minutes, Lloyd flinched with every step. He thought he heard a noise, or he thought he felt PK activity, or he thought he saw something move. He was someplace he wasn't supposed to be, and each second he waited for someone to notice.

<<Quit walking like that or we're never going to get anywhere,>> Aron sent.

<<How am I walking?>>

<<Like a nervous hunchback. Try to relax.>>

<<Okay,>> Lloyd sent. He managed to take four steps before he heard something to his left and jerked his head to look at it. There was nothing there.

<<Look, think of it this way,>> Aron sent. <<They know we're here but they don't necessarily know who we are or what we look like. Act like you're not doing anything suspicious and no one will notice you.>>

<<But I *am* doing something suspicious!>>

<<Boiling blood, man, you stayed in that church way too long. You don't know anything about *life.*>>

<<Sneaking around and trying not to be seen is life?>>

Aron didn't reply for a minute, and then Lloyd realized what he had said.

<<Sorry, Aron, I forget ...>>

<<I know,>> Aron said. <<But after we're done here, hopefully you won't forget again.>>

Lloyd tried to walk at a normal pace, sticking one hand inside a damp pocket so he'd look casual. They walked near a road they had seen not long after they left the others.

<<Fuel station up ahead,>> Aron sent. <<Their payment system must be wired somehow.>>

<<Are they open?>>

<<Probably. I don't see any cars there, but everything's pretty bright.>>

They hadn't seen a single car since they came to the road. Most of the people on Bermuda worked for the church, and most of them went to bed early.

They stopped about a quarter mile from the fuel station. There still weren't any cars at the pumps, but Lloyd thought he saw someone walking around inside.

<<Should I do a scan?>> he sent.

<<No,>> Aron said. <<At this range, a scan would leave a pretty big footprint. That would get their attention fast. Do you have any money?>>

<<I've got a card that's still good.>> Lloyd sent.

<<Go in and buy something to eat. Something sweet. With cream filling. I haven't had any cream filling in a long time. But look around. Take your time before you make a selection.>>

<<Okay,>> Lloyd said.

<<And check if the attendant's got any talent while you're at it.>>

<<Got it.>> Lloyd left Aron behind and went to get some snacks.

The fuel station was clean and bright, and the attendant was in her late teens. She smiled at Lloyd when he entered but didn't say anything, so Lloyd took a slow look around.

There was a simple test that adepts sometimes used to check for people who have the talent. It's not definitive, but it's a quick, dirty, and pretty reliable. Any wizard, with enough training, learns how to sense PK activity happening around them. While most PK spells involve manipulating matter at some level, it's possible to send out a quick burst of pure psycho-kinetic energy. This burst has no effect on the physical world, but a wizard who is near it will see it as something like a brief flash, and feel it like a strange, light slap in the area where they normally sense PK activity. It's an odd, slightly unpleasant sensation, and it's usually enough to draw a reaction from any wizard who senses it.

Using the counters of the mini-mart as cover so he wouldn't have to see the flash, Lloyd set off a burst just to the attendant's right. Then he took a few steps and peered over at her. She was staring at a magazine on the counter in front of her. He turned away briefly and set off a flash just above the magazine. When he looked at her again, she hadn't moved.

That was enough for Lloyd. He picked up two packages of something that looked tremendously processed, completely unhealthy, and also quite yummy, and took them to the counter.

When he was outside he didn't see Aron, but he knew better than to just stand there and look around for him. He started walking back in the direction he'd come. When he was a half-mile away from the station, Aron abruptly appeared next to him.

<<Where did you learn to move so quiet ...>> Lloyd started, but then he stopped. <<Never mind.>>

<<The place is perfect,>> Aron said. <<There's a comm box in the back. If Spree can't jack into that, then all her equipment wasn't worth saving.>>

By sunrise they still hadn't been found.

<<I'm not sure I like this plan,>> Lloyd sent to Kale as they were preparing to separate. <<It seems like I'm more likely to be captured.>>

<<It's a little late to decide you don't want to take any risks.>>

<<True.>>

<<Just make sure you're late for your appointment. The more time we have, the better. And always, *always* keep Amelia with you.>>

<<Is that you being overprotective again?>>

<<Yeah,>> Kale sent. <<But this time, I'm protecting you.>>

His orders were to go with Amelia, stick to the roads, and walk to Hamilton, coming into the town from the north. Lloyd didn't like being in the open like that, especially since the first cars of the morning were already out, but Aron reminded him that sneaking through people's back yards looked a lot more suspicious than walking along a road.

<<They're not going to do anything to you,>> Aron had sent. <<After all, you're walking right to them. What more could they want?>>

It looked like rain clouds might be gathering to the west as Lloyd and Amelia set off down the road. Lloyd hoped they could get to Hamilton ahead of the rain—his clothes had barely dried. But he was under orders not to hurry, so he didn't.

They walked for a half hour without saying anything. Then they were passing more and more buildings, most of them white, pink, or light blue, and Lloyd felt a heavy sensation in his gut.

"How far do you think we're going to get?" he asked.

"Before what?"

"Before we're stopped."

"Oh, I'm not too worried about that," Amelia said. "Why should they stop you when you're going where they want you to be?"

Lloyd forced out a chuckle. "That's what Aron said."

"Then we must be right."

"Okay." He stared at his feet as he walked.

"Which one is ours?" Kale said, looking over row after row of small, round cars.

"413," Spree said.

"And where is that?"

"Don't no know," she said placidly. "Old eyes just gon' have to look 'til they find it." She looked at Nesbitt. "Young eyes, too."

They walked through four rows of cars before Kale found it, a little blue car with the number "413" painted on its rear bumper.

"Here it is," he said, and was already climbing in when the others arrived.

He waved an ID card in front of the dashboard, and the engine puttered to life. He tried not to show Spree that he was impressed.

"Hey, Faltergast," Nesbitt said. "The car has only two seats."

Jason M. Hardy

"Guess I'll have to leave one of you behind," Kale said, and smiled broadly at Nesbitt.

"Funny," Nesbitt said. "How do you expect me to keep up?"

"Take a moped," Kale said, waving at a line of bikes on the other side of the rental lot.

"Spree get one of them lined up for me?"

Spree looked at Kale, then and Nesbitt. Her hair, which normally had some long spikes on top these days, lay flat on her head, which Kale found disconcerting.

"Nope," she said.

"Just take one." Kale paused. "Though I guess you didn't learn the hotwire trick in church."

Nesbitt grinned. "Not in church, I didn't." Then he turned and jogged to the bikes.

He stopped when he was halfway there. "I gotta say, you guys are a lot more fun to hang out with than the adepts." Then he went back to work.

"He think that a compliment?" Spree said.

"It's something," he said. "Come on, we're wasting our charge."

Bermuda may have lost many of its tourists, but the buildings of Hamilton still presented their best face to the world. They were all clean, the streets were clear and pedestrian-friendly, and palm trees swayed in the breeze.

Kale sped by Amelia and Lloyd as they walked toward Hamilton, but they didn't see him. Good. The less they knew about what he was up to, the better. He hoped Nesbitt would have enough sense not to rev his moped engine as he passed them.

There were a half-dozen churches scattered about the east side of Hamilton, formerly belonging to a variety of denominations, but now they were all CMC. According to Spree's information, they needed to go to the Wesley Church just down the road from the main cathedral. Kale felt like driving right in front of the cathedral, daring them to do something about his presence, but there really wasn't any reason to taunt them. They'd let him run around for this long, he shouldn't push his luck.

The church was a simple affair, white and ponderous. There was steady traffic into and out of the building, some people wearing robes, others in suits. The door kept opening and closing, showing glimpses of a fluorescent-lit interior with desks and cubicles, looking nothing like a house of worship.

Kale passed the church and parked a block east.

"Stay here," he said to Spree and Nesbitt as he climbed out of the car. "It's probably best that we stay separate. In case descriptions are circulating."

"Security all adepts here," Spree said. "They don't no pass 'round photos of perps. They want to know who we are, it don't no matter if we together or separate. They check our minds, then they know if they care about us. And they don't no know me, anyway. Nobody no know me. You made sure of that."

"They can find me if they want to," Nesbitt said. "It might be fun."

"Fine. Then we'll separate so if I get caught, you'll still be safe. Whatever explanation you want is fine with me, as long as you agree that you'll wait a bit before you go in."

"Whatever you say," Spree said.

Kale got out and walked the church. He knew how security in a building like this would work. There would be two or three adepts assigned to do a quick scan of anyone who came in. They'd mainly be looking at surface thoughts—anyone thinking anything that looked troublesome would be stopped. If they were attentive, they'd notice when someone unfamiliar walked in and give that person a more detailed scan. On a normal day, the security would probably be a little lax, but the arrival of Kale's boat had likely put the guards on a higher level of alert.

He decided on a fairly simple trick. He picked someone who walked by the white church but not in it, then did a fast copy of that person's uppermost brain patterns. Anyone who looked into Kale's head for more than a second or two would know his copy was a fake—he put in on a loop, one moment's thoughts repeating over and over. But a second was all he would need to convince the guards that he was someone familiar and benign. At least, he hoped it was.

He walked into the church at full stride, no hesitation. He didn't feel the scan when it came, but he also didn't feel or hear any alarm. The coating he'd layered over his thoughts had done the job.

The inside of the building looked nothing like a church, except for the stained glass windows on every wall. The interior walls had been stripped out, leaving one large, echoing room. Grey carpet covered the floor, and cubicle walls turned the room into a maze. As was the case with many bureaucratic labyrinths, there was no clear indication of where to start.

Kale walked over to cubicle nearest to him and stuck his head over the top of the wall. He smiled at the scowling man sitting at his desk.

"Hi. I need to pick up a badge."

"I don't have any badges," the man said.

"Do you know where I should go?"

"No. There's lots of different kinds of badges, so lots of people have them."

Kale waited for the man to ask him what kind of badge he needed so he could direct Kale to the appropriate place, but the man had returned his attention to the screen in front of him.

"It's a custodial badge," Kale said helpfully.

The man made a sweeping wave, a gesture that covered nearly every cubicle in the building. "Number 135. Scott. Tamara Scott. Go talk to her."

Kale said thanks and walked away, while the man in the cubicle muttered something about locations too close to the doors.

Kale had to ask two other people for help before he found cubicle 135, but when he did it was occupied by a friendly looking woman who smiled and asked him to sit down before he said anything.

"What can I do for you?" she asked.

"My name is Kale Phillips," he said. "I'm supposed to pick up a badge."

"Okay. I hope it's a custodial badge, because that's all I got, honey."

"Yes, it is."

She sorted through a black box on her desk, then pulled out a small square of plastic. "Okay, this is you. Smile real nice, would you?"

Kale smiled, and something near the woman's screen flashed. She dropped the badge into a small slot, and it popped out with Kale's picture printed across the left half.

"All right, Mr. Phillips, there you are. Says here you're supposed to be cleaning the cathedral grounds in about half an hour, so you should be on your way."

"Thank you very much, Ms. Scott." Kale stood and looked over the cubicle walls so he could find his way out.

"And remember, Mr. Phillips, your badge is only good to get you by the boys with the guns. If you're at the cathedral, you better think nice thoughts the whole time or else someone's bound to notice." She smiled broadly, so Kale smiled back.

When he walked out of the church, he let the guards see his actual thoughts, with no disguise other than the slight alteration that he thought of himself as Kale Phillips. If everything was going to work, the guards would need to know that Phillips' badge had been picked up. He thought they'd let him go once they knew he had it, and he was right. For the time being, they were content to know where he was instead of stopping him. They probably hoped he thought he was getting away with something.

Lloyd and Amelia waited out a brief rainstorm in a gazebo in the middle of Victoria Park. A cobblestone path wound over grass and past a few trees, including the occasional palm. Lloyd stared at the palms to make sure he didn't forget that he was far from home.

The rain fell thick and hard but lasted for less than half an hour. When it passed, the air felt thicker, and everything sparkled in the just-emerged sunlight. The tops of the palm leaves were so shiny it looked like they had been varnished.

Lloyd stared at the palm trees for so long he forgot to check the time.

"We're fifteen minutes late for the appointment," Amelia said. "We can probably go now."

"Okay." He stood up. The park had emptied during the rain shower, but now a few people were starting to walk along the path. None of them seemed concerned by Lloyd's presence. "Let's see how far we get."

The cathedral was only a block away, and its thick, square tower had been visible for most of Lloyd and Amelia's walk to the city. The building was grey stone, large and heavy, with a steep red roof. According to Spree's research, they shouldn't enter the main building—instead, they walked around the back to a small black door next to a brass sign that read "Office of the Premier Adept."

Lloyd felt like he was gasping for air, inhaling more water than oxygen. He looked over at Amelia, hoping her normally impassive demeanor would calm him, but her eyes bounced back and forth like rubber balls, looking at the sign, then the door, then to the side, then the sign again.

"Holy crap," she said.

"Yeah," Lloyd said. "Okay."

He didn't bother with a shield. He knew he was good, but he also knew the people around Dugwu would be much, much better. If they wanted to read him, they would. Any shield he put up would just make them angry.

He pressed the small black button underneath the sign and waited, unguarded and open.

The door opened, moving at a smooth, regular speed, revealing a room with a red carpet, brown leather furniture, and an old wooden desk. An adept sat behind the desk, radiating power.

"Come in," she said. She had white hair, a round face, and looked like the kind of woman who might have a plate of cookies waiting for any visitors.

Lloyd took a breath and walked in. He stepped to the desk, prepared to speak, and hoped his voice did not stick in his throat.

It didn't. "We have an appointment to see the Premier Adept."

"Your name?"

"Courtney Whitaker."

The adept's eyes did not move from Lloyd's face. "Of course, Mr. Whitaker. Down that hallway, first door on your right. Please make yourself comfortable." She made no mention of their lateness.

"Thank you." Lloyd tried to keep a measured pace down the hallway, not too fast, not too slow. The first door on the right was wood, solid with a red tinge to it. It opened easily.

The room on the other side had a round table surrounded by six chairs. A long table lined the wall opposite the door. There were no windows and no visible source of light.

Amelia closed the door behind her as she entered. "Too easy," she said.

"We haven't accomplished anything yet," Lloyd said. He sat in one of the chairs that faced the door and waited.

The room was bare. No pictures on the wall, no electronic devices, no paper, no pens. Not even a floral arrangement. But it was a room used by powerful adepts, people who had no need for any communication tools besides their own heads and who also could make the room look however they pleased at a moment's notice. Lloyd thought about designing some picture of his own to give him something to look at and calm his nerves, but then worried that the adepts here would find such an effort presumptuous.

He sat in his chair, lightly rocking back and forth, for five minutes. The only noise in the room was a light squeak from his movement.

Then the door opened. A man walked in, dressed in black adept robes. He had traces of brown hair above his ears and on the back of his head, but most of his scalp was shiny. He moved with a deliberate slowness, smooth and efficient. When he sat opposite Lloyd, his chair made no sound.

"Of all the names you could have selected," the man said, "'Courtney Whitaker' was perhaps the most foolish. Even more foolish than using your own. How did you think we would react to that?"

"Curiously, I hoped," Lloyd said. "I hoped you'd want to know who would schedule a meeting using that name—and how that name was placed in your system."

"Oh, I'll admit, the way you broke into the network here was impressive. I have people still going over the system, looking for any tracks your hacker left behind, and they haven't found a trace. Whoever did it is quite good. But did you really think we would let you get anywhere near the Premier Adept just because we were curious about you?"

"I thought it would be worth a shot."

"It failed," the man said. He had a low voice, and a way of speaking that made everything he said sound like an indisputable fact, like the narrator of the educational films Lloyd had watched during his training. "So now we have two rebels—Lloyd Hsu, leader of the splinter sect on Long Island, and Amelia Diaz, granddaughter of Armando and diligent member of the Islip Liberation Front—here on Bermuda. And the question is, what do we do with you?"

"Why do anything with us at all?"

"You have led several adepts astray along with your own apostasy, Hsu."

"Then kick me out of the church," Lloyd said, and tried not to flinch at the pain in his gut when he said it. "I've already pretty much removed myself."

"If it were just about you, that would be acceptable," the adept said. "But you have been a harmful influence on several others, and by all appearances you will continue to be a bad influence if left alone. We cannot have that."

"Then give me a church trial," Lloyd said. "My dispute is with Grand Adept Malvoin Serl, which means the case will have to be heard by the Grand Adept's superior. Premier Adept Eliazer Dugwu."

The adept leaned forward. "Ah. So that's the game. Well, I suppose I underestimated you. You didn't use Whitaker's name because you thought it would get you in to see the Premier

Adept—you just wanted our attention. I suppose that is at least somewhat more clever than I at first thought."

Lloyd didn't say anything.

"But I'm sure you'll understand that a personal hearing with the Premier Adept is quite impossible," the adept continued. "He is far too busy to attend to every such dispute. He has delegates to handle such things."

"That's not good enough," Lloyd said.

"It will have to do," the adept said.

Lloyd looked over to Amelia and started to say something, but he stopped. She didn't look right. The nerves she had displayed outside the building seemed to have gotten worse. Her right leg was bouncing constantly, occasionally so high that her entire foot came off the floor. She was making a series of small scratches in the arm of her chair, fraying the leather where her fingernails were the sharpest.

"Who would this delegate be, then?" Lloyd said.

"Me, of course," the adept said. "That's why I'm here—to offer judgment and decide on your ultimate disposition."

Chapter Forty-seven

Kale was trimming a hedge, moving slowly so that the job could last a good three hours or more. Now that the rain had cleared, the day had become warm and humid. Many of the other custodians working outside had their shirts off, but Kale's wasn't about to risk a sunburn just to gain a bit of comfort. If circumstances were different he could cast a cooling spell, or create a UV screen around himself, but he didn't have any attention to spare. Everything had to be focused on the task at hand.

"Something needs to happen soon or I'm going to get blisters on my hands," he muttered.

Spree's voice came back as a slightly distorted grumble in his ear. "If you getting blisters be the worst thing that happens today, we done all right," she said.

"Where are you?" he asked.

"Not far. Over on Front Street, watching the water. Nesbitt boy's keeping an eye on me. We ready when you want."

"Okay. Don't talk too much—no sense in tipping them off."

He had a small microphone on one of his shirt buttons, and a tiny receiver in his right ear. Radio technology had worked for him once, and he hoped it would go unnoticed for a while here.

Short as it had been, the conversation had been reassuring. He felt blind and deaf, standing there cutting the hedge, with his mind tightly contained within his skull. He wanted to eavesdrop on Hsu and Amelia, he wanted to scan the mansion behind the cathedral and try to find Dugwu, he wanted to do so many things besides just stand and wait. He was all but certain, though, that he had been watched from the moment he picked up his badge, and any PK activity from him would be monitored. He had to stay completely inside himself, no matter how crazy that made him. He had to wait for the signal.

"Let me be very clear," the adept said. "Not only have you not provided a single reason why I should let you talk to the Premier Adept, but you haven't really given me a reason to let you out of this room."

"Is that a threat?" Lloyd asked.

"Yes," the adept said. "I thought that was pretty obvious. You are a rogue PK, you have spread misinformation about the church, and you seem quite prepared to repeat slanders about the Premier Adept."

"And for that the church is prepared to kill me."

The adept smiled without making his face look a bit friendlier. "You're far too literal. We might not keep you in this exact room—any secure room will do."

"What would I have to do to keep that from happening? Promise to be good?"

"No. We're past the point where we can rely on promises from you. If you submit to a brief procedure, though, we will not have to rely on your word."

"Really? The church has perfected behavior modification?"

"No, I'm afraid not. But we have become rather accomplished at memory erasing."

Lloyd glanced quickly at Amelia. She had calmed down a little was still jittery. She kept thumping her fingers on the table for a period of time, then stopping when the noise annoyed her, then starting again.

He returned his attention to the adept. "So you'll erase my memory of what Serl told me, and probably what I found out about Terrin. Anything else? Would I have to forget about Courtney too?"

"I'm afraid the procedure lacks precision," the adept said. "It's likely we'd just clear your memories of the past eighteen months and be done with it."

"Ah," Lloyd said. "Well, if that's the case I think I'll pass."

"Then we'll find a nice place where you can think about what steps you need to take to repent of your past actions."

Lloyd leaned back in his chair. It creaked. He still hadn't heard a noise from the other adept's chair. Had he chosen the wrong seat, or was he just not graceful?

"You know what I find interesting?" Lloyd said. "That in all this you've told me to repent and accused me of spreading slander, but never once did you say 'The Premier Adept didn't do what you said he did.' Not once."

The adept started to answer, but he was interrupted by an odd, wordless noise from Amelia, something between a bark and a cough. She wasn't really sitting anymore, she was leaning so far forward she was actually standing, her hands against the table.

"I can't stay on this island," she said, and her voice shook.

"You'll be fine here," the adept said. "It's paradise, after all."

"I can't stay here!" she said, her voice more shrill. "I didn't come here to—I wasn't part of this! I'm not even part of your church! You can't keep me here!"

"Then you'll opt for the procedure," the adept said.

Amelia jumped forward, almost climbing on top of the table. "You will stay out of my head! Stay out! Out!"

"You don't have the talent," the adept said. "I could wipe you clean any time I want."

"Not while I'm standing here," Lloyd said.

Amelia was moving more now, pacing back and forth across the room. "You're not keeping me! You have no right! You're not! You're not you're not you're not!"

"If your friend cannot calm down I'm going to have to sedate her."

Lloyd stood up and put a hand on Amelia's shoulder. "Amelia," he said. "It's okay. Calm down. We won't have to stay here forever."

"I wouldn't say that," the adept said. "I'd just say there's no reason to panic about it, since that won't change anything."

"He's already made up his mind!" Amelia said, her voice rising to an ever-higher pitch. "He's already made up his *mind*!"

"Amelia ..." Lloyd said.

"No!" Amelia said, pushing his hand off her shoulder. "Don't try to calm me down! Don't try to tell me it's all okay!"

"All right, that's enough," the adept said.

"You keep your mind away from me," Amelia said, pointing at the adept with a shaking finger. Her voice sounded like it was about to hit a pitch beyond human hearing. "Stop, stop stop sto—"

She froze. Her finger stopped shaking. Slowly, her body leaned forward and fell into the table, now that her muscles couldn't balance her anymore. Her nose and right cheek rested on the polished brown table.

"Oops," the adept said. "Almost forgot to keep letting her breathe." He looked at her and furrowed his brow slightly.

Then the adept crumbled to the floor as if his legs had been cut off from under him. He'd been too focused on containing Amelia, so he never saw the blow coming at him from outside the room. As the adept fell, Amelia inhaled like a vacuum.

"I hope you're okay," Lloyd said to Amelia, "because we need to move."

She'd done it. Now Kale could only hope that she was okay.

Spree had heard the signal, Amelia setting off a transmitter that was something like a dog whistle. She had passed word on to Kale, and he was finally free to act. He lashed out, putting a pinch on the brain stem of the adept who had been in the room with Lloyd and Amelia, sending him off to a nice late-morning nap. Something he never would have gotten away with unless the adept was distracted. Then Kale started running.

The air around him was on fire. An alarm from the residence building flashed—it was silent and colorless, but it pulsed in a way Kale felt in the back of his skull. Messages flashed back and forth, individualized in ways that made them impossible for Kale to intercept. Kale knew a lot of them were about him.

He ran around to the front of the cathedral—highest volume of people there, most accessible doors. He was inside, and the cathedral was bright, lighter than any church he'd been in recently. Maybe they'd turned up the lights for him.

He made his way around the edge of the chapel, looking for a staircase up. He found one about a hundred feet from the entrance, simple grey stone steps. He took them three at a time.

The reception area was to the left, so Lloyd went right. Amelia was right behind him—the paralysis the adept had laid on her wasn't having any after-effects, and she was perfectly calm now that the need for a distraction had passed.

"The important thing is that we don't hit any dead ends," he said as he ran.

"Spree is aware of that," Amelia said. "She said there's no guarantee that the blueprints are current. But there should be stairs at the end of the hall."

"It's probably only a matter of time before they figure out we're using wireless and shut us down," Lloyd said. "If there's any really, really important things we should know, she should tell you now."

Amelia didn't reply. Lloyd turned and saw her mouth moving, but no sound coming out. It was a subtle quiet spell, it had slipped between them without him noticing.

He swatted it away.

"Sorry," he said. "Could you say that again?"

"This building has three floors, two stairways. Our choices are limited, and they'll have sealed off most places quick. We're not going to be able to run for long."

Two attacks came at once. One was a shriek, a mental scream that speared Lloyd's skull for a second until he cast a low-range pitch that canceled it out. That let the second attack work a bit longer, an odd spell that made Lloyd's ankles and knees feel like they were solidifying. It slowed him enough that he was briefly stopped in mid-step, until he fed as much strength as he could to his legs and shattered the spell with an almost audible crack.

Amelia passed him while he was frozen. It was one benefit of not having the talent—she wouldn't be as easy to target from a distance.

They were on the second floor, and it was dark. No one was using it, so no one had bothered to turn on any wizard light.

"Dugwu's not here," he said. "Let's double back and go up higher."

He took one step toward the stairs, then saw a tinge of blue in the air. He stopped.

"They've blocked it," he said. He focused on the wall, trying to find a way to break it. He may have taken a few chips off, but it healed itself quickly. It reminded Lloyd of the barriers that had surrounded Courtney over the border wall, and the memory felt like a swift, low kick.

"The other stairway is probably blocked, too," he said. "We're going to have to stay here and make some noise."

Stay public, Kale told himself. The private areas, the places he wasn't supposed to be, were the ones most likely to have the best defenses. The easier it was for most people to get through an area, the easier it would be for him as well.

That meant he had to deal with a lot of low-level PKs who wanted to interfere with him. They weren't up to the job, though. Their presumptuousness annoyed him, but he tried to keep from permanently damaging any of them. He didn't even knock most of them out, as bodies suddenly falling to the ground tended to be disruptive. A quick mental block seemed to be the best solution, leaving them standing in place, wondering what they had just been doing and why.

The second level of the chapel hadn't been much more than a balcony with a few small rooms scattered here and there. But he'd found a way up to a third level, and that seemed to hold more promise. The hallways were more secluded, the doors and walls were clean, and everything looked the way it did in places where high-ranking leaders spent their time.

The attacks came as soon as he stepped into the hallway. It was a wide range of attacks, too many for Kale to name. They came like waves in a storm, moving in from three or four different directions, trying to push him back. He stood firm, shattering each attack as it came, but he couldn't move forward. They came too fast. It was almost physical, the pounding rhythm of the assaults. He scanned as much of the area as he could, looking for any of the sources of the attacks, but they were well hidden.

He might have been able to stand there all day, locked in a stalemate, waiting for the hidden adepts to tire, but he didn't have that kind of time. He could hold out against cathedral security, but he was pretty sure Hsu couldn't.

He'd have to find another way to do this. He went back to the stairway.

As soon as he'd taken two steps down, the attacks stopped. They wanted to keep him off that floor—if he was anywhere else, he was someone else's concern.

That was good. It would give him a minute to think. Not long, though—the third floor adepts had probably already told other adepts in the cathedral to come get him.

The public byways had gotten him this far, but now it was probably time to hit some less-traveled roads.

Amelia tried to focus, keeping her mind on the here and now, but she couldn't stop thinking about how much fun she was having.

She had infiltrated the halls of power, she'd gotten to display her acting skills with her fake panic attack in front of the bald adept, and now she was trying to find out how annoying she could be. It would be just plain wrong for her to not enjoy this—especially since, once it was all over, there was a good chance she wouldn't be doing anything fun for a good long time.

At the moment, she was looking at the glass globes used to diffuse wizard light that were spread along the ceiling.

Then she had it.

"The ceiling," she said. "We should go for the ceiling."

Lloyd smiled. "Of course. They can't put a barrier across the entire floor. At least, I don't think they can."

"So how do we get through?"

Lloyd didn't answer. His eyes were unfocused, and he didn't look steady on his feet.

"Lloyd?"

Suddenly all Amelia's hair felt like it was standing on end, and there was a blast of wind even though the air didn't move. She closed her eyes and braced herself, but it passed quickly. When she opened here eyes again, Lloyd was back to normal.

"What was that?"

"I'm not sure," Lloyd said. "But they're getting more active. Come on—what are we going to do about the ceiling?"

"Give me a second." She pressed a small button clipped to her waistband. "Spree, what's the ceiling here made of?"

"Hard-ass concrete," Spree said. "With some tile and stone around it."

"So we need something hard and sharp."

"Kale's head not no available? Or that too thick?"

"He's not here, unfortunately. Thanks, Spree." Amelia pressed the button again, terminating the connection.

"If we can find a fireplace on this level, that would help a lot," she said.

"Okay, come on," Lloyd said.

They ran down the hall, and doors opened before them. Lloyd was making all this look easy—until she actually looked at him. He was sweating, and the skin around his eyes had darkened.

The fourth room they looked in had a fireplace but no poker.

"Closet," Amelia said, pointing to a narrow door on the same wall as the fireplace, and ran toward it.

There were two doors to the room, and both of them slammed shut. Amelia jumped.

"Security," Lloyd said in a heavy voice. "We'll have to stay in here for now." His eyes lost their focus again.

Amelia took that to mean that she was on her own for the moment. She continued on toward the closet and hoped it was unlocked.

It was. And inside there were brooms, mops, sponges, and a few metal-handled tools. Including a poker. She grabbed it and ran back into the room.

There was a table in the back of the room, and she made one jump onto the seat of a chair, then a second to the table. Holding the poker in an underhand grip, she heaved upward and spiked the ceiling.

Tiles cracked, and one of them fell on her head. She lowered the poker, then walloped the ceiling again.

The poker flew out of her hands. She tried to grab after it as it moved away from her, but it was too fast. It hit the wall about fifteen feet from her and dropped to the floor.

She jumped off the table and ran after it, grabbing it and heading back to the dent she had made. The poker tugged in her hand as soon as she grabbed it, but she managed to hold on to it. But then it heaved a second time, and it was out of her hands.

"Dammit, Lloyd can you do something about this?" she yelled.

"Probably," Lloyd said. "Hold on."

Around the room picture frames shuddered, and a vase of flowers crashed to the floor.

"Go!" Lloyd said. "Now!"

Amelia was back in position with the poker, and she slammed it into the ceiling again. She was through the outer tile and into the plaster. She went again. And again. Dust fell on her head with each blow.

Then Lloyd yelled and staggered backward, taking a few steps before falling to the ground. Just as he went down, the poker jumped out of Amelia's hands again and flew away.

She had to decide if she should recover the poker or check on Lloyd. She ran toward the adept.

"What happened?" she asked as she grabbed his shoulders. "You okay?'

"How deep did you get?" Lloyd asked, his eyes bleary. "How deep is the hole?"

"Not very," Amelia said. "Inch, inch and a half."

"Okay. Get the poker and take off your shirt."

"What?"

"To protect your hands. Hurry!" Lloyd winced, and parts of his face seemed to squish and distort. His hands came to his forehead, he closed his eyes, and even Amelia, with her total lack of talent, could feel the power that waved out of him.

He opened his eyes. "At most I gave us fifteen seconds. Move!"

Amelia ran across the room, crossing her arms to take off her shirt as she moved. She grabbed the poker and held her shirt in one hand and the poker in the other.

"Hold the poker with both hands, use the shirt to cover your hands. Put the point of the poker in the hole."

Amelia did as he said, and as soon as it was in place the poker started spinning. The heat built up quickly, even through the fabric of her shirt, and a thin trail of smoke drifted up.

"Let go!" Lloyd said. "I've got it now."

Amelia dropped her hands and immediately ran to dip her shirt in one of the intact vases in the room. It came out wet, and she covered her stinging hands with it. Then she looked to see how the poker was doing.

It was still spinning, spitting out dust as it drilled through the ceiling. But the handle was shaking, and sweat was running down Lloyd's face.

"Lloyd?" Amelia said.

"I'm losing it!" he said.

Amelia moved, dropping her shirt and grabbing a chair. The poker was wobbling more now. If she hit it with the wrong angle, she wouldn't do a bit of good.

She heaved it upward, hitting the handle of the poker with the seat, driving it deeper into the ceiling. Her arms shivered with the force of the blow. The chair clattered to the floor, and the poker fell on top of it. And there was a small shaft of light illuminating the pieces of dust hovering above the poker.

She looked up. It was a hole about as wide as a ballpoint pen. But it was a hole.

"We're through!" she said.

Lloyd glanced up. He wiped his forehead with his wrist.

"Okay," he said. "Hide under a table."

"Will that really help?"

"Can't hurt," he said.

Amelia rolled under one of the side tables and then watched as Lloyd poured hell through the hole in the ceiling.

Kale was on the roof, disguised as a pigeon. It wasn't a great disguise. To anyone on the ground, he still looked like Kale Faltergast. And any PK who took more than a cursory look at him would discover an impressive depth of talent. But his disguise was built to prevent anyone from taking a close look at him. A routine scan, even basic security spells, would detect only a pigeon where Kale stood. Hopefully that would be enough.

He could see the storm cloud disappearing to the east from here, and the roof was still wet with rain. He had hoped to find a ledge or a balcony next to a third-floor window, but there wasn't one. Luckily, he had his gardening shears.

He could also see the building behind the cathedral, the building where Amelia and Lloyd were supposed to be. Spree had said he had heard from them not long ago, but she didn't have any more reports for him. In fact, when he called her she didn't say anything at all—the adepts here must have discovered they were using wireless tools. He was cut off, and it was all he could do to keep from scanning the building and finding Amelia.

Then one of the rooms in the nearby building exploded. It was a third-floor room, and a ball of flame pierced by lightning was inside, growing, filling the room. It reached the windows and they exploded, and Kale instinctively raised a shield to keep the glass shards off him.

Amelia was over there. At least, that's where she was supposed to be. He could jump off the roof and fly, or at least glide, that short distance. He could check on her, rescue her if she was in trouble. And waste the opportunity that was sitting in front of him. Possibly the only opportunity he'd get.

He felt power rush by him when the room exploded. He knew there were adepts around the building, around the area, turning their attention and power to the room, seeing what was happening and quickly extinguishing the fires. It was a reflex, the quick look at a loud noise. Soon, they'd all be looking where they were supposed to. He couldn't wait for that to happen.

He ran along the roof edge, making sure his feet didn't slip, and ran to where he knew he needed to be. He sent a wave of sound ahead of him, high-pitched and keening, at the frequency Spree had provided. He heard the sound of shattering glass, so he jumped off the roof.

He couldn't make a wind strong enough to blow him in, and he couldn't assemble enough solid matter out of thin air to slide him in the right direction. That was why he had a rope tied around his waist.

He jumped out far, the rope stretched behind him, then grew taut with a tug on the harness Kale wore under his jumpsuit. He swung down and backward, rushing toward the cathedral and through the shattered window in front of him. A quick spell burned the rope around his waist, breaking it, and Kale flew into the building and landed on glass-strewn carpet in a clumsy roll.

He was bombarded as soon as he hit the floor, spells he couldn't identify coming from at least three different directions. He blocked them, trying to get to his feet at the same time, but one of them penetrated his shields too deeply, staggering him back, sending him to the floor. He lashed out, a sweeping, broad blow, a simple fist of air that would dissolve as it went through shields and then reform itself. He hoped it made an impact, but he didn't have time to watch.

He pushed himself up again, looking across the room, seeing several floor-to-ceiling bookshelves, a podium displaying a large copy of the scriptures, desks and chairs, and behind the desk a man standing, a man in a dark robe with gold braiding, a man with a firm bearing, a sharp nose, and a high forehead. His hands were at his sides, and he looked like he was receiving a normal visitor into his office.

Kale didn't approach him. There were more spells coming in, more defenses he had to mount, heat and cold and electricity bearing down on him, and he wasn't sure he could put out his defenses quick enough, but he did, staying on his feet and feeling the effects disintegrate in front of him. They were fast and strong, but he had been doing this longer than they had.

Then there was a stab, a type of spell Kale hadn't seen before, and it cut through his defenses and came right for his chest before Kale found a way to push it down. But he couldn't get rid of it entirely; it sliced into a piece of his leg, and his knee felt warm and wet.

Kale was angry, and he shook the entire room. It was a spell he didn't have a name for, one he couldn't describe if asked, but it made the floor bounce and the walls wobble, and it gave him a moment's rest while the others in the room stumbled.

Kale found one of the guards in that time, an adept hidden behind an illusory bookshelf, and gave him a pinch in the brain that would put him out for a few minutes. Then he kept and eye on Eliazer Dugwu while he repaired his bleeding leg.

Dugwu was back on his feet quickly, still looking utterly impassive. Kale wasn't sure if any of the spells had come from Dugwu himself, or if he'd been able to rely solely on his security to this point.

"Eliazer," he said. "Good to see you."

Dugwu didn't say anything. He sent a spell, and then Kale knew for sure that Dugwu hadn't sent anything before, because this spell, this typhoon that sprang up around him, took all his effort to counter. He couldn't shatter it like the others, couldn't push it aside. He could only keep it away from him while he whittled it down.

Another spell, this one from a security adept, wandered its way through while Kale was busy with the swirling, pummeling air around him. It was electric, aimed at his head, designed to mess up the signals in his head temporarily or possibly permanently. Kale didn't notice it until he felt the hair on the back of his neck standing up, when it was almost too late. He sent out a positive charge to counteract it, and shocks ran up and down his neck to the base of his skull, sharp pinches, but they stayed out of his skull. His mind was intact.

And angry. Angry at himself for letting a spell through, angry at Dugwu for not talking, angry that he had to do what he was doing. He stood straight, his arms starting to rise, his hands in tight fists, and he stilled the air around him. He didn't sweep the spell away, he didn't shatter it. He just stopped it, canceled it, so one second there was a typhoon around him, and the next the air was still. He felt some spells coming from the adepts around him, but they couldn't touch him. He started walking toward Dugwu.

"None of this has to happen, Eliazer," Kale said. "We don't even need to talk about the past and all the things that happened after Harry died. All we need to talk about is what's happening now, and what's been happening on the Island and the Guatemala. People have been dying, Eliazer, and there's a fair amount of people who want to know why."

Dugwu still didn't say anything. His arms were folded now, his mouth was stern, but there was something in his eyes. Kale Faltergast, one of the Six, one of the most powerful PKs in the world, was standing in front of him in his full power, and Eliazer Dugwu did not seem to be scared. If anything, there was a trace of amusement in his eyes.

Kale took a chance. Normally Dugwu would have a first-class shield up around his thoughts and emotions, but their exchange of spells had been draining, and when you got into a battle like that the thought shields were the first thing you dropped, since no one usually had the time or the energy to read anyone else. Kale made a quick stab, sharp but deep into Dugwu's mind, to see how much he could get.

It only lasted a fraction of a second, but when Kale understood what he had seen, his hands fell to his side. He had to work hard to keep his mouth from falling open.

"Holy God," he said.

Then he moved. There was nothing more to be done here, and he would only be inviting more trouble by staying. He ran to the window he came through and leaped out.

Below him was the concrete walk that edged the cathedral, and his head was quickly rushing toward it. He put his hands in front of him by reflex and sent a message on such a broad wave that even some non-PKs might hear it. That didn't matter, as long as Hsu got it.

<<GET OUT!>> he sent.

Chapter Forty-eight

When the message came Lloyd was on the verge of giving up. His distraction had worked too well. When the room above him exploded, a wave of energy flowed into it, extinguishing flames and canceling electricity, quickly undoing everything he had done. Then, once the chaos above was controlled, church adepts focused on the source.

The first attacks had been primitive, sweeping blows trying to catch Lloyd off guard and knock him down or out. He warded them off easily enough, though he forgot to protect Amelia until a low swipe took her feet out from under her and brought her to the ground. He moved next to her, helped her back to her feet, and enlarged his shield to protect them both.

The next attacks were fewer in number but more intense. The adepts in the hall were closing in. There was cold, there were windows shattering across the room and glass shards swirling in the air, and there was a strange quality to the air that kept any noise from traveling farther than a foot or so. Lloyd could hear himself breathe, but not much else.

He tried to make a single shield that would keep everything out, but the adepts outside kept knocking it down, or throwing spells he had never seen before and had no idea how to cancel. There was a blistering burn that appeared on the back of his hand, the stabbing pain that he felt deep in his gut, and the continuing silence. After a while he was on the floor, hunched around his knees, and he didn't know how he got there. He felt Amelia's arm near his, and he hoped she was better protected than he was. He was repelling more blows than he absorbed, but too many were getting through. Soon the adepts would be able to just walk into the room, and Lloyd wouldn't be able to stop them. He didn't know what would happen then. He wondered what he'd be like with the memory of the past two years wiped away.

Then the message came through, the screaming thought from Kale. The words ricocheted around his head as if Kale had been standing right next to Lloyd.

"We have to leave!" Lloyd said. "We've gotta go!" He heard himself speak, but nothing reached Amelia. She said huddled next to him. Blood covered the back of both her hands.

He grabbed her wrist and pulled as he stood up. She looked at him, but she didn't focus. When she came to her feet, she wobbled unsteadily.

There was really only one way out—the windows. The adepts had cleared all the glass out of them, which meant that people on the ground would likely be waiting for them before they landed. That didn't leave Lloyd with many options.

Leading Amelia through the room, he grabbed a chair and heaved it toward the window so it could crash on the ground outside. It wouldn't fool anyone for long, but the sight of an object flying out a window was usually enough to startle anyone, no matter how much talent they had.

Then Lloyd stretched his thoughts. It was a common meditation exercise, like stretching your muscles, but a long time ago Aron found out that it could have an effect like throwing your voice—if you could let some of your thoughts wander freely away from your mind, it became harder for other PKs to tell exactly where you were.

Lloyd kept his thoughts innocent, thinking only of the different parts of the room he was in. Then he took a deep breath and started running forward. Amelia was right behind him.

Lloyd dropped several barriers he had been holding because he knew what would happen. The door closest to him didn't just fly open—it splintered. Lloyd charged through the flying pieces of wood that bounced off his shield and ran into the hallway.

Immediately there were twelve of him. Twelve Lloyds leading twelve Amelias in a hallway with four adepts surging forward. Lloyd wanted to run straight for the nearest staircase, but straight lines wouldn't help. The simpler his movements, the easier it would be for the adepts to tell who was real and who wasn't. He needed to weave.

He slalomed through the hallway, dodging around images of himself who staggered like he did, watching the adepts try to blast the images away or just reach out and touch them to tell which ones were real. Once, a short, barrel-chested adept brushed the real Lloyd with his hand, but before the adept could react Lloyd spun, his elbow smashing into the adept's face and sending him to the ground. The other three adepts reacted quickly, spells coming from three directions, and some of them got through, giving Lloyd a stabbing pain in his back and a tingling sensation in both knees. But he sent of a shower of colors and kept moving, and soon the chaos was restored. And the whole time, he came closer and closer to the stairs.

When he was at the top, he didn't hesitate. He pulled Amelia forward and went down, taking four steps at a time, his feet barely touching a step before he launched himself forward again. There were more adepts on the stairs, coming up to help, and Lloyd hit them so quickly that he almost didn't feel them, barreling over them and moving on. He saw Amelia move ahead of him briefly and kick someone in the chest. She limped for a few steps after that.

Then they were on the first floor, and there were more. Too many more. They had the hallway blocked, with spells and with their own presence, and Lloyd didn't have enough to get through them. The adepts from upstairs came down with thumping steps.

Making air firm enough to lift an entire person takes time and effort, but pulling enough together to make a cushion can literally be done on the fly. Kale's landing on the sidewalk next to the cathedral wasn't exactly soft, but he came away conscious and unbroken, which was all he needed. He was on his feet immediately, running toward the outbuilding.

He wasn't alone. The alarm was up, and adepts from all over were coming after him. He could tell by what they were throwing at him that none of them knew whom they were dealing with. Despite this, some of them were strong, and Kale had all he could handle, including a small cloud around his head that made him sneeze twenty times in a row.

But he was making progress, approaching the continuing stream of people running into and out of the outbuilding. He had firespouts popping up all over, the same thing he'd done in Manhattan back when he was in a mood to commemorate what had happened in Antigua. He had put up half a dozen of them, orange columns rising higher than the cathedral spire, blazing light and crackling with heat. He wanted to make new ones, but there were too many people moving too fast. He couldn't make sure any new spouts would be in the clear.

The spouts he had managed were causing a nice amount of chaos, but people were learning to just move around them. He needed something more to help keep them occupied.

At that moment, something else happened.

Spree's cart barreled onto the grass near Kale. Nesbitt was sitting in the passenger seat, a machine gun on his shoulder and a grin on his face.

<<Aim low, dammit!>> Kale sent. He thought he saw Nesbitt nod briefly. Then Nesbitt pulled the trigger down and held it there.

There was a long, repeated spit, and then colors appeared everywhere. Red and purple splatted on the outbuilding near the door, yellow and green and blue on the sidewalk, orange on the legs of an adept near Kale. The adept dropped to the ground, grabbing her legs in pain, but Kale then saw the surprised look on her face as she saw the liquid color hardening. It stung, but that's about all the damage the wax bullets would do.

It was a good distraction. Nesbitt drew a lot of attention from the adepts, so much that he had to stop firing for a time while he assembled his own defenses. Kale saw the cart rock back and forth, and he knew it was being pummeled.

He'd help soon, but now he had to use what Nesbitt had given him. He ran forward, past one of his firespouts, putting a pinch on the brain stem of one of the adepts in his way so he collapsed before he got to the door of the outbuilding. Kale reached the open door and ran through.

Lloyd couldn't move back, so he went ahead, but it was like moving through quicksand. There was so much coming at him, and some of it made it through, slowing him down and putting pain in places he didn't know could hurt. Each step seemed like it took a full minute, and he knew the adepts on the stairs would be on top of him soon, and he didn't have enough spells to protect him.

Then they fell. They fell like bowling pins. One of them even flew into the wall and hit it, arms and legs spread, like a hapless bird against a window. It was as if something had exploded in the hallway, and Lloyd didn't know how it hadn't touched him.

<<MOVE!>> Kale sent, and Lloyd didn't know he had stopped. He put himself into a run, and now he could go, sprinting by the fallen adepts. And there he was, an old man in a jumpsuit, waving him forward. Amelia was ahead of him now, trailing blood behind her but running strong. Kale just kept waving.

Lloyd ran past him and out the building. The lawn was chaos. Columns of fire seared the sky, and there were colors everywhere, new ones popping up all the time.

He didn't know where to go. He ran toward the street, mainly because it was away from the cathedral.

Then a cart was in front of him, a cart with a crazy man firing a gun, aiming everywhere but at Lloyd. Lloyd almost stopped running—his reflexes told him not to run toward people with guns—but then he saw Aron's smile above the gun, and he kept moving. He jumped into the back of the cart and watched as sparks exploded behind it, a shower of yellow-gold stars falling into the road behind him. He hoped what he was seeing was a spell that had been broken, but all he knew was that he wasn't the one who had broken it.

The cart was moving forward, and Lloyd dimly realized he wasn't the only person in the back seat. Reflexes took over—he was in a moving vehicle, he was under attack, so he shielded. He wanted the cart protected. He might as well be back on the Island, keeping the van safe as they rushed away from the wall. It was familiar territory.

He heard a sound like hail hitting the roof. Dents appeared above him, and then there was a hole, a puncture as a small rock flew through. It caught Aron in the left shoulder and lodged there. Aron closed his eyes in pain but didn't make a sound.

"Amelia, take the gun," he heard Kale say. "Aron, let me see."

Lloyd didn't pay much attention to what Kale did next. He couldn't let more rocks through. Couldn't let anything more through. It was like the empty apartment building in Far Rockaway, the blurry hours he spent holding up the roof against all the USNA had to offer, hours when he couldn't remember anything his own body felt, when his whole mind went into the shield above him. He felt more rocks fall, and they bounced off the power of his mind like acorns hitting a tent wall.

The rocks stopped. The adepts immediately switched tactics. But the cart was still moving forward, making progress. Moving away.

They tried electricity, but they didn't know who they were dealing with. Electricity was Lloyd's element. Every bolt they sent toward him disappeared, absorbed. The church adepts saw what was happening soon enough and stopped sending lightning.

Next came ice. It was a low attack, lower than Lloyd expected, and then there was a wide, thin sheet of ice on the road. And then a wind, and the card was spinning.

<<Melt it!>> Kale sent, and Lloyd responded with heat on the road, turning ice to water and water to steam.

<<Not so hot!>> Kale sent. <<You'll puncture the tires!>>

Lloyd obeyed, and the road was now wet but not icy. The cart had stopped moving, sitting sideways with the two rear tires off the road. Lloyd heard Spree take a breath, and then the cart was moving again.

There was more, more wind, more rocks, and a dozen metal pipes rolling in the road ahead of them. The wind was deflected, the rocks bounced away harmlessly, and the pipes flew over the car, a spiraling mass of metal, and Lloyd wasn't sure how much of it he did, but he was pretty sure it was some of it. And when he looked forward, he saw the ocean.

They were driving straight for it. They were off the road, surrounded by tall grass, and sand was in front of them. Lloyd might have been imagining it, he might have just been tired, but he thought there were less attacks now. But they wouldn't let them off so easy, would they?

The cart stopped. Lloyd looked around frantically, wondering what he had missed, and he saw the others getting out of the cart.

"Come on, Lloyd," Amelia said. "It's time to get wet."

Lloyd wasn't sure what she meant, but he got out of the cart and followed the others. He had to run to keep up. The sun was high overhead, there were a few people scattered on the beach in front of them, and the five of them ran into the ocean in their clothes.

Lloyd kept moving to knee level, to waist level, to chest level, then he floated. The water was as warm as it had been the previous night, warmer even. Too comfortable. He turned as he floated, looking behind him to see what the adepts on the island had in store for him.

<<They're not coming,>> Kale sent.

<<What?>>

<<They're not coming after us. The adepts on the island.>>

<<That's it?>>

<<Yes,>> Kale said. <<They did what they wanted to do. They protected Dugwu and they kept us from getting into their secret files, if they have any. Sure, they might want to arrest us, but it would be a pain to keep us incarcerated for any length of time. They mainly want us gone, and we're leaving. They won't chase us because they think we failed.>>

<<Did we?>>

Lloyd felt the cold amusement radiate from Kale. He thought maybe it came with a trace of fear, but Lloyd couldn't think of a reason why that would be.

<<No,>> Kale sent. <<We didn't fail.>>

Chapter Forty-nine

It was summer in Manhattan. The sun found its way through narrow streets and lit up street-side trees and playlots. Stone stoops were warm, metal exteriors hot to the touch. People were still reminding themselves how much fun it was to not have to think about which coat to wear, and they hadn't started complaining about the heat. Restaurants reclaimed sections of sidewalk with plastic tables and chairs, and pedestrians grew re-accustomed to squeezing themselves through tight spaces.

In the park, though, everything opened up. People walked slower, swung their arms more, and breathed air that was fresher than normal.

What was a skating rink in winter was a café in warmer weather, a clutch of umbrella-covered tables holding food that was a half-step better than what was sold from the carts scattered throughout the park. An order of fries here cost as much as Kale normally spent on food for an entire day, but he liked the city view and the warm breezes. And the gyros.

He was halfway through his sandwich when he was cast in shadow. He didn't bother to look up.

"I wasn't sure you'd be here," Kale said.

The familiar baritone voice was not friendly. "I've been here every month for more than half a year. You're the one who didn't show."

Kale nodded as he ate a fry. "I've been busy."

"You want to tell me about it?"

"Yes," he said. "I do." Then he looked up, right into Andy's unchanged face. "Sit down. Eat something."

"I'm not hungry," Andy said, but he sat down. "You've been a busy man," he said.

"I always am. I just happened to be doing some things recently that you would notice."

"I'm not sure what to ask you first—how you managed to piece it together, or how you managed to convince anyone that it was true."

"That's what I'm here for. I thought you'd want to know," Kale said.

"I'm assuming you think you found something on your trip to Bermuda last fall. Though from the accounts of the event that found their way to me, you really didn't get anything. So what happened?"

Kale leaned back in his chair. Andy was sitting forward, frowning, his arms folded on the table. It made Kale smile.

"When was the last time you've had a situation like this, something you didn't know about or couldn't control?" Kale said.

"Oh, for God's sake, Kale."

"All right, all right. Here's what happened. The whole time we were in Bermuda, Dugwu knew we were there. Serl had sent word ahead of us. We acted like they weren't expecting us, but they knew. And they let us get close—why drag us in if we'd just waltz in on our own? Anyway, we got close enough that a few rash moves put me right in front of Eliazer Dugwu.

"That meant one of two things," Kale continued. "they either underestimated my power or overestimated their own. Because generally, you put me in front of just about any PK on the planet not named Drauer, and I'm going to overwhelm them. But they didn't seem worried.

"I wondered about that the whole time we were there, why it went as smooth as it did. It was like the invasion of the Rockaways—look underneath the chaos of that day, and you'll see it was remarkably easy."

Andy didn't look at him. He kept his eyes down, but there was a hint of a smile now tugging at his lips.

"You noticed that?" Andy said.

"I noticed that."

"That's not enough, though. That's not enough to prove anything."

"True," Kale said. "When we were in Bermuda, I thought it was too easy, but I didn't have any idea why. I didn't guess. Nothing happened until I was standing in front of Dugwu. There were adepts all around, throwing spell after spell after me, and it kept me busy but still wasn't much of a threat. And Dugwu was just standing there, doing nothing, but totally unconcerned. Totally confident. So I wondered, what's he got going that I don't know about? So I did a quick read, a nice short stab, in and out. Dugwu may never have noticed, I don't know. But I found what was making him so confident. Why he wasn't worried. And it was you."

"Really," Drauer said, not making it a question.

"Yes. He knew Anderson Drauer had his back. He was thinking that his boss would take care of him."

"His boss?"

Kale shrugged. "The correlation between ideas and words is never perfect, but that's close enough."

"That's an odd idea for him to have," Andy said. "And it isn't proof of anything."

Kale slapped the table in front of him. No one turned to look, since the sound of it didn't travel more than a couple feet. Andy looked up, though.

"Are you really going to do this?" Kale said. "Are you still going to sit there and pretend this isn't happening? You played your game, you fooled everyone for a long time, but do you have to insult me by still playing now? After everything else?"

The frown returned to Andy's face as Kale spoke. He looked down again.

"That wasn't enough to prove anything," he said.

"No," Kale said, calm again. "You're right. It wasn't. But then I knew what to look for. I knew that communication from you would be going out to Bermuda. So I watched for it. And Serl watched for it. And others watched for it. And lo and behold, we saw it. Encoded in more ways that we could hope to crack, but with a definite signature. Your signature. And with everything else—with Slane Olsen's stories from Guatemala, with Malvoin Serl's stories of how Hampton had been run—it was enough. People believed."

"And now you have your own church."

Kale laughed. "Not my church. No, no, no. I'm still unaffiliated. Not even a new church. A friend of mine says it's the same church, just put back to the way it should be, the way Harry wanted it. Before you got your hands on it."

Andy looked up. Abruptly, the frown disappeared. He smiled, the confident half-smile Kale remembered from their teen years, when Andy would propose any number of ridiculous, grandiose plans and then guarantee he could pull them off.

"It was a good run," he said. "The way I count it, I had more than three-quarters of all the PKs in the Western Hemisphere reporting to me in one way or another. And I could set them against each other, put them through exercises, to see who really had ability. It was working well. I didn't need to expand the nation any more—with the church, I had all the territory I needed. All the people I needed."

"And if some people had to die, oh well."

"They generally died devoted to causes they firmly believed in. Not a bad way to go."

"Except their causes were lies."

"Not at all. My nation is real, Harry's church is real. The ideas behind them are real. The only issue is there were some leadership issues of which people were not aware."

Kale drummed his fingers on the table. He felt a slow burning inside his gut, but it wasn't time to let it out yet.

"It was quite an operation, though," Kale said. "This whole fulfillment of the prophecies. You even had to bring down one of your own buildings."

"I had wanted to redevelop that block anyway."

"It was you then? I didn't recognize your signature."

"I thought you might be watching. It was a group effort, quite some time in the planning. It was a good crew."

"Did you reward them to keep them quiet, or just kill them?"

Andy kept smiling but didn't answer the question.

"But here's the real question—why go to all the effort? You dragged out this poor kid Whitaker who didn't know his ass from his elbow, made him a prophet—"

"Which wasn't easy, believe me," Andy interjected. "Eliazer said Mal had to put in a lot of work to get the kid to show anything once the invasion started."

"—and then you killed him. Built him up and killed him."

"Yes."

"Why?"

Andy was silent for a moment. "Because the prophecies had always been a pain in the ass," he finally said. "A rallying point for all these young adepts. They all came into the church fully convinced that it was their destiny to bring my nation down. It was inconvenient. So I thought it was time to show them that the prophecies weren't all they were cracked up to be. And in the process, I'd find some good leaders, develop some new skills."

"Sounds like fun," Kale said.

"It was business," Andy said. "Like everything else."

"That's the problem. There's some people in that church who don't see it as a business and would prefer for it to run like a religion. And once they found out what was going on—well, you saw what happened."

"Indeed. I've lost a third of my clergy already, and the number keeps going up."

"Get used to it," Kale said.

"I'd worry about the church more, but you're even causing me problems here. Too many media outlets have picked up the story, and there are some of my own people who aren't happy about the whole operation. People who have difficulty with the big picture."

"People who don't like you working both sides of the fence, you mean," Kale said.

"Describe it however you want. I thought you should know, though, just how much trouble you're causing me."

"Did you think I'd feel bad about that?"

Andy sighed. "No."

"It's going to continue. Hampton's under new leadership now. And they're not reporting to Bermuda—the leadership of the church will likely shift to Guatemala."

"My control of the church is the only reason Hampton still exists," Andy said. "Do you think that handful of adepts and a few parishioners could have held me off for so long? Do something the entire *nation* of Mexico couldn't pull off? I could've taken Hampton any time I wanted it, but I left it alone for one reason—I already had it. Now that I don't ..."

"You'll leave it alone," said a new voice.

Andy whirled and looked at the short, serious man standing to his left. "Who the hell are you?" he said. "Kale, get the damn shield back up and—"

"He's supposed to hear," Kale said. "He's my guest. Which puts him, let me remind you, under the same protections we give each other."

"You didn't say anything about having a guest," Andy muttered.

"I'm saying it now. This is Lloyd Hsu of Hampton Cathedral."

Andy looked carefully at Hsu. "This is him," he said.

"You'll keep your hands off Hampton," Hsu said. "If you make any move against us, with everything we're doing there, everyone will know that the things we're saying are true and you're coming against us as a cover-up. You've got a number of people still supporting you because they think we're making it all up. Move against us, and you shut me up, but you lose all those people. Gain the Island, lose a few million people. Your call."

Andy was silent again. Then, as Kale thought he might, he smiled.

"Not too many adepts play politics," Andy said. "It's never been one of their gifts. I'm not used to them doing it, but I suppose I should start." He nodded. "Hampton is yours for now. First, because it's a small, mostly barren piece of land, and second because you're right. But I've been playing the political game for longer than you have. Don't assume that brute force is the only tool I've got." He stood. "Thanks for coming, Kale." He walked away with long strides.

"Wait," Hsu said.

Andy turned, his lips thin.

"Courtney. Was he—anyone? Did you pick him for a reason? Was he just someone you picked at random?"

Andy stared Hsu down for a few seconds, but Hsu didn't waver.

"He wasn't anyone," Andy said. Then he turned away again.

Kale looked at Hsu. His hand was shaking.

"You hid it well," he said.

"I was just talking to Anderson Bloody Drauer," Hsu said. "Good hell." That was the strongest oath Kale had ever heard him utter.

"He's just a guy," Kale said. "A guy with more PKs at his command than anyone in the world, a guy who could probably destroy most of the world with a stroke of his pen, yes. But just a guy."

"Just a guy. So why didn't he kill me? Kill us?"

"Gentlemen's agreement."

"With Drauer? And he keeps it?"

"Yeah," Kale said. "He usually keeps his word. He's just a guy, you know?"

"But what is he going to do? He's not just going to sit back with all the news that's been coming out. He's going to respond somehow. What do we do?"

Kale shrugged. "I don't know. He probably has a good half-dozen contingency plans, and he's choosing between them right now. He may start taking action before we get home. Who knows?"

"We can't ... Look at all these people. How many there are. If he wants to take us, he'll take us. He'll overrun the whole Island."

"Andy hasn't had any real opposition for a number of years now. We'll hope he's rusty."

Hsu stared at the table. He looked like he was about to hyperventilate.

"And we have the Creator on our side," Kale said, though his voice sounded thin, even to him.

"That wasn't enough to save High Adept Kroll. That wasn't enough to save Courtney. Or all those people in Guatemala."

Kale tried to come up with a good answer. He looked at the trees, and the sky, and the sunlight glinting off high windows to the east. He wished he had Andy's or Harry's confidence, that he could speak firmly about what they were going to do and what would happen. But he couldn't say what he didn't feel.

"We'll do what we can," he said, then stuffed his gyro into his mouth.

Epilogue

There was work waiting for Lloyd when he returned to Hampton from Manhattan, because there was always work. Adepts clamored for assignments, and parishioners who had been angry with Serl were now enthusiastic members who wanted to rebuild their community.

Lloyd had no idea how much of the Grand Adept's work was involved in temporal matters. He had to worry about boats that were coming in and going out, stores of food and the management of the church's farmland on the Island, the condition of the buildings in the cathedral campus—they had moved back there— and so on and so forth. He could have spent the rest of the week, of the month, of his life responding to urgent requests from people on the Island and trying to keep up.

He didn't know how Grand Adept Serl had done it, and the Grand Adept wasn't around to tell him. Serl had cooperated some and shared some of his experiences, but he didn't adjust to all the changes happening around him. One night he slipped away, likely to Bermuda, to rejoin the church structure he understood.

The division in the church was growing. The nets called Hampton the first splinter of the Church of the Miraculous Creator, even though Lloyd explained to Slane more than once that they weren't really a splinter, but that they were restoring the church to what it should be (each time, Slane waved him off and said that sort of nuance wasn't easy to capture). The parish in San Jose Pinula broke off soon afterward and expressed an interest in operating jointly with Hampton Cathedral. That, of course, was no surprise, but the real shock came when all of Guatemala City followed San Jose Pinula's lead. Rafael had been busy with others besides Lloyd, getting people into the places where they were needed.

The more the news spread, the more parishes splintered off the main church. Dozens of churches across Canada had contacted

Lloyd about his efforts, and Rafael regularly reported on churches across Central and South America that were breaking away. Not all of them allied themselves to what was now called the Hampton-Guatemala axis, but many did. The growth was phenomenal— Lloyd believed that within the year, his so-called splinter group would be as big as the Bermuda church, which he liked to think of as the rogue CMC. People occasionally said he should give the church a new name, like the Restored CMC, but Lloyd would have none of that. This was the Church of the Miraculous Creator, he told people. The real one.

Rafael Diego had accepted the mantle of Premier Adept, then quickly discarded the title. He would have been happy without any title at all, but Lloyd told him he needed to be called something just to keep things clear. After a bit of wrangling, Rafael agreed to be called Adept Diego, Church Steward. Lloyd and all other cathedral heads who joined Rafael's order called themselves assistant stewards.

The change in title did not, sadly, reduce the amount of work for Lloyd, and papers were always waiting for him and demanding his attention. Most of the time he didn't know how to handle any of the requests, and too often he found himself staring blankly at a paper in his hand or a form on a screen.

Thankfully, Rowan Birch was there, now with no other title besides adept. He offered what help he could, but many of the administrative matters were beyond anything he had seen. And some of the fire had gone out of his eyes—he offered advice where he could, but when days grew late, Lloyd could see his eyes glazing and his attention wandering. Lloyd wasn't sure what Birch wanted to do with himself now, but church administration didn't seem to be it.

About a month after Kale took him into Manhattan to meet Anderson Drauer, Lloyd decided to make a change. One morning he walked into his office (for the moment he was using the apartment Birch had assigned him to upon his return to Hampton, but it still felt too lavish) and saw the stack of papers and decided not to pick any of them up. He walked out and went to the classroom building and sat in on a class on the use of the talent in agriculture. He listened for a while as Adept Pujo led the class in a discussion about ways to maximize crop harvests and ensure efficient food distribution. That turned to a discussion about the church's responsibility to help the poor while promoting self-reliance, and Lloyd joined in enthusiastically. Of course, the whole class deferred to his opinions as soon as he offered them, but Lloyd hoped that, with more exposure to him, that might change.

That became the first change in the way he did things. He spent at least three hours per week in a classroom, preferably listening and occasionally commenting instead of teaching. Other things didn't get done during that time, and that was fine.

Except to the people who wanted those things done, who started to get increasingly impatient with the business left unfinished. Lloyd needed to find a way to deal with them, and Kale suggested Nilda. She had been a bureaucrat in the USNA, Kale said, and the USNA turned out the best bureaucrats on earth. Nilda became Lloyd's chief of administration, and the paperwork dwindled.

This gave Lloyd a brilliant idea. If Kale was willing to find a place for Nilda, he could maybe find a place for himself. After all, the church could really use another one of the Six helping them get back on track.

"No," Kale said. "No, no, no, no, absolutely not. I like you, you're a good boy, and I know Harry would have liked you, but no. No."

"But I thought—I thought you made your choice. I thought you'd decided to be with us."

"No, I didn't. I decided that the past few years showed me how right I've been about everything. I function best on my own."

Lloyd knew it wasn't worth pushing the point. "But you'll help me when I ask, won't you?"

Kale thought about that for a small moment. "I'll help you when I want," he said, but he smiled, and it was warmer than usual.

If Kale wasn't available, others were. Everyone who had been there for the sit-in were willing to do just about anything Lloyd asked. They were a little too pliant, too eager to do whatever he asked just because of who he was. He knew he couldn't encourage that.

It helped that some old faces came back. Stel Grant, Archie Gwin, and others who had left Hampton asked Lloyd if they could come back, and he welcomed them. They knew him before he became a steward, and they talked to him, for the most part, like they did back then. They told him when he was pompous, they told him when he was wrong, they told him when he needed to shut up and listen. They were invaluable.

Amelia was good for that, too. Ever since they got back from the Island, she was a little nicer to him than she used to be, but that didn't mean her edge had worn down. She was happy to call him an idiot when he was acting like an idiot, and often when he wasn't, but she usually did it with a smile on her face. Some of her contentment was due to the re-invigoration of the ILF, which was active in spreading all the anti-USNA information that had emerged recently. They had established closer ties with Mira Corwin in the city, and they were having more of an effect within USNA borders than ever. Amelia loved it. She still wasn't surrounded in luxury, as the Island was still the Island and remained poor in many resources. But, as she often told Lloyd, the work she was doing was more fun when people around you respected you and you could actually see some results of your work.

Lloyd enjoyed having Amelia around, and he was as pleased as she was with the progress of the ILF and the church. All of it would have been even better if Aron came back, something Lloyd mentioned every time he saw him. Aron kept saying he was happy that Lloyd was leading the church on Hampton now, and he was even happier that Lloyd had discontinued the policy of hunting down rogue adepts, meaning Aron was free to move out of the border wastes. He settled in East Islip, keeping a decent buffer between himself and the cathedral, but he was close enough that Lloyd saw him fairly often. The wariness and bitterness Lloyd had seen in Aron when he first found him in the wastes started to fade, but Aron didn't show any interest in the church. Not in Dugwu's version, not in Rafael Diego's version.

"If God wants me, he knows where to find me," he said once. "Until then, it's probably best if we leave each other alone."

"Maybe God's using me to ask you to come back," Lloyd replied. "Maybe this is your invitation."

Aron tilted his head to the side and thought for a moment, then smiled.

"Nah," he said.

It was disappointing, but at least Lloyd had Aron as another voice to talk to. Life on the Island even started to be peaceful, especially once the administrative duties were under control and Lloyd found time for teaching, meditating, and listening. While he believed in the church and the good work it did, he found that the events of the past few years had put a distance between him and God, which was not something a church leader should have. It worried him for the first months he spent on the job, because he could speak with utter conviction about matters of good works and helping the less fortunate and so forth, but when it came to matters of faith and God's love he found himself thinking about Courtney and stumbling over his words.

But it came back. As he went out to the Island and helped build communities and brought food to people who needed it and used Aron to introduce him to some border rats and offer what services he could, he thought he occasionally felt glimpses of God nearby. They were fleeting, often too much like the accounts of ghosts who vanished when you looked at them, but it happened enough that Lloyd could not help but believe it was real. Visions of Whitaker's face at the end helped keep him grounded in the cruelty of the world, but he understood the machinations behind his execution and the horrible web Courtney had been snared in—a web that had nothing to do with the workings of God, and something for which God should not take the blame.

Everything, then, would have been truly peaceful if it wasn't for the shadow to the west. There were some days, when the air was clear and Lloyd was in the upper floors of the cathedral, that he could see a few distant buildings. The city was there, full of Drauer's people, waiting to sweep down on him and take the Island if the whim ever hit them. Months passed and the hammer blow didn't fall, but that did nothing to convince Lloyd it wasn't poised.

There wasn't a day that passed that he didn't think about it, not a day he didn't wait for Spree to call him and tell him the troops had crossed the wall and were moving east. It was a threat that kept him moving, making sure he did everything he could to build up the church. He met with Slane regularly, telling her what he was doing, putting out information so that if they were ever wiped away, the story would be there. People would know about how Drauer had manipulated everything and killed Courtney, and hopefully they would hold him accountable.

That wasn't quite enough to make Lloyd feel calm, but it gave him a sense of purpose, The more time Drauer could give him, the more he could do. With Dugwu's church shrinking and the restored CMC growing, there could be a day when Hampton was as strong as Serl's phantom cathedral was supposed to be. It had been a long road already, and there was much more to go, but if the work continued, and if the story was told right, Anderson Drauer and his nation might finally have a proper opposition.

THE END

Acknowledgments

Many conversations over the course of many years helped shape the perspectives and ideas in this book. If there are flaws or problems with the ideas, it's because I'm still working to understand, not due to any flaws in these good people: Jeff Anderson, Keri Anderson, Joe Bennett, Randall Bills, Tara Bills, Sam Brunson, Jamie Brunson, Loren Coleman, Kimo Esplin, Bernie Fish, Michelle Fish, Jill Garrett, Rob Garrett, Peter Lewis, Greg Merkley, Kym Mellen, Vance Mellen, David Robertson.

My entire family should also be on that list, so here they are: James, Nedra, David, Lindy, Brigham, Elissa, Megan, Gretchen, Katrina, Jenica, Iris, and Lauren. Special thanks to James and Iris, who served as first readers of the manuscript.

Art Lyons not only has been very influential on my thought process, but he read an early version of the manuscript.

Special thanks to Neil, Scott, Alan, Mimi, Carol, and other names I might be forgetting.

Extra special thanks to Kat, who is a sounding board, a first reader, a patient spouse, and a good friend through everything. And a pretty smart cookie to boot. And to Finn, who has taught me about new ways of looking at life.

About the Author

Jason M. Hardy has written about aliens, futuristic trolls with shotguns, giant stompy robots, and Chicago politics. He clearly enjoys strange realms of the impossible. His work has appeared in the award-winning anthologies *The Corps* and *Spells & Chrome*, and he is the author of four novels, including *The Scorpion Jar* and *Drops of Corruption*. He is currently the line developer for the popular *Shadowrun* role-playing game.

He lives in Chicago with his wife and son.